Praise f...
bests...

"Popular roma...
the emotions t...

—*Publishers Weekly*

"[Macomber] demonstrates her impressive skills with characterization and her flair for humor."

—*RT Book Reviews*

"Macomber…is no stranger to the *New York Times* bestseller list. She knows how to please her audience."

—*Oregon Statesman Journal*

"Whether [Debbie Macomber] is writing lighthearted romps or more serious relationship books, her novels are always engaging stories that accurately capture the foibles of real-life men and women with warmth and humor."

—*Milwaukee Journal Sentinel*

Praise for the novels of *New York Times* bestselling author RaeAnne Thayne

"In Thayne's latest, her beautiful, honest storytelling goes straight to the heart. Her characters are authentically vulnerable and the light, amusing banter between them adds to the sweet warmth of this story… [A] moving yet powerful romance."

—*RT Book Reviews* on *Wild Iris Ridge*

"Thayne's series starter introduces the Colorado town of Hope's Crossing in what can be described as a cozy romance… [A] gentle, easy read."

—*Publishers Weekly* on *Blackberry Summer*

"Thayne, once again, delivers a heartfelt story of a caring community and a caring romance between adults who have triumphed over tragedies."

—*Booklist* on *Woodrose Mountain*

DEBBIE MACOMBER

A Little Bit Country

RAEANNE THAYNE

BLACKBERRY SUMMER

MIRA

ISBN-13: 978-0-7783-1825-5

Recycling programs
for this product may
not exist in your area.

A Little Bit Country
Copyright © 1990 by Debbie Macomber

Blackberry Summer
Copyright © 2011 by RaeAnne Thayne

For questions and comments about the quality of this book, please contact us at
CustomerService@Harlequin.com.

www.MIRABooks.com

Printed in U.S.A.

CONTENTS

A LITTLE BIT COUNTRY

Debbie Macomber

Also by Debbie Macomber

Blossom Street Books

The Shop on Blossom Street
A Good Yarn
Susannah's Garden
Back on Blossom Street
Twenty Wishes
Summer on Blossom Street
Hannah's List
The Knitting Diaries
   "The Twenty-First Wish"
A Turn in the Road

Cedar Cove Books

16 Lighthouse Road
204 Rosewood Lane
311 Pelican Court
44 Cranberry Point
50 Harbor Street
6 Rainier Drive
74 Seaside Avenue
8 Sandpiper Way
92 Pacific Boulevard
1022 Evergreen Place
Christmas in Cedar Cove
   (5-B Poppy Lane and
   A Cedar Cove Christmas)
1105 Yakima Street
1225 Christmas Tree Lane

Dakota Series

Dakota Born
Dakota Home
Always Dakota
Buffalo Valley

The Manning Family

The Manning Sisters
The Manning Brides
The Manning Grooms

Christmas Books

A Gift to Last
On a Snowy Night
Home for the Holidays
Glad Tidings
Christmas Wishes
Small Town Christmas
When Christmas Comes
   (now retitled Trading
   Christmas)
There's Something About
   Christmas
Christmas Letters
The Perfect Christmas
Choir of Angels
   (Shirley, Goodness and Mercy,
   Those Christmas Angels and
   Where Angels Go)
Call Me Mrs. Miracle

Heart of Texas Series

VOLUME 1
   (Lonesome Cowboy and
   Texas Two-Step)
VOLUME 2
   (Caroline's Child and
   Dr. Texas)
VOLUME 3
   (Nell's Cowboy and
   Lone Star Baby)
Promise, Texas
Return to Promise

One

"Help! Fire!" Rorie Campbell cried as she leaped out of the small foreign car. Smoke billowed from beneath the hood, rising like a burnt offering to a disgruntled god. Rorie ran across the road, and a black-and-white cow ambled through the pasture toward her, stopping at the split-rail fence. Soulful brown eyes studied her, as if the cow wondered what all the commotion was about.

"It's not even my car," Rorie said, pointing in the direction of the vehicle. "All of a sudden smoke started coming out."

The cow regarded her blankly, chewing its cud, then returned lazily to the shade of a huge oak tree.

"I think it's on fire. Dan's going to kill me for this," Rorie muttered as she watched the uninterested animal saunter away. "I don't know what to do." There was no water in sight and even if there had been, Rorie didn't have any way of hauling it to the car. She was so desperate, she was talking to a cow—and she'd almost expected the creature to advise her.

"Howdy."

Rorie whirled around to discover a man astride a chestnut stallion. Silhouetted against the warm afternoon sun, he looked like an apparition smiling down at her from the side of the hill opposite Dan's car.

"Hello." Rorie's faith in a benign destiny increased tenfold in that moment. "Boy, am I glad to see another human being." She'd been on this road for the past two hours and hadn't encountered another car in either direction.

"What seems to be the problem?" Leather creaked as the man swung out of the saddle with an ease that bespoke years of experience.

"I…I don't know," Rorie said, flapping her hands in frustration. "Everything was going just great when all of a sudden the car started smoking like crazy."

"That's steam."

"Steam! You mean the car isn't on fire?"

The man flipped the reins over his horse's head and walked toward the hood of the sports car. It was then that Rorie realized the man wasn't a man at all, but a boy. Sixteen, or possibly a little older. Not that Rorie was particular. She was just grateful someone had stopped. "A friend of mine insisted I drive his MGB up to Seattle." She sighed. "I should've known that if anything went wrong, I'd be at a total loss about what to do. I should've known…"

The boy whipped a large blue-starred hankie from the hip pocket of his faded jeans and used it to protect his hand while he raised the hood of her car. The instant he did, a great white cloud of steam swirled up like mist from a graveyard in a horror movie.

"I…thought I'd take the scenic route," Rorie explained, frantically waving her hand in front of her face to dispel the vapor. "The man at the gas station a hundred miles back said this is beautiful country. He said I'd miss some of the best scenery in Oregon if I stuck to the freeway." Rorie knew she was chattering, but she'd never experienced this type of situation before or felt quite so helpless.

"It's not only the best scenery in the state, it tops the whole country, if you ask me," the boy murmured absently while he examined several black hoses beneath the raised hood.

Rorie looked at her watch and moaned. If she wasn't in Seattle before six, she'd lose her hotel reservation. This vacation wasn't starting out well—not at all. And she'd had such high expectations for the next two weeks.

"I think you've got a leak in your water pump," the teenager stated, sounding as though he knew what he was talking about. "But it's hard to tell with all that fancy stuff they got in these foreign cars. Clay can tell you for sure."

"Clay?"

"My brother."

"Is he a mechanic?" Rorie's hopes soared.

"He's done his share of working on cars, but he's not a mechanic."

Rorie gnawed on her lower lip as her spirits plummeted again. Her first concern was getting to a phone. She'd make the necessary arrangements to have the car repaired and then call the hotel to ask if they'd hold her room. Depending on how close she was to the nearest town, Rorie figured it would take an hour for a tow truck to arrive and then another for it to get her car to a garage. Once there, the repairs shouldn't take too long. Just how hard could it be to fix a water pump?

"How far is it to a phone?"

The young man grinned and pointed toward his horse. "Just over that ridge…"

Rorie relaxed. At least that part wasn't going to be much of a problem.

"…about ten miles," he finished.

"Ten miles?" Rorie leaned her weight against the side of the car. This was the last time she'd ever take the scenic route and the last time she'd ever let Dan talk her into borrowing his car!

"Don't worry, you won't have to walk. Venture can handle both of us. You don't look like you weigh much."

"Venture?" Rorie was beginning to feel like an echo.

"My horse."

Rorie's gaze shifted to the stallion, who had lowered his head to sample the tall hillside grass. Now that she had a chance to study him, she realized what an extraordinarily large animal he was. Rorie hadn't been on the back of a horse since she was a child. Somehow, the experience of riding a pony in a slow circle with a bunch of other six-year-olds didn't lend her much confidence now.

"You...you want me to ride double with you?" She was wearing a summer dress and mounting a horse might prove...interesting. She eyed the stallion, wondering how she could manage to climb into the saddle and still maintain her dignity.

"You wearing a dress and all could make that difficult." The boy rubbed the side of his jaw, frowning doubtfully.

"I could wait here until someone else comes along," she offered.

He used his index finger to set his snap-brim hat further back on his head. "You might do that," he drawled, "but it could be another day or so—if you're lucky."

"Oh, dear!"

"I suppose I could head back to the house and grab the pickup," he suggested.

It sounded like a stroke of genius to Rorie. "Would you? Listen, I'd be more than happy to pay you for your time."

He gave her an odd look. "Why would you want to do that? I'm only doing the neighborly thing."

Rorie smiled at him. She'd lived in San Francisco most of her life. She loved everything about the City by the Bay, but she couldn't have named the couple in the apartment next door had her life depended on it. People in the city kept to themselves.

"By the way," he said, wiping his hands with the bright blue handkerchief, "the name's Skip. Skip Franklin."

Rorie eagerly shook his hand, overwhelmingly grateful that he'd happened along when he did. "Rorie Campbell."

"Pleased to meet you, ma'am."

"Me too, Skip."

The teenager grinned. "Now you stay right here and I'll be back before you know it." He paused, apparently considering something else. "You'll be all right by yourself, won't you?"

"Oh, sure, don't worry about me." She braced her feet wide apart and held up her hands in the classic karate position. "I can take care of myself. I've had three self-defence lessons."

Skip chuckled, ambled toward Venture and swung up into the saddle. Within minutes he'd disappeared over the ridge.

Rorie watched him until he was out of sight, then walked over to the grassy hillside and sat down, arranging her dress carefully around her knees. The cow she'd been conversing with earlier glanced in her direction and Rorie felt obliged to explain. "He's gone for help," she called out. "Said it was the neighborly thing to do."

The animal mooed loudly.

Rorie smiled. "I thought so, too."

An hour passed, and it seemed the longest of Rorie's life. With the sun out in full force now, she felt as if she was wilting more by the minute. Just when she began to suspect that Skip Franklin had been a figment of her overwrought imagination, she heard a loud chugging sound. She leaped to her feet and, shading her eyes with her hand, looked down the road. It was Skip, sitting on a huge piece of farm equipment, heading straight toward her.

Rorie gulped. Her gallant rescuer had come to get her on a tractor!

Skip removed his hat and waved it. Even from this distance, she could see his grin.

Rorie feebly returned the gesture, but her smile felt brittle. Of the two modes of transportation, she would have preferred the stallion. Good grief, there was only one seat on the tractor. Where exactly did Skip plan for her to sit? On the engine?

Once he'd reached the car, he parked the tractor directly in front of it. "Clay said we should tow the car to our place instead of leaving it on the road. You don't mind, do you?"

"Whatever he thinks is best."

"He'll be along any minute," Skip explained, jumping down from his perch. He used a hook and chain to connect the sports car to the tractor. "Clay had a couple of things he needed to do first."

Rorie nodded, grateful her options weren't so limited, after all.

A few minutes later, she heard the sound of another vehicle. This time it was a late-model truck in critical need of a paint job. Rust showed through on the left front fender, which had been badly dented.

"That's Clay now," Skip announced, nodding toward the winding road.

Rorie busied herself brushing bits of grass from the skirt of her dress. When she'd finished, she looked up to see a tall muscular man sliding from the driver's side of the pickup. He was dressed in jeans and a denim shirt, and his hat was pulled low over his forehead, shading his eyes. Rorie's breath caught in her throat as she noticed his grace of movement—a thoroughly masculine grace.

Something about Clay Franklin grabbed her imagination. He embodied everything she'd ever linked with the idea of an outdoorsman, a man's man. She could imagine him taming a wilderness or forging an empire. In his clearly defined features she sensed a strength that reminded her of the land itself. The spellbinding quality of his steel-gray eyes drew her own and held them for a long moment. His nose had a slight curve, as though it had been broken once. He smiled, and a tingling sensation Rorie couldn't explain skittered down her spine.

His eyes still looked straight into hers and his hands rested on his lean hips. "Looks as if you've got yourself into a predicament here." His voice was low, husky—and slightly amused.

His words seemed to wrap themselves around Rorie's throat, choking off any intelligent reply. Her lips parted, but to her embarrassment nothing came out.

Clay smiled and the fine lines that fanned out from the corners of his eyes crinkled appealingly.

"Skip thinks it might be the water pump," she said, pointing at the MGB. The words came out weak and rusty and Rorie felt even more foolish. She'd never had a man affect her this way. He wasn't really even handsome. Not like Dan Rogers. No, Clay wasn't the least bit like Dan, who was urbane and polished—and very proud of his little MGB.

"From the sounds of it, Skip's probably right." Clay walked over to the car, which his brother had connected to the tractor. He twisted the same black hose Skip had earlier and shook his head. Next he checked to see that the bumper of Dan's car was securely fastened to the chain. He nodded, lightly slapping his brother's back in approval. "Nice work."

Skip beamed under his praise.

"I assume you're interested in finding a phone. There's one at the house you're welcome to use," Clay said, looking at Rorie.

"Thank you." Her heart pounded in her ears and her stomach felt queasy. This reaction was so unusual for her. Normally she was a calm, levelheaded twenty-four-year-old, not a flighty teenager who didn't know how to act when an attractive male happened to glance in her direction.

Clay walked around to the passenger side of the pickup and held open the door. He waited for Rorie, then gave her his hand to help her climb inside. The simple action touched her; it had been a long time since anyone had shown her such unselfconscious courtesy.

Then Clay walked to the driver's side and hoisted himself in. He started the engine, which roared to life immediately, and shifted gears.

"I apologize for any inconvenience I've caused you," Rorie said stiffly, after several moments of silence.

"It's no problem," Clay murmured, concentrating on his driving, doing just the speed limit and not a fraction more.

They'd been driving for about ten minutes when Clay turned off the road and through a huge log archway with ELK RUN lettered across the top. Lush green pastures flanked the private road, and several horses were grazing calmly in one of them. Rorie knew next to nothing about horse breeds, but whatever these were revealed a grace and beauty that was apparent even to her untrained eye.

The next thing Rorie noticed was the large two-story house with a wide wraparound veranda on which a white wicker swing swayed gently. Budding rosebushes lined the meandering brick walkway.

"It's beautiful," she said softly. Rorie would have expected something like this in the bluegrass hills of Kentucky, not on the back roads of Oregon.

Clay made no comment.

He drove past the house and around the back toward the largest stable Rorie had ever seen. The sprawling wood structure must have had room for thirty or more horses.

"You raise horses?" she said.

A smile moved through his eyes like distant light. "That's one way of putting it. Elk Run is a stud farm."

"Quarter horses?"

That was the only breed that came to mind.

"No. American Saddlebreds."

"I don't think I've ever heard of them before."

"Probably not," Clay said, not unkindly.

He parked the truck, helped Rorie down and led her toward the back of the house.

"Mary," he called, holding the screen door for Rorie to precede him into the large country kitchen. She was met with the smell of cinnamon and apples. The delectable aroma came from a freshly baked pie, cooling on the counter. A black Labrador retriever slept on a braided rug. He raised his head and thumped his tail gently when Clay stepped over to him and bent down to scratch the dog's ears. "This is Blue."

"Hi, Blue," Rorie said, realizing the dog had probably been a childhood pet. He looked well advanced in years.

"Mary doesn't seem to be around."

"Mary's your wife?"

"Housekeeper," Clay informed her. "I'm not married."

That small piece of information gladdened Rorie's heart and she instantly felt foolish. Okay, so she was attracted to this man with eyes as gray as a San Francisco sky, but that didn't change a thing. If her plans went according to schedule, she'd be in and out of his life within hours.

"Mary's probably upstairs," Clay said when the house-keeper didn't answer. "There's a phone on the wall." He pointed to the other side of the kitchen.

While Rorie retrieved her AT&T card from her eel-skin wallet, Clay crossed to the refrigerator and took out a brightly colored ceramic pitcher.

"Iced tea?" he asked.

"Please." Her throat felt parched. She had to swallow several times before she could make her call.

As she spoke on the phone, Clay took two tall glasses from a cupboard and half filled them with ice cubes. He poured in the tea, then added thin slices of lemon.

Rorie finished her conversation and walked over to the table. Sitting opposite Clay, she reached for the drink he'd prepared. "That was my hotel in Seattle. They won't be able to hold the room past six."

"I'm sure there'll be space in another," he said confidently.

Rorie nodded, although she thought that was unlikely. She was on her way to a writers' conference, one for which she'd paid a hefty fee, and she hated to miss one minute of it. Every hotel in the city was said to be filled.

"I'll call the garage in Nightingale for you," Clay offered.

"Is that close by?"

"About five miles down the road."

Rorie was relieved. She'd never heard of Nightingale and was grateful to learn it had a garage. After all, the place was barely large enough to rate a mention on the road map.

"Old Joe's been working on cars most of his life. He'll do a good job for you."

Rorie nodded again, not knowing how else to respond. Clay quickly strode to the phone, punched out the number and talked for a few minutes. He was frowning when he replaced the receiver. Rorie wanted to question him, but before she could, he grabbed an impossibly thin phone book and dialed a second number. His frown was deeper by the time he'd completed the call.

"I've got more bad news for you."

"Oh?" Rorie's heart had planted itself somewhere between her chest and her throat. She didn't like the way Clay was frowning, or the concern she heard in his voice. "What's wrong now?"

"Old Joe's gone fishing and isn't expected back this month. The mechanic in Riversdale, which is about sixty miles south of here, says that if it is your pump it'll take at least four days to ship a replacement."

Two

"Four days!" Rorie felt the color drain from her face. "But that's impossible! I can't possibly wait that long."

"Seems to me," Clay said in his smooth drawl, "you don't have much choice. George tells me he could have the water pump within a day if you weren't driving a foreign job."

"Surely there's someone else I could call."

Clay seemed to mull that over; then he shrugged. "Go ahead and give it a try if you like, but it isn't going to do you any good. If the shop in Riversdale can't get the part until Saturday, what makes you think someone else can do it any faster?"

Clay's calm acceptance of the situation infuriated Rorie. If she stayed here four days, in the middle of nowhere, she'd completely miss the writers' conference, which she'd been planning to attend for months. She'd scheduled her entire vacation around it. She'd made arrangements to travel to Victoria on British Columbia's Vancouver Island after the conference and on the way home take a leisurely trip down the coast.

Clay handed her the phone book, and feeling defeated Rorie thumbed through the brief yellow pages until she came to the section headed Automobile Repair. Only a handful were listed and none of them promised quick service, she noted.

"Yes, well," she muttered, expelling her breath, "there doesn't seem to be any other option." Discouraged, she set the directory back on the counter. "You and your brother have been most helpful and I want you to know how much I appreciate everything you've done. Now if you could recommend a hotel in…what was the name of the town again?"

"Nightingale."

"Right," she said, with a wobbly smile, which was the best she could do at the moment. "Actually, anyplace that's clean will be fine."

Clay rubbed the side of his jaw. "I'm afraid that's going to present another problem."

"Now what? Has the manager gone fishing with Old Joe?" Rorie did her best to keep the sarcasm out of her voice, but it was difficult. Obviously the people in the community of…Nightingale didn't take their responsibilities too seriously. If they were on the job when someone happened to need them, it was probably by coincidence.

"A fishing trip isn't the problem this time," Clay explained, his expression thoughtful. "Nightingale doesn't have a hotel."

"What?" Rorie exploded. "No hotel…but there must be."

"We don't get much traffic through here. People usually stick to the freeway."

If he was implying that *she* should have done so, Rorie couldn't have agreed with him more. She might have seen some lovely scenery, but look where this little side trip had taken her! Her entire vacation was about to be ruined. She slowly released her breath, trying hard to maintain her composure, which was cracking more with every passing minute.

"What about Riversdale? Surely they have a hotel?"

Clay nodded. "They do. It's a real nice one, but I suspect it's full."

"Full? I thought you just told me people don't often take this route."

"Tourists don't."

"Then how could the hotel possibly be full?"

"The Jerome family."

"I beg your pardon?"

"The Jerome family is having a big reunion. People are coming from all over the country. Jed was telling me the other day that a cousin of his is driving out from Boston. The overflow will more than likely fill up Riversdale's only hotel."

One phone call confirmed Clay's suspicion.

"Terrific," Rorie murmured, her hand still on the receiver. The way things were beginning to look, she'd end up sleeping on a park bench—if Nightingale even had a park.

The back door opened and Skip wandered in, obviously pleased about something. He poured himself a glass of iced tea and leaned against the counter, glancing from Rorie to Clay and then back again.

"What's happening?" he asked, when no one volunteered any information.

"Nothing much," Rorie said. "Getting the water pump for my car is going to take four days and it seems the only hotel within a sixty-mile radius is booked full for the next two weeks and—"

"That's no problem. You can stay here," Skip inserted quickly, his blue eyes flashing with eagerness. "We'd love to have you, wouldn't we, Clay?"

Rorie spoke before the elder Franklin had an opportunity to answer. "No, really, I appreciate the offer, but I can't inconvenience you any more than I already have."

"She wouldn't be an inconvenience, would she?" Once more Skip directed the question to his older brother. "Tell her she wouldn't, Clay."

"I can't stay here," she returned, without giving Clay the chance to echo his brother's invitation. She didn't know these people. And, more important, they didn't know her and Rorie refused to impose on them further.

Clay gazed into her eyes and a slow smile turned up the edges of his mouth. "It's up to you, Rorie. You're welcome on Elk Run if you want to stay."

"But you've done so much. I really couldn't—"

"There's plenty of room," Skip announced ardently.

Those baby-blue eyes of his would melt the strongest resolve, Rorie mused.

"There's three bedrooms upstairs that are sitting empty. And you wouldn't need to worry about staying with two bachelors, because Mary's here—she has a cottage across the way."

It seemed inconceivable to Rorie that this family would take her in just like that. But, given her options, her arguments for refusing their offer were weak, to say the least. "You don't even know me."

"We know all we need to, don't we, Clay?" Skip glanced at his older brother, seeking his support.

"You're welcome to stay here, if you like," Clay repeated, his gaze continuing to hold Rorie's.

Again she was struck by the compelling quality of this man. He had a stubborn jaw and she doubted there were many confrontations where he walked away a loser. She'd always prided herself on her ability to read people. And her instincts told her firmly that Clay Franklin could be trusted. She sensed he was scrupulously honest, utterly dependable—and she already knew he was generous to a fault.

"I'd be most grateful," she said, swallowing a surge of tears at the Franklins' uncomplicated kindness to a complete stranger. "But, please, let me do something to make up for all the trouble I've caused you."

"It's no trouble," Skip said, looking as if he wanted to jump up and click his heels in jubilation.

Clay frowned as he watched his younger brother.

"Really," Rorie stressed. "If there's anything I can do, I'd be more than happy to lend a hand."

"Do you know anything about computers?"

"A little," she said. "We use them at the library."

"You're a librarian?"

Rorie nodded and brushed a stray dark curl from her forehead. "I specialize in children's literature." Someday she hoped to have her own work published. That had been her reason for attending the conference in Seattle. Three of the top children's authors in the country were slated to speak. "If you have a computer system, I'd be happy to do whatever I can…"

"Clay bought a new one last winter," Skip informed her proudly. "He has a program that records horse breeding and pedigrees up to the fourth and fifth generation."

A heavyset woman Rorie assumed was the housekeeper entered the kitchen, hauling a mop and bucket. She inspected Rorie with a measuring glance and seemed to find her lacking. She grumbled something about city girls as she sidled past Skip.

"Didn't know you'd decided to hold a convention right in the middle of my kitchen."

"Mary," Clay said, "this is Rorie Campbell, from San Francisco. Her car broke down, so she'll be staying with us for the next few days. Could you see that a bed is made up for her?"

The older woman's wide face broke into a network of frown lines.

"Oh, please, I can do that myself," Rorie said quickly.

Mary nodded. "Sheets are in the closet at the top of the stairs."

"Rorie is our guest." Clay didn't raise his voice, but his displeasure was evident in every syllable.

Mary shrugged, muttering, "I got my own things to do. If the girl claims she can make a bed, then let her."

Rorie couldn't contain her smile.

"You want to invite some city slicker to stay, then fine, but I got more important matters to attend to before I make up a bed for her." With that, Mary marched out of the kitchen.

"Mary's like family," Skip explained. "It's just her way to be sassy. She doesn't mean anything by it."

"I'm sure she doesn't," Rorie said, smiling so Clay and Skip would know she wasn't offended. She gathered that the Franklins' housekeeper didn't hold a high opinion of anyone from the city and briefly wondered why.

"I'll get your suitcase from the car," Skip said, heading for the door.

Clay finished his drink and set the glass on the counter. "I've got to get back to work," he told her, pausing for a moment before he added, "You won't be bored by yourself, will you?"

"Not at all. Don't worry about me."

Clay nodded. "Dinner's at six."

"I'll be ready."

Rorie picked up the empty glasses and put them by the sink. While she waited for Skip to carry in her luggage, she phoned Dan. Unfortunately he was in a meeting and couldn't be reached, so she left a message, explaining that she'd been delayed and would call again. She felt strangely reluctant to give him the Franklins' phone number, but decided there was no reason not to do so. She also decided not to examine that feeling too closely.

Skip had returned by the time she'd hung up. "Clay says you can have Mom and Dad's old room," the teenager announced on his way through the door. He hauled her large suitcase in one hand and her flight bag was slung over his shoulder. "Their room's at the other end of the house. They were killed in an accident five years ago."

"But—"

"Their room's got the best view."

"Skip, really, any bedroom will do... I don't want your parents' room."

"But that's the one Clay wants for you." He bounded up the curving stairway with the energy reserved for the young.

Rorie followed him more slowly. She slid her hand along the polished banister and glanced into the living room. A large natural-rock fireplace dominated one wall. The furniture was built of solid oak, made comfortable with thick chintz-covered cushions. Several braided rugs were placed here and there on the polished wood floor. A piano with well-worn ivory keys stood to one side. The collection of family photographs displayed on top of it immediately caught her eye. She recognized a much younger Clay in what had to be his high-school graduation photo. The largest picture in an ornate brass frame was of a middle-aged couple, obviously Clay and Skip's parents.

Skip paused at the top of the stairway and looked over his shoulder. "My grandfather built this house more than fifty years ago."

"It's magnificent."

"We think so," he admitted, eyes shining with pride.

The master bedroom, which was at the end of the hallway, opened onto a balcony that presented an unobstructed panorama of the entire valley. Rolling green pastures stretched as far as the eye could see. Rorie felt instantly drawn to this unfamiliar rural beauty. She drew a deep breath, and the thought flashed through her mind that it must be comforting to wake up to this serene landscape day after day.

"Everyone loves it here," Skip said from behind her.

"I can understand why."

"Well, I suppose I should get back to work," he said regretfully, setting her suitcases on the double bed. A colorful quilt lay folded at its foot.

Rorie turned toward him, smiling. "Thank you, Skip. I hate to think what would've happened to me if you hadn't come along when you did."

He blushed and started backing out of the room, taking small steps as though he was loath to leave her. "I'll see you at dinner, okay?"

Rorie smiled again. "I'll look forward to it."

"Bye for now." He raised his right hand in a farewell gesture, then whirled around and dashed down the hallway. She could hear his feet pounding on the stairs.

It took Rorie only a few minutes to hang her things in the bare closet. When she'd finished, she went back to the kitchen, where Mary was busy peeling potatoes at the stainless steel sink.

"I'd like to help, if I could."

"Fine," the housekeeper answered gruffly. She took another potato peeler out of a nearby drawer, slapping it down on the counter. "I suppose that's your fancy sports car in the yard."

"The water pump has to be replaced...I think," Rorie

answered, not bothering to mention that the MGB wasn't actually hers.

"Humph," was Mary's only response.

Rorie sighed and reached for a large potato. "The mechanic in Riversdale said it would take until Saturday to get a replacement part."

For the second time, Mary answered her with a gruff-sounding *humph.* "If then! Saturday or next Thursday or a month from now, it's all the same to George. Fact is, you could end up staying here all summer."

Three

Mary's words echoed in Rorie's head as she joined Clay and Skip at the dinner table that evening. She stood just inside the dining room, dressed in a summer skirt and a cotton-knit cream-colored sweater, and announced, "I can't stay any longer than four days."

Clay regarded her blankly. "I have no intention of holding you prisoner, Rorie."

"I know, but Mary told me that if I'm counting on George what's-his-name to fix the MG, I could end up spending the summer here. I've got to get back to San Francisco—I have a job there." She realized how nonsensical her little speech sounded, as if that last bit about having a job explained everything.

"If you want, I'll keep after George to make sure he doesn't forget about it."

"Please." Rorie felt a little better for having spoken her mind.

"And the Greyhound bus comes through on Mondays," Skip said reassuringly. "If you had to, you could take that back to California and return later for your friend's car."

"The bus," she repeated. "I *could* take the bus." As it

was, the first half of her vacation was ruined, but it'd be nice to salvage what she could of the rest.

Both men were seated, but as Rorie approached the table Skip rose noisily to his feet, rushed around to the opposite side and pulled out a chair for her.

"Thank you," she said, smiling up at him. His dark hair was wet and slicked down close to his head. He'd changed out of his work clothes and into what appeared to be his Sunday best—a dress shirt, tie and pearl-gray slacks. With a good deal of ceremony, he pushed in her chair. As he leaned toward her, it was all Rorie could do to keep from grimacing at the overpowering scent of his spicy after-shave. He must have drenched himself in the stuff.

Clay's gaze seemed to tug at hers and when Rorie glanced in his direction, she saw that he was doing his utmost not to laugh. He clearly found his brother's antics amusing, though he took pains not to hurt Skip's feelings, but Rorie wasn't sure how she should react. Skip was only in his teens, and she didn't want to encourage any romantic fantasies he might have.

"I hope you're hungry," Skip said, once he'd reclaimed his chair. "Mary puts on a good feed."

"I'm starved," Rorie admitted, eyeing the numerous serving dishes spread out on the table.

Clay handed her a large platter of fried chicken. That was followed by mashed potatoes, gravy, rolls, fresh green beans, a mixed green salad, milk and a variety of preserves. By the time they'd finished passing around the food, there wasn't any space left on Rorie's oversize plate.

"Don't forget to leave room for dessert," Clay commented, again with that slow, easy drawl of his. Here Skip was practically doing cartwheels to attract her attention and all Clay needed to do was look at her and she became light-headed. Rorie couldn't understand it. From the moment Clay Franklin had stepped down from his pickup, she hadn't been the same.

"After dinner I thought I'd take you up to the stable and introduce you to King Genius," Skip said, waving a chicken leg.

"I'd be happy to meet him."

"Once you do, you'll feel like you did when you stood on the balcony in the big bedroom and looked at the valley."

Obviously this King wasn't a foreman, as Rorie had first assumed. More than likely, he was one of the horses she'd seen earlier grazing on the pasture in front of the house.

"I don't think it would be a good idea to take Rorie around Hercules," Clay warned his younger brother.

"Of course not." But it looked as if Skip wanted to argue.

"Who's Hercules?"

"Clay's stallion," Skip explained. "He has a tendency to act up if Clay isn't around."

Rorie could only guess what "act up" meant, but even if Skip didn't intend to heed Clay's advice, she gladly would. Other than that pony ride when she was six, Rorie hadn't been near a horse. One thing was certain; she planned to steer a wide path around the creature, no matter how much Skip encouraged her. The largest pet she'd ever owned had been a guinea pig.

"When Hercules first came to Elk Run, the man who brought him said he was mean-spirited and untrainable. He wanted him destroyed, but Clay insisted on working with the stallion."

"Now he's your own personal horse?" Rorie asked Clay.

He nodded. "We've got an understanding."

"But it's only between them," Skip added. "Hercules doesn't like anyone else getting close."

"He doesn't have anything to worry about as far as I'm concerned," Rorie was quick to assure both brothers. "I'll give him as much space as he needs."

Clay grinned, and once again she felt her heart turn over. This strange affinity with Clay was affirmed in the look he gave her. Unexpected thoughts of Dan Rogers sprang to mind. Dan was a divorced stockbroker she'd been seeing steadily for the past few months. Rorie enjoyed Dan's company and had recently come to believe she was falling in love with him. Now she knew differently. She couldn't be this powerfully drawn to Clay Franklin if Dan was anything more than a good friend. One of the reasons Rorie had decided on this vacation was to test her feelings for Dan. Two days out of San Francisco, and she had her answer.

Deliberately Rorie pulled her gaze from Clay, wanting to attribute everything she was experiencing to the clean scent of country air.

Skip's deep blue eyes sparkled with pride as he started to tell Rorie about Elk Run's other champion horses. "But you'll love the King best. He was the five-gaited world champion four years running. Clay put him out to stud four years ago. National Show Horses are commanding top dollar and we've produced three of the best. King's the sire, naturally."

"Do all the horses I saw in the pasture belong to you?"

"We board several," Skip answered. "Some of the others are brought here from around the country for Clay to break and train."

"You break horses?" She couldn't conceal her sudden alarm. The image of Clay sitting on a wild bronco that bucked and heaved in a furious effort to unseat him did funny things to Rorie's stomach.

"Breaking horses isn't exactly the way Hollywood pictures show it," Clay explained.

Rorie was about to ask him more when Skip planted his elbows on the table and leaned forward. Once again Rorie was assaulted by the overpowering scent of his aftershave. She did her best to smile, but if he remained in that position much longer, her eyes would start watering. Already she could feel a sneeze tickling her nose.

"How old are you, Rorie?" he asked.

The question was so unexpected that she was too surprised to answer immediately. Then she said, "Twenty-four."

"And you live in San Francisco. Is your family there, too?"

"No. My parents moved to Arizona and my brother's going to school back east."

"And you're not engaged or anything?"

As Rorie shook her head, Clay shot his brother an exasperated look. "Are you interviewing Rorie for the *Independent*?"

"No. I was just curious."

"She's too old for you, little brother."

"I don't know about that," Skip returned fervently. "I've always liked my women more mature. Besides, Rorie's kind of cute."

"Kind of?"

Skip shrugged. "You know what I mean. She doesn't act like a city girl…much."

Rorie's eyes flew from one brother to the next. They were talking as if she wasn't even in the room, and that annoyed her—especially since she was the main topic of conversation.

Unaware of her reaction, Skip helped himself to another

roll. "Actually, I thought she might be closer to twenty. With some women it's hard to tell."

"I'll take that as a compliment," Rorie muttered to no one in particular.

"My apologies, Rorie," Clay said contritely. "We were being rude."

She took time buttering her biscuit. "Apology accepted."

"How old do you think I am?" Skip asked her, his eyes wide and hopeful.

It was Rorie's nature to be kind, and besides, Skip had saved her from an unknown fate. "Twenty," she answered with barely a pause.

The younger Franklin straightened and sent his brother a smirk. "I was seventeen last week."

"That surprises me," Rorie continued, setting aside her butter knife and swallowing a smile. "I could've sworn you were much older."

Looking even more pleased with himself, Skip cleared his throat. "Lots of girls think that."

"Don't I remember you telling me you're helping Luke Rivers tonight?" Clay reminded his brother.

Skip's face fell. "I guess I did."

"If Rorie doesn't mind, I'll introduce her to King."

Clay's offer appeared to surprise Skip, and Rorie studied the boy, a little worried now about causing problems between the two brothers. Nor did she want to disappoint Skip, who had offered first.

"But I thought…" Skip began, then swallowed. "You want to take Rorie?"

Clay's eyes narrowed, and when he spoke, his voice was cool. "That's what I just said. Is there a problem?"

"No…of course not." Skip stuffed half a biscuit in his mouth and shook his head vigorously. After a moment of chewing, he said, "Clay will show you around the stable."

His words were measured and even, but his gaze held his
brother's.

"I heard," Rorie said gently. She could only speculate
on what was going on between them, but obviously something was amiss. There'd been more than a hint of surprise
in Skip's eyes at Clay's offer. She noticed that the younger
Franklin seemed angry. Because his vanity was bruised?
Rorie supposed so. "I could wait until tomorrow if you
want, Skip," she suggested.

"No, that's all right," he answered, lowering his eyes.
"Clay can do it, since that's what he seems to want."

When they finished the meal, Rorie cleared the table,
but Mary refused to let her help with cleaning up the
kitchen.

"You'd just be in the way," she grumbled, though her
eyes weren't unfriendly. "Besides, I heard the boys were
showing you the barn."

"I'll do the dishes tomorrow night then."

Mary murmured a response, then asked brusquely,
"How was the apple pie?"

"Absolutely delicious."

A satisfied smile touched the edges of the woman's
mouth. "Good. I did things a little differently this time,
and I was just wondering."

Clay led Rorie out the back door and across the yard toward the barn. The minute Rorie walked through the enor-
mous double doors she felt she'd entered another world.
The wonderful smells of leather and liniments and saddle
soap mingled with the fragrance of fresh hay and the pun-
gent odor of the horses themselves. Rorie found it surprisingly pleasant. Flashes of bright color from halters and
blankets captured her attention, as did the gleam of steel
bits against the far wall.

"King's over here," Clay said, guiding her with a firm hand beneath her elbow.

When Clay opened the top of the stall door, the most magnificent creature Rorie had ever seen turned to face them. He was a deep chestnut color, so sleek and powerful it took her breath away. This splendid horse seemed to know he was royalty. He regarded Rorie with a keen eye, as though he expected her to show him the proper respect and curtsy. For a wild moment, Rorie was tempted to do exactly that.

"I brought a young lady for you to impress," Clay told the stallion.

King took a couple of steps back and pawed the ground.

"He really is something," Rorie whispered, once she'd found her voice. "Did you raise him from a colt?"

Clay nodded.

Rorie was about to ask him more when they heard frantic whinnying from the other side of the aisle.

Clay looked almost apologetic. "If you haven't already guessed, that's Hercules. He doesn't like being ignored." He walked to the stall opposite King's and opened the upper half of the door. Instantly the black stallion stuck his head out and complained about the lack of attention in a loud snort, which brought an involuntary smile to Rorie's mouth. "I was bringing Rorie over to meet you, too, so don't get your nose out of joint," Clay chastised.

"Hi," Rorie said, and raised her right hand in a stiff greeting. It amused her that Clay talked to his animals as if he honestly expected them to understand his remarks and join in the conversation. But then who was she to criticize? Only a few hours earlier, she'd been conversing with a cow.

"You don't need to be frightened of him," Clay told her when she stood, unmoving, a good distance from the stall. Taking into consideration what Skip had mentioned earlier about the moody stallion, Rorie decided to stay where she was.

Clay ran his hand down the side of Hercules's neck, and his touch seemed to appease the stallion's obviously delicate ego.

Looking around her, Rorie was impressed by the size of the barn. "How many stalls are there altogether?"

"Thirty-six regular and four foaling. But this is only a small part of Elk Run." He led her outside to a large arena and pointed at a building on the opposite side. "My office is over there, if you'd like to see it."

Rorie nodded, and they crossed to the office. Clay opened the door for her. Inside, the first thing she noticed was the collection of championship ribbons and photographs displayed on the walls. A large trophy case was filled with a variety of awards. When he saw her interest in the computer, Clay explained the system he'd had installed and how it would aid him in the future.

"This looks pretty straightforward," Rorie told him.

"I've been meaning to hire a high-school kid to enter the data for me so I can get started, but I haven't got around to it yet."

Rorie sorted through the file folders. There were only a few hours of work and her typing skills were good. "There's no need to pay anyone. If I'm going to be imposing on your hospitality, the least I can do is enter this into the computer for you."

"Rorie, that isn't necessary. I don't want you to spend your time stuck here in the office doing all that tedious typing."

"It'll give me something productive to do instead of fretting over how long it's taking to get the MG repaired."

He glanced at her, his expression concerned. "All right, if you insist, but it really isn't necessary, you know."

"I do insist." Rorie clasped her hands behind her back and decided to change the subject. "What's that?" she asked, gesturing toward a large room off the office. Floor-to-ceiling windows looked out over the arena.

"The observation room."

"So you can have your own private shows?"

"In a manner of speaking. Would you like to go down there?"

"Oh, yes!"

Inside the arena, Rorie saw that it was much bigger than it had appeared from above. They'd been walking around for several minutes when Clay checked his watch and frowned. "I hate to cut this short, but I've got a meeting in town. Normally I wouldn't leave company."

"Oh, please," she said hurriedly, "don't worry about it. I mean, it's not as though I was expected or anything. I hardly consider myself company."

Still Clay seemed regretful. "I'll walk you back to the house."

He left in the pickup a couple of minutes later. The place was quiet; Mary had apparently finished in the kitchen and retired to her own quarters, a cottage not far from the main house. Skip, who had returned from helping his friend, was busy talking on the phone. He smiled when he saw Rorie, without interrupting his conversation.

Rorie moved into the living room and idly picked up a magazine, leafing through it. Restless and bored, she read a heated article on the pros and cons of a new medication used for equine worming, although she couldn't have described what it said.

When Skip was finished on the phone, he suggested they play cribbage. Not until after ten did Rorie realize she was unconsciously waiting for Clay's return. But she wasn't quite sure why.

Skip yawned rather pointedly and Rorie took the hint.

"I suppose I should think about heading up to bed," she said, putting down the deck of playing cards.

"Yeah, it seems to be that time," he answered, yawning again.

"I didn't intend to keep you up so late."

"Oh, that's no problem. It's just that we start our days early around here. But you sleep in. We don't expect you to get up before the sun just because we do."

By Rorie's rough calculation, getting up before the sun meant Clay and Skip started their workday between four-thirty and five in the morning.

Skip must have read the look in her eyes, because he chuckled and said, "You get used to it."

Rorie followed him up the stairs, and they said their good-nights. But even after a warm bath, she couldn't sleep. Wearing her flower-sprigged cotton pajamas, she sat on the bed with the light still on and thought about how different everything was from what she'd planned. She was supposed to be in Seattle now, at a cocktail party arranged for the first night of the conference; she'd hoped to talk to several of the authors there. But she'd missed that, and the likelihood of attending even one workshop was dim. Instead she'd made an unscheduled detour onto a stud farm and stumbled upon a handsome rancher.

She grinned. Things could be worse. Much worse.

An hour later, Rorie heard a noise outside, behind the house. Clay must be home. She smiled, oddly pleased that he was back. Yawning, she reached for the lamp on the bedside table and turned it off.

The discordant noise came again.

Rorie frowned. This time, whatever was making the racket didn't sound the least bit like a pickup truck parking, or anything else she could readily identify. The dog was barking intermittently.

Grabbing her housecoat from the foot of the bed and tucking her feet into fuzzy slippers, Rorie went downstairs to investigate.

As she stood in the kitchen, she could tell that the clamor was coming from the barn. A problem with the horses?

Not knowing what else to do, she scrambled up the stairs and hurried from room to room until she found Skip's bedroom.

The teenager lay sprawled across his bed, snoring loudly.

"Skip," she cried, "something's wrong with the horses!"

He continued to snore.

"Skip," she cried, louder this time. "Wake up!"

He remained deep in sleep.

"Skip, please, oh, please, wake up!" Rorie pleaded, shaking him so hard he'd probably have bruises in the morning. "I'm from the city. Remember? I don't know what to do."

The thumps and bangs coming from the barn were growing fiercer and Blue's barking more frantic. Perhaps there was a fire. Oh, dear Lord, she prayed, not that. Rorie raced halfway down the stairs, paused and then reversed her direction.

"Skip," she yelled. "Skip!" Rorie heard the panic in her own voice. "Someone's got to do something!"

No one else seemed to think so.

Nearly frantic now, Rorie dashed back down the stairs and across the yard. Trembling, she entered the barn. A lone electric light shone from the ceiling, dimly illuminating the area.

Several of the stalls' upper doors were open and Rorie

could sense the horses becoming increasingly restless. Walking on tiptoe, she moved slowly toward the source of the noise, somewhere in the middle of the stable. The horses were curious and their cries brought Rorie's heart straight to her throat.

"Nice horsey, nice horsey," she repeated soothingly over and over until she reached the stall those unearthly sounds were coming from.

The upper half of the door was open and Rorie flattened herself against it before daring to peek inside. She saw a speckled gray mare, head thrown back and teeth bared, neighing loudly, ceaselessly. Rorie quickly jerked away and resumed her position against the outside of the door. She didn't know much about horses, but she knew this one was in dire trouble.

Running out of the stable, Rorie picked up the hem of her robe and sprinted toward the house. She'd find a way to wake Skip or die trying.

She was breathless by the time she got to the yard. That was when she saw Clay's battered blue truck.

"Clay," she screamed, halting in the middle of the moonlit yard. "Oh, Clay."

He was at her side instantly, his hands roughly gripping her shoulders. "Rorie, what is it?"

She was so glad to see him, she hugged his waist and only just resisted bursting into tears. Her shoulders were heaving and her voice shook uncontrollably. "There's trouble in the barn...."

Four

Clay ran toward the barn with Rorie right behind him. He paused to flip a switch, flooding the interior with bright light.

The gray mare in the center stall continued to neigh and thrash around. Rorie found it astonishing that the walls had remained intact. The noise of the animal's pain echoed through the stable, reflected by the rising anxiety of the other horses.

Clay took one look at the mare and released a low groan, then muttered something under his breath.

"What's wrong?" Rorie cried.

"It seems Star Bright is about to become a mother."

"But why isn't she in one of the foaling stalls?"

"Because two different vets palpated her and said she wasn't in foal."

"But…"

"She's already had six foals and her stomach's so stretched she looks pregnant even when she isn't." Clay opened the stall door and entered. Rorie's hand flew to her heart. Good grief, he could get killed in there!

"What do you want me to do?" she said.

Clay shook his head. "This is no place for you. Get back

to the house and stay there." His brow furrowed, every line a testament to his hard, outdoor life.

"But shouldn't I be phoning a vet?"

"It's too late for that."

"Boiling water—I could get that for you." She wanted to help; she just had no idea how.

"Boiling water?" he repeated. "What the hell would I need that for?"

"I don't know," she confessed with a shrug, "but they always seem to need it in the movies."

Clay gave an exasperated sigh. "Rorie, please, just go to the house."

She made it all the way to the barn door, then abruptly turned back. If anyone had asked why she felt it so necessary to remain with Clay, she wouldn't have been able to answer. But something kept her there, something far stronger than the threat of Clay's temper.

She marched to the center stall, her head and shoulders held stiff and straight. She stood with her feet braced, prepared for an argument.

"Clay," she said, "I'm not leaving."

"Listen, Rorie, you're a city girl. This isn't going to be pretty."

"I'm a woman, too. The sight of a little blood isn't enough to make me faint."

Clay was doing his best to calm the frightened mare, but without much success. The tension in the air seemed to crackle like static electricity.

"I haven't got time to argue with you," he said through clenched teeth.

"Good."

Star Bright heaved her neck backward and gave a deep groan that seemed to reverberate in the stall like the boom of a cannon.

"Poor little mother," Rorie whispered in a soothing voice. Led by instinct, she carefully unlatched the stall door and slipped inside.

Clay sent her a look hot enough to peel paint. "Get out of here before you get hurt." His voice was low and urgent.

Star Bright reacted to his tension immediately, jerking about, her body twitching convulsively. One of her hooves caught Clay in the forearm and, almost immediately, blood seeped through his sleeve. Rorie bit her lip to suppress a cry of alarm, but if Clay felt any pain he didn't show it.

"Hold her head," Clay said sharply.

Somehow Rorie found the courage to do as he asked. Star Bright groaned once more and her pleading eyes looked directly into Rorie's, seeming to beg for help. The mare's lips pulled back from her teeth as she flailed her head to and fro, shaking Rorie in the process.

"Whoa, girl," Rorie said softly, gaining control. "It's painful, isn't it, but soon you'll have a beautiful baby to show off to the world."

"Foal," Clay corrected from behind the mare.

"A beautiful foal." Rorie stroked the sweat-dampened neck, doing what she could to reassure the frightened horse.

"Keep talking to her," Clay whispered.

Rorie kept up a running dialogue for several tense minutes, but there was only so much she could find to say on such short acquaintance. When she ran out of ideas, she started to sing in a soft, lilting voice. She began with lullabies her mother had once sung to her, then followed those with a few childhood ditties. Her singing lasted only minutes, but Rorie's lungs felt close to collapse.

Suddenly the mare's water broke. Clay wasn't saying much, but he began to work quickly, although she couldn't see what he was doing. Star Bright tossed her neck in the final throes of birth and Rorie watched, fascinated, as two hooves and front legs emerged, followed by a white nose.

The mare lifted her head, eager to see. Clay tugged gently, and within seconds, the foal was free. Rorie's heart pounded like a locomotive struggling up a steep hill as Clay's strong hands completed the task.

"A filly," he announced, a smile lighting his face. He reached for a rag and wiped his hands and arms.

Star Bright turned her head to view her offspring. "See?" Rorie told the mare, her eyes moist with relief. "Didn't I tell you it would all be worth it?"

The mare nickered. Her newborn filly was gray, like her mother, and finely marked with white streaks on her nose, mane and tail. Rorie was touched to her very soul by the sight. Tears blurred her vision and ran down her flushed cheeks. She blotted them with her sleeve so Clay couldn't see them, and silently chided herself for being such a sentimental fool.

It was almost another hour before they left Star Bright's stall. The mare, who stood guard over her long-legged baby, seemed content and utterly pleased with herself. As they prepared to leave, Rorie whispered in her ear.

"What was that all about?" Clay wanted to know, latching the stall door.

"I just told her she'd done a good job."

"That she did," Clay whispered. A moment later, he added, "And so did you, Rorie. I was grateful for your help."

Once more tears sprang to her eyes. She responded with a nod, unable to trust her voice. Her heart was racing with exhilaration. She couldn't remember a time she'd felt more excited. It was well past midnight, but she'd never felt less sleepy.

"Rorie?" He was staring at her, his eyes bright with concern.

She owed him an explanation, although she couldn't fully explain this sudden burst of emotion. "It was so… beautiful." She brushed the hair from her face and smiled up at him, hoping he wouldn't think she was just a foolish city girl. She wasn't sure why it mattered, but she doubted that any man had seen her looking worse, although Rorie was well aware that she didn't possess a classic beauty. She was usually referred to as cute, with her slightly turned-up nose and dark brown eyes.

"I understand." He walked to the sink against the barn's opposite wall and busily washed his hands, then splashed water on his face. When he'd finished, Rorie handed him a towel hanging on a nearby hook.

"Thanks."

"I don't know how to describe it," she said, after a fruitless effort to find the words to explain all the feeling that had surged up inside her.

"It's the same for me every time I witness a birth," Clay told her. He looked at her then and gently touched her face, letting his finger glide along her jaw. All the world went still as his eyes caressed hers. There was a primitive wonder in the experience of birth, a wonder that struck deep within the soul. For the first time, Rorie understood this. And sharing it with Clay seemed to intensify the attraction she already felt for him. During that brief time in the stall, just before Star Bright delivered her foal, Rorie had felt closer to Clay than she ever had to any other man. It was as though her heart had taken flight and joined his in a moment of sheer challenge and joy. That was a silly romantic thought, she realized. But it seemed so incredible to her that she could feel anything this strong for a man she'd known for mere hours.

"I've got a name for her," Clay said, hanging up the towel. "What do you think of Nightsong?"

"Nightsong," Rorie repeated softly. "I like it."

"In honor of the woman who sang to her mother."

Rorie nodded as emotion clogged her throat. "Does this mean I did all right for a city slicker?"

"You did more than all right."

"Thanks for not sending me away... I probably would've gone if you'd insisted."

They left the barn, and Clay draped his arm across her shoulders as though he'd been doing it for years. Rorie was grateful for his touch because, somehow, it helped ground the unfamiliar feelings and sensations.

As they strolled across the yard, she noticed that the sky was filled with a thousand glittering stars, brighter than any she'd ever seen in the city. She paused midstep to gaze up at them.

Clay's quiet voice didn't dispel the serenity. "It's a lovely night, isn't it?"

Rorie wanted to hold on to each exquisite minute and make it last a lifetime. A nod was all she could manage as she reminded herself that this time with Clay was about to end. They would walk into the house and Clay would probably thank her again. Then she'd climb the stairs to her room and that would be all there was.

"How about some coffee?" he asked once they'd entered the kitchen. Blue left his rug and wandered over to Clay. "The way I feel now, it would be a waste of time to go to bed."

"Me, too." Rorie leaped at the suggestion, pleased that he wanted to delay their parting, too. And when she did return to her room, she knew the adrenaline in her system would make sleep impossible, anyway.

Clay was reaching up for the canister of coffee, when Rorie suddenly noticed the bloodstain on his sleeve and remembered Star Bright's kick.

"Clay, you need to take care of that cut."

From the surprised way he glanced at his arm, she guessed that he, too, had forgotten about the injury. "Yes, I suppose I should." Then he calmly returned to his task.

"Let me clean it for you," Rorie offered, joining him at the kitchen counter.

"If you like." He led her into the bathroom down the hall and took a variety of medical supplies from the cabinet above the sink. "Do you want to do it here or in the kitchen?"

"Here is fine."

Clay sat on the edge of the bath and unfastened the cuff, then rolled back his sleeve.

"Oh, Clay," Rorie whispered when she saw the angry torn flesh just above his elbow. Gently her fingers tested the edges, wondering if he needed stitches. He winced slightly at her probing fingers.

"Sorry."

"Just put some antiseptic on it and it'll be all right."

"But this is really deep—you should probably have a doctor look at it."

"Rorie, I'm as tough as old leather. This kind of thing happens all the time. I'll recover."

"I don't doubt that," she said primly.

"Then put on a bandage and be done with it."

"But—"

"I've been injured often enough to know when a cut needs a doctor's attention."

She hesitated, then conceded that he was probably right. She filled the sink with warm tap water and took care to clean the wound thoroughly. All the while, Rorie was conscious of Clay's eyes moving over her face, solemnly perusing the chin-length, dark brown hair and the big dark eyes that—judging by a glance in the mirror—

still displayed a hint of vulnerability. She was tall, almost five-eight, her figure willowy. But if Clay found anything attractive about her, he didn't mention it. Her throat muscles squeezed shut, and, although she was grateful for the silence between them, it confused her.

"You missed your vocation," he told her as she rinsed the bloody cloth. "You should've been a nurse."

"I toyed with the idea when I was ten, but decided I liked books better."

His shoulders were tense, Rorie noted, and she tried to be as gentle as possible. A muscle leaped in his jaw.

"Am I…hurting you?"

"No," he answered, his voice curt.

After that, he was an excellent patient. He didn't complain when she dabbed on the antiseptic, although she was sure it must have stung like crazy. He cooperated when she wrapped the gauze around his arm, lifting and lowering it when she asked him to. The silence continued as she secured the bandage with adhesive tape. Rorie had the feeling that he wanted to escape the close confines of the bathroom as quickly as possible.

"I hope that stays."

He stood up and flexed his elbow a couple of times. "It's fine. You do good work."

"I'm glad you think so."

"The coffee's probably ready by now." He spoke quickly, as if eager to be gone.

She sighed. "I could use a cup."

She put the medical supplies neatly back inside the cabinet, while Clay returned to the kitchen. Rorie could smell the freshly made coffee even before she entered the room.

He was leaning against the counter, sipping a cup of the fragrant coffee, waiting for her.

"It's been quite a night, hasn't it?" she murmured, adding cream and sugar to the mug he'd poured for her.

A certain tension hung in the air, and Rorie couldn't explain or understand it. Only ten minutes earlier, they'd walked across the yard, spellbound by the stars, and Clay had laid his arm across her shoulders. He'd smiled down on her so tenderly. Now he looked as if he couldn't wait to get away from her.

"Have I done anything wrong?" she asked outright.

"Rorie, no." He set his mug aside and gripped her shoulders with both hands. "There's something so intimate and…earthy in what we shared." His eyes were intense, strangely darker. "Wanting you this way isn't right."

Rorie felt a tremor work through him as he lifted his hands to her face. His callused thumbs lightly caressed her cheeks.

"I feel like I've known you all my life," he whispered hoarsely, his expression uncertain.

"It's…been the same for me, from the moment you stepped out of the truck."

Clay smiled, and Rorie thought her knees would melt. She put her coffee down and as soon as she did Clay eased her into his arms, his hands on her shoulders. Her heart stopped, then jolted back to frenzied life.

"I'm going to kiss you…."

He made the statement almost a question. "Yes," she whispered, letting him know she'd welcome his touch. Her stomach fluttered as he slowly lowered his mouth to hers.

Rorie had never wanted a man's kiss more. His moist lips glided over hers in a series of gentle explorations. He drew her closer until their bodies were pressed tight.

"Oh, Rorie," he breathed, dragging his mouth from hers. "You taste so good… I was afraid of that." His mouth found the pulse in her throat and lingered there.

"This afternoon I thought I'd cry when the car broke down and now…now I'm glad…so glad," she said.

He kissed her again, nibbling on her lower lip, gently drawing it between his teeth. Rorie could hardly breathe, her heart was pounding so hard. She slumped against him, delighting in the rise and fall of his broad chest. His hands moved down her back with slow restraint, but paused when he reached the curve of her hips.

He tensed. "I think we should say good-night."

A protest sprang to her lips, but before she could voice it, Clay said, "Now."

She looked at him, dazed. The last thing she wanted to do was leave him. "What about my coffee?"

"That was just an excuse and we both know it."

Rorie said nothing.

The silence between them seemed to throb for endless minutes.

"Good night, Clay," she finally whispered. She broke away, but his hand caught her fingers, and with a groan he pulled her back into his arms.

"What the hell," he muttered fiercely, "sending you upstairs isn't going to help. Nothing's going to change."

His words brought confusion, but Rorie didn't question him, didn't want to. What she longed for was the warmth and security she'd discovered in his arms.

"Come on," he whispered, after he'd kissed her once more. He led her through the living room and outside to the porch, where the swing moved gently in the night breeze.

Rorie sat beside him and he wrapped his arm around her. She nestled her head against his shoulder, savoring these precious moments.

"I'll never forget this night."

"Neither will I," Clay promised, kissing her again.

* * *

Rorie awoke when the sun settled on her face and refused to leave her alone. Keeping her eyes closed, she smiled contentedly, basking in the memory of her night with Clay. They'd sat on the swing and talked for hours. Talked and kissed and laughed and touched...

Sitting up, Rorie raised her hands high above her head and stretched, arching her spine. She looked at her watch on the nightstand and was shocked to see that it was after eleven. By the time she'd climbed the stairs for bed the sky had been dappled with faint shreds of light. She suspected Clay hadn't even bothered to sleep.

Tossing aside the blankets, Rorie slid to the floor, anxious to shower and dress. Anxious to see him again. Fifteen minutes later, she was on her way down the stairs.

Mary, who was dusting in the living room, nodded when she saw Rorie. Then the housekeeper resumed her task, but not before she'd muttered something about how city folks were prone to sleeping their lives away.

"Good morning, Mary," Rorie greeted her cheerfully.

"'Mornin'."

"Where is everyone?"

"Where they ought to be this time of day. Working."

"Yes, I know, but where?"

"Outside."

Rorie had trouble hiding her smile.

"I heard about you helping last night," Mary added gruffly. "Seems you did all right for a city girl."

"Thank you, Mary. You don't do half bad for a country girl, either."

The housekeeper seemed uncomfortable with the praise, despite the lightness of Rorie's tone. "I suppose you want me to cook you some fancy breakfast."

"Good heavens, no, you're busy. I'll just make myself some toast."

"That's hardly enough to fill a growing girl," Mary complained.

"It'll suit me fine."

Once her toast was ready, Rorie carried it outside. If she couldn't find Clay, she wanted to check on Nightsong.

"Rorie."

She turned to discover Skip walking toward her, in animated conversation with a blonde. His girlfriend, she guessed. He waved and Rorie returned the gesture, smiling. The sun was glorious and the day held marvelous promise.

"I didn't think you were ever going to wake up," Skip said.

"I'm sorry—I don't usually sleep this late."

"Clay told me how you helped him deliver Star Bright's filly. You could've knocked me over with a feather when I heard."

Rorie nodded, her heart warming with the memory. "Well, I tried to get you up. It would've been easier to wake a dead man than to get you out of bed last night."

Skip looked slightly embarrassed. "Sorry about that, but I generally don't wake up too easily once I'm asleep." As he spoke, he slipped his arm around the blonde girl's shoulders. "Rorie, I want you to meet Kate Logan."

"Hello, Kate." Rorie held out a hand and Kate shook it politely.

"Hello, Rorie," she said. "Clay and Skip told me about your car troubles. I hope everything turns out all right for you."

"I'm sure it will. Do you live around here?" Rorie already knew she was going to like her. At a closer glance, she saw that Kate was older than she'd first assumed.

Maybe her own age, which gave credence to Skip's comment about liking older, more mature women.

"I don't live far," Kate said. "The Circle L is down the road, only a few miles from here."

"She's going to be living *with* us in the near future," Skip put in, gazing fondly at Kate.

The young woman's cheeks reddened and she smiled shyly.

"Oh?" Skip couldn't possibly mean he planned to marry her, Rorie thought. Good heavens, he was still in high school.

He must have seen Rorie's puzzled frown, and hurried to explain. "Not me," he said with a short laugh. "Kate is Clay's fiancée."

Five

"You and Clay are…engaged," Rorie murmured as shock waves coursed through her blood. They stopped with a thud at her heart and spread out in ripples of dismay.

Somehow Rorie managed a smile, her outward composure unbroken. She was even able to offer her congratulations. To all appearances, nothing was wrong. No one would've known that those few simple words had destroyed a night she'd planned to treasure all her life.

"I hope you and Clay will be very happy," Rorie said—and she meant it. She'd just been introduced to Kate Logan, but already Rorie knew that this sweet, friendly woman was exactly the kind of wife a man like Clay would need.

"Skip's rushing things a little," Kate pointed out, but the glint of love in her eyes contradicted her words. "Clay hasn't even given me an engagement ring yet."

"But you and Clay have been talking about getting married, haven't you?" Skip pressed. "And you're crazy about him."

Kate blushed prettily. "I've loved Clay from the time I was in fifth grade. I wrote his name all over my books. Of course, Clay wouldn't have anything to do with me, not when he was a big important high-schooler and I was just the pesky little girl next door. It took a while for him to notice me—like ten years." She gave a small laugh. "We've been dating steadily for the past two."

"But you and Clay *are* going to get married, right?" Skip continued, clearly wanting to prove his point.

"Eventually, but we haven't set a date, although I'm sure it'll be soon," Kate answered, casting a sharp look at Rorie.

The tightness that had gripped Rorie's throat eased and she struggled to keep her smile intact. It was impossible not to like Kate, but that didn't lessen the ache in Rorie's heart.

"The wedding's inevitable," Skip said offhandedly, "so I wasn't exaggerating when I said you were Clay's fiancée, now was I?"

Kate smiled. "I suppose not. We love each other, and have for years. We're just waiting for the right time." Her eyes held Rorie's, assessing her, but she didn't seem worried about competition.

Rorie supposed she should be pleased about that, at least.

"I was taking Kate over to see Nightsong," Skip explained to Rorie.

"I actually came to Elk Run to meet you," the other woman said. "Clay stopped by last night and told me about your car. I felt terrible for you. Your whole vacation's been ruined. You must be awfully upset."

"These things happen," Rorie said with a shrug. "Being upset isn't going to ship that part any faster. All I can do is accept the facts."

Kate nodded sympathetically. "Skip was about to show me the filly. You'll come with us, won't you?"

Rorie nodded, unable to excuse herself without sounding rude. If there'd been a way, she would have retreated, wanting only to lick her wounds in private. Instead, hoping she sounded more enthusiastic than she felt, she mumbled, "I was headed in that direction myself."

Skip led the way to the barn, which was alive with activity. Clay had explained that Elk Run employed five men full-time, none of whom lived on the premises. Two men mucking out stalls paused when Skip and the women entered the building. Skip introduced Rorie and they touched the tips of their hats in greeting.

"I don't understand Clay," Skip said as they approached the mare's stall. "When we bought Star Bright a few years back, all Clay could do was complain about that silly name. He even talked about getting her registration changed."

"Star Bright's a perfectly good name," Kate insisted, her sunny blue eyes intent on the newborn foal.

Nightsong was standing now on knobby, skinny legs that threatened to buckle, greedily feasting from her mother.

"Oh, she really is lovely, isn't she?" Kate whispered.

Rorie hadn't been able to stop looking at the filly from the moment they'd reached the stall. Finished with her breakfast, Nightsong gazed around, fascinated by everything she surveyed. She returned Rorie's look, not vacantly, but as though she recognized the woman who'd been there at her birth.

Rorie couldn't even identify all the emotions she suddenly felt. Some of these feelings were so new she couldn't put a name to them, but they gripped her heart and squeezed tight.

"What I can't understand," Skip muttered, "is why Clay would go and call her Nightsong when he hates the name Star Bright. It doesn't sound like anything he'd ever come up with on his own, yet he says he did."

"I know," Kate agreed, "but I'm glad, because the name suits her." She sighed. "Clay's always been so practical when it comes to names for his horses, but Nightsong has such a romantic flavor, don't you think?"

Skip chuckled. "You know what Clay thinks about romance, and that makes it even more confusing. But Nightsong she is, and she's bound to bring us a pretty penny in a year or two. Her father was a Polish Arabian, and with Star Bright's bloodlines Nightsong will command big bucks as a National Show Horse."

"Skip." Clay's curt voice interrupted them. He strode from the arena leading a bay mare. The horse's coat gleamed with sweat, turning its color the shade of an oak leaf in autumn. One of the stablemen approached to take the reins. Then Clay removed his hat, wiping his brow with his forearm, and Rorie noticed the now-grimy bandage she'd applied last night. No, this morning.

She stared hungrily at his sun-bronzed face, a face that revealed more than a hint of impatience. The lines around his mouth were etched deep with poorly disguised regrets. Rorie recognized them, even if the others didn't.

Clay stopped short when he saw Kate, his eyes narrowing.

"'Morning, Kate."

"Hello, Clay."

Then his gaze moved, slowly and reluctantly, to Rorie. The remorse she'd already sensed in him seemed unmistakable.

"I hope you slept well," was all he said to her.

"Fine." She detected a tautness along his jawline and decided he was probably concerned that she'd say or do something to embarrass him in front of his fiancée. Rorie wouldn't, but not because she was worried about him. Her sense of fair play wouldn't allow her to hurt Kate, who so obviously adored this man.

"We're just admiring Nightsong," Kate explained, her expression tender as she smiled up at him.

"I can't understand why you'd name her that," Skip said, his mouth twitching with barely suppressed laughter. "You always pick names like Brutus and Firepower, but Nightsong? I think you're going soft on us." Considering himself particularly funny, Skip chuckled and added, "I suppose that's what love does to a man."

Kate's lashes brushed against the high arch of her cheek and she smiled, her pleasure so keen it was like a physical touch.

"Didn't I ask you to water the horses several hours ago?" Clay asked in a tone that could have chipped rock.

"Yes, but—"

"Then kindly see to it. The farrier will be here any minute."

The humor left Skip's eyes; he was clearly upset by Clay's anger. He looked from his brother to the two women and then back at Clay again. Hot color rose into his neck and invaded his face. "All right," he muttered. "Excuse me for living." Then he stormed out of the barn, slapping his hat against his thigh in an outburst of anger.

Kate waited until Skip was out of the barn. "Clay, what's wrong?"

"He should've done what I told him long before now. Those horses in the pasture are thirsty because of his neglect."

"I'm the one you should be angry with, not Skip." Kate's voice was contrite. "I should never have stopped in without calling first, but I...wanted to meet Rorie."

"You've only been here a few minutes," Clay insisted, his anger in check now. "Skip had plenty of time to complete his chores before you arrived."

Rorie tossed invisible daggers at Clay, annoyed with

him for taking his irritation out on his younger brother.
Skip had introduced her to Clay's fiancée. *That* was what
really bothered him if he'd been willing to admit it—which
he clearly wasn't.

"We came here to see Nightsong," Kate said again. "I'm
glad you named her that, no matter what Skip thinks." She
wrapped her arm around his waist, and rested her head
against his broad chest. "He was just teasing you and you
know how he loves to do that."

Clay gave her an absent smile, but his gaze settled with
disturbing ease on Rorie. She met his eyes boldly, deny-
ing the emotions churning furiously inside her. The plea
for patience and understanding he sent her was so obvious
that Rorie wondered how anyone seeing it wouldn't know
what was happening.

As though she'd suddenly remembered something, Kate
dropped her arm and glanced hurriedly at her watch. She
groaned. "I promised Dad I'd meet him for lunch today.
He's getting together with the other Town Council members in one of those horribly boring meetings. He needs
me as an excuse to get away." She stopped abruptly, a chagrined expression on her face. "I guess that tells you how
informal everything is in Nightingale, doesn't it, Rorie?"

"The town seems to be doing very well." She didn't
know if that was true or not, but it sounded polite.

"He just hates these things, but he likes the prestige of
being a Council member—something I tease him about."

"I'll walk you to your car," Clay offered.

"Oh, there's no need. You're busy. Besides, I wanted to
talk to Rorie and arrange to meet her tomorrow and show
her around town. I certainly hope you remembered to invite her to the Grange dance tomorrow night. I'm sure
Luke would be willing to escort her."

"Oh, I couldn't possibly intrude," Rorie blurted.

"Nonsense, you'd be more than welcome. And don't worry about having the right kind of clothes for a square dance, either, because I've got more outfits than I know what to do with. We're about the same size," Kate said, eyeing her. "Perhaps you're a little taller, but not so much that you couldn't wear my skirts."

Rorie smiled blandly, realizing it wouldn't do any good to decline the invitation. But good heavens, square dancing? Her?

"Knowing you and Skip," Kate chastised Clay, "poor Rorie will be stuck on Elk Run for the next four days bored out of her mind. The least I can do is see that she's entertained."

"That's thoughtful of you," Rorie said. The sooner she got back on the road, the safer her heart would be, and if Kate Logan was willing to help her kill time, then all the better.

"I thought I'd give you a tour of our little town in the morning," Kate went on. "It's small, but the people are friendly."

"I'd love to see Nightingale."

"Clay." The brusque voice of a farmhand interrupted them. "Could you come here a minute?"

Clay turned to the man and nodded. "I have to find out what Don needs," he said quietly. As he met Rorie's eyes, a speculative look flashed into his own.

She nearly flinched, wondering what emotion her face had betrayed. From the minute Clay had walked into the barn, she'd been careful to school her expression, not wanting him to read anything into her words or actions. She'd tried to look cool and unconcerned, as if the night they'd shared had never happened.

"You two will have to excuse me." Weary amusement

turned up the corners of his mouth and Rorie realized he'd readily seen through her guise.

"Of course," Kate said. "I'll see you later, sweetheart."

Clay nodded abruptly and departed with firm purposeful strides.

Kate started walking toward the yard. Rorie followed, eager to escape the barn and all the memories associated with it.

"Clay told us you're a librarian," Kate said when she reached the Ford parked in the curving driveway. "If you want, I can take you to our library. We built a new one last year and we're rather proud of it. I know it's small compared to where you probably work, but I think you'll like what we've done."

"I'd love to see it." Libraries were often the heart of a community, and if the citizens of Nightingale had seen fit to upgrade theirs, it was apparent they shared Rorie's love of books.

"I'll pick you up around ten tomorrow, if that's convenient?"

"That'd be fine."

"Plan on spending the afternoon with me and we'll meet Clay and Skip at the dance later."

Rorie agreed, although her enthusiasm was decidedly low. The last thing she wanted was to be at some social event with Clay. Never mind how Dan would tease her if he ever discovered she'd spent part of her vacation square dancing with the folks at the Grange.

"Bye for now," Kate said.

"Bye," Rorie murmured, waving. She stood in the yard until Kate's car was out of sight. Not sure what else to do, she wandered back into the house, where Mary was busy with preparations for lunch.

"Can I help?" she asked.

In response, Mary scurried to a drawer and once again handed her a peeler. Rorie started carefully whittling away at a firm red apple she'd scooped from a large bowlful of them.

"I don't suppose you know anything about cooking?" Mary demanded, pointing her own peeler at Rorie.

"I've managed to keep from starving for the last few years," she retorted idly.

The merest hint of amusement flashed into the older woman's weathered face. "If I was judging your talents in the kitchen on looks alone, I think you'd starve a man to death within a week."

Despite her glum spirits, Rorie laughed. "If you're telling me you think I'm thin, watch out, Mary, because I'm likely to throw my arms around your neck and kiss you."

The other woman threw her a grin. Several peaceful minutes passed while they peeled apple after apple.

"I got a call from my sister," Mary said hesitantly, her eyes darting to Rorie, then back to her task. "She's coming to Riversdale and wants to know if I can drive over and see her. She's only going to be in Oregon one day."

This was the most Mary had said to Rorie since her arrival. It pleased her that the older woman was lowering her guard and extending a friendly hand.

"I'd like to visit with my sister."

"I certainly think you should." It took Rorie another minute to figure out where Mary was heading with this meandering conversation. Then suddenly she understood. "Oh, you're looking for someone to do the cooking while you're away."

Mary shrugged as if it didn't concern her one way or the other. "Just for the evening meal, two nights from now. I could manage lunch for the hands before I leave. It's supper I'm worried about. There's only Clay and Skip who need to be fed—the other men go home in the evenings."

"Well, relax, because I'm sure I can manage one dinner without killing off the menfolk."

"You're sure?"

Mary was so completely serious that Rorie laughed outright. "Since my abilities do seem to worry you, how would you feel if I invited Kate Logan over to help?"

Mary nodded and sighed. "I'd rest easier."

Rorie stayed in the kitchen until the lunch dishes had been put away. Mary thanked her for helping, then went home to watch her daily soap operas.

Feeling a little lost, Rorie wandered outside and into the stable. Since Clay had already shown her the computer, she decided to spend the afternoon working in his office.

The area was deserted, which went some distance toward reassuring her—but then, she'd assumed it would be. From what she'd observed, a stud farm was a busy place and Clay was bound to be occupied elsewhere. That suited Rorie just fine. She hoped to avoid him as much as possible. In three days she'd be out of his life, leaving hardly a trace, and that was the way she wanted it.

Rorie sat typing in data for about an hour before her neck and shoulders began to cramp. She paused, flexing her muscles, then rotated her head to relieve the building tightness.

"How long have you been here?"

The rough male voice behind her startled Rorie. Her hand flew to her heart and she expelled a shaky breath. "Clay! You frightened me."

"How long?" he repeated.

"An hour or so." She glanced at her watch and nodded.

Clay advanced a step toward her, his mouth a thin line of impatience. "I suppose you're looking for an apology."

Rorie didn't answer. She'd learned not to expect anything from him.

"I'll tell you right now that you're not going to get one," he finished gruffly.

Six

"You don't owe me anything, Clay," Rorie said, struggling to make her voice light. Clay looked driven to the limits of exhaustion. Dark shadows had formed beneath his eyes and fatigue lines fanned out from their corners. His shoulders sagged slightly, as if the weight he carried was more than he could bear. He studied her wearily, then turned away, stalking to the other side of the office. His shoulders heaved as he drew in a shuddering breath.

"I know I should feel some regrets, but God help me, Rorie, I don't."

"Clay, listen…"

He turned to face her then, and drove his fingers into his hair with such force Rorie winced. "I'd like to explain about Kate and me."

"No." Under no circumstances did Rorie want to listen to his explanations or excuses. She didn't have a lot of room to be judgmental herself. She had, after all, been dating a man steadily for the past few months. "Don't. Please don't say anything. It isn't necessary."

He ignored her request. "Kate and I have known each other all our lives."

"Clay, stop." She pushed out the chair and stood up, wanting only to escape.

"For the last two years, it's been understood by everyone around us that Kate and I would eventually get married. I didn't even question the right or wrong of it, just calmly accepted the fact. A man needs someone to share his life."

"Kate will make you a wonderful wife," she said, feeling both disillusioned and indignant, but she refused to let him know how much his indiscretion had hurt her. "If you owe anyone an apology, it's Kate, not me."

His responding frown was brooding and dark. "I know." He drew his fingers across his eyes, and she could feel his exhaustion. "The last thing in the world I want is to hurt Kate."

"Then don't."

He stared at her, and Rorie made herself send him a smile, although she feared it was more flippant than reassuring. "There's no reason for Kate to find out. What good would it do? She'd only end up feeling betrayed. Last night was a tiny impropriety and best forgotten, don't you agree?" Walking seemed to help, and Rorie paced the office, her fingers brushing the stack of books and papers on his cluttered desk.

"I don't know what's best anymore," Clay admitted quietly.

"I do," Rorie said with unwavering confidence, still struggling to make light of the incident. "Think about it, Clay. We were alone together for hours—we shared something beautiful with Star Bright and…her foal. And we shared a few stolen kisses under the stars. If anything's to blame, it's the moonlight. We're strangers, Clay. You don't know me and I don't know you." Afraid to look him directly in the eye, Rorie lowered her gaze and waited, breathless, for his next words.

"So it was the moonlight?" His voice was hoarse and painfully raw.

"Of course," she lied. "What else could it have been?"

"Yes, what else could it have been?" he echoed, then turned and walked out of the office.

It suddenly seemed as though the room's light had dimmed. Rorie felt so weak, she sank into the chair, shocked by how deeply the encounter had disturbed her.

Typing proved to be a distraction and Rorie left the office a couple of hours later with a feeling of accomplishment. She'd been able to enter several time-consuming pages of data into the computer. The routine work was a relief because it meant she had no time to think.

The kitchen smelled of roasting beef and simmering apple crisp when Rorie let herself in the back door. It was an oddly pleasant combination of scents. Mary was nowhere to be seen.

While she thought of it, Rorie reached for the telephone book and called the number listed for the garage in Riversdale.

"Hello," she said when a gruff male voice answered. "This is Rorie Campbell...the woman with the broken water pump. The one in Nightingale."

"Yeah, Miss Campbell, what can I do for you?"

"I just wanted to be sure there wasn't any problem in ordering the part. I don't know if Clay...Mr. Franklin told you, but I'm more or less stuck here until the car's repaired. I'd like to get back on the road as soon as possible—I'm sure you understand."

"Lady, I can't make that pump come any faster than what it already is."

"Well, I just wanted to check that you'd been able to order one."

"It's on its way, at least that's what the guy in Los Angeles told me. They're shipping it by overnight freight to Portland. I've arranged for a man to pick it up the following day, but it's going to take him some time to get it to me."

"But that's only three days."

"You called too late yesterday for me to phone the order in. Lady, there's only so much I can do."

"I know. I'm sorry if I sound impatient."

"The whole world's impatient. Listen, I'll call you the minute it arrives."

She sighed. "Thanks, I'd appreciate it."

"Clay got your car here without a hitch, so don't worry about that—he saved you a bundle on towing charges. Shipping costs and long-distance phone bills are going to be plenty high, though."

Rorie hadn't even noticed that Dan's shiny sports car wasn't in the yard where Skip had originally left it. "So you'll be calling me within the next day or two?" she asked, trying to hide the anxiety in her voice. And trying not to consider the state of her finances, already depleted by this disastrous vacation.

"Right. I'll call as soon as it comes in."

"Thank you. I appreciate it," she said again.

"No problem," the mechanic muttered, obviously eager to end their conversation.

When the call was finished, Rorie toyed with the idea of phoning Dan next. She'd been half expecting to hear from him, since she'd left the Franklins' number with his secretary the day before. He hadn't phoned her back. But there was nothing new to tell him, so she decided not to call a second time.

Hesitantly Rorie replaced the telephone receiver, pleased that everything was under control—everything except her heart.

* * *

Dinner that evening was a strained affair. If it hadn't been for Skip, who seemed oblivious to the tension between her and Clay, Rorie didn't think she could have endured it. Clay hardly said a word throughout the meal. But Skip seemed more than eager to carry the conversation and Rorie did her best to lighten the mood, wondering all the time whether Clay saw through her facade.

"While you're here, Rorie," Skip said with a sudden burst of enthusiasm, "you should learn how to ride."

"No, thank you," she said pointedly, holding up her hand, as though fending off the suggestion. An introduction to King and Hercules was as far as she was willing to go.

"Rain Magic would suit you nicely."

"Rain Magic?"

"That's a silly name Kate thought up, and Clay went along with it," Skip explained. "He's gentle, but smart—the gelding I mean, not Clay." The younger Franklin laughed heartily at his own attempt at humor.

Clay smiled, but Rorie wasn't fooled; he hadn't been amused by the joke, nor, she suspected, was he pleased by the reference to Kate.

"No, thanks, Skip," she said, hoping to bring the subject to a close. "I'm really not interested." There, that said it plainly enough.

"Are you afraid?"

"A little," she admitted truthfully. "I prefer my horses on a merry-go-round. I'm a city girl, remember?"

"But even girls from San Francisco have been known to climb on the back of a horse. It'll be good for you, Rorie. Trust me—it's time to broaden your horizons."

"Thanks, but no thanks," she told him, emphasizing

her point by biting down on a crisp carrot stick with a loud crunch.

"Rorie, I insist. You aren't going to get hurt—I wouldn't let that happen, and Rain Magic is as gentle as they come. In fact—" he wiggled his eyebrows up and down "—if you want, we can ride double until you feel more secure."

Rorie laughed. "Skip, honestly."

"All right, you can ride alone, and I'll lead you around in a circle. For as long as you want."

Rorie shook her head and, amused at the mental picture that scenario presented, laughed again.

"Leave it," Clay said with sudden sharpness. "If Rorie doesn't want to ride, drop it, okay?"

Skip's shocked gaze flew from Rorie to his brother. "I was just having fun, Clay."

His older brother gripped his water goblet so hard Rorie thought the glass might shatter. "Enough is enough. She said she wasn't interested and that should be the end of it."

The astounded look left Skip's features, but his eyes narrowed and he stiffened his shoulders in a display of righteous indignation. "What's with you, Clay?" he shouted. "You've been acting like a wounded bear all day, growling at everyone. Who made *you* king of the universe all of a sudden?"

"If you'll excuse me, I'll bring in the apple crisp," Rorie said, and hurriedly rose to her feet, not wanting to be caught in the cross fire between the two brothers. Whatever they had to say wasn't meant for her ears.

The exchange that followed ended quickly, Rorie noted gratefully from inside the kitchen. Their voices were raised and then there was a hush followed by laughter. Rorie relaxed and picked up the dessert, carrying it into the dining room along with a carton of vanilla ice cream.

"I apologize, Rorie," Clay said soberly when she reentered the room. "Skip's right, I've been cross and unreasonable all day. I hope my sour mood hasn't ruined your dinner."

"Of course not," she murmured, giving him a smile.

Clay stood up to serve the dessert, spooning generous helpings of apple crisp and ice cream into each bowl.

Skip chattered aimlessly, commenting on one subject and then bouncing to another without any logical connection, his thoughts darting this way and that.

"What time are you going over to Kate's tonight?" he casually asked Clay.

"I won't be. She's got some meeting with the women's group from the Grange. They're decorating for the dance tomorrow night."

"Now that you mention it, I seem to remember Kate saying something about being busy tonight." Without a pause he turned to Rorie. "You'll be coming, I hope. The Grange is putting on a square dance—the biggest one of the year, and they usually do it up good."

"Kate already invited me. I'll be going with her," Rorie explained, although she hadn't the slightest idea how to square dance. Generally she enjoyed dancing, although she hadn't gone for several months because Dan wasn't keen on it.

"You could drive there with us if you wanted," Skip offered. "I'd kinda like to walk in there with you on my arm. You'd cause quite a stir with the men, especially Luke Rivers—he's the foreman at the Logan place. Most girls go all goo-goo-eyed over him."

Clay's spoon clanged loudly against the side of his glass dish and he murmured an apology.

"I'm sorry, Skip," Rorie said gently. "I told Kate I'd drive over with her."

"Darn," Skip muttered.

The meal was completed in silence. Once, when Rorie happened to glance up, her eyes met Clay's. Her heart felt as though it might hammer its way out of her chest. She was oppressively aware of the chemistry between them. It simmered in Rorie's veins and she could tell that Clay felt everything she did. Throughout dinner, she'd been all too conscious of the swift stolen glances Clay had sent in her direction. She'd sent a few of her own, though she'd tried hard not to. But it was impossible to be in the same room with this man and not react to him.

A thousand times in the next couple of hours, Rorie told herself that everything would be fine as soon as she could leave. Life would return to normal then.

When the dishes were finished, Skip challenged her to a game of cribbage, and grateful for the escape Rorie accepted. Skip sat with his back to his brother, and every time Rorie played her hand, she found her eyes wandering across the room to where Clay sat reading. To all outward appearances, he was relaxed and comfortable, but she knew he felt as tense as she did. She knew he was equally aware of the electricity that sparked between them.

Rorie's fingers shook as she counted out her cards.

"Fifteen eight," Skip corrected. "You forgot two points."

Her eyes fell to the extra ten, and she blinked. "I guess I did."

Skip heaved a sigh. "I don't think your mind's on the game tonight."

"I guess not," she admitted wryly. "If you'll excuse me, I think I'll go up to bed." She threw him an apologetic smile and reached for her coffee cup. Skip was right; her mind hadn't been on the game at all. Instead, her thoughts had been on a man who owed his loyalties to another woman—a woman whose roots were intricately bound with his. A woman Rorie had liked and respected from the moment they met.

Feeling depressed, she bade the two men good-night and carried her cup to the kitchen. Dutifully, she rinsed it out and set it beside the sink, but when she turned around Clay was standing in the doorway, blocking her exit.

"Where's Skip?" she asked a little breathlessly. Heat seemed to throb between them and she retreated a step in a futile effort to escape.

"He went upstairs."

She blinked and faked a yawn. "I was headed in that direction myself."

Clay buried one hand in his jeans pocket. "Do you know what happened tonight at dinner?"

Not finding her voice, Rorie shook her head.

"I was jealous," he said from between clenched teeth. "You were laughing and joking with Skip and I wanted it to be *me* your eyes were shining for. Me. No one else." He stopped abruptly and shook his head. "Jealous of a seventeen-year-old boy… I can't believe it myself."

Seven

Rorie decided to wear a dress for her outing with Kate Logan. Although she rose early, both Skip and Clay had eaten breakfast and left the house by the time she came downstairs. Which was just as well, Rorie thought.

Mary stood at the stove, frying chunks of beef for a luncheon stew. "I spoke to Clay about your cooking dinner later this week. He says that'll be fine if you're still around, but the way he sees it, you'll be on your way in a day or two."

Rorie poured herself a cup of coffee. "I'll be happy to do it if I'm here. Otherwise, I'm sure Kate Logan would be more than pleased."

Mary turned to face her, mouth open as if to comment. Instead her eyes widened in appreciation. "My, my, you look pretty enough to hog-tie a man's heart."

"Thank you, Mary," Rorie answered, grinning.

"I suppose you got yourself a sweetheart back there in San Francisco?" she asked, watching her closely. "A pretty girl like you is bound to attract plenty of men."

Rorie paused to think about her answer. She briefly considered mentioning Dan, but decided against it. She'd planned this separation to gain a perspective on their relationship. And within hours of arriving at Elk Run, Rorie had found her answer. Dan would always be a special friend—but nothing more.

"The question shouldn't require a week's thought," Mary grumbled, stirring the large pot of simmering beef.

"Sorry…I was mulling something over."

"Then there is someone?"

She shook her head. "No."

The answer didn't seem to please Mary, because she frowned. "When did you say that fancy car of yours was going to be fixed?"

The abrupt question caught Rorie by surprise. Mary was openly concerned about the attraction between her and Clay. The housekeeper, who probably knew Clay as well as anyone did, clearly wasn't blind to what had been happening—and just as clearly didn't like it.

"The mechanic in Riversdale said it should be finished the day after tomorrow if all goes well."

"Good!" Mary proclaimed with a fierce nod, then turned back to her stew.

Rorie couldn't help smiling at the older woman's astuteness. Mary was telling her that the sooner she was off Elk Run the better for everyone concerned. Rorie had to agree.

Kate Logan arrived promptly at ten. She wore tight-fitting jeans, red checkered western shirt and a white silk scarf knotted at her throat. Her long honey-colored hair was woven into thick braids that fell over her shoulders. At first glance, Kate looked closer to sixteen than the twenty-four Rorie knew her to be.

Kate greeted her with a warm smile. "Rorie, there wasn't any need to wear something so nice. I should've told you to dress casually."

Rorie's shoulders slumped. "I brought along more

dresses than jeans. Am I overdressed? I could change," she said hesitantly.

"Oh, no, you look lovely…" But for the first time, Kate seemed worried. The doubt that played across her features would have been amusing if Rorie hadn't already been suffering from such a potent bout of guilt. It was all too obvious that Kate viewed Rorie as a threat.

If Clay Franklin had chosen that moment to walk into the kitchen, Rorie would've called him every foul name she could think of. She was furious with him for doing this to her—and to Kate.

"I wear a lot of dresses because of my job at the library," Rorie rushed to explain. "I also date quite a bit. I've been seeing someone—Dan Rogers—for a while now. In fact, it's his car I was driving."

"You're dating someone special?" Kate asked, sounding relieved.

"Yes, Dan and I've been going out for several months."

Mary coughed noisily and sent Rorie an accusing glare; Rorie ignored her. "Shouldn't we be leaving?"

"Oh, sure, any time you're ready." When they were outside, Kate turned to face Rorie. Looking uncomfortable, she slipped her hands into the back pockets of her jeans. "I've embarrassed you and I'm sorry. I didn't mean to imply that I didn't trust you and Clay."

"There's no need for an apology. I'm sure I wouldn't react any differently if Clay was *my* fiancé."

Kate shook her head. "But I feel as if I *should* apologize. I'm not going to be the kind of wife Clay wants if I can't trust him around a pretty girl once in a while."

Had the earth cracked open just then, Rorie would gladly have fallen in. That had to be preferable to looking at Kate and feeling the things she did about Clay Franklin.

"Don't have any worries about me," she said, dismissing the issue as nonchalantly as she could. "I'll be out of everyone's hair in a day or two."

"Oh, Rorie, please, I don't want you to rush off because I had a silly attack of jealousy. Now I feel terrible."

"Don't, please. I have to leave… I want to leave. My vacation's on hold until I can get my car repaired and there's so much I'd planned to see and do." She dug in her bag for a brochure. "Have you ever been up to Victoria on Vancouver Island?"

"Once, but I was only five, too young to remember much of anything," Kate told her, scanning the pamphlet. "This does sound like fun. Maybe this is where Clay and I should have our honeymoon."

"It'd be perfect for that," Rorie murmured. Her heart constricted with a sudden flash of pain, but she ruthlessly forced down her emotions, praying Kate hadn't noticed. "I'm looking forward to visiting Canada. By the way, Mary's driving to Riversdale to visit her sister later in the week. She's asked me to take charge of cooking dinner if I'm still here. Would you like to help? We could have a good time and really get to know each other."

"Oh, that would be great." Kate slipped her arm around Rorie's waist and gave her an enthusiastic squeeze. "Thank you, Rorie. I know you're trying to reassure me, and I appreciate it."

That had been exactly Rorie's intent.

"It probably sounds selfish," Kate continued, "but I'm glad your car broke down when it did. Without any difficulty at all, I can see us becoming the best of friends."

Rorie could, too, but that only added to her growing sense of uneasiness.

Nightingale was a sleepy kind of town. Businesses lined both sides of Main Street, with a beauty shop, an insurance agency, Nellie's Café and a service station on one side, a grocery store, pharmacy and five-and-dime on the other. Rorie had the impression that things happened in their own time in Nightingale, Oregon. Few places could have been more unlike San Francisco, where people always seemed to be rushing. Here, no one seemed to feel any need to hurry. It was as though this town, with its population of fifteen hundred, existed in a time warp. Rorie found the relaxed pace unexpectedly pleasant.

"The library is across from the high school on Maple Street," Kate explained as she parked her Ford on Main. "That way, students have easy access."

Rorie climbed out of the car, automatically pressing down the door lock.

"You don't have to do that here. There hasn't been a vehicle stolen in...oh, at least twenty years."

Rorie's eyes must have revealed her surprise, because Kate went on, "Actually, we had trouble passing our last bond issue for a new patrol car. People couldn't see the need since there hasn't been a felony committed in over two years. About the worst thing that goes on is when Harry Ackerman gets drunk. That happens once or twice a year and he's arrested for disturbing the peace." She grinned sheepishly. "He sings old love songs to Nellie at the top of his lungs in front of the café. They were apparently sweet on each other a long time back. Nellie married someone else and Harry never got over the loss of his one true love."

Looping the strap of her bag over her shoulder, Rorie looked around the quiet streets.

"The fire and police station are in the same building," Kate pointed out next. "And there's a really nice restaurant on Oak. If you want, we could have lunch there."

"Only if you let me treat."

"I wouldn't hear of it," Kate said with a shake of her head that sent her braids flying. "You're my guest."

Rorie decided not to argue, asking another question instead. "Where do the ranchers get their supplies?" It seemed to her that type of store would do a thriving business, yet she hadn't seen one.

"At Garner's Feed and Supply. It's on the outskirts of town—I'll take you past on the way out. In fact, we should take a driving tour so you can see a little more of Nightingale. Main Street is only a small part of it."

By the time Kate and Rorie walked over to Maple and the library, Rorie's head was swimming with the names of all the people Kate had insisted on introducing. It seemed everyone had heard about her car problems and was eager to talk to her. Several mentioned the Grange dance that night and said they'd be looking for her there.

"You're really going to be impressed with the library," Kate promised as they walked the two streets over to Maple. "Dad and the others worked hard to get the levy passed so we could build it. People here tend to be tight-fisted. Dad says they squeeze a nickel so hard, the buffalo belches."

Rorie laughed outright at that.

The library was the largest building in town, a sprawling one-story structure with lots of windows. The hours were posted on the double glass doors, and Rorie noted that the library wouldn't open until the middle of the afternoon, still several hours away.

"It doesn't seem to be open," she said, disappointed.

"Oh, don't worry, I've got a key. All the volunteers do." Kate rummaged in her bag and took out a large key ring. She opened the door, pushing it wide for Rorie to enter first.

"Mrs. Halldorfson retired last year, a month after the

building was finished," Kate told her, flipping on the lights, "and the town's budget wouldn't stretch to hire a new full-time librarian. So a number of parents and teachers are taking turns volunteering. We've got a workable schedule, unless someone goes on vacation, which, I hate to admit, has been happening all summer."

"You don't have a full-time librarian?" Rorie couldn't disguise her astonishment. "Why go to all the trouble and expense of building a modern facility if you can't afford a librarian?"

"You'll have to ask Town Council that," Kate returned, shrugging. "It doesn't make much sense, does it? But you see, Mrs. Halldorfson was only part-time and the Council seems to think that's what her replacement should be."

"That doesn't make sense, either."

"Especially when you consider that the new library is twice the size of the old one."

Rorie had to bite her tongue to keep from saying more. But she was appalled at the waste, the missed opportunities.

"We've been advertising for months for a part-time librarian, but so far we haven't found anyone interested. Not that I blame them—one look at the size of the job and no one wants to tackle it alone."

"A library is more than a place to check books in and out," Rorie said, gesturing dramatically. Her voice rose despite herself. This was an issue close to her heart, and polite silence was practically impossible. "A library can be the heart of a community. It can be a place for classes, community services, all kinds of things. Don't non-profit organizations use it for meetings?"

"I'm afraid not," Kate answered. "Everyone gets together at Nellie's when there's any kind of meeting. Nellie serves great pies," she added, as though that explained everything.

Realizing that she'd climbed onto her soapbox, Rorie dropped her hands and shrugged. "It's a very nice building, Kate, and you have every reason to be proud. I didn't mean to sound so righteous."

"But you're absolutely correct," Kate said thoughtfully. "We're not using the library to its full potential, are we? Volunteers can only do so much. As it is, the library's only open three afternoons a week." She sighed expressively. "To be honest, I think Dad and the other members of the Town Council are expecting Mrs. Halldorfson to come back in the fall, but that's unfair to her. She's served the community for over twenty years. She deserves to retire in peace without being blackmailed into coming back because we can't find a replacement."

"Well, I hope you find someone soon."

"I hope so, too," Kate murmured.

They ate a leisurely lunch, and as she'd promised, Kate gave Rorie a tour of the town. After showing her several churches, the elementary school where she taught second grade and some of the nicer homes on the hill, Kate ended the tour on the outskirts of town near Garner's Feed and Supply.

"Luke's here," Kate said, easing into the parking place next to a dusty pickup truck.

"Luke?"

"Our foreman. I don't know what Dad would do without him. He runs the ranch and has for years—ever since I was in high school. Dad's retirement age now, and he's more than willing to let Luke take charge."

Kate got out of the car and leaned against the front fender, crossing her arms over her chest. Rorie joined her.

"He'll be out in a minute," Kate said.

True to her word, a tall, deeply tanned man appeared with a sack of grain slung over his shoulder. His eyes were so dark they gleamed like onyx, taking in everything around him, but revealing little of his own thoughts. His strong square chin was balanced by a high intelligent brow. He was lean and muscular and strikingly handsome.

"Need any help, stranger?" Kate asked with a laugh.

"You offering?"

"Nope."

Luke chuckled. "That's what I figured. You wouldn't want to ruin those pretty nails of yours now, would you?"

"I didn't stop by to be insulted by you," Kate chastised, clearly enjoying the exchange. "I wanted you to meet Rorie Campbell—she's the one Clay was telling us about the other night, whose car broke down."

"I remember." For the first time the foreman's gaze left Kate. He tossed the sack of grain into the back of the truck and used his teeth to tug his glove free from his right hand. Then he presented his long callused fingers to Rorie. "Pleased to meet you, ma'am."

"The pleasure's mine." Rorie remembered where she'd heard the name. Skip had mentioned Luke Rivers when he'd told her about the Grange square dance. He'd said something about all the girls being attracted to the foreman. Rorie could understand why.

They exchanged a brief handshake before Luke's attention slid back to Kate. His eyes softened perceptibly.

"Luke's like a brother to me," Kate said fondly.

He frowned at that, but didn't comment.

"We're going to let you escort us to the dance tonight," she informed him.

"What about Clay?"

"Oh, he'll meet us there. I thought the three of us could go over together."

Rorie wasn't fooled. Kate was setting her up with Luke, who didn't look any too pleased at having his evening arranged for him.

"Kate, listen," she began, "I'd really rather skip the dance tonight. I've never done any square dancing in my life—"

"That doesn't matter," Kate interrupted. "Luke will be glad to show you. Won't you, Luke?"

"Sure," he mumbled, with the enthusiasm of a man offered the choice between hanging and a firing squad.

"Honestly, Luke!" Kate gave an embarrassed laugh.

"Listen," Rorie said quickly. "It's obvious Luke has his own plans for tonight. I don't want to intrude—"

He surprised her by turning toward her, his eyes searching hers. "I'd be happy to escort you, Rorie."

"I'm likely to step all over your toes… I really think I should sit the whole thing out."

"Nonsense," Kate cried. "Luke won't let you do that and neither will I!"

"We'll enjoy ourselves," the foreman said. "Leave everything to me."

Rorie nodded reluctantly.

A moment of awkward silence fell over the trio. "Well, I suppose I should get Rorie back to Circle L and see about finding her a dress," Kate said, smiling. She playfully tossed her car keys in the air and caught them deftly.

Luke tipped his hat when they both returned to the car. Rorie didn't mention his name until they were back on the road.

"Luke really is attractive, isn't he?" she asked, closely watching Kate.

The other woman nodded eagerly. "It surprises me that he's not married. There are plenty of girls around Nightingale who'd be more than willing, believe me. At every

Grange dance, the ladies flirt with him like crazy. I love to tease him about it—he really hates that. But I wish Luke *would* get married—I don't like the idea of him living his life alone. It's time he thought about settling down and starting a family. He was thirty last month, but when I said something about it, he nearly bit my head off."

Rorie nibbled on her lower lip. She inhaled a deep breath and released it slowly. Her guess was that Luke Rivers had his heart set on someone special, and that someone was engaged to another man. God help him, Rorie thought. She knew exactly how he felt.

The music was already playing by the time Luke, Kate and Rorie arrived at the Grange Hall in Luke's ten-year-old four-door sedan. Rorie tried to force some enthusiasm for this outing, but had little success. She hadn't exchanged more than a few words with the foreman during the entire drive. He, apparently, didn't like this arranged-date business any better than she did. But they were stuck with each other, and Rorie at least was determined to make the best of it.

They entered the hall and were greeted by the cheery voice of the male caller:

Rope the cow, brand the calf
Swing your sweetheart, once and a half...

Rorie hadn't known what to expect, but she was surprised by the smooth-stepping, smartly dressed dancers who twirled around the floor following the caller's directions. She felt more daunted than ever by the evening ahead of her. And to worsen matters, Kate had insisted Rorie borrow one of her outfits. Although Rorie liked the bright blue colors, she felt awkward and self-conscious in the billowing skirts.

The Grange itself was bigger than Rorie had anticipated. On the stage stood the caller and several fiddlers. Refreshment tables lined one wall and the polished dance floor was so crowded Rorie wondered how anyone could move without bumping into others. The entire meeting hall was alive with energy and music, and despite herself, she felt her mood lift. Her toes started tapping out rhythms almost of their own accord. Given time, she'd be out there, too, joining the vibrant, laughing dancers. It was unavoidable, anyway. She knew Kate wouldn't allow her to sit sedately in the background and watch. Neither would Clay and Skip, who'd just arrived.

"Oh, my feet are moving already." Kate was squirming with eagerness. Clay smiled indulgently, tucked his arm around her waist and the two of them stepped onto the dance floor. He glanced back once at Rorie, before a circle of eight opened up to admit them.

"Shall we?" Luke asked, eyeing the dance floor.

He didn't sound too enthusiastic and Rorie didn't blame him. "Would it be all right if we sat out the first couple of dances?" she asked. "I'd like to get more into the swing of things."

"No problem."

Luke looked almost grateful for the respite, which didn't lend Rorie much confidence. No doubt he assumed this city slicker was going to make a fool of herself and of him—and she probably would. When he escorted her to the row of chairs, Rorie made the mistake of sitting down. Instantly her skirts leaped up into her face. Embarrassed, she pushed them down, then tucked the material under her thighs in an effort to tame the layers of stiff petticoats.

"Hello, Luke." A pretty blonde with sparkling blue eyes

sauntered over. "I didn't know if you'd show tonight or not. Glad you did."

"Beth Hammond, this is Rorie Campbell."

Rorie nodded. "It's nice to meet you, Beth."

"Oh, I heard about you at the drugstore yesterday. You're the gal with the broken-down sports car, aren't you?"

"That's me." By now it shouldn't have surprised Rorie that everyone knew about her troubles.

"I hope everything turns out okay."

"Thanks." Although Beth was speaking to Rorie, her eyes didn't leave Luke. It was patently obvious that she expected an invitation to dance.

"Luke, why don't you dance with Beth?" Rorie suggested. "That way I'll gather a few pointers from watching the two of you."

"What a good idea," Beth chirped eagerly. "We'll stay on the outskirts of the crowd so you can see how it's done. Be sure and listen to Charlie—he's the caller. Then you'll see what each step is."

Rorie nodded agreeably.

Luke gave Rorie a long sober look. "You're sure?"

"Positive."

All join hands, circle right around
Stop in place at your hometown...

Studying the dancers, Rorie quickly picked up the terms *do se do, allemande left* and *allemande right* and a number of others, which she struggled to keep track of. By the end of the dance, her foot was tapping out the lively beat of the fiddlers' music and a smile formed as she listened to the perfectly rhyming words.

"Rorie," Skip said, suddenly standing in front of her. "May I have the pleasure of this dance?"

"I...I don't think I'm ready yet."

"Nonsense." Without listening to her protest, he grabbed her hand and hauled her to her feet.

"Skip, I'll embarrass you," she protested in a low whisper. "I've never done this before."

"You've got to start sometime." He tucked his arm around her waist and led her close to the stage.

"We got a newcomer, Charlie," Skip called out, "so make this one simple."

Charlie gave Skip a thumbs-up and reached for the microphone. "We'll go a bit slower this time," Charlie announced to his happy audience. "Miss Rorie Campbell from San Francisco has joined us and it's her first time on the floor."

Rorie wanted to curl up and die as a hundred faces turned to stare at her. But the dancers were shouting and cheering their welcome and Rorie shyly raised her hand, smiling into the crowd.

Getting through that first series of steps was the most difficult, but soon Rorie was in the middle of the floor, stepping and twirling—and laughing. Something she'd always assumed to be a silly, outdated activity turned out to be great fun.

By the time Skip led her back to her chair, she was breathless. "Want some punch?" he asked. Rorie nodded eagerly. Her throat felt parched.

When Skip left her, Luke Rivers appeared at her side. "You did just great," he said sincerely.

"For a city girl, you mean," she teased.

"As good as anyone."

"Thanks."

"I suspect I owe you an apology, Rorie."

"Because you didn't want to make a fool of yourself with me on the dance floor?" she asked with a light laugh. "That's understandable. Kate and Clay practically threw me in your lap. I'm sure you had other plans for tonight, and I'm sorry for your sake that we got stuck with each other."

Luke grinned. "Trust me, I've had plenty of envious looks from around the room. Any of a dozen different men would be more than happy to be 'stuck' with you."

That went a long way toward boosting her ego. She would have commented, but Skip came back just then carrying a paper cup filled with bright pink punch. A teenage girl was beside him, clutching his free arm and smiling dreamily up at him.

"I'm going to dance with Caroline now, okay?" he said to Rorie.

"That's fine," she answered, smiling, "and thank you for braving the dance floor with me." Skip blushed as he slipped an arm around Caroline's waist and hurried her off.

"You game?" Luke nodded toward the dancing couples.

Rorie didn't hesitate. She swallowed the punch in three giant gulps, and gave him her hand. Together they moved onto the crowded floor.

By the end of the third set of dances, Rorie had twirled around with so many different partners, she lost track of them. She'd caught sight of Clay only once, and when he saw her he waved. Returning the gesture, she promptly missed her footing and nearly fell into her partner's waiting arms. The tall sheriff's deputy was all too happy to have her throw herself at him and told her as much, to Rorie's embarrassment.

Although it was only ten o'clock, Rorie was exhausted

and so warm the perspiration ran in rivulets down her face
and neck. She had to escape. Several times, she'd tried to
sit out a dance, but no one would listen to her excuses.

In an effort to catch her breath and cool down, Rorie
took advantage of a break between sets to wander outside.
The night air was refreshing. Quite a few other people had
apparently had the same idea; the field that served as a
car park was crowded with groups and strolling couples.

As she made her way through the dimly lit field, she
saw a handful of men passing around a flask of whis-
key and entertaining each other with off-color jokes. She
steered a wide circle around them and headed toward
Luke's parked car, deciding it was far enough away to
discourage anyone from following her. In her eagerness
to escape, she nearly stumbled over a couple locked in a
passionate embrace against the side of a pickup.

Rorie mumbled an apology when the pair glanced up
at her, irritation written all over their young faces. Good
grief, she'd only wanted a few minutes alone in order to
get a breath of fresh air—she hadn't expected to walk
through an obstacle course!

When she finally arrived at Luke Rivers's car, she
leaned on the fender and slowly inhaled the clean country air. All her assumptions about this evening had been
wrong. She'd been so sure she'd feel lonely and bored and
out of place. And she'd felt none of those things. If she
were to tell Dan about the Grange dance, he'd laugh at
the idea of having such a grand time with a bunch of what
he'd refer to as "country bumpkins." The thought annoyed
her. These were good, friendly, fun-loving people. They'd
taken her under their wing, expressed their welcome without reserve, and now they were showing her an uncomplicated lifestyle that had more appeal than Rorie would
have believed possible.

"I thought I'd find you out here."

Rorie's whole body tensed as she recognized the voice of the man who'd joined her.

"Hello, Clay."

Eight

Rorie injected a cheerful note into her voice. She turned around, half expecting Kate to be with him. The two had been inseparable from the minute Clay had arrived. It was just as well that Kate was around, since her presence prevented Clay and Rorie from giving in to any temptation.

Clay's hands settled on her shoulders and Rorie flinched involuntarily at his touch. With noticeable regret, Clay dropped his hands.

"Are you having a good time?" he asked.

She nodded. "I didn't think I would, which tells you how prejudiced I've been about country life, but I've been pleasantly surprised."

"I'm glad." His hands clenched briefly at his sides, then he flexed his fingers a couple of times. "I would've danced with you myself, but—"

She stopped him abruptly. "Clay, no. Don't explain…it isn't necessary. I understand."

His eyes held hers with such tenderness that she had to look away. The magical quality was in the air again—Rorie could feel it as forcefully as if the stars had spelled it out across the heavens.

"I don't think you do understand, Rorie," Clay said,

"but it doesn't matter. You'll be gone in a couple of days and both our lives will go back to the way they were meant to be."

Rorie agreed with a quick nod. It was too tempting, standing in the moonlight with Clay. Much too tempting. The memory of another night in which they'd stood and gazed at the stars returned with powerful intensity. Rorie realized that even talking to each other, alone like this, was dangerous.

"Won't Kate be looking for you?" she asked carefully.

"No. Luke Rivers is dancing with her."

For a moment she closed her eyes, not daring to look up at Clay. "I guess I'll be going inside now. I just came out to catch my breath and cool down a little."

"Dance with me first—here in the moonlight."

A protest rose within her, but the instant Clay slid his arms around her waist, Rorie felt herself give in. Kate would have him the rest of her life, but Rorie only had these few hours. Almost against her will, her hands found his shoulders, slipping around his neck with an ease that brought a sigh of pleasure to her lips. Being held by Clay shouldn't feel this good.

"Oh, Rorie," he moaned as she settled into his embrace.

They fitted together as if they'd been created for each other. His chin touched the top of her head and he caressed her hair with his jaw.

"This is a mistake," Rorie murmured, closing her eyes, savoring the warm, secure feel of his arms.

"I know…"

But neither seemed willing to release the other.

His mouth grazed her temple and he kissed her there. "God help me, Rorie, what am I going to do? I haven't been able to stop thinking about you. I can't sleep, I hardly eat…" His voice was raw, almost savage.

"Oh, please," she said with a soft cry. "We can't…we mustn't even talk like this." His gray eyes smoldered above hers, and their breaths merged as his mouth hovered so close to her own.

"I vowed I wouldn't touch you again."

Rorie looked away. She'd made the same promise to herself. But it wasn't in her to deny him now, although her mind searched frantically for the words to convince him how wrong they were to risk hurting Kate—and each other.

His hands drifted up from her shoulders, his fingertips skimming the sides of her neck, trailing over her cheeks and through the softness of her hair. He placed his index finger over her lips, gently stroking them apart.

Rorie moaned. She moistened her lips with the tip of her tongue. Clay's left hand dug into her shoulders as her tongue caressed the length of his finger, drawing it into her mouth and sucking it gently. She needed him so much in that moment, she could have wept.

"Just this once…for these few minutes," he pleaded, "let me pretend you're mine." His hands cupped her face and slowly brought her mouth to his, smothering her whimper of part welcome, part protest.

A long series of kisses followed. Deep, relentless, searching kisses that sent her heart soaring. Kisses that only made the coming loneliness more painful. A sob swelled within her and tears burned her eyes as she twisted away and tore her mouth from his.

"No," she cried, covering her face with her hands and turning her back to him. "Please, Clay. We shouldn't be doing this."

He was silent for so long that Rorie suspected he'd left her. She inhaled a deep, calming breath and dropped her hands limply to her sides.

"It would be so easy to love you, Rorie."

"No," she whispered, shaking her head vigorously as she faced him again. "I'm not the right person for you—it's too late for that. You've got Kate." She couldn't keep the pain out of her voice. Anything between them was hopeless, futile. Within a day or two her car would be repaired and she'd vanish from his life as suddenly as she'd appeared.

Clay fell silent, his shoulders stiff and resolute as he stood silhouetted against the light of the Grange Hall. His face was masked by shadows and Rorie couldn't read his thoughts. He drew in a harsh breath.

"You're right, Rorie. We can't allow this...attraction between us to get out of hand. I promise you, by all I hold dear, that I won't kiss you again."

"I'll...do my part, too," she assured him, feeling better now that they'd made this agreement.

His hand reached for hers and clasped it warmly. "Come on, I'll walk you back to the hall. We're going to be all right. We'll do what we have to do."

Clay's tone told her he meant it. Relieved, Rorie silently made the same promise to herself.

Rorie slept late the next morning, later than she would have thought possible. Mary was busy with lunch preparations by the time she made her way downstairs.

"Did you enjoy yourself last night?" Mary immediately asked.

In response, Rorie curtsied and danced a few steps with an imaginary partner, clapping her hands.

Mary tried to hide a smile at Rorie's antics. "Oh, get away with you now. All I was looking for was a yes or a no."

"I had a great time."

"It was nothing like those city hotspots, I'll wager."

"You're right about that," Rorie told her, pouring herself a cup of coffee.

"You seeing Kate today?"

Rorie shook her head and popped a piece of bread in the toaster. "She's got a doctor's appointment this morning and a teachers' meeting this afternoon. She's going to stop by later if she has a chance, but if not I'll be seeing her for sure tomorrow." Rorie intended to spend as much time as she could with Clay's fiancée. She genuinely enjoyed her company, and being with her served two useful purposes. It helped keep Rorie occupied, and it prevented her from being alone with Clay.

"What are you going to do today, then?" Mary asked, frowning.

Rorie laughed. "Don't worry. Whatever it is, I promise to stay out of your way."

The housekeeper gave a snort of amusement—or was it relief?

"Actually, I thought I'd finish putting the data Clay needs for his pedigree-research program into the computer. There isn't much left and I should be done by this afternoon."

"So if someone comes looking for you, that's where you'll be?"

"That's where I'll be," Rorie echoed. She didn't know who would "come looking for her," as Mary put it. The housekeeper made it sound as though a posse was due to arrive any minute demanding to know where the Franklin men were hiding Rorie Campbell.

Taking her coffee cup with her, Rorie walked across the yard and into the barn. Once more, she was impressed with all the activity that went on there. She'd come to know several of the men by their first names and returned their greetings with a smile and a wave.

As before, she found the office empty. She set down her cup while she turned on the computer and collected Clay's data. She'd just started to type it in when she heard someone enter the room. Pausing, she twisted around.

"Rorie."

"Clay."

They were awkward with each other now. Almost afraid.

"I didn't realize you were here."

She stood abruptly. "I'll leave…"

"No. I came up to get something. I'll be gone in a minute."

She nodded and sat back down. "Okay."

He walked briskly to his desk and sifted through the untidy stacks of paper. His gaze didn't waver from the task, but his jaw was tight, his teeth clenched. Impatience marked his every move. "Kate told me you're involved with a man in San Francisco. I…didn't know."

"I'm not exactly involved with him—at least not in the way you're implying. His name is Dan Rogers, and we've been seeing each other for about six months. He's divorced. The MG is his."

Clay's mouth thinned, but he still didn't look at her. "Are you in love with him?"

"No."

Lowering his head, Clay rubbed his hand over his eyes. "I had no right to ask you that. None. Forgive me, Rorie." Then, clutching his papers, he stalked out of the office without a backward glance.

Rorie was so shaken by the encounter that when she went back to her typing, she made three mistakes in a row and had to stop to regain her composure.

When the phone rang, she ignored it, knowing Mary

or one of the men would answer it. Soon afterward, she heard running footsteps behind her and swivelled around in the chair.

A breathless Skip bolted into the room. Shoulders heaving, he pointed in the direction of the telephone. "It's for you," he panted.

"Me?" It could only be Dan.

He nodded several times, his hand braced theatrically against his heart.

She picked up the extension. "Hello," she said, her fingers closing tightly around the receiver. "This is Rorie Campbell."

"Miss Campbell," came the unmistakable voice of George, the mechanic in Riversdale, "let me put it to you like this. I've got good news and bad news."

"Now what?" she cried, pushing her hair off her forehead with an impatient hand. She had to get out of Elk Run.

"My man picked up the water pump for your car in Portland just like we planned."

"Good."

George sighed heavily. "There's a minor problem, though."

"Minor?" she repeated hopefully.

"Well, not that minor actually."

"Oh, great... Listen, George, I'd prefer not to play guessing games with you. Just tell me what happened and how long it's going to be before I can get out of here."

"I'm sorry, Miss Campbell, but they shipped the wrong part. It'll be two, possibly three more days."

Nine

"What's the matter?" Skip asked when Rorie indignantly replaced the receiver.

She crossed her arms over her chest and breathed deeply, battling down the angry frustration that boiled inside her. The problem wasn't George's fault, or Skip's, or Kate's, or anyone else's.

"Rorie?" Skip asked again.

"They shipped the wrong part for the car," she said flatly. "I'm going to be stuck here for another two or possibly three days."

Skip didn't look the least bit perturbed at this information. "Gee, Rorie, that's not so terrible. We like having you around—and you like it here, don't you?"

"Yes, but…" How could she explain that her reservations had nothing to do with their company, the farm or even with country life? She couldn't very well blurt out that she was falling in love with his brother, that she had to escape before she ruined their lives.

"But what?" Skip asked.

"My vacation."

"I know you had other plans, but you can relax and enjoy yourself here just as well, can't you?"

She didn't attempt to answer him, but closed her eyes and nodded, faintly.

"Well, listen, I've got to get back to work. Do you need me for anything?"

She shook her head. When the office door closed, Rorie sat down in front of the computer again and poised her fingers over the keyboard. She sat like that, unmoving, for several minutes as her thoughts churned. What was she going to do? Every time she came near Clay the attraction was so strong that trying to ignore it was like swimming upstream. Rorie had planned on leaving Elk Run the following day. Now she was trapped here for God only knew how much longer.

She got up suddenly and started pacing the office floor. Dan hadn't called her, either. She might have vanished from the face of the earth as far as he was concerned. The stupid car was his, after all, and the least he could do was make some effort to find out what had happened. Rorie knew she wasn't being entirely reasonable, but she was caught up in the momentum of her anger and frustration.

Impulsively she snatched up the telephone receiver, had the operator charge the call to her San Francisco number and dialed Dan's office.

"Rorie, thank God you phoned," Dan said.

The worry in his voice appeased her a little. "The least you could've done was call me back," she fumed.

"I tried. My secretary apparently wrote down the wrong number. I've been waiting all this time for you to call me again. Why didn't you? What on earth is going on?"

She told him in detail, from the stalled car to her recent conversation with the mechanic. She didn't tell him about Clay Franklin and the way he made her feel.

"Rorie, baby, I'm so sorry."

She nodded mutely, close to tears. If she wasn't so dangerously close to falling in love with Clay, none of this would seem such a disaster.

The silence lengthened while Dan apparently mulled things over. "Shall I come and get you?" he finally asked.

"With what?" she asked with surprising calm. "My car? You were the one who convinced me it would never make this trip. Besides, how would you get the MG back?"

"I'd figured something out. Listen, I can't let you sit around in some backwoods farm town. I'll borrow a car or rent one." He hesitated, then expelled his breath in a short burst of impatience. "Damn, forget that. I can't come."

"You can't?"

"I've got a meeting tomorrow afternoon. It's important—I can't miss it. I'm sorry, Rorie, I really am, but there's nothing I can do."

"Don't worry about it," she said, defeat causing her voice to dip slightly. "I understand." In a crazy kind of way she did. Dan was a rising stockbroker, so career moves were critical to him, more important than rescuing Rorie, the woman he claimed to love… Somehow Rorie couldn't picture Clay making the same decision. In her heart she knew Clay would come for her the second she asked.

They spoke for a few more minutes before Rorie ended the conversation. She felt trapped, as though the walls were closing in around her. So far she and Clay had managed to disguise their feelings, but they wouldn't be able to keep it up much longer before someone guessed. Kate wasn't blind, and neither was Mary.

"Rorie?" Clay called her name as he burst into the office. "What happened? Skip told me you were all upset—something about the car? What is it?"

"George called." She whirled around and pointed toward the phone. "The water pump arrived just like it was supposed to—but it's the wrong one."

Clay dropped his gaze, then removed his hat and wiped his forehead. "I'm sorry."

"I am, too, but that doesn't help, does it?" The conversation with Dan hadn't improved matters, and taking her frustration out on Clay wasn't going to change anything, either. "I'm stuck here, and this is the last place on earth I want to be."

"Do you think I like it any better?" he challenged.

Rorie blinked wildly at the tears that burned for release.

"I wish to God your car had broken down a hundred miles from Elk Run," he said. "Before you bombarded your way into my home, my life was set. I knew what I wanted, where I was headed. In the course of a few days you've upended my whole world."

Emotion clogged Rorie's throat at the unfairness of his accusations. She hadn't asked for the MGB to break down where it had. The minute she could, she planned to get out of his life and back to her own.

No, she decided, they couldn't wait that long—it was much too painful for them both. She had to leave now. "I'll pack my things and be gone before evening."

"Just where do you plan to go?"

Rorie didn't know. "Somewhere…anywhere." She had to leave for his sake, as well as hers.

"Go back inside the house, Rorie, before I say or do something else I'll regret. You're right—we can't be in the same room together. At least not alone."

She started to walk past him, eyes downcast, her heart heavy with misery. Unexpectedly his hand shot out and caught her fingers, stopping her.

"I didn't mean what I said." His voice rasped, warm and hoarse. "None of it. Forgive me, Rorie."

Her heart raced when his hand touched hers. It took all the restraint Rorie could muster, which at the moment wasn't much, to resist throwing herself into his arms and holding on for the rest of her life.

"Forgive me, too," she whispered.

"Forgive you?" he asked, incredulous. "No, Rorie. I'll thank God every day of my life for having met you." With that, he released her fingers, slowly, reluctantly. "Go now, before I make an even bigger fool of myself."

Rorie ran from the office as though a raging fire were licking at her heels, threatening to consume her.

And in a way, it was.

For two days, Rorie managed to stay completely out of his way. They saw each other only briefly and always in the company of others. Rorie was sure they gave Academy Award performances every time they were together. They laughed and teased and joked and the only one who seemed to suspect things weren't quite right was Mary.

Rorie was grateful the housekeeper didn't question her, but the looks she gave Rorie were frowningly thoughtful.

Three days after the Grange dance, Mary's sister arrived in Riversdale. Revealing more excitement than Rorie had seen in their acquaintance, Mary fussed with her hair and dress, and as soon as she'd finished the lunch dishes she was off.

Putting on Mary's well-worn apron, Rorie looped the long strands around her waist twice and set to work. Kate joined her mid-afternoon, carrying a large bag of ingredients for the dessert she was going to prepare.

"I've been cooking from the moment Mary left," Rorie told Kate, pushing the damp hair from her forehead as she stirred wine into a simmering sauce. Rorie intended to dazzle Clay and Skip with her one speciality—seafood fettuccine. She hadn't admitted to Mary how limited her repertoire of dishes was, although the housekeeper had repeatedly quizzed her about what she planned to make for dinner. Rorie had insisted it was a surprise. She'd decided that this rich and tasty dish stood a good chance of impressing the Franklin men.

"And I'm making Clay his favorite dessert—homemade lemon meringue pie." Kate reached for the grocery bag on the kitchen counter and six bright yellow lemons rolled out.

Rorie was impressed. The one and only time she'd tried to bake a lemon pie, she'd used a pudding mix. Apparently, Kate took the homemade part seriously.

"Whatever you're cooking smells wonderful," Kate said, stepping over to the stove. Crab, large succulent shrimp and small bite-sized pieces of sole were waiting in the refrigerator, to be added to the sauce just before the dish was served.

Kate was busy whipping up a pie crust when the phone rang several minutes later. She glanced anxiously at the wall, her fingers sticky with flour and lard.

Rorie looked over at her. "Do you suppose I should answer that?"

"You'd better. Clay usually relies on Mary to catch the phone for him."

Rorie lifted the receiver before the next peal. "Elk Run."

"That Miss Campbell?"

Rorie immediately recognized the voice of the mechanic from Riversdale. "Yes, this is Rorie Campbell."

"Remember I promised I'd call you when the part arrived? Well, it's here, all safe and sound, so you can stop fretting. Just came in a few minutes ago—haven't even had a chance to take it out of the box. Thought you'd want to know."

"It's the right one this time?"

"Here, I'll check it now... Yup, this is it."

Rorie wasn't sure what she felt. Relief, yes, but regret, too. "Thank you. Thank you very much."

"It's a little late for me to be starting the job this afternoon. My son's playing a Little League game and I promised him I'd be there. I'll get to this first thing in the morning and should be finished before noon. Give me a call before you head over here and I'll make sure everything's running the way it should."

"Yes, I'll do that. Thanks again." Slowly Rorie replaced the receiver. She leaned against the wall sighing deeply. At Kate's questioning gaze, she smiled weakly and explained, "That was the mechanic. The water pump for my car arrived and he's going to be working on it first thing in the morning."

"Rorie, that's great."

"I think so, too." She did—and she didn't. Part of her longed to flee Elk Run, and another part of her realized that no matter how far she traveled, no matter how many years passed, she'd never forget these days with Clay Franklin.

"Then tonight's going to be your last evening here," Kate murmured. "Selfish as it sounds, I really hate the thought of you leaving."

"We can keep in touch."

"Oh, yes, I'd like that. I'll send you a wedding invitation."

That reminder was the last thing Rorie needed. But once she was on the road again, she could start forgetting, she told herself grimly.

"Since this is going to be your last night, we should make it special," Kate announced brightly. "We're going to use the best china and set out the crystal wineglasses."

Rorie laughed, imagining Mary's face when she heard about it.

Even as she spoke, Kate was walking toward the dining-room china cabinet. In a few minutes, she'd set the table, cooked the sauce for the pie and poured it into the cooling pie shell that sat on the counter. The woman was a marvel!

Rorie was busy adding the final touches to the fettuccine when Clay and Skip came in through the back door.

"When's dinner?" Skip wanted to know. "I'm starved."

"Soon." Rorie tested the boiling noodles to be sure they'd cooked all the way through but weren't overdone.

"Upstairs with the both of you," Kate said, shooing them out of the kitchen. "I want you to change into something nice."

"We're supposed to dress up for dinner?" Skip complained. He'd obviously recovered from any need to impress her with his sartorial elegance, Rorie noted, remembering that he'd worn his Sunday best that first night. "We already washed—what more do you want?"

"For you to change your clothes. We're having a celebration tonight."

"We are?" The boy looked from Kate to Rorie and then back again.

"That's right," Kate continued, undaunted by his lack of enthusiasm. "And when we're through with dinner, there's going to be a farewell party for Rorie. We're going to send her off country-style."

"Rorie's leaving?" Skip sounded shocked. "But she just got here."

"The repair shop from Riversdale called. Her car will be finished tomorrow and she'll be on her way."

Clay's eyes burned into Rorie's. She tried to avoid looking at him, but when she did chance to meet his gaze, she could feel his distress. His jaw went rigid, and his mouth tightened as though he was bracing himself against Kate's words.

"Now hurry up, you two. Dinner's nearly ready," Kate said with a laugh. "Rorie's been cooking her heart out all afternoon."

Both men disappeared and Rorie set out the fresh green salad she'd made earlier, along with the seven-grain dinner rolls she'd warmed in the oven.

Once everyone was seated at the table and waiting, Rorie ceremonially carried in the platter of fettuccine, thick with seafood. She'd spent at least ten minutes arranging it to look as attractive as possible.

"Whatever it is smells good," Skip called out as she entered the dining room. "I'm so hungry I could eat a horse."

"Funny, Skip, very funny," Kate said.

Rorie set the serving dish in the middle of the table and stepped back, anticipating their praise.

Skip raised himself halfway out of his seat as he glared at her masterpiece. "That's it?" His voice was filled with disappointment.

Rorie blinked, uncertain how she should respond.

"You've been cooking all afternoon and you mean to tell me that's everything?"

"It's seafood fettuccine," she explained.

"It just looks like a bunch of noodles to me."

Ten

"I'll have another piece of lemon pie," Skip said, eagerly extending his plate.

"If you're still hungry, Skip," Clay remarked casually, "there are a few dinner rolls left."

Skip's gaze darted to the small wicker basket and he wrinkled his nose. "No, thanks. Too many seeds in those things. I got one caught in my tooth earlier and spent five minutes trying to suck it out."

Rorie did her best to smile.

Skip must have noticed how miserable she was because he added, "The salad was real good though. What kind of dressing was that?"

"Vinaigrette."

"Really? It tasted fruity."

"It was raspberry flavored."

Skip's eyes widened. "I've never heard of that kind of vinegar. Did you buy it here in Nightingale?"

"Not exactly. I got the ingredients while Kate and I were out the other day and mixed it up last night."

"*That* tasted real good." Which was Skip's less-than-subtle method of telling her nothing else had. He'd barely touched the main course. Clay had made a show of asking for seconds, but Rorie was all too aware that his display of enthusiasm had been an effort to salve her injured ego.

Rorie wasn't fooled—no one had enjoyed her special dinner. Even old Blue had turned his nose up at it when she'd offered him a taste of the leftovers.

Clay and Skip did hard physical work; they didn't sit in an office all day like Dan and the other men she knew. She should have realized that Clay and his brother required a more substantial meal than noodles swimming in a creamy sauce. Rorie wished she'd discussed her menu with either Mary or Kate. A tiny voice inside her suggested that Kate might have said something to warn her...

"Anyone else for more pie?" Kate was asking.

Clay nodded and cast a guilty glance in Rorie's direction. "I could go for a second piece myself."

"The pie was delicious," Rorie told Kate, meaning it. She was willing to admit Kate's dessert had been the highlight of the meal.

"Kate's one of the best cooks in the entire country," Skip announced, licking the back of his fork. "Her lemon pie won a blue ribbon at the county fair last year." He leaned forward, planting his elbows on the table. "She's got a barbecue sauce so tangy and good that when she cooks up spareribs I just can't stop eating 'em." His face fell as though he was thinking about those ribs now and would have gladly traded all of Rorie's fancy city food for a plateful.

"I'd like the fettuccine recipe if you'd give it to me," Kate told Rorie, obviously attempting to change the subject and spare Rorie's feelings. Perhaps she felt a little guilty, too, for not giving her any helpful suggestions.

Skip stared at Kate as if she'd volunteered to muck out the stalls.

"I'll write it down before I leave."

"Since Rorie and Kate put so much time and effort into the meal, I think Skip and I could be convinced to do our part and wash the dishes."

"We could?" Skip protested.

"It's the least we can do," Clay returned flatly, frowning at his younger brother.

Rorie was all too aware of Clay's ploy. He wanted to get into the kitchen so they could find something else to eat without being conspicuous about it. Something plain and basic, no doubt, like roast-beef sandwiches.

"Listen, you guys," Rorie said brightly. "I'm sorry about dinner. I can see everyone's still hungry. You're all going out of your way to reassure me, but it isn't necessary."

"I don't know what you're talking about, Rorie. Dinner was excellent," Clay said, patting his stomach.

Rorie nearly laughed out loud. "Why don't we call for a pizza?" she said, pleased with her solution. "I bungled dinner, so that's the least I can do to make it up to you."

Three faces stared at her blankly.

"Rorie," Clay said gently. "The closest pizza parlour is thirty miles from here."

"Oh."

Undeterred, Skip leaped to his feet. "No problem… You phone in the order and I'll go get it."

Empty pizza boxes littered the living-room floor, along with several abandoned soft-drink cans.

Skip lay on his back staring up at the ceiling. "Anyone for a little music?" he asked lazily.

"Sure." Kate got to her feet and sat down at the piano. As her nimble fingers ran over the keyboard, the rich sounds echoed against the walls. "Some Lee Greenwood?"

"All *right*," Skip called out with a yell, punching his

fist into the air. He thrust two fingers in his mouth and gave a shrill whistle.

"Who?" Rorie asked once the commotion had died down.

"He's a country singer," Clay explained. Blue ambled to his side, settling down at his feet. Clay gently stroked his back.

"I guess I haven't heard of him," Rorie murmured.

Once more she discovered three pairs of eyes studying her curiously.

"What about Johnny Cash?" Kate suggested next. "You probably know who he is."

"Oh, sure." Rorie looped her arms over her bent knees and lowered her voice to a gravelly pitch. "I hear that train a comin'."

Skip let loose with another whistle and Rorie laughed at his boisterous antics. Clay left the room; he returned a moment later with a guitar, then seated himself on the floor again, beside Blue. Skip crawled across the braided rug in the center of the room and retrieved a harmonica from the mantel. Soon Kate and the two men were making their own brand of music—country songs, from the traditional to the more recent. Rorie didn't know a single one, but she clapped her hands and tapped her foot to the lively beat.

"Sing for Rorie," Skip shouted to Clay and Kate. "Let's show her what she's been missing."

Clay's rich baritone joined Kate's lilting soprano, and Rorie's hands and feet stopped moving. Her eyes darted from one to the other in openmouthed wonder at the beautiful harmony of their two voices, male and female. It was as though they'd been singing together all their lives. She realized they probably had.

When they finished, Rorie blinked back tears, too dumbfounded for a moment to speak. "That was wonderful," she told them and her voice caught with emotion.

"Kate and Clay sing duets at church all the time," Skip explained. "They're good, aren't they?"

Rorie nodded, gazing at the two of them. Clay and Kate were right for each other—they belonged together, and once she was gone they would blend their lives as beautifully as they had their voices. Rorie happened to catch Kate's eye. The other woman slipped her arms around Clay's waist and rested her head against his shoulder, laying claim to this man and silently letting Rorie know it. Rorie couldn't blame Kate. In like circumstances she would have done the same.

"Do you sing, Rorie?" Kate asked, leaving Clay and sliding onto the piano bench.

"A little, and I play some piano." Actually her own singing voice wasn't half bad. She'd participated in several singing groups while she was in high school and had taken five years of piano lessons.

"Please sing something for us." Rorie recognized a hint of challenge in the words.

"Okay." She replaced Kate at the piano seat and started out with a little satirical ditty she remembered from her college days. Skip hooted as she knew he would at the clever words, and all three rewarded her with a round of applause.

"Play some more," Kate encouraged. "It's nice to have someone else do the playing for a change." She sat next to Clay on the floor, once again resting her head against his shoulder. If it hadn't been for the guitar in his hands, Rorie knew he would've placed his arm around her and drawn her even closer. It would have been the natural thing to do.

"I don't know the songs you usually sing, though." Rorie

was more than a little reluctant now. She'd never heard of this Greenwood person they seemed to like so well.

"Play what you know," Kate said, "and we'll join in."

After a few seconds' thought, Rorie nodded. "This is a song by Billy Joel. I'm sure you've heard of him—his songs are more rock than country, but I think you'll recognize the music." Rorie was only a few measures into the ballad before she realized that Kate, Clay and Skip had never heard this song.

She stopped playing. "What about Whitney Houston?"

Skip repeated the name a couple of times before his eyes lit up with recognition. "Hasn't she done Coke commercials?"

"Right," Rorie said, laughing. "She's had several big hits."

Kate slowly shook her head. "Sorry, I don't think I can remember the words to her songs."

"Barbra Streisand?"

"I thought she was an actress," Skip said with a puzzled frown. "You mean she sings, too?"

Reluctantly Rorie rose from the piano seat. "Kate, you'll have to take over. It seems you three are a whole lot country and I'm a little bit rock and roll."

"We'll make you into a country girl yet!" Skip insisted, sliding the harmonica across his mouth with an ease Rorie envied.

Clay glanced at his watch. "We aren't going to be able to convert Rorie within the next twelve hours."

A gloom settled over them as Kate took Rorie's place at the piano.

"Are you sure we can't talk you into staying a few extra days?" Skip asked. "We're just getting to know each other."

Rorie shook her head, more determined than ever to leave as soon as she could.

"It would be a shame for you to miss the county fair next weekend. Maybe you could stop here on your way back through Oregon, after your trip to Canada," Kate added. "Clay and I are singing, and we're scheduled for the square dance competition, too."

"Yeah," Skip cried. "And we've got pig races planned again this year."

"Pig races?" Rorie echoed faintly.

"I know it sounds silly, but it's really fun. We take the ten fastest pigs in the area and let them race toward a bowl of Oreos. No joke—cookies! Everyone bets on who'll win and we all have a lot of fun." Skip's eyes shone with eagerness. "Please think about it, anyway, Rorie."

"Mary's entering her apple pie again," Clay put in. "She's been after that blue ribbon for six years."

A hundred reasons to fade out of their lives flew across Rorie's mind like particles of dust in the wind. And yet the offer was tempting. She tried, unsuccessfully, to read Clay's eyes, her own filled with a silent appeal. This was a decision she needed help making. But Clay wasn't helping. The thought of never seeing him again was like pouring salt onto an open wound; still, it was a reality she'd have to face sooner or later.

So Rorie volunteered the only excuse she could come up with at the moment. "I don't have the time. I'm sorry, but I'd be cutting it too close to get back to San Francisco for work Monday morning."

"Not if you canceled part of your trip to Canada and came back on Friday," Skip pointed out. "You didn't think you'd have a good time at the square dance, either, but you did, remember?"

It wasn't a matter of having a good time. So much more was involved…though the pig races actually sounded like fun. The very idea of such an activity would have astounded her only a week before, Rorie reflected. She could just imagine what Dan would say.

"Rorie?" Skip pressed. "What do you think?"

"I...I don't know."

"The county fair is about as good as it gets around Nightingale."

"I don't want to impose on your hospitality again." Clay still wasn't giving her any help with this decision.

"But having you stay with us isn't a problem," Skip insisted. "As long as you promise to stay out of the kitchen, you're welcome to stick around all summer. Isn't that right, Clay?"

His hesitation was so slight that Rorie doubted anyone else had noticed it. "Naturally Rorie's welcome to visit us any time she wants."

"If staying with these two drives you crazy," Kate inserted, "you could stay at my house. In fact, I'd love it if you did."

Rorie dropped her gaze, fearing what she might see in Clay's eyes. She sensed his indecision as she struggled with her own. She had to leave. Yet she wanted to stay....

"I think I should take the rest of my vacation in Victoria," she finally told them.

"I know you're worried about getting back in time for work, but Skip's right. If you left Victoria one day early, then you could be here for the fair," Kate suggested again, but her offer didn't sound as sincere as it had earlier.

"Rorie said she doesn't have the time," Clay said after an awkward silence. "I think we should respect her decision."

"You sound as if you don't want her to come back," Skip accused.

"No," Clay murmured, his eyes meeting hers. "I want her here, but Rorie should try to salvage some of the vacation she planned. She has to do what she think's best."

Rorie could feel his eyes moving over her hair and her face in loving appraisal. She tensed and prayed that Kate and Skip weren't aware of it.

During the next hour, Skip tried repeatedly to convince Rorie to visit on her way back or even to stay until the fair. As far as Skip could see, there wasn't much reason to go to Canada now, anyway. But Rorie resisted. Walking away from Clay once was going to be painful enough. Rorie didn't know if she could do it twice.

Skip was yawning by the time they decided to call an end to the evening. With little more than a mumbled goodnight, he hurried up the stairs, abandoning the others.

Rorie and Kate took a few extra minutes to straighten the living room, while Clay drove his pickup around to the front of the house. "I'd better burn the evidence before Mary sees these pizza boxes," Rorie joked. "She'll have my hide once she hears about dinner."

Kate laughed good-naturedly as she collected her belongings. When they heard Clay's truck, she put down her bags and ran to Rorie. "You'll call me before you leave tomorrow?"

Rorie nodded and hugged her back.

"If something happens and you change your mind about the fair, please know that you're welcome to stay with me and Dad—we'd enjoy the company."

"Thank you, Kate."

The house felt empty and silent once Kate had left with Clay. Rorie knew it would be useless to go upstairs and try to sleep. Instead she went out to the front porch, where she'd sat in the swing with Clay that first night. She sank down on the steps, one arm wrapped around a post, and gazed upward. The skies were glittered with the light of countless stars—stars that shone with a clarity and brightness one couldn't see in the city.

Clay belonged to this land, this farm, this small town. Rorie was a city girl to the marrow of her bones. This evening had proved the hopelessness of any dream that she and Clay might have of finding happiness together. There was his commitment to Kate. And there was the fact that he and Rorie were too different, their tastes too dissimilar. She certainly couldn't picture him making a life away from Elk Run.

Clay had accepted the hopelessness of it, too. That was the reason he agreed she should travel to Canada. This evening Rorie had sensed a desperation in him that rivaled her own.

It was a night filled with insights. Sitting under the heavens, she was beginning to understand some important things about life. For perhaps the first time, she'd fallen in love. During the past six days she'd tried to deny what she was feeling, but on the eve of her departure it seemed silly to lie to herself any longer. Rorie couldn't believe something like this had actually happened to her. Meeting someone and falling in love with him in the space of a few days was an experience reserved for novels and movies. This wasn't like her normal sane, sensible self at all. Rorie had always thought she was too levelheaded to fall so easily in love.

Until she met Clay Franklin.

On the wings of one soul-searching realization came another. Love wasn't what she'd expected. She'd assumed it meant a strong sensual passion that overwhelmed the lovers and left them powerless before it. But in the past few days, she'd learned that love marked the soul as well as the body.

Clay would forever be a part of her. Since that first night when Nightsong was born, her heart had never felt more alive. Yet within a few hours she would walk away from the man she loved and consider herself blessed to have shared these days with him.

A tear rolled down the side of her face, surprising her. This wasn't a time for sadness, but joy. She'd discovered a deep inner strength she hadn't known she possessed. She wiped the moisture away and rested her head against the post, her eyes fixed on the heavens.

The footsteps behind Rorie didn't startle her. She'd known Clay would come to her this one last time.

Eleven

Clay draped his arm over Rorie's shoulders and joined her in gazing up at the sky. Neither spoke for several minutes, as though they feared words would destroy the tranquil mood. Rorie stared, transfixed by the glittering display. Like her love for this man, the stars would remain forever distant, unattainable, but certain and unchanging.

A ragged sigh escaped her lips. "All my life I've believed that everything that befalls us has a purpose."

"I've always thought that, too," Clay whispered.

"Everything in life is deliberate."

"Our final hours together you're going to become philosophical?" He rested his chin on her head, gently ruffling her hair. "Are you sad, Rorie?"

"Oh, no," she denied quickly. "I can't be... I feel strange, but I don't know if I can find the words to explain it. I'm leaving tomorrow and I realize we'll probably never see each other again. I have no regrets—not a single one—and yet I think my heart is breaking."

His hand tightened on her shoulder in silent protest as if he found the idea of relinquishing her more than he could bear.

"We can't defy reality," she told him. "Nothing's going

to change in the next few hours. The water pump on the car will be replaced, and I'll go back to my life. The way you'll go back to yours."

"I have this gut feeling there's going to be a hole the size of the Grand Canyon in mine the minute you drive away." He dropped his arm and moved away from her. His eyes held a weary sadness, but Rorie found an acceptance there, too.

"I'm an uncomplicated man," he said evenly. "I'm probably nothing like the sophisticated man you're dating in San Francisco."

Her thoughts flew to Dan, so cosmopolitan and…superficial, and she recognized the truth in Clay's words. The two men were poles apart. Dan's interests revolved around his career and his car, but he was genuinely kind, and it was that quality that had attracted Rorie.

"Elk Run's given me a good deal of satisfaction over the years. My life's work is here and, God willing, some day my son will carry on the breeding programs I've started. Everything I've ever dreamed of has always been within my grasp." He paused, holding in a long sigh and releasing it slowly. "And then you came," he whispered, and a brief smile crossed his lips, "and, within a matter of days, I'm reeling from the effects. Suddenly I'm left doubting what's really important in my life."

Rorie lowered her eyes. "Who'd have believed a silly water pump would be responsible for all this wretched soul-searching?"

"I've always been the type of man who's known what he wants, but you make me feel like a schoolboy no older than Skip. I don't know what to do anymore, Rorie. In a few hours, you'll be leaving and part of me says if you do, I'll regret it the rest of my life."

"I can't stay." Their little dinner party had shown her

how different their worlds actually were. She wouldn't fit into his life and he'd be an alien in hers. But Kate... Kate belonged to his world.

Clay rubbed his hands across his eyes and harshly drew in a breath. "I know you feel you should leave, but that doesn't mean I have to like it."

"The pull to stay is there for me, too," she whispered.

"And it's tearing both of us apart."

Rorie shook her head. "Don't you see? So much good has come out of meeting you, Clay." Her voice was strong. She had to make him understand that she'd always be grateful for the things he'd taught her. "In some ways I grew up tonight. I feel I'm doing what's right for both of us, although it's more painful than anything I've ever known."

He looked at her with such undisguised love that she ached.

"Let me hold you once more," he said softly. "Give me that, at least."

Rorie shook her head. "I can't...I'm sorry, Clay, but this is how it has to be with us. I'm so weak where you're concerned. I couldn't bear to let you touch me now and then leave tomorrow."

His eyes drifted shut as he yielded to her wisdom. "I don't know that I could, either."

They were only a few feet apart, but it seemed vast worlds stood between them.

"More than anything I want you to remember me fondly, without any bitterness," Rorie told him, discovering as she spoke the words how much she meant them.

Clay nodded. "Be happy, Rorie, for my sake."

Rorie realized that contentment would be a long time coming without this man in her life, but she would find it eventually. She prayed that he'd marry Kate the way he'd planned. The other woman was the perfect wife for him—unlike herself. A thread of agony twisted around Rorie's heart.

She turned to leave him, afraid she'd dissolve into tears if she remained much longer. "Goodbye, Clay."

"Goodbye, Rorie."

She rushed past him and hurried up the stairs.

The following morning, both Clay and Skip had left the house by the time Rorie entered the kitchen.

"Good morning, Mary," she said with a note of false cheer in her voice. "How did the visit with your sister go?"

"Fine."

Rorie stepped around the housekeeper to reach the coffeepot and poured herself a cup. A plume of steam rose enticingly to her nostrils and she took a tentative sip.

"I found those pizza boxes you were trying so hard to hide from me," Mary grumbled as she wiped her hands on her apron. "You fed these good men restaurant pizza?"

Unable to stop herself, Rorie chuckled at the housekeeper's indignation. "Guilty as charged. Mary, you should've known better than to leave their fate in my evil hands."

"Near as I can figure, the closest pizza parlour is a half-hour away. Did you drive over and get it yourself or did you send Skip?"

"Actually he volunteered," she admitted reluctantly. "Dinner didn't exactly turn out the way I'd hoped."

The housekeeper snickered. "I should've guessed. You city slickers don't know nothing about serving up a decent meal to your menfolk."

Rorie gave a hefty sigh of agreement. "The only thing for me to do is stay on another couple of months and have you teach me." As she expected, the housekeeper opened her mouth to protest. "Unfortunately," Rorie continued, cutting Mary off before she could launch into her arguments, "I'm hoping to be gone by this afternoon."

Mary's response was a surprise. The older woman's expression grew troubled and intense.

"I suspected you'd be going soon enough," she said in a tight voice, pulling out a chair. She sat down heavily and brushed wisps of gray hair from her forehead. Her weathered face was thoughtful. "It's for the best, you know."

"I knew you'd be glad to get rid of me."

Mary shrugged. "It's other reasons that make it right for you to leave. You know what I'm talking about, even if you don't want to admit it to me. As a person you tend to grow on folks. Like I said before, for a city girl, you ain't half bad."

Rorie took a banana from the fruit bowl in the center of the table. "For a stud farm, stuck out here in the middle of nowhere, this place isn't half bad, either," she said, trying to lighten the mood, which had taken an unexpected turn toward the serious. "The people are friendly and the apple pie's been exceptional."

Mary ignored the compliment on her pie. "By people, I suppose you're referring to Clay. You're going to miss him, aren't you, girl?"

The banana found its way back into the bowl and with it went her cheerful facade. "Yes. I'll miss Clay."

The older woman's frown deepened. "From the things I've been noticing, he's going to be yearning for you, as well. But it's for the best," she said again. "For the best."

Rorie nodded and her voice wavered. "Yes…but it isn't easy."

The housekeeper gave her a lopsided smile as she gently patted Rorie's hand. "I know that, too, but you're doing the right thing. You'll forget him soon enough."

A strong protest rose in her breast, closing off her throat.

She wouldn't forget Clay. Ever. How could she forget the man who had so unselfishly taught her such valuable lessons about life and love? Lessons about herself.

"Kate Logan's the right woman for Clay," Mary said abruptly.

Those few words cut Rorie to the quick. Hearing another person voice the truth made it almost unbearably painful.

"I…hope they're very happy."

"Kate loves him. She has from the time she was knee-high to a June bug. And there's something you don't know. Years back, when Clay was in college, he fell in love with a girl from Seattle. She'd been born and raised in the city. Clay loved her, wanted to marry her, even brought her to Elk Run to meet the family. She stayed a couple of days, and the whole time, she was as restless as water on a hot skillet. Apparently she had words with Clay because the next thing I knew, she'd packed her bags and headed home. Clay never said much about her after that, but she hurt him bad. It wasn't until Kate got home from college that Clay thought seriously about marriage again."

Mary's story explained a lot about Clay.

"Now, I know I'm just an old woman who likes her soaps and Saturday-night bingo. Most folks don't think I've got a lick of sense, and that's all right. What others choose to assume don't bother me much." She paused, and shook her head. "But Kate Logan's about the kindest, dearest person this town has ever seen. People like her—they can't help themselves. She's always got a kind word and there's no one in this world she's too good for. She cares about the people in this community. Those kids she teaches over at the grade school love her like nothing you've ever seen. And she loves them. When it came to building that fancy library, it was Kate who worked so hard convincing folks they'd be doing what was best for Nightingale by voting for that bond issue."

Rorie kept her face averted. She didn't need Mary to tell her Kate was a good person; she'd seen the evidence of it herself.

"What most folks don't know is that Kate's seen plenty of pain in her own life. She watched her mother die a slow death from cancer. Took care of her most of the time herself, nursing Nora when she should've been off at college having fun like other nineteen-year-olds. Her family needed her and she was there. Kate gave old man Logan a reason to go on living when Nora passed away. She still lives with him, and it's long past time for her to be a carefree adult on her own. Kate's a good person clean through." Mary hesitated, then drew in a solemn breath. "Now, you may think I'm nothing but a meddling old fool. But I'm saying it's a good thing you're leaving Elk Run before you break that girl's heart. She's got a chance now for some happiness, and God knows she deserves it. If she loses Clay, I can tell you it'd break her heart. She's too good to have that happen to her over some fancy city girl who's only passing through."

Rorie winced at the way Mary described her.

"I'm a plain talker," Mary said on the end of an abrupt laugh. "Always have been, always will be. Knowing Clay—and I do, as well as his mother did, God rest her soul—he'll pine for you awhile, but eventually everything will fall back into place. The way it was before you arrived."

Tears stung Rorie's eyes. She felt miserable as it was, and Mary wasn't helping. She'd already assured the housekeeper she was leaving, but Mary apparently wanted to be damn sure she didn't change her mind. The woman didn't understand...but then again, maybe she did.

"Have you ever been in love, Mary?"

"Once," came the curt reply. "Hurt so much the first time I never chanced it again."

"Are you sorry you lived your life alone now?" That was what Rorie saw for herself. Oh, she knew she was being melodramatic and over-emotional, but she couldn't imagine loving any man as much as she did Clay.

Mary lifted one shoulder in a shrug. "Some days I have plenty of regrets, but then on others it ain't so bad. I'd like to have had a child, but God saw to it that I was around when Clay and Skip needed someone…. That made up for what I missed."

"They consider you family."

"Yeah, I suppose they do." Mary pushed out her chair and stood up. "Well, I better get back to work. Those men expect a decent lunch. I imagine they're near starved after the dinner you fed them last night."

Despite her heartache, Rorie smiled and finished her coffee. "And I'd better get upstairs and pack the rest of my things. The mechanic said my car would be ready around noon."

On her way to the bedroom, Rorie paused at the framed photograph of Clay's parents that sat on the piano. She'd passed it a number of times and had given it little more than a fleeting glance. Now it suddenly demanded her attention, and she stopped in front of it.

A tremor went through her hand as she lightly ran her finger along the brass frame. Clay's mother smiled serenely into the camera, her gray eyes so like her son's that Rorie felt a knot in her stomach. Those same eyes seemed to reach across eternity and call out to Rorie, plead with her. Rorie's own eyes narrowed, certain her imagination was playing havoc with her troubled mind. She focused her attention on the woman's hair. That, too, was the same dark shade as Clay's, brushed away from her face in a carefully styled chignon. Clay had never mentioned his parents to her, not once, but studying the photograph Rorie knew intuitively that he'd shared a close relationship with his mother. Blue wandered out from the kitchen and stood at Rorie's side as though offering consolation. Grateful, she bent down to pet him.

Looking back at the photograph, Rorie noted that Skip resembled his father, with the same dancing blue eyes that revealed more than a hint of devilry.

Rorie continued to study both parents, but it was Clay's mother who captured her attention over and over again.

The phone ringing in the distance startled her, and her wrist was shaking when she set the picture back on the piano.

"Phone's for you," Mary shouted from the kitchen.

Rorie assumed it was George at the repair shop in Riversdale; she'd been waiting all morning to hear from him.

"Hello," she said, her fingers closing tightly around the receiver. Her biggest fear was that something had happened to delay her departure a second time.

"Miss Campbell," said the mechanic, "everything's fine. I got that part in and working for you without a hitch."

"Thank God," she murmured. Her hold on the telephone receiver relaxed, a little.

"I've got a man I could spare if you'd like to have your car delivered to Elk Run. But you've got to understand fifty miles is a fair distance and I'm afraid I'll have to charge you extra for it."

"That's fine," Rorie said eagerly, not even bothering to ask the amount. "How soon can he be here?"

Twelve

"So you're really going," Skip said as he picked up Rorie's bags. "Somehow I figured I might've talked you into staying on for the county fair."

"You seem intent on bringing me to ruin, Skip Franklin. I'm afraid I'd bet all my hard-earned cash on those pig races you were telling me about," Rorie teased. Standing in the middle of the master bedroom, she surveyed it to be sure she hadn't forgotten anything.

A pang of wistfulness settled over her as she slowly looked around. Not for the first time, Rorie felt the love and warmth emanating from these brightly papered walls. Lazily, almost lovingly, she ran her fingertips along the top of the dresser, letting her hand linger there a moment, unwilling to pull herself away. This bedroom represented so much of what she was leaving behind. It was difficult to walk away.

Skip stood in the doorway impatiently waiting for her. "Kate phoned and said she's coming over. She wants to say goodbye."

"I'll be happy to see her one last time." Rorie wished Skip would leave so she could delay her parting with this room a little longer. Until now, Rorie hadn't realized how much sleeping in Clay's parents' room had meant to her. Her appreciation had come too late.

"Mary's packing a lunch for you," Skip announced with a wry chuckle, "and knowing Mary, it'll be enough to last you a week."

Rorie smiled and reluctantly followed him down the stairs. As Skip had claimed, the housekeeper had prepared two large bags, which sat waiting on the kitchen table.

"Might as well take those with you, too," Mary muttered gruffly. "I hate the thought of you eating restaurant food. This, at least, will stick to your ribs."

"Goodbye, Mary," Rorie said softly, touched by the housekeeper's thoughtfulness. On impulse she hugged the older woman. "Thank you for everything—including our talk this morning." The impromptu embrace surprised Rorie as much as it obviously did Mary.

"You drive careful now, you hear?" the housekeeper responded, squeezing Rorie tightly and patting her back several times.

"I will, I promise."

"A letter now and again wouldn't be amiss."

"All right," Rorie agreed, and used her sleeve to blot tears from the corners of her eyes. These people had touched her in so many ways. Leaving them was even more difficult than she'd imagined.

The housekeeper rubbed the heel of her hand over her right eye. "Time for you to get on the road. What are you doing standing in the kitchen chitchatting with me?" she asked brusquely.

"I'm going, I'm going." Mary's gruff voice didn't fool Rorie. The housekeeper's exterior might be a little crusty, and her tongue a bit surly, but she didn't succeed in disguising a generous, loving heart.

"I don't know where Clay is," Skip complained after

he'd loaded the luggage into the MG's trunk. "I thought he'd want to see you before you left. I wonder where he got off to."

"I'm…sure he's got better things to do than say good-bye to me."

"No way," Skip said, frowning. "I'm going to see if I can find him."

Rorie's first reaction was to stop Skip, then she quickly decided against it. If she made too much of a fuss, Skip might suspect something. She understood what had prompted Clay to stay away from the house all morning, and in truth she was grateful. Leaving Elk Run was hard enough without prolonging the agony in lengthy farewells.

Skip hesitated, kicking at the dirt with the pointed toe of his cowboy boot. "You two didn't have a fight or anything, did you?"

"No. What makes you ask?"

Skip shrugged. "Well… It's just that every time I walked into a room with the two of you, I could feel something. If it wasn't for Kate, I'd think my big brother was interested in you."

"I'm sure you're imagining things."

"I suppose so," Skip said with a nod, dismissing the notion. "Ever since you got here, though, Clay's been acting weird."

"How do you mean?"

"Sort of cranky."

"My unexpected arrival added to his problems, don't you think?" In so many ways it was the truth, and she felt guilty about that. The responsibilities for the farm and for raising Skip were sobering enough; he didn't need her there to wreak havoc with his personal life.

"You weren't any problem," Skip answered sharply. "In

fact, having you around was fun. The only trouble is you didn't stay long enough."

"Thank you, Skip." Once again she felt her throat clog with tears. She was touched by his sweet, simple hospitality and reminded of how much she'd miss him.

"I still kinda wish you were going to stay for the fair," he mumbled. "You'd have a good time, I guarantee it. We may not have all the fancy entertainment you do in San Francisco, but when we do a county fair, we do it big."

"I'm sure it'll be great fun."

Skip braced his foot against the bumper of the faded blue pickup, apparently forgetting his earlier decision to seek out Clay, which was just as well.

"You don't like the country much, do you, Rorie?"

"Oh, but I do," she said. "It's a different way of life, though. Here on Elk Run, I feel like a duck in a pond full of swans."

Skip laughed. "I suppose folks there in the big city don't think much of the country."

"No one has time to think," Rorie said with a small laugh.

"That doesn't make any sense. Everyone's got thoughts."

Rorie nodded, not knowing how to explain something so complex. When Skip had spent some time in the city, he'd figure out what she meant.

"The one thing I've noticed more than anything is how quiet it is here," she said pensively, looking around, burning into her memory each detail of the farmhouse and the yard.

"I like the quiet. Some places, the noise is so bad I worry about ear damage," Skip said.

"I imagine if I lived here, I'd grow accustomed to the silence, too. But to be honest, I hadn't realized how much I enjoy the sounds of the city. There's something invigorating about the clang of the trolley cars or the foghorn on the Bay early in the morning."

Skip frowned and shook his head. "You honestly like all that racket?"

Rorie nodded. "It's more than that. The city's exciting. I hadn't really known how much living there meant to me before coming to Elk Run." Rorie wasn't sure how to describe the aroma of freshly baked sourdough bread, or the perfumed scent of budding rosebushes in Golden Gate Park, to someone who'd never experienced them. Country life had its appeal, she couldn't deny that, but she belonged to the city. At least, that was what she told herself over and over again.

"Ah," Skip said, and his foot dropped from the bumper with a thud, "here's Clay now."

Rorie tensed, clasping her hands in front of her. Clay's lengthy strides quickly diminished the distance between the barn and the yard. Each stride was filled with purpose, as though he longed to get this polite farewell over with.

Rorie straightened and walked toward him. "I'll be leaving in a couple of minutes," she said softly.

"Kate's coming to say goodbye," Skip added.

Rorie noted how Clay's eyes didn't quite meet her own. He seemed to focus instead on the car behind her. They'd already said everything there was to say and this final parting only compounded the pain.

"Saying thank you seems so inadequate," Rorie told him in a voice that wasn't entirely steady. "I've appreciated your hospitality more than you'll ever know." Hesitantly she held out her hand to him.

Clay's hard fingers curled around her own, his touch light and impersonal. Rorie swallowed hard, unable to hold back the emotion churning so violently inside her.

His expression was completely impassive, but she

sensed that he held on to his self-control with the thinnest of threads. In that moment, Rorie felt the longing in him and knew that he recognized it in her, too.

"Oh, Clay…" she whispered, her eyes brimming with tears. The impulse to move into his arms was like a huge wave, threatening to sweep over her, and she didn't know how much longer she'd have the strength to resist.

"Don't look at me like that," Clay muttered grimly.

"I…can't help it." But he belonged to Kate and nothing was likely to change that.

He took a step toward her and stopped himself, suddenly remembering they weren't alone.

"Skip, go hold Thunder for Don. Don's trying to paste-worm him, and he's getting dragged all over the stall." Clay's words were low-pitched, sharp, full of demand.

"But, Clay, Rorie's about to—"

"Do it."

Mumbling something unintelligible, Skip trudged off to the barn.

The minute his brother was out of sight, Clay caught Rorie's shoulders, his fingers rough and urgent through the thin cotton of her blouse. The next instant, she was locked against him. The kiss was inevitable, Rorie knew, but when his mouth settled over hers she wanted to weep for the joy she found in his arms. He kissed her temple, her cheek, her mouth, until she clung to him with hungry abandon. They were standing in the middle of the yard in full view of farmhands, but Clay didn't seem to care and Rorie wasn't about to object.

"I told myself I wouldn't do this," he whispered huskily.

Rorie's heart constricted.

At the sound of a car in the distance, Clay abruptly dropped his arms, freeing her. His fingers tangled in her hair as if he had to touch her one last time.

"I was a fool to think I could politely shake your hand and let you leave. We're more than casual friends and I can't pretend otherwise—to hell with the consequences."

Tears flooded Rorie's eyes as she stared up at Clay. Then, from behind him, she saw the cloud of dust that announced Kate's arrival. She inhaled a deep breath in an effort to compose herself and, wiping her damp cheeks with the back of one hand, forced a smile.

Clay released a ragged sigh as he trailed a callused hand down the side of her face. "Goodbye, Rorie," he whispered. With that, he turned and walked away.

Thick fog swirled around Rorie as she paused to catch her breath on the path in Golden Gate Park. She bent forward and planted her hands on her knees, driving the oxygen into her heaving lungs. Not once in the two weeks she'd been on vacation had she followed her jogging routine, and now she was paying the penalty. The muscles in her calves and thighs protested the strenuous exercise and her heart seemed about to explode. Her biggest problem was trying to keep up with Dan, who'd run ahead, unwilling to slow his pace to match hers.

"Rorie?"

"Over here." Her voice was barely more than a choked whisper. She meant to raise her hand and signal to him, but even that required more effort than she could manage. Seeing a bench in the distance, she stumbled over and collapsed into it. Leaning back, she stretched out her legs.

"You *are* out of shape," Dan teased, handing her a small towel.

Rorie wiped the perspiration from her face and smiled her appreciation. "I can't believe two weeks would make such a difference." She'd been back in San Francisco only a couple of days. Other than dropping off the MG at Dan's place, this was the first time they'd had a chance to get together.

Dan stood next to her, hardly out of breath—even after a three-mile workout.

"Two weeks *is* a long time," he said with the hint of a smile. "I suppose you didn't keep up with your vitamin program, either," he chastised gently. "Well, Rorie, it's obvious how much you need me."

She chose to ignore that comment. "I used to consider myself in top physical condition. Not anymore. Good grief, I thought my heart was going to give out two miles back."

Dan, blond and debonair, was appealingly handsome in a clean-cut boyish way. He draped the towel around his neck and grasped the ends. Rorie's eyes were drawn to his hands, with their finely manicured nails and long tapered fingers. Stockbroker fingers. Nice hands. Friendly hands.

Still, Rorie couldn't help comparing them with another pair of male hands, darkly tanned from hours in the sun and roughly callused. Gentle hands. Working hands.

"I meant what I said about you needing me," Dan murmured, watching her closely. "It's time we got serious, Rorie. Time we made some important decisions about our future."

When she least expected it, he slid closer on the bench beside her. With his so smooth fingers, he cupped her face, his thumbs stroking her flushed cheeks. "I did a lot of thinking while you were away."

She covered his fingers with her own, praying for an easier way to say what she must. They'd been seeing each other for months and she hated to hurt him, but it would be even crueler to lead him on. When they'd started dating, Dan had been looking for a casual relationship. He'd recently been divorced and wasn't ready for a new emotional commitment.

"Oh, Dan, I think I know what you're going to say. Please don't."

He paused, searching her face intently. "What do you mean?"

"I did some thinking while I was away, too, and I realized that although I'll always treasure your friendship, we can't ever be more than friends."

His dark eyes ignited with resistance. "What happened to you on this vacation, Rorie? You left, and two weeks later you returned a completely different woman."

"You're exaggerating," Rorie objected weakly. She knew she *was* different, from the inside out.

"You've hardly said a word to me about your trip," Dan complained, in a tone that suggested he felt hurt by her reticence. "All you've said is that the car broke down in the Oregon outback and you were stuck on some farm for days until a part could be delivered. You don't blame me for that, do you? I had no idea there was anything wrong with the water pump."

She laughed at his description of Nightingale as the outback.

"You completely missed the writers' conference, didn't you?"

"That couldn't be helped, but I enjoyed the rest of my vacation. Victoria was like stepping into a small piece of England," she said, in an effort to divert his attention from the time she'd spent on the Franklin farm. Victoria had been lovely, but unfortunately she hadn't been in the proper mood to appreciate its special beauty.

"You didn't so much as mail me a postcard."

"I know," she said with a twinge of guilt.

"I was lonesome without you," Dan said slowly, running his hand over her hair. "Nothing felt right with you gone."

Rorie knew it had taken a lot for him to admit that, and it made what she had to tell him all the more difficult.

"Dan, please," she said, breaking away from him and standing. "I...I don't love you."

"But we're friends."

"Of course."

He seemed both pleased and relieved by that. "Good friends?" he coaxed.

Rorie nodded, wondering where this was leading.

"Then there's really no problem, is there?" he asked, his voice gaining enthusiasm. "You went away, and I realized how much I love you, and you came back deciding you value my friendship. That, at least, is a beginning."

"Dan, honestly!"

"Well, isn't it?"

"Our relationship isn't going anywhere," she told him, desperate to clarify the issue. Dan was a good person and he deserved someone who was crazy in love with him. The way she was with Clay.

To Rorie's surprise, Dan drew her forward and kissed her. Startled, she stood placidly in his arms, feeling his warm mouth move over hers. She experienced no feeling, no excitement, nothing. Kissing Dan held all the appeal of drinking flat soda.

Frustrated, he tried to deepen the kiss.

Rorie braced her hands against his chest and tried to pull herself free. He released her immediately, then stepped back, frowning. "Okay, okay, we've got our work cut out for us. But the electricity will come, in time."

Somehow Rorie doubted that.

Dan dropped her off in front of her apartment. "Can I see you soon?" he asked, his hands clenching the steering wheel. He didn't look at her but stared straight ahead as though he feared her answer.

Rorie hesitated. "I'm not going to fall in love with you, Dan, and I don't want to take advantage of your feelings. I think it'd be best if you started seeing someone else."

He appeared to consider that for an awkward moment. "But the decision should be mine, shouldn't it?"

"Yes, but—"

"Then leave everything to me, and stop worrying. If I choose to waste my time on you, that's my problem, not yours. I think you're going to change your mind, Rorie. Because I love you enough for both of us."

"Oh, Dan." Her shoulders sagged with defeat. He hadn't believed a single word she'd said.

"Now don't look so depressed. How about a movie on Sunday? It's been a while since we've done that."

Exhausted, she shook her head. "Dan, no."

"I insist, so stop arguing."

She didn't have the energy to argue. "All right," she murmured. He'd soon learn she meant what she'd said. "All right."

"Good. I'll pick you up at six."

Rorie climbed out of the MG and closed the door, turning to give Dan a limp wave. She paused in the foyer of her apartment building to unlock her mailbox.

There was a handful of envelopes. Absently, she shuffled through a leaflet from a prominent department store, an envelope with a Kentucky postmark and an electric bill. It wasn't until she was inside her apartment that Rorie noticed the letter postmarked Nightingale, Oregon.

Thirteen

Rorie set the letter on her kitchen counter and stared at it for a moment. Her chest felt as if a dead weight were pressing against it. Her heart was pounding and her stomach churned. The post-office box number for the return address didn't tell her much. The letter could as easily be from Kate as Clay. It could even be from Mary.

Taking a deep, calming breath, Rorie reached for the envelope from Kentucky first. The return address told her nothing—she didn't know anyone who lived in that state.

The slip of paper inside confused her, too. She read it several times, not understanding. It appeared to be registration papers for Nightsong, from the National Show Horse Association. Rorie Campbell was listed as owner, with Clay's name as breeder. The date of Nightsong's birth was also recorded. Rorie slumped into a kitchen chair and battled an attack of memories and tears.

Clay was giving her Nightsong.

It was Nightsong who'd brought them together and it was through Nightsong that they'd remain linked. Life would go on; the loss of one couple's love wouldn't alter the course of history. But now there was something—a single piece of paper—that would connect her to Clay, something that gave testimony to their sacrifice.

Rorie had needed that and Clay had apparently known it.

They'd made the right decision, Rorie told herself for the hundredth time. Clay's action confirmed it.

Clay was wide-open spaces and sleek, well-trained horses, while she thrived in the crowded city.

His strength came from his devotion to the land; hers came from the love of children and literature and the desire to create her own stories.

They were dissimilar in every way—and alike. In the most important matters, the most telling, they were actually very much alike. Neither of them was willing to claim happiness at the expense of someone else.

Tears spilled down her cheeks, and sniffling, Rorie wiped them aside. The drops dampened her fingertips as she picked up the second envelope, blurring the return address. But even before she opened it, Rorie realized the letter was from Kate. Clay wouldn't write her, and everything Mary had wanted to say she'd already said the morning Rorie left Elk Run.

Three handwritten sheets slipped easily from the envelope, with Kate's evenly slanted signature at the bottom of the last.

The letter was filled with chatty news about Nightingale and some of the people Rorie had met. There were so many, and connecting names with faces taxed her memory. Kate wrote about the county fair, telling Rorie that she'd missed a very exciting pig race. The biggest news of all was that after years of trying, Mary had finally won a blue ribbon for her apple pie—an honor long overdue in Kate's opinion.

Toward the end of the letter, Clay's fiancée casually mentioned that Clay would be in San Francisco the first week of September for a horse show. The American Saddlebreds from Elk Run were well-known throughout the Pacific coast for their fire and elegance. Clay had high hopes of repeating last year's wins in the Five Gaited and Fine Harness Championships.

Rorie's pulse shifted into overdrive and her fingers tightened on the letter. Clay was coming to San Francisco. He hadn't said anything about the show to Rorie—although he must've known about it long before she'd left Nightingale.

Kate went on to say that she'd asked Clay if he planned to look up Rorie while he was in town, but he'd claimed there wouldn't be time. Kate was sure Rorie would understand and not take offense. She closed by saying that her father might also be attending the horse show and, if he did, Kate would try to talk him into letting her tag along. Kate promised she'd phone Rorie the minute she arrived in town, if she could swing it with her father.

Not until Rorie folded the letter to return it to the envelope did she notice the postscript on the back of the last page. She turned over the sheet of pink stationery. The words seemed to jump off the page: Kate was planning an October wedding and would send Rorie an invitation. She ended with, "Write soon."

Rorie's breath caught in her lungs. An October wedding... In only a few weeks, Kate would belong to Clay. Rorie closed her eyes as her heart squeezed into a knot of pain. It wasn't that she hadn't known this was coming. Kate and Clay's wedding was inevitable, but Rorie hadn't thought Clay would go through with it quite so soon. With trembling hands, she set the letter aside.

"Rorie, love, I can't honestly believe you want to go to a horse show," Dan complained, scanning the entertainment section of the Friday-evening paper. They sat in the minuscule living room in her apartment and sipped their coffee while they tossed around ideas for something to do.

Rorie smiled blandly, praying Dan couldn't read her thoughts. He'd offered several suggestions for the night's amusement, but Rorie had rejected each one. Until she pretended to hit upon the idea of attending the horse show…

"A horse show?" he repeated. "You never told me you were interested in horses."

"It would be fun, don't you think?"

"Not particularly."

"But, Dan, it's time to broaden our horizons—we might learn something."

"Does this mean you're going to insist we attend a demolition derby next weekend?"

"Of course not. I read an article about this horse show and I just thought we'd enjoy the gaited classes and harness competitions. Apparently, lots of Saddlebreds and National Show Horses are going to be performing. Doesn't that interest you?"

"No."

Rorie shrugged, slowly releasing a sigh. "Then a movie's fine," she said, not even trying to hide her disappointment. They'd seen each other only a handful of times since Rorie's return. Rorie wouldn't be going out with him tonight if he hadn't persisted. She hoped he'd get the message and start dating other women, but that didn't seem to be happening.

"I have no idea why you'd want to see a horse show," Dan said once more.

For the past few days the newspapers had been filled with information regarding the country-wide show in which Kate had said several of Elk Run's horses would be participating. In all the years she'd lived in San Francisco, Rorie couldn't remember reading about a single equine exhibition, but then she hadn't exactly been looking for one, either.

If Dan refused to go with her, Rorie was determined to attend the event on her own. She didn't have any intention of seeking out Clay, but the opportunity to see him, even from a distance, was too tempting to let pass. It would probably be the last time she'd ever see him.

"I don't know what's got into you lately, Rorie," Dan muttered. "Just when I think our lives are on track, you throw me for a loop."

"I said a movie was fine." Her tone was testier than she meant it to be, but Dan had been harping on the same subject for weeks and she was tired of it.

If he didn't want her company, he should start dating someone else. She wasn't going to suddenly decide she was madly in love with him, as he seemed to expect. Again and again, Dan phoned to tell her he loved her, that his love was enough for both of them. She always stopped him there, unable to imagine spending the rest of her life with him. If she couldn't have Clay—and she couldn't—then she wasn't willing to settle for anyone else.

"I'm talking about a lot more than seeing a movie." He laid the newspaper aside and seemed to carefully consider his next words.

"Really, Dan, you're making a mountain out of a molehill," Rorie said. "Just because I wanted to do something a little out of the ordinary…"

"Eating at an Armenian restaurant is a little out of the ordinary," he said, frowning, "but horse shows… I can't even begin to understand why you'd want to watch a bunch of animals running around in circles."

"Well, you keep insisting I've changed," she said flippantly. If she'd known Dan was going to react so strongly to her suggestion, she'd never have made it. "I guess this only goes to prove you're right."

"How much writing have you done in the past month?"

The question was completely unexpected. She answered him with a shrug, hoping he'd drop the subject, knowing he wouldn't.

"None, right? I've seen you sitting at your computer, staring into space with that sad look on your face. I remember how you used to talk about your stories. Your eyes would light up. Enthusiasm would just spill out of you." His hand reached for hers, tightly squeezing her fingers. "What happened to you, Rorie? Where's the joy? Where's the energy?"

"You're imagining things," she said, nearly leaping to her feet in an effort to sidestep the issues he was raising. She grabbed her purse and a light sweater, eager to escape the apartment, which suddenly felt too small. "Are you going to take me to that movie, or are you going to sit here and ask questions I have no intention of answering?"

Dan stood, smiling faintly. "I don't know what happened while you were on vacation, and it's not important that I know, but whatever it was hurt you badly."

Rorie tried to deny it, but couldn't force the lie past her tongue. She swallowed and turned her head away, eyes burning.

"You won't be able to keep pretending forever. Put whatever it is behind you. If you want to talk about it, I've got a sympathetic ear and a sturdy shoulder. I'm your friend, Rorie."

"Dan, please…"

"I know you're not in love with me," he said quietly. "I suspect you met someone else while you were away, but that doesn't matter to me. Whatever happened during those two weeks is over."

"Dan…"

He took her hand, pulling her back onto the sofa, then sitting down beside her. She couldn't look at him.

"Given time, you'll learn to love me," he cajoled, holding her hand, his voice filled with kindness. "We're already good friends, and that's a lot more than some people have when they marry." He raised her fingers to his mouth and kissed them lightly. "I'm not looking for passion. I had that with my first wife. I learned the hard way that desire is a poor foundation for a solid marriage."

"We've talked about this before," Rorie protested. "I can't marry you, Dan, not when I feel the way I do about… someone else." Her mouth trembled with the effort to suppress tears. Dan was right. As much as she hadn't wanted to face the truth, she'd been heartbroken from the moment she'd left Nightingale.

She'd tried to forget Clay, believing that was the best thing for them both, yet she cherished the memories, knowing those few brief days were all she'd ever have of this man she loved.

"You don't have to decide right now," Dan assured her.

"There isn't anything to decide," she persisted.

His fingers continued to caress hers, and when he spoke his voice was thick. "At least you've admitted there is someone else."

"Was," she corrected.

"I take it there isn't any chance the two of you—"

"None," she blurted, unwilling to discuss anything that had to do with Clay.

"I know it's painful for you right now, but all I ask is that you seriously consider my proposal. My only wish is to take care of you and make you smile again. Help you forget."

His mouth sought hers, and though his kiss wasn't unpleasant, it generated no more excitement than before, no rush of adrenaline, no urgency. She hadn't minded Dan's kisses in the past, but until she met Clay she hadn't known the warmth and magic a man's touch could create.

Dan must have read her thoughts, because he said in a soothing voice, "The passion will come in time—you shouldn't even look for it now, but it'll be there. Maybe not this month or the next, but you'll feel it eventually, I promise."

Rorie brushed the hair from her face, confused and uncertain. Clay was marrying Kate in just a few weeks. Her own life stretched before her, lonely and barren—surely she deserved some happiness, too. Beyond a doubt, Rorie knew Clay would want her to build a good life for herself. But if she married Dan, it would be an act of selfishness, and she feared she'd end up hurting him.

"Think about it," Dan urged. "That's all I ask."

"Dan…"

"Just consider it. I know the score and I'm willing to take the risk, so you don't have to worry about me. I'm a big boy." He rubbed his thumb against the inside of her wrist. "Now, promise me you'll think honestly about us getting married."

Rorie nodded, although she already knew what her answer would have to be.

Dan heaved a sigh. "Now, are you really interested in that horse show, or are we going to a movie?"

"The movie." There was no use tormenting herself with thoughts of Clay. He belonged to Kate in the same way that he belonged to the country. Rorie had no claim to either.

The film Dan chose was surprisingly good, a comedy, which was just what Rorie needed to lift her spirits. Afterward, they dined at an Italian restaurant and drank wine and discussed politics. Dan went out of his way to be the perfect companion, making no demands on her, and Rorie was grateful.

It was still relatively early when he drove her back to her apartment, and he eagerly accepted her invitation for coffee. As he eased the MG into a narrow space in front of her building, he suddenly paused, frowning.

"Do you have new neighbors?"

"Not that I know of. Why?"

Dan nodded toward the battered blue pickup across the street. "Whoever drives that piece of junk is about to bring down the neighborhood property values."

Fourteen

"Clay." His name escaped Rorie's lips on a rush of excitement. She jerked open the car door and stepped onto the sidewalk, her legs trembling, her pulse thundering.

"Rorie?" Dan called, agitated. "Who is this man?"

She hardly heard him. A door slammed in the distance and Rorie whirled around and saw that Clay had been sitting inside his truck, apparently waiting for her to return. He'd been parked in the shadows, and she hadn't noticed him.

Dan joined her on the pavement and placed his hand possessively on her shoulder. His grip was the only thing that rooted her in reality, his hand the restraining force that prevented her from flying into Clay's arms.

"Who is this guy?" Dan asked a second time.

Rorie opened her mouth to explain and realized she couldn't, not in a few words. "A…friend," she whispered, but that seemed so inadequate.

"He's a cowboy!" Dan hissed, making it sound as though Clay's close-fitting jeans and jacket were the garb of a man just released from jail.

Clay crossed the street and his long strides made short work of the distance separating him from Rorie.

"Hello, Rorie."

She heard the faint catch in his voice. "Clay."

A muscle moved in his cheek as he looked past her to Dan, who squared the shoulders of his Brooks Brothers suit. No one spoke, until Rorie saw that Clay was waiting for an introduction.

"Clay Franklin, this is Dan Rogers. Dan is the stockbroker I...I mentioned before. It was his sports car I was driving."

Clay nodded. "I remember now." His gaze slid away from Rorie to the man at her side.

Dan stepped around Rorie and accepted Clay's hand. She noticed that when Dan dropped his arm to his side, he flexed his fingers a couple of times, as though to restore the circulation. Rorie smiled to herself. Clay's handshake was the solid one of a man accustomed to working with his hands. When Dan shook hands, it was little more than a polite business greeting, an archaic but necessary exchange.

"Clay and his brother, Skip, were the family who helped me when the MG broke down," Rorie explained to Dan.

"Ah, yes, I remember your saying something about that now."

"I was about to make a pot of coffee," Rorie went on, unable to take her eyes off Clay. She drank in the sight of him, painfully noting the crow's-feet that fanned out from the corners of his eyes. She couldn't remember their being quite so pronounced before.

"Yes, by all means join us." Dan's invitation lacked any real welcome.

Clay said nothing. He just stood there looking at her. Almost no emotion showed in his face, but she could feel the battle that raged inside him. He loved her still, and everything about him told her that.

"Please join us," she whispered.

Any lingering hope that Dan would take the hint and make his excuses faded as he slipped his arm protectively around Rorie's shoulders. "I picked up some Swiss mocha coffee beans earlier," he said, "and Rorie was going to make a pot of that."

"Swiss mocha coffee?" Clay repeated, blinking quizzically.

"Decaffeinated, naturally," Dan hurried to add.

Clay arched his brows expressively, as if to say that made all the difference in the world.

With Dan glued to her side, Rorie reluctantly led the way into her building. "Have you been here long?" she asked Clay while they stood waiting for the elevator.

"About an hour."

"Oh, Clay…" Rorie felt terrible, although it wasn't her fault; she hadn't known he intended to stop by. Perhaps he hadn't known himself and had been lured to her apartment the same way she'd been contemplating the horse show.

"You should have phoned." Dan's comment was casual, but it contained a hint of accusation. "But then, I suppose, you folks tend to drop in on each other all the time. Things are more casual in the country, aren't they?"

Rorie sent Dan a furious glare. He returned her look blankly, as if to say he had no idea what could have angered her. Rorie was grateful that the elevator arrived just then.

Clay didn't comment on Dan's observation and the three stepped inside, facing the doors as they slowly closed.

"When you weren't home, I asked the neighbors if they knew where you'd gone," Clay said.

"The neighbors?" Dan echoed, making no effort to disguise his astonishment.

"What did they tell you?" Rorie asked.

Clay smiled briefly, then sobered when he glanced at

Dan. "They said they didn't know *who* lived next door, never mind where you'd gone."

"Frankly, I'm surprised they answered the door at all," Dan said conversationally. "There's a big difference between what goes on in small towns and big cities."

Dan spoke like a teacher to a grade-school pupil. Rorie wanted to kick him, but reacting in anger would only increase the embarrassment. She marveled at Clay's tolerance.

"Things are done differently here," Dan continued. "Few people have anything to do with their neighbors. People prefer to mind their own business. Getting involved leads to problems."

Clay rubbed the side of his face. "It seems to me *not* getting involved would lead to even bigger problems."

"I'm grateful Clay and Skip were there when *your* car broke down," Rorie said to Dan, hoping to put an end to this tiresome discussion. "Otherwise I don't know what would have happened. I could still be on that road waiting for someone to stop and help me," she said, forcing the joke.

"Yes," Dan admitted, clearing his throat. "I suppose I should thank you for assisting Rorie."

"And I suppose I should accept your thanks," Clay returned.

"How's Mary?" Rorie asked, quickly changing the subject as the elevator slid to a stop at her floor.

Humor sparked in Clay's gray eyes. "Mary's strutting around proud as a peacock ever since she won a blue ribbon at the county fair."

"She has reason to be proud." Rorie could just picture her. Knowing Mary, she was probably wearing the ribbon pinned to her apron. "What about Skip?" Rorie asked next, hungry for news about each one. She took the keys from her bag and systematically began unlocking the three bolts on her apartment door.

"Fine. He started school last week—he's a senior this year."

Rorie already knew that, but she nodded.

"Kate sends you her best," Clay said next, his voice carefully nonchalant.

"Tell her I said hello, too."

"She hasn't heard from you. No one has."

"I know. I'm sorry. She wrote after I got home from Canada, but I haven't had a chance to answer." On several occasions, Rorie had tried to make herself sit down and write Kate a letter. But she couldn't. At the end of her second week back home, she'd decided it was better for everyone involved if she didn't keep in touch with Kate. When the wedding invitation came, Rorie planned to mail an appropriate gift, and that would be the end of it.

Once they were inside the apartment, Rorie hung up her sweater and purse and motioned for both men to sit down. "It'll only take a minute to put on the coffee."

"Do you need me to grind the beans?" Dan asked, obviously eager to assist her.

"No, thanks. I don't need any help." His offer was an excuse to question her about Clay, and Rorie wanted to avoid that if she could. At least for now.

Her apartment had never felt more cramped than it did when she rejoined the two men in her tiny living room. Clay rose to his feet as she entered, and the simple courtly gesture made her want to weep. He was telling her that he respected her and that…he cared for her…would always care for her.

The area was just large enough for one sofa and a coffee table. Her desk and computer stood against the other wall. Rorie pulled the chair away from the desk, turned it to face her guests and perched on the edge. Only then did Clay sit back down.

"So," Dan said with a heavy sigh. "Rorie never did tell me what it is you do in...in..."

"Nightingale," Rorie and Clay said together.

"Oh, yes, Nightingale," Dan murmured, clearing his throat. "I take it you're some kind of farmer? Do you grow soybeans or wheat?"

"Clay owns a stud farm, where he raises American Saddlebreds," Rorie said.

Dan looked as if she'd punched him in the stomach. He'd obviously made the connection between Clay and her earlier interest in attending the horse show.

"I see," he breathed, and his voice shook a little. "Horses. So you're involved with horses."

Clay glanced at him curiously.

"How's Nightsong?" Rorie asked, before Dan could say anything else. Just thinking about the foal with her wide curious eyes and long wobbly legs produced a feeling of tenderness in Rorie.

"She's a rare beauty," Clay told her softly, "showing more promise every day."

Rorie longed to tell Clay how much it had meant to her that he'd registered Nightsong in her name, how she cherished that gesture more than anything in her life. She also knew that Clay would never sell the foal, but would keep and love her all her life.

An awkward silence followed, and in an effort to smooth matters over she explained to Dan, "Clay was gone one night when Star Bright—one of the broodmares—went into labor...if that's what they call it in horses?" she asked Clay.

He nodded.

"Anyway, I couldn't wake Skip, and I didn't know where Mary was sleeping and something had to be done—quick."

Dan leaned forward, his eyes revealing his shock. "You don't mean to tell me *you* delivered the foal?"

"Not exactly." Rorie wished now that she hadn't said anything to Dan about that night. No one could possibly understand what she and Clay had shared in those few hours. Trying to convey the experience to someone else only diminished its significance.

"I'll get the coffee," Rorie said, standing. "I'm sure it's ready."

From her kitchen, she could hear Dan and Clay talking, although she couldn't make out their words. She filled three cups and placed them on a tray, together with cream and sugar, then carried it into the living room.

Once more Clay stood. He took the tray out of her hands and set it on the coffee table. Rorie handed Dan the first cup and saucer and Clay the second. He looked uncomfortable as he accepted it.

"I'm sorry, Clay, you prefer a mug, don't you?" The cup seemed frail and tiny, impractical, cradled in his strong hand.

"It doesn't matter. If I'm going to be drinking Swiss mocha coffee, I might as well do it from a china cup." He smiled into her eyes, and Rorie couldn't help reciprocating.

"Eaten any seafood fettuccine lately?" she teased.

"Can't say I have."

"It's my favorite dinner," Dan inserted, apparently feeling left out of the conversation. "We had linguini tonight, but Rorie's favorite is sushi."

Her eye caught Clay's and she saw that the corner of his mouth quirked with barely restrained humor. She could just imagine what the people of Nightingale would think of a sushi bar. Skip would probably turn up his nose, insisting that the small pieces of seaweed and raw fish looked like bait.

The coffee seemed to command everyone's attention for the next minute or so.

"I'm still reeling from the news of your adventures on this stud farm," Dan commented, laughing lightly. "You could have knocked me over with a feather when you said you'd helped deliver a foal. I would never have believed it of you, Rorie."

"I brought a picture of Nightsong," Clay said, cautiously putting down his coffee cup. He unsnapped the pocket of his wide-yoked shirt and withdrew two color photographs, which he handed to Rorie. "I meant to show these to you earlier...but I got sidetracked."

"Oh, Clay," she breathed, studying the filly with her gleaming chestnut coat. "She's grown so much in just the past month," she said, her voice full of wonder.

"I thought you'd be impressed."

Reluctantly Rorie shared the pictures with Dan, who barely glanced at them before giving them back to Clay.

"Most men carry around pictures of their wife and kids," Dan stated, his eyes darting to Clay and then Rorie.

Rorie supposed this comment was Dan's less-than-subtle attempt to find out if Clay was married. Taking a deep breath, she said, "Clay's engaged to a neighbor—Kate Logan."

"I see." Apparently he did, because he set aside his coffee cup, and got up to stand behind Rorie. Hands resting on her shoulders, he leaned forward and brushed his mouth over her cheek. "Rorie and I have been talking about getting married ourselves, haven't we, darling?"

Fifteen

No emotion revealed itself on Clay's face, but Rorie could sense the tight rein he kept on himself. Dan's words had dismayed him.

"Is that true, Rorie?" he said after a moment.

Dan's fingers tightened almost painfully on her shoulders. "Just tonight we were talking about getting married. Tell him, darling."

Her eyes refused to leave Clay's. She *had* been talking to Dan about marriage, although she had no intention of accepting his offer. Dan knew where he stood, knew she was in love with another man. But nothing would be accomplished by telling Clay that she'd always love him, especially since he was marrying Kate in a few weeks. "Yes, Dan has proposed."

"I'm crazy about Rorie and have been for months," Dan announced, squarely facing his competition. He spoke for a few more minutes, outlining his goals. Within another ten years, he planned to be financially secure and hoped to retire.

"Dan's got a bright future," Rorie echoed.

"I see." Clay replaced his coffee cup on the tray, then

glanced at his watch and rose to his feet. "I suppose I should head back to the Cow Palace."

"How...how are you doing in the show?" Rorie asked, distraught, not wanting him to leave. Kate would have him the rest of their lives; surely a few more minutes with him wouldn't matter. "Kate wrote that you were going after several championships."

"I'm doing exactly as I expected." The words were clipped, as though he was impatient to get away.

Rorie knew she couldn't keep him any longer. Clay's face was stern with purpose—and resignation. "I'll see you out," she told him.

"I'll come with you," Dan said.

She whirled around and glared at him. "No, you won't."

"Good to see you again, Rorie," Clay said, standing just inside her apartment, his hand on the door. His mouth was hard and flat and he held himself rigid, eyes avoiding hers. He stepped forward and shook Dan's hand.

"It was a pleasure," Dan said in a tone that conveyed exactly the opposite.

"Same here." Clay dropped his hand.

"I'm glad you came by," Rorie told him quietly. "It was...nice seeing you." The words sounded inane, meaningless.

He nodded brusquely, opened the door and walked into the hallway.

"Clay," she said, following him out, her heart hammering so loudly it seemed to echo off the walls.

He stopped and slowly turned around.

Now that she had his attention, Rorie didn't know what to say. "Listen, I'm sorry about the way Dan was acting."

He shook off her apology. "Don't worry about it."

Her fingers tightened on the doorknob, and she wondered if this was really the end. "Will I see you again?" she asked despite herself.

"I don't think so," he answered hoarsely. He looked past her as though he could see through the apartment door and into her living room where Dan was waiting. "Do you honestly love this guy?"

"He's…he's been a good friend."

Clay took two steps toward her, then stopped. As if it was against his better judgment, he raised his hand and lightly drew his finger down the side of her face. Rorie closed her eyes at the wealth of sensation the simple action provoked.

"Be happy, Rorie. That's all I want for you."

The rain hit during the last week of September, and the dreary dark afternoons suited Rorie's mood. Normally autumn was a productive time for her, but she remained tormented with what she felt sure was a terminal case of writer's block. She sat at her desk, her computer humming merrily as she read over the accumulation of an entire weekend's work.

One measly sentence.

There'd been a time when she could write four or five pages a night after coming home from the library. Perhaps the problem was the story she'd chosen. She wanted to write about a filly named Nightsong, but every time she started, her memories of the real Nightsong invaded her thoughts, crippling her imagination.

Here it was Monday night and she sat staring at the screen, convinced nothing she wrote had any merit. The only reason she kept trying was that Dan had pressured her into it. He seemed to believe her world would right itself once Rorie was back to creating her warm, lighthearted children's stories.

The phone rang and, grateful for a reprieve, Rorie hurried into the kitchen to answer it.

"Is this Miss Rorie Campbell of San Francisco, California?"

"Yes, it is." Her heart tripped with anxiety. In a matter of two seconds, every horrible scenario of what could have happened to her parents or her brother darted through Rorie's mind.

"This is Devin Logan calling."

He paused, as though expecting her to recognize the name. Rorie didn't. "Yes?"

"Devin Logan," he repeated, "from the Nightingale, Oregon, Town Council." He paused. "I believe you're acquainted with my daughter, Kate."

"Yes, I remember Kate." If her heart continued at this pace Rorie thought she'd keel over in a dead faint. Just as her pulse had started to slow, it shot up again. "Has anything happened?"

"The Council meeting adjourned about ten minutes ago. Are you referring to that?"

"No...no, I mean has anything happened to Kate?"

"Not that I'm aware of. Do you know something I don't?"

"I don't think so." This entire conversation was driving her crazy.

Devin Logan cleared his throat, and when he spoke his voice dropped to a deeper pitch. "I'm phoning in an official capacity," he said. "We voted at the Town Council meeting tonight to employ a full-time librarian."

He paused again, and, not knowing what else to say, Rorie murmured, "Congratulations. Kate mentioned that the library was currently being run by part-time volunteers."

"It was decided to offer *you* the position."

Rorie nearly dropped the receiver. "I beg your pardon?"

"My daughter managed to convince the Council that we need a full-time librarian for our new building. She also persuaded us that you're the woman for the job."

"But…" Hardly able to take in what she was hearing, Rorie slumped against the kitchen wall, glad of its support. Logan's next remark was even more surprising.

"We'll match whatever the San Francisco library is paying you and throw in a house in town—rent-free."

"I…" Rorie's mind was buzzing. Kate obviously thought she was doing her a favor, when in fact being so close to Clay would be utter torment.

"Miss Campbell?"

"I'm honored," she said quickly, still reeling with astonishment, "truly honored, but I'm going to have to decline."

A moment of silence followed. "All right…I'm authorized to enhance the offer by ten percent over the amount you're currently earning, but that's our final bid. You'd be making as much money as the fire chief, and he's not about to let the Council pay a librarian more than he's bringing home."

"Mr. Logan, please, the salary isn't the reason I'm turning down your generous offer. I…I want you to know how much I appreciate your offering me the job. Thank you, and thank Kate on my behalf, but I can't accept."

Another, longer silence vibrated across the line, as though he couldn't believe what she was telling him.

"You're positive you want to refuse? Miss Campbell, we're being more than reasonable…more than generous."

"I realize that. In fact, I'm flattered by your proposal, but I can't possibly accept this position."

"Kate had the feeling you'd leap at the job."

"She was mistaken."

"I see. Well, then, it was good talking to you. I'm sorry

we didn't get a chance to meet while you were in Nightingale. Perhaps next time."

"Perhaps." Only there wouldn't be a next time.

Rorie kept her hand on the receiver long after she'd hung up. Her back was pressed against the kitchen wall, her eyes closed.

She'd regained a little of her composure when the doorbell chimed. A glance at the wall clock told her it was Dan, who'd promised to drop by that evening. She straightened, forcing a smile, and slowly walked to the door.

Dan entered with a flourish, handing her a small white bag.

"What's this?" she asked.

"Frozen yogurt. Just the thing for a girl with a hot keyboard. How's the writing going?" He leaned forward to kiss her cheek.

Rorie walked into the kitchen and set the container in the freezer compartment of her refrigerator. "It's not. If you don't mind, I'll eat this later."

"Rorie." Dan caught her by her shoulders and studied her face. "You're as pale as chalk. What's wrong?"

"I...I just got off the phone. I was offered another job—as head librarian..."

"But, darling, that's wonderful!"

"...in Nightingale, Oregon."

The change in Dan's expression was almost comical. "And? What did you tell them?"

"I refused."

He gave a great sigh of relief. His eyes glowed and he hugged her impulsively. "Does this mean what I think it does? Are you finally over that cowpoke, Rorie? Will you finally consent to be my wife?"

Rorie lowered her gaze. "Oh, Dan, don't you understand? I'll never get over Clay. Not next week, not next

month, not next year." Her voice was filled with pain, and
with conviction. Everyone seemed to assume that, in time,
she'd forget about Clay Franklin, but she wouldn't.

Dan's smile faded, and he dropped his arms to his sides.
"I see." Leaning against the counter, he sighed pensively
and said, "I'd do just about anything in this world for you,
Rorie, but I think it's time we faced a few truths."

Rorie had wanted to confront them long before now.

"You're never going to love me the way you do that
horseman. We can't go on like this. It isn't doing either of
us any good to pretend your feelings are going to change."

He looked so grim and discouraged that she didn't point
out that *he* was the one who'd been pretending.

"I'm so sorry to hurt you—it's the last thing I ever
wanted to do," she told him sincerely.

"It isn't as if I didn't know," he admitted. "You've been
honest with me from the start. I can't be less than honest
with you. That country boy loves you. I knew it the minute he walked across the street without even noticing the
traffic. The whole world would know," he said ruefully.
"All he has to do is look at you and everything about him
shouts his feelings. He may be engaged to another woman,
but it's you he loves."

"I wouldn't fit into his world."

"But, Rorie, you're lost and confused in your own."

She bit her lower lip and nodded. Until Dan said it, she
hadn't recognized how true that was. But it didn't change
the fact that Clay belonged to Kate. And she was marrying him within the month.

"I'm sorry," Dan said, completely serious, "but the wedding's off."

She nearly laughed out loud at Dan's announcement. No
wedding had ever been planned. He'd asked her to marry
him at least ten times since she'd returned from her va-

cation, and each time she'd refused. Instead of wearing her down as he'd hoped, Dan had finally come to accept her decision. Rorie felt relieved, but she was sorry to lose her friend.

"I didn't mean to lead you on," she told him, genuinely contrite.

He shrugged. "The pain will only last for a while. I'm 'a keeper' as the girls in the office like to tell me. I guess it's time I put out the word that I'm available." He wiggled his eyebrows, striving for some humor.

"You've been such a good friend."

He cupped her face and gently kissed her. "Yes, I know. Now don't let that yogurt go to waste—you're too thin as it is."

She smiled and nodded. When she let him out of the apartment, Rorie bolted the door then leaned against it, feeling drained, but curiously calm.

Dan had been gone only a few minutes when Rorie's phone rang again. She hurried into the kitchen to answer it.

"Rorie? This is Kate Logan."

"Kate! How are you?"

"Rotten, but I didn't call to talk about me. I want to know exactly why you're refusing to be Nightingale's librarian—after everything I went through. I can't believe you, Rorie. How can you do this to Clay? Don't you love him?"

Sixteen

"Kate," Rorie demanded. "What are you talking about?"

"You and Clay," she said sharply, sounding quite unlike her usual self. "Now, do you love him or not? I've got to know."

This day had been sliding steadily downhill from the moment Rorie had climbed out of bed that morning. To admit her feelings for Clay would only hurt Kate, and Rorie had tried so hard to avoid upsetting the other woman.

"Well?" Kate said with a sob. "The least you can do is answer me!"

"Oh, Kate," Rorie said, her heart in her throat, "why are you asking me if I love Clay? He's engaged to you. It shouldn't matter one little bit if I love him or not. I'm out of your lives and I intend to stay out."

"But he loves you."

The tears in Kate's voice tore at Rorie's already battered heart. She would've given anything to spare her friend this pain. "I know," she whispered.

"Doesn't that mean anything to you?"

Only the world and everything in it. "Yes," she murmured, her voice growing stronger.

"Then how could you do this to him?"

"Do what?" Rorie didn't understand.

"Hurt him this way!"

"Kate," Rorie pleaded. "I have no idea what you're talking about—I'd never intentionally hurt Clay. If you insist on knowing, I do love him, with all my heart, but he's your fiancé. You loved him long before I even knew him."

Kate's short laugh was riddled with sarcasm. "What is this? First come, first served?"

"Of course not—"

"For your information, Clay isn't my fiancé anymore," Kate blurted, her voice trembling. "He hasn't been in weeks... since before he went to San Francisco for the horse show."

Rorie's head came up so fast she wondered whether she'd dislocated her neck. "He isn't?"

"That's...that's what I just told you."

"But I thought... I assumed..."

"I know what you assumed—that much is obvious— but it isn't like that now and it hasn't been in a long time."

"But you love Clay," Rorie muttered, feeling lightheaded.

"I've loved him from the time I was in pigtails. I love him enough to want to see him happy. Why...why do you think I talked my fool head off to a bunch of hard-nosed Council members? Why do you think I ranted and raved about what a fantastic librarian you are? I as good as told them you're the only person who could possibly assume full responsibility for the new library. Do you honestly think I did all that for the fun of it?"

"No, but, Kate, surely you understand why I have to refuse. I just couldn't bear to come between you and—"

Kate wouldn't allow her to finish, and when she spoke, her voice was high and almost hysterical. "Well, if you believe that, Rorie Campbell, then you've got a lot to learn about me...and even more about Clay Franklin."

"Kate, I'm sorry. Please listen to me. There's so much I don't understand. We've got to talk, because I can't make head or tail out of what you're telling me and I've got to know—"

"If you have anything to say to me, Rorie Campbell, then you can do it to my face. Now, I'm telling Dad and everyone else on the Council that you've accepted the position we so generously offered you. The job starts in two weeks and you'd damn well better be here. Understand?"

Rorie's car left a dusty trail on the long, curving driveway that led to the Circle L Ranch. It'd been a week since the telephone call from Kate, and Rorie still had trouble assimilating what the other woman had told her. Their conversation repeated itself over and over in her mind, until nothing made sense. But one thing stood out: Kate was no longer engaged to Clay.

Rorie was going to him, running as fast as she could, but first she had to settle matters with his former fiancée.

The sun had begun to descend in an autumn sky when Rorie parked her car at the Logan ranch and climbed out. Rotating her neck and shoulders to relieve some of the tension there, Rorie looked around, wondering if anyone was home. She'd been on the road most of the day, so she was exhausted. And exhilarated.

Luke Rivers strolled out of the barn, and stopped when he saw Rorie. His smile deepened. It could've been Rorie's imagination, but she sensed that the hard edge was missing from his look, as though life had unexpectedly tossed him a good turn.

"So you're back," he said by way of greeting.

Rorie nodded, then reached inside the car for her purse. "Is Kate here?"

"She'll be back any minute. Usually gets home from

the school around four. Come inside and I'll get you a cup of coffee."

"Thanks." At the moment, coffee sounded like nectar from the gods.

Luke opened the kitchen door for her. "I understand you're going to be Nightingale's new librarian," he said, following her into the house.

"Yes." But that wasn't the reason she'd come back, and they both knew it.

"Good." Luke took two mugs from the cupboard and filled them from a coffeepot that sat on the stove. He placed Rorie's cup on the table, then pulled out a chair for her.

"Thanks, Luke."

The sound of an approaching vehicle drew his attention. He parted the lace curtain at the kitchen window and looked out.

"That's Kate now," he said, his gaze lingering on the driveway. "Listen, if I don't get a chance to talk to you later, I want you to know I'm glad you're here. I've got a few things to thank you for. If it hadn't been for you, I might've turned into a crotchety old saddle bum."

Before Rorie could ask what he meant, he was gone.

Kate burst into the kitchen a minute later and hugged Rorie as though they were long-lost sisters. "I don't know when I've been happier to see anyone!"

Rorie's face must have shown her surprise because Kate hurried to add, "I suppose you think I'm a crazy woman after the way I talked to you on the phone last week. I don't blame you, but…well, I was upset, to put it mildly, and my thinking was a little confused." She threw her purse on the counter and reached inside the cupboard for a mug. She poured the coffee very slowly, as if she needed time to gather her thoughts.

Rorie's mind was whirling with questions she couldn't

wait for Kate to answer. "Did I understand you correctly the other night? Did you tell me you and Clay are no longer engaged?"

Kate wasn't able to disguise the flash of pain that leaped into her deep blue eyes. She dropped her gaze and nodded. "We haven't been in weeks."

"But…"

Kate sat down across the table from Rorie and folded her hands around the mug. "The thing is, Rorie, I knew how you two felt about each other since the night of the Grange dance. A blind man would've known you and Clay had fallen in love, but it was so much easier for me to pretend otherwise." Her finger traced the rim of the mug. "I thought that once you went home, everything would go back to the way it was before…."

"I was hoping for the same thing. Kate, you've got to believe me when I tell you I would've done anything in the world to spare you this. When I learned you and Clay were engaged I wanted to—"

"Die," Kate finished for her. "I know exactly how you must have felt, because that's the way I felt later. The night of the Grange dance, Clay kept looking at you. Every time you danced with a new partner, he scowled. He might have had me at his side, but his eyes followed you all over the hall."

"He loves you, too," Rorie told her. "That's what makes this all so difficult."

"No, he doesn't," Kate answered flatly, without a hint of doubt. "I accepted that a long time before you ever arrived. Oh, he respects and likes me, and to Clay's way of thinking that was enough." She hesitated, frowning. "To my way of thinking, it was, too. We probably would've married and been content. But everything changed when Clay met you. You hit him right between the eyes, Rorie—a direct hit."

"I'm sure he feels more for you than admiration…."

"No." Kate rummaged in her purse for a tissue. "He told me as much himself, but like I said, it wasn't something I didn't already know. You see, I was so crazy about Clay, I was willing to take whatever he offered me, even if it was only second-best." She swabbed at the tears that sprang so readily to her eyes and paused in an effort to gather her composure. "I'm sorry. It's still so painful. But you see, through all of this, I've learned a great deal about what it means to love someone."

Rorie's own eyes welled with involuntary tears, which she hurriedly brushed aside. Then Kate's fingers clasped hers and squeezed tight in a gesture of reassurance.

"I learned that loving people means placing their happiness before your own. That's the way you love Clay, and it's the way he loves you." Kate squared her shoulders and inhaled a quavery breath.

"Kate, please, this isn't necessary."

"Yes, it is, because what I've got to say next is the hardest part. I need to ask your forgiveness for that terrible letter I wrote after you left Nightingale. I don't have any excuse except that I was insane with jealousy."

"Letter? You wrote me a terrible letter?" The only one Rorie had received was the chatty note that had told her about Mary's prize-winning ribbon and made mention of the upcoming wedding.

"I used a subtle form of viciousness," Kate replied, her voice filled with self-contempt.

Rorie discounted the possibility that Kate could ever be malicious. "The only letter I got from you wasn't the least bit terrible."

Kate lowered her eyes to her hands, neatly folded on

the table. Her grip tightened until Rorie was sure her nails would cut her palms.

"I lied in that letter," Kate continued. "When I told you that Clay wouldn't have time for you while he was at the horse show, I was trying to imply that you didn't mean anything to him anymore. I wanted you to think you'd slipped from his mind when nothing could have been further from the truth."

"Don't feel bad about it. I'm not so sure I wouldn't have done the same thing."

"No, Rorie, you wouldn't have. That letter was an underhand attempt to hold on to Clay… I was losing him more and more each day and I thought…I hoped that if you believed we were going to be married in October, then… Oh, I don't know, my thinking was so warped and desperate."

"Your emotions were running high at the time." Rorie's had been, too; she understood Kate's pain because she'd been in so much pain herself.

"But I was pretending to be your friend when in reality I almost hated you." Kate paused, her shoulders shaking with emotion. "That was the crazy part. I couldn't help liking you and wanting to be your friend, and at the same time I was eaten alive with jealousy and selfish resentment."

"It's not in you to hate anyone, Kate."

"I…I didn't think it was, either, but I was wrong. I can be a terrible person, Rorie. Facing up to that hasn't been easy." She took a deep, shuddering breath.

"Then…a few days after I mailed that letter to you, Clay came over to the house wanting to talk. Almost immediately I realized I'd lost him. Nothing I could say or do would change the way he felt about you. I said some awful things to Clay that night…. He's forgiven me, but I need your forgiveness, too."

"Oh, Kate, of course, but it isn't necessary. I understand. I truly do."

"Thank you," she murmured, dabbing her eyes with the crumpled tissue. "Now I've got that off my chest, I feel a whole lot better."

"But if Clay had broken your engagement when he came to San Francisco, why didn't he say anything to me?"

Kate shrugged. "I don't know what happened while he was gone, but he hasn't been himself since. He never has been a talkative person, but he seemed to draw even further into himself when he came back. He's working himself into an early grave, everyone says. Mary's concerned about him—we all are. Mary said if you didn't come soon, she was going after you herself."

"Mary said that?" The housekeeper had been the very person who'd convinced Rorie she was doing the right thing by getting out of Clay's life.

"Well, are you going to him? Or are you planning to stick around here and listen to me blubber all day? If you give me any more time," she said, forcing a laugh, "I'll manage to make an even bigger fool of myself than I already have." Kate stood abruptly, pushing back the kitchen chair. Her arms were folded around her waist, her eyes bright with tears.

"Kate," Rorie murmured, "you are a dear, dear friend. I owe you more than it's possible to repay."

"The only thing you owe me is one godchild—and about fifty years of happiness with Clay Franklin. Now get out of here before I start weeping in earnest."

Kate opened the kitchen door and Rorie gave her an impulsive hug before hurrying out.

Luke Rivers was standing in the yard, apparently waiting for her. When she came out of the house he sauntered over to her car and held open the driver's door. "Did everything go all right with Kate?"

Rorie nodded.

"Well," he said soberly, "there may be more rough waters ahead for her. She doesn't know it yet, but I'm buying out the Circle L." Then he smiled, his eyes crinkling. "She's going to be fine, though. I'll make sure of that." He extended his hand, gripping hers in a firm handshake. "Let me be the first to welcome you to our community."

"Thank you."

He touched the rim of his hat in farewell, then glanced toward the house. "I think I'll go inside and see how Kate's doing."

Rorie's gaze skipped from the foreman to the house and then back again. "You do that." If Luke Rivers had anything to say about it, Kate wouldn't be suffering from a broken heart for long. Rorie had suspected Luke was in love with Kate. But, like her, he was caught in a trap, unable to reveal his feelings. Perhaps now Kate's eyes would be opened—Rorie fervently hoped so.

The drive from the Logans' place to the Franklins' took no more than a few minutes. Rorie parked her car behind the house, her heart pounding. When she climbed out, the only one there to greet her was Mary.

"About time you got here," the housekeeper complained, marching down the porch steps with a vengeance.

"Could this be the apple-pie blue-ribbon holder of Nightingale, Oregon?"

Mary actually blushed, and Rorie laughed. "I thought you'd never want to see the likes of me again," she teased.

"Fiddlesticks." The weathered face broke into a smile.

"I'm still a city girl," Rorie warned.

"That's fine, 'cause you got the heart of a country girl."

Wiping her hands dry on her apron, Mary reached for Rorie and hugged her.

After one brief, bone-crushing squeeze, she set her free. "I'm a meddling old woman, sure enough, and I suspect the good Lord intends to teach me more than one lesson in the next year or two. I'd best tell you that I never should've said those things I did about Kate being the right woman for Clay."

"Mary, you spoke out of concern. I know that."

"Clay doesn't love Kate," she continued undaunted, "but my heavens, he does love you. That boy's been pining his heart out for want of you. He hasn't been the same from the minute you drove out of here all those weeks ago."

Rorie had suffered, too, but she didn't mention that to Mary. Instead, she slipped her arm around the housekeeper's broad waist and together they strolled toward the house.

"Clay's gone for the day, but he'll be back within the hour."

"An hour," Rorie repeated. She'd waited all this time; another sixty minutes shouldn't matter.

"Dinner will be ready then, and it's not like Clay or Skip to miss a meal. Dinner's been at six every night since I've been cooking for this family, and that's a good many years now." Mary's mouth formed a lopsided grin. "Now what we'll do is this. You be in the dining room waiting for him and I'll tell him he's got company."

"But won't he notice my car?" Rorie twisted around, gesturing at her old white Toyota—her own car this time—parked within plain sight.

Mary shook her head. "I doubt it. He's never seen your car, so far as I know, only that fancy sports car. Anyway, the boy's been working himself so hard, he'll be too tired to notice much of anything."

Mary opened the back door and Rorie stepped inside

the kitchen. As she did, the house seemed to fold its arms around her in welcome. She paused, breathing in the scent of roast beef and homemade biscuits. It might not be sourdough and Golden Gate Park roses, but it felt right. More than right.

"Do you need me to do anything?" Rorie asked.

Mary frowned, then nodded. "There's just one thing I want you to do—make Clay happy."

"Oh, Mary, I intend to start doing that the second he walks through that door."

An hour later, almost to the minute, Rorie heard Skip and Clay come into the kitchen.

"What's for dinner?" Skip asked immediately.

"It's on the table. Now wash your hands."

Rorie heard the teenager grumble as he headed down the hallway to the bathroom.

"How'd the trip go?" Mary asked Clay.

He mumbled something Rorie couldn't hear.

"The new librarian stopped by to say hello. Old man Logan and Kate sent her over—thought you might like to meet her."

"I don't. I hope you got rid of her. I'm in no mood for company."

"Nope," Mary said. "Fact is, I invited her to stay for dinner. The least you can do is wipe that frown off your face and go introduce yourself."

Rorie stood just inside the dining room, her heart ready to explode. By the time Clay stepped into the room, tears had blurred her vision and she could hardly make out the tall, familiar figure that blocked the doorway.

She heard his swift intake of breath, and the next thing she knew she was crushed in Clay's loving arms.

Seventeen

Rorie was locked so securely in Clay's arms that for a moment she couldn't draw a breath. But that didn't matter. What mattered was that she was being hugged by the man she loved and he was holding on to her as though he didn't plan to ever let her go.

Clay kissed her again and again, the way a starving man took his first bites of food, initially hesitant, then eager. The palms of Rorie's hands were pressed against his chest and she felt the quick surge of his heart. His own hand was gentle on her hair, caressing it, running his fingers through it.

"Rorie…Rorie, I can't believe you're here."

Rorie felt the power of his emotions, and they were strong enough to rock her, body and soul. This man loved her. He was honest and hardworking, she knew all that, but even more, Clay Franklin was *good,* with an unselfishness and a loyalty that had touched her profoundly. In an age of ambitious, hardhearted, vain men, she had inadvertently stumbled on this rare man of character. Her life would never be the same.

Clay exhaled a deep sigh, and his hands framed her face as he pulled his head back to gaze into her eyes. The lines that marked his face seemed more deeply incised now, and she felt another pang of sorrow for the pain he'd endured.

"Mary wasn't teasing me, was she? You *are* the new librarian?"

Rorie nodded, smiling up at him, her happiness shining from her eyes. "There's no going back for me. I've moved out of my apartment, packed everything I own and quit my job with barely a week's notice."

Rorie had fallen in love with Clay, caught in the magic of one special night when a foal had been born. But her feelings stretched far beyond the events of a single evening and the few short days they'd spent together. Her love for Clay had become an essential part of her. Rorie adored him and would feel that way for as long as her heart continued to beat.

Clay's frown deepened and his features tightened briefly. "What about Dan? I thought you were going to marry him."

"I couldn't," she said, then smiled tenderly, tracing his face with her hands, loving the feel of him beneath her fingertips.

"But—"

"Clay," she interrupted, "why didn't you tell me when I saw you in San Francisco that you'd broken your engagement to Kate?" Her eyes clouded with anguish at the memory, at the anxiety they'd caused each other. It had been such senseless heartache, and they'd wasted precious time. "Couldn't you see how miserable I was?"

A grimace of pain moved across his features. "All I noticed was how right you and that stockbroker looked together. You both kept telling me what a bright future he had. I couldn't begin to offer you the things he could. And if that wasn't enough, it was all too apparent that Dan was in love with you." Gently Clay smoothed her hair away from her temple. "I could understand what it meant to love you, and, between the two of us, he seemed the better man."

Rorie lowered her face, pressing her forehead against the hollow of his shoulder. She groaned in frustration. "How could you even *think* such a thing, when I love you so much?"

Clay moved her face so he could meet her eyes. "But, Rorie…" He stopped and a muscle jerked in his jaw. "Dan can give you far more than I'll ever be able to. He's got connections, background, education. A few years down the road, he's going to be very wealthy—success is written all over him. He may have his faults, but basically he's a fine man."

"He *is* a good person and he's going to make some woman a good husband. But it won't be me."

"He could give you the kinds of things I may never be able to afford…."

"Clay Franklin, do you love me or not?"

Clay exhaled slowly, watching her. "You know the answer to that."

"Then stop arguing with me. I don't love Dan Rogers. I love you."

Still his frown persisted. "You belong in the city."

"I belong with you," she countered.

He said nothing for a long moment. "I can't argue with that," he whispered, his voice husky with emotion. "You do belong here, because God help me, I haven't got the strength to let you walk away a second time."

Clay kissed her again, his mouth sliding over hers as though he still couldn't believe she was in his arms. She held on to him with all her strength, soaking up his love. She was at home in his arms. It was where she belonged and where she planned to stay.

The sound of someone entering the room filtered through to Rorie's consciousness, but she couldn't bring herself to move out of Clay's arms.

"Rorie!" Skip cried, his voice high and excited, "What are you doing here?"

Rorie finally released Clay and turned toward the teenager who had come to her rescue that August afternoon.

"Hello, Skip," she said softly. Clay slipped his arm around her waist and she smiled up at him, needing his touch to anchor her in the reality of their love.

"Are you back for good?" Skip wanted to know.

She nodded, but before she could answer Clay said, "Meet Nightingale's new librarian." His arm tightened around her.

The smile that lit the teenager's eyes was telling. "So you're going to stick around this time." He blew out a gusty sigh. "It's a damn good thing, because since you left, my brother's been as hard to live with as a rattlesnake."

"I'd say that was a bit of an exaggeration," Clay muttered, clearly not approving of his brother's choice of description.

"You shouldn't have gone," Skip said, sighing again. "Especially before the county fair."

Rorie laughed. "You're never going to forgive me for missing that, are you?"

"You should've been here, Rorie. It was great."

"I'll be here next summer," she promised.

"The fact is, Rorie's going to be around for a lifetime of summers," Clay informed his brother. "We're going to be married as soon as we can arrange it." His eyes held hers but they were filled with questions, as if he half expected her, even now, to refuse him.

Rorie swallowed the emotion that bobbed so readily to

the surface and nodded wildly, telling him with one look that she'd marry him anytime he wanted.

Skip crossed his arms over his chest and gave them a smug look. "I knew something was going on between the two of you. Every time I was around you guys it was like getting zapped with one of those stun guns."

"We were that obvious?" It still troubled Rorie that Kate had known, especially since both she and Clay had tried so hard to hide their feelings.

Skip's shrug was carefree. "I don't think so, but I don't care about love and all that."

"Give it time, little brother," Clay murmured, "because when it hits, it'll knock you for a loop."

Mary stepped into the room, carrying a platter of meat. "So the two of you are getting hitched?"

Their laughter signaled a welcome release from all the tensions of the past weeks. Clay pulled out Rorie's chair, then sat down beside her. His hand reached for hers, lacing their fingers together. "Yes," he said, still smiling, "we'll be married as soon as we can get the license and talk to the pastor."

Mary pushed the basket of biscuits closer to Skip. "Well, you don't need to fret—I'll stay for a couple more years until I can teach this child the proper way to feed a man. She may be pretty to look at, but she don't know beans about whipping up a decent meal."

"I'd appreciate that, Mary," Rorie said. "I could do with a few cooking lessons."

The housekeeper's smile broadened. "Now, go ahead and eat before the potatoes get cold and the gravy gets lumpy."

Skip didn't need any further inducement. He helped himself to the biscuits, piling three on the edge of his plate.

Mary playfully slapped his hand. "I've got apple pie for dessert, so don't go filling yourselves up on my buttermilk biscuits." Her good humor was evident as she surveyed the table, glancing at everyone's plate, then bustled back to the kitchen.

Rorie did her best to sample a little of everything. Although the meal was delicious, she was too excited to do anything as mundane as eat.

After dinner, Skip made himself scarce. Mary delivered a tray with two coffee cups to the living room, where Clay and Rorie sat close together on the couch. "You two have lots to talk about, so you might as well drink this while you're doing it."

"Thank you, Mary," Clay said, exchanging a smile with Rorie.

The older woman set the tray down, then patted the fine gray hair at the sides of her head. "I want you to know how pleased I am for you both. Have you set the date yet?"

"We're talking about that now," Clay answered. "We're going to call Rorie's family in Arizona this evening and discuss it with them."

Mary nodded. "She's not the woman I would've chosen for you, her being a city girl and all, but she'll make you happy."

Clay's hand clasped Rorie's. "I know."

"She's got a generous soul." The housekeeper looked at Rorie and her gaze softened. "Fill this house with children—and with love. It's been quiet far too long."

The phone rang in the kitchen and, with a regretful glance over her shoulder, Mary hurried to answer it. A moment later, she stuck her head around the kitchen door.

"It's for you, Clay. Long distance."

Clay's grimace was apologetic. "I'd better get it."

"You don't need to worry that I'll leave," Rorie said with a laugh. "You're stuck with me for a lot of years, Clay Franklin."

He kissed her before he stood up, then headed toward the kitchen. Rorie sighed and leaned back, cradling her mug. By chance, her gaze fell on the photograph of Clay's parents, which rested on top of the piano. Once more, Rorie felt the pull of his mother's eyes. She smiled now, understanding so many things. The day she'd planned to leave Elk Run, this same photograph had captured her attention. The moment she'd walked into this house, Rorie had belonged to Clay and he to her. Somehow, looking at his mother's picture, she'd sensed that. She belonged to this home and this family.

Clay returned a few minutes later, with Blue trailing him. "Just a call from the owner of one of the horses I board," he said, as he sat down beside Rorie and placed his arm around her shoulders. His eyes followed hers to the photo. "Mom would have liked you."

Rorie sipped her coffee and smiled. "I know I would have loved her." Setting her cup aside, she reached up and threw both arms around Clay's neck. Gazing into his eyes, she brought his mouth down to hers.

Perhaps it was her imagination or an optical illusion—in fact, Rorie was sure of it. But she could have sworn the elegant woman in the photograph smiled.

* * * * *

Also available from RaeAnne Thayne and HQN Books

Look for her next book

BLACKBERRY SUMMER

RaeAnne Thayne

As always, to my wonderful husband and children, who fill my life with laughter and love. Special thanks to Nicole Jordan for a hundred different things, but mostly for believing in me.

One

"We are each of us angels with one wing. And we can only fly embracing each other."
—Luciano de Crescenzo

Lousy, stupid horoscope.

Claire Bradford stood with one hand on the doorway and the other clutching her coffee go-cup as she stared at the chaotic mess inside her store.

According to the stars—at least according to the horoscope in the *Hope Gazette* she'd scanned while standing in line at her friend Maura's coffee shop for her morning buzz after dropping the kids off at school—she was supposed to prepare herself for something fun and exciting headed her way today. She had been thinking more along the lines of a few dozen new customers at her bead store or maybe a big commission on one of her more intricate custom pieces.

Discovering that String Fever had been burglarized during the night didn't exactly fit her personal definition of either fun or exciting.

Beads covered the beige berber in a glittery, jumbled disaster as apparently someone had yanked out an entire vast display of tiny clear drawers and dumped their contents all over the floor. Her cash register drawer was open and the small amount of cash she kept on hand to make change was missing. Her office door had been left ajar, too, something she never did, and even from here, she could see a big, dusty, empty spot on her desk where her computer should be.

She could handle the material loss and her computer was automatically backed up off-site several times a day. The mess, on the other hand, would be a nightmare to clean up. Claire gave a tiny whimper and closed her eyes, dreading the hours and days of work ahead of her, re-sorting all those scattered beads into their hundreds of proper compartments. String Fever was hanging by a thread anyway in the uncertain economy. How could she afford the time and energy involved in setting things to rights again?

Chester whined beside her, his basset hound features even more morose than usual. He was uncanny at picking up her emotions. She scratched behind his acres-long ears. "I know, buddy. Sucks, doesn't it?"

She dug in her coat pockets to find where she'd stowed her cell phone so that she could dial 9-1-1. She had only punched in one number before the phone vibrated in her hand and suddenly the nuclear meltdown alert ringtone she had programmed for her mother sounded its death knell through the empty store.

Yeah, not much fun or excitement there, either. Rotten horoscope.

Chester whined again. He hated that ringtone as much as she did. Claire swallowed her groan and despite thirty-six years of better instincts, she hit the talk button to accept the call. Ruth Tatum had trained her daughter well. "Mom, I can't talk right now. Sorry. The store has been robbed. I'll call you back as soon as I can, okay?"

"Robbed? You've got to be kidding!"

"Really, Mom? You think I'd joke about something like this?"

"How would I know?" Ruth went on the defensive, as she did so well. "You've always had a weird sense of humor."

Yeah. That was her. Making up stories about her store being robbed just to go for the cheap laugh. "I'm not joking. The store really has been robbed."

"That's terrible! What did they take?"

"I don't know yet. I just walked in the door and barely had a chance to even react before you called. I need to go so I can call the police, Mom."

"Well, call me as soon as you can and tell me what's going on. Do you need me to come down there?"

Sure, like she needed to stick a couple dozen earring hooks in her eyeballs. "Not right now. Thanks for the offer, though. I'll call you later."

She hung up and quickly dialed the police.

"Hope's Crossing Emergency Dispatch. What is the nature of your emergency?"

She recognized the dispatcher as a neighbor and one of her frequent customers, Donna Mazell, though her voice seemed pitched a little higher than normal.

"Hey, Donna. This is Claire at String Fever. I need to report a crime. I just came in to open my store and discovered an apparent burglary."

"Oh, lordy be. Not another one!"

"Another one?"

"You're the fourth store in town to report a break-in today. We've got ourselves a genuine crime spree! The guys are going *crazy* trying to stay on top of everything."

Hope's Crossing, Colorado, had a population of only five thousand year-round residents, although those numbers swelled in the wintertime to ten times that with skiers and those who owned vacation homes or condos in the canyon near the vast Silver Strike Ski Resort. Still, Claire knew the town's police force consisted of only eight officers, supplemented by deputies from the county sheriff's department when the need arose.

"Can you spare somebody to send here?"

"Oh, sure. No problem. The new chief is just down the street at Pinecone Property Management, but I think he's wrapping things up there. I'll give him a holler and tell him to head over to the store first chance he has."

"Thanks, Donna."

"Tell me they didn't take those gorgeous Czech crystals you bought for Genevieve Beaumont's wedding gown."

Her stomach took another dive. "Oh, I hope not. It took me two months to import those through Customs. I don't know if I'll have time to get more and finish the design before the wedding."

"Keeping my fingers crossed here. I'll call Riley right now and tell him to head over there when he's done over at the real estate office."

"Thanks, Donna."

"You bet. Give me another call if somebody doesn't show up in the next ten, fifteen minutes or so. And don't touch anything."

"Yeah, I watch television. I know that much. I'll wait outside with Chester until Riley can get here."

"It's freezing, darlin'. You can't wait outside in this weather and neither can that dog. He's not as young as he used to be. The chief won't care if you grab a chair inside and sit down until he can make it, just as long as you keep Chester close so he doesn't go mucking around the crime scene."

Too much restless energy zinged through her for her to

sit calmly and wait for the police, so she remained standing in the doorway, horrified all over again that someone would be so malicious. Stealing from her was one thing. They could have the money and her computer, she didn't care about that. But why make such a mess? This blatant vandalism was intended to gouge and wound—causing trouble for trouble's sake, something she had never understood.

Why would someone want to be so hurtful? And why *her?* She tried hard to be kind to most people she came in contact with. Sure, she had a few disgruntled customers at the store who seemed to think it a crime that she expected to make at least some profit for all the resources of time and energy she poured into String Fever. But she couldn't imagine any of them being so vindictive as to trash her store just for the fun of it.

She forced herself to do a little of the circle breathing her best friend, Alex, was always trying to convince her to practice and shifted her gaze out the wide store windows at Hope's Crossing's Main Street. The morning seemed gray and cheerless, a dreary sort of day. Even though it was mid-April, spring took its dear sweet time arriving in the Colorado high country.

The weather forecasters were predicting a late snowstorm would be moving in later that evening. The ski resort would appreciate a few more inches for the diehard skiers who opted to spend their spring break hanging on to the last struggling days of winter instead of heading to the beach. By this time of year, she was heartily sick of more snow, but at least a little fresh powder would cover the tired, gray piles out there.

Despite the cold and the promise of a storm, she could see a pretty good Monday morning crowd at the Center of Hope Café across the way. She'd noticed the same story at Dog-Eared Books & Brew.

Of course, none of those shoppers would be heading her direction anytime soon, not with the Closed sign still firmly turned in the doorway.

The thought had barely formed in her mind when the door behind her opened with a musical chime. Claire opened her mouth to explain the store was still closed and then shut it again, her spirits sinking even more.

Her fun and exciting morning only needed this, she thought as she watched her ex-husband's new wife burst through, looking pert and cute and glowing with pregnancy hormones.

"Hi, Claire!" Holly Vestry Bradford chirped, beaming the smile her orthodontist father had worked tirelessly to perfect as she unbuttoned her red wool peacoat and stamped snow off her black UGGs.

Chester grunted and plopped onto his belly, never a big fan of Holly's.

"Um, this really isn't a good time," Claire began. She wasn't at all in the mood to be sociable right now, especially not to Holly, who seemed to bring out the worst in her, despite her best efforts.

"Oh, my word!" Holly exclaimed. "What happened in here?"

Claire had made a firm policy for the last two years—since Jeff moved out and put an official end to their marriage that had been broken for much longer than that—to be as gracious as she could stand to Holly. "I think we were robbed," she said, without a hint of the sarcastic retort she wanted to make.

"Oh, no! Have you called the police?"

"I just did. They're on the way."

"Oh, Claire. I'm so sorry."

She didn't know which she disliked more: the sense of invasion from the robbery, contemplating the endless work putting the store back in order, or being on the receiving end of Holly Bradford's pity.

"I'm sure everything will be okay. My insurance should cover any losses. But I have to ask you not to touch anything, okay? We can't mess up the crime scene."

"Crime scene. That sounds so scary! Right out of *CSI: Miami!* Where's Horatio?"

Was she ever this young when she was twenty-five? Claire wondered, then answered her own rhetorical question. No. By then, she'd already been married for over a year, had given birth to Macy and had been working two jobs to put Jeff through medical school.

"I'm sorry things are in such disarray." She tried on a smile and found she still had one or two in reserve. "Maybe you can come back later today after I've had a chance to start cleaning things up."

"Don't you worry about that. I didn't need anything urgent. I guess Macy probably told you about our crazy shopping trip to Vail, didn't she?"

"She might have mentioned it." Twenty or thirty times. Her twelve-year-old daughter adored her stepmother. Why wouldn't she? Holly was the big sister Macy had always wanted. She was fun and young and hip. Holly had read all the *Twilight* books and had MySpace, Twitter *and* Facebook accounts.

Claire tried hard not to resent their bond. Macy loved her mother, too, although sometimes she didn't act very much like she did as she tested her wings on her way to adolescence.

"That girl is a shopping maniac!" Holly gushed. "Jeff just cut us loose with his credit cards while he and Owen went snowboarding and Macy helped me buy a whole new maternity wardrobe. When we got back home and I started opening all those bags, I realized what I really need now are some killer accessories to distract people from my big fat belly."

Right. Although she was five months along in her pregnancy, Holly could still probably fit into a size 4 pair of jeans, at least if they were low cut.

"You know you look beautiful, no matter what you're wearing. But new jewelry is always nice." Particularly when it was handcrafted out of the pricey Venetian glass beads Holly liked, the ones that netted String Fever a healthy profit. "I'll be glad to help you with some ideas after the store opens later today, if you don't mind coming back."

"No problem. I've got nothing else on my schedule today."

Oh, that she could say the same. Claire summoned another smile. "I'll try to call you after the police clear the store for me to reopen."

"You're so sweet to me. Thank you so much, Claire."

Before she quite knew what she intended, Holly grabbed her in a hug and Claire had no real choice but to endure it and even hug her back a little before she quickly eased out of the embrace.

She didn't really dislike Holly. The situation was just so awkward, living in the same town with her and Jeff, bumping into each other all the time, sharing concentric circles of friends.

No matter how much Jeff claimed Holly had nothing to do with his unilateral decision to leave the marriage and no matter how much Claire knew she bore equal responsibility for the problems and the distance that had grown between them those last few years, Jeff had started living his little cliché—dating the young, beautiful receptionist in his orthopedic surgery practice—just a few weeks after their divorce was final. He'd married her six months after that and now they were starting their own family.

Whether Claire liked the situation or not, they were all three coparenting the children. When Owen and Macy were with their father, Holly was a major influence in their lives and for the sake of her children, Claire couldn't afford to be bitter or spiteful. Nor could she move away from Hope's Crossing, not when she had a business here and not when Macy and Owen needed their father in their lives more than just on weekends.

"Are you sure you're okay?" Holly asked. "Maybe I should stay with you while the police come. You know, for moral support."

"That's really not necessary," she started to say, but the last word was barely out when the bells on the door chimed out again. She and Holly both turned at the sound and despite everything—especially whatever shred of good sense she had left—the day suddenly seemed far less bleak.

The town's brand-new chief of police stood in the doorway, dark-haired and gorgeous and almost ridiculously male looming over the glittery beads strewn across the floor. He wore jeans and a light blue dress shirt and tie and beneath his unzipped official Hope's Crossing Police Department parka, she saw a badge flash on one hip and a handgun at the other.

The chief took a long look around at the carnage and shook his head slowly. "What am I going to do with you, Claire? I turn my back for fifteen years or so and just look at the trouble you get yourself into."

In spite of everything, she had to laugh. Apparently Riley hadn't lost his uncanny ability to tweak that weird sense of humor her mother had been talking about. He stepped toward her, his arms wide, and without even thinking, she walked into them. Unlike Holly's brief embrace, this one was warm and familiar and completely natural, and for the first time all morning she felt as if she had something solid to hang on to.

Too soon, he eased away to study her and she was suddenly painfully aware of every single one of her thirty-six years and the two kids and divorce she had in her back pocket.

"You look terrific, Claire. How long has it been?"

She never could resist that smile, even when he was only her best friend's annoying kid brother who thought his sole purpose on earth was to taunt and tease and basically do his best to drive her and Alex crazy. This little flutter of attraction couldn't be appropriate, not with all the water that had flowed under their respective bridges. Especially not when her life and her store were in crisis.

"I'm not sure. A few years anyway. That's what happens when you head off to the coast and leave everybody behind."

"Word on the street is that you finally dumped Dr. Idiot. About damn time. You were always too good for him, even back in the day. I don't know what you ever saw in a little weasel like him."

About thirty seconds too late, Claire remembered with a mix of horror and a tiny, petty secret amusement she knew she ought to be ashamed to entertain that Holly was still hovering around. With an inward wince, she shifted to direct his attention toward the other woman.

"Oh. Riley, um, have you met Holly, Jeff's new wife? Holly, this is Riley McKnight, former town hellion and now the new chief of police in Hope's Crossing."

With her color high and her mouth pursed, Holly looked as if she might have been choking on an 8-millimeter rounded bicone.

"Sorry, ma'am." Riley offered an apologetic smile, even

as he held his crossed fingers behind his back so that only Claire could see. "Claire's an old friend and I'm afraid I spoke without thinking."

Holly didn't seem to know how to respond, whether to defend her spouse or let the awkwardness of the moment pass. She looked ruffled and insecure and terribly young, even though Riley at thirty-three would only be eight years older.

Finally she must have decided to ignore him completely. Instead, she spoke in a stiff voice to Claire. "I guess you don't need me to stick around, then?"

"I think I'll be okay." Now she was ashamed of that brief moment of small-minded amusement. "Thanks, though. It was really, uh, great of you to offer your moral support, Holly. I'll let you know when the store opens again and we can start working on those accessories for your new maternity wardrobe."

"Don't worry. We can do it another day. I guess I'll see you tonight at Owen's play, then? Jeff and I can save you and Macy a seat if you want."

She supposed she deserved that little dig, intentional or not, the reminder that Claire would be arriving at the annual Spring Fling pageant at Hope's Crossing Elementary with her twelve-year-old daughter as her date while Holly would be comfortably ensconced next to her handsome and successful orthopedic surgeon husband.

"Thanks, but I don't know what time I'll get there."

"We'll save a seat for you guys anyway. I'm sure Macy will want to see me wearing one of the new sweaters we bought."

"No doubt," Claire answered calmly. "I'll see you later, then."

As soon as Holly left the store, Claire managed to shrug out from under Riley's arm, trying not to notice how much colder she felt away from him. Her store had been robbed, for heaven's sake. This wasn't exactly the time for a warm, fuzzy happy reunion.

"Donna Mazell told me when I phoned dispatch that String Fever wasn't the only store that was hit during the night."

He nodded, even as he reached down to scratch Chester's jowls. "Apparently the town's criminal element had itself a busy Sunday night. At last count, four businesses were burglarized."

"I have a security system. Why wasn't the alarm tripped? The security company should have responded."

"That's a good question. I'm going to take a guess here that you're with Topflight Security."

"Yes."

"I'm thinking it might not be a coincidence that every other business that was hit in the night also happens to be with Topflight Security. That's just one of the angles we're going to be working in our investigation."

She frowned. "Surely you don't think someone there had anything to do with this?" The owner of the security company was a friend and she couldn't even contemplate that he or any of his employees might have been involved.

"One of the good things about being away from town all these years, I guess, is that I can come back without a lot of preconceptions. Right now I don't know what to think. We're looking into the possibility that their computer system had been hacked to allow someone access to the businesses without alerting Topflight, but we don't know yet. At this point, we're just adding everything to the pot and we'll sort through it later. What time did your store close yesterday?"

"During the shoulder seasons in the spring and fall, we

stay closed on Sundays. It could have been robbed at any time from Saturday night to this morning."

"Let's take a look at the damage. Have you figured out what's missing yet?"

"My office computer is gone. It was a fairly new iMac I bought only about six months ago. The drawer for the cash register was emptied, but I only keep about fifty dollars in change there overnight. I took care of the night deposit myself Saturday before I went home."

She was grateful for that at least. The weekend had been crazy, between running Owen to his dress rehearsal and her mother asking her at the last minute to pick up a couple of prescriptions for her, but she clearly remembered going to the drive-up at the bank and dropping off the deposit.

"Did they take anything else?"

"To be honest with you, I haven't looked very carefully. I didn't want to mess up the evidence."

"Go ahead and walk through, see what else might be missing."

The thieves hadn't touched the locked glass-fronted cabinet where she kept the pricier Czech crystals Donna had been talking about and some of the handcrafted Venetian glass, or some of more valuable finished jewelry pieces either she or Evie had made or she sold on consignment for her customers. It was still intact. She did see three empty hooks on the wall where she had hung a few of the less valuable custom necklaces she had created. One good thing about that—she would instantly recognize her own pieces if the thieves were stupid enough to flaunt their loot around town.

She walked through the retail section of the store and the workroom where she kept beading equipment for her customers to use on-site—bead boards and looms, reamers, cutters. Nothing else appeared to be missing.

She headed into her office last and suddenly gasped.

Riley was there in an instant. "Whoa." His gaze sharpened on the wedding dress still hanging in the protective bag, both slashed to tatters with what looked like a pair of her own scissors from the workroom. "Now that's interesting."

Interesting? She could come up with a hundred different adjectives and that particular one wasn't among them.

"That's a designer wedding dress," she moaned. "I've had it for only two days so I could customize the beadwork on the bodice. It was a huge commission."

A commission she could now see imploding—along with possibly the store's entire future. "Who would be so destructive?"

"Wild guess here, but maybe somebody who's not too crazy about the bride. Who did the gown belong to?" he asked.

"Genevieve Beaumont. The mayor's daughter."

Her grand society wedding to the son of one of the region's richest bachelors was still eight months away. Maybe Gen would have time to order a replacement gown between now and then and Claire could still have time to finish the beadwork.

Or maybe the somewhat spoiled bride-to-be would decide to sue Claire for every penny she eked out of the store, for whatever breach in security had potentially ruined Genevieve's big day.

Chester nudged her leg with his head and she wanted to sink to the floor in the middle of all those spilled beads, gather him in her arms and indulge in a big, soggy pity party. The emotions clogged her throat and burned behind her eyes, but she blinked them back and swallowed hard. She had no time to indulge in tears, not now when she had such a mess to clean up—and especially not in front of the new chief of police, for heaven's sake.

"This is a nightmare. It makes no sense. Why just destroy the dress when they didn't even bother to take the crystals? They're worth a fortune."

"I don't know the answer to that yet. But I promise you, Claire, I'll find out."

Riley might have been an annoying little pest when he was younger and a hell-on-wheels troublemaker when he hit his teen years, but all she had heard over the years from Alex and the rest of his family indicated he had shaped up from his wayward youth and truly found his calling with police work.

Most people in Hope's Crossing seemed to think the town was lucky he had agreed to give up his life as an undercover detective in the Bay Area to come back, although she had heard rumors there was discontent in the police department over his hiring.

"Tell me what else I can do to help you, then."

"Just sit tight while I finish processing the scene. Maybe you and your dog here could head over to Maura's place for coffee or something. I might be here a while."

"I'd rather stay, if you don't mind. We'll do our best to keep out of your way."

"Not a problem. I'm glad to have the company. I only wish it were under better circumstances."

For the next hour, she had a front-row seat as Riley worked the scene—collecting evidence, lifting fingerprints, taking photos.

It was a bit of a jarring dichotomy trying to reconcile the pain in the neck she remembered with this wholly competent officer of the law. Mixed in there was the wild, angry teenager he'd been after his parents' divorce, but by then she'd been living in Boulder for college and had only heard everything secondhand about his drinking, smoking and more.

The Riley she remembered was the one who had hidden a voice-activated tape recorder in his sister's room during one of Claire's frequent sleepovers at the McKnight home so he could overhear what she and Alex talked and giggled about.

Their conversation had inevitably centered around boys, of course, because they were probably twelve or thirteen at the time and beginning to be obsessed with the opposite sex. Claire had just started to notice the smartest, cutest boy in the grade ahead of her, Jeff Bradford. Alexandra at the time had been enamored with the quarterback on the freshman football team, Jason Kolpecki.

They had talked long into the night about their current crushes with no clue that Riley, the sneak, had recorded all of it—and then threatened to share the tape recording with the boys in question if they didn't meet his demands, a mortifying prospect.

It was probably a good thing those who weren't thrilled about Riley's return didn't know their new chief of police had once included blackmail in his repertoire. She and Alex had spent every Saturday for two months taking over his customary duty of mowing and edging the McKnights' lawn in exchange for Riley's promise to destroy the tape.

All the teasing and mischief of their childhood seemed worlds away, buried deep under the weight of all that had come later. Her father's scandalous death, her mother's subsequent breakdowns, *his* father's midlife crisis that had decimated his family and Riley's own wild youth.

Sometimes she thought she would give anything to go back to that peaceful time, when the only thing she had to worry about in junior high was her algebra grade and Riley leaking to Jeff Bradford that she had a crush on him.

After another half hour while he spent considerable time on his cell phone with, she assumed, officers working the other crime scenes, he finally collected the last evidence and loaded everything into a bag.

"That should do it," he said. "I'm going to send everything here to the crime lab and hopefully we can get a print or two."

"Thanks, Riley. I really appreciate everything you've done."

"No problem. I hope to have information for you as soon as possible."

He gave her the big, broad, charming smile he had perfected as the youngest and only boy in a family of five sisters, the same smile that helped him wiggle out of more trouble than she cared to think about.

A little sizzle of attraction sparked through her, just like the flickering lights floating down the mountainside in the hands of skiers during the annual Christmas Eve candle festival at the resort. She frowned, especially when he stepped a little closer and reached for her hand.

"It really is terrific to see you, Claire. When things settle a little, what do you say I take you up to the resort for dinner so we can catch up under better circumstances?"

Okay, she had been out of the dating scene for pretty much *ever,* since she had started seeing Jeff when she was fifteen, but that sounded suspiciously like Riley McKnight was asking her out.

"Uh." Brilliant answer, she knew. She couldn't help it—she couldn't remember the last time anything beyond leaving her grocery list at home managed to fluster her. Surely she must have misunderstood. He was just being polite, wasn't he?

"It was only a simple dinner invitation, Claire." A dimple quirked at the edge of his mouth. "I didn't intend to send you into a panic."

She forced a bland smile and reminded herself this was pesky Riley McKnight. "The day you send me into a panic is the day I dye my hair purple and join a punk-rock band."

"Now *that* I would love to see."

Too late, she remembered that he never backed down from a challenge. Once when they were kids, Alex had been grounded for a month when she dared her brother to ride his bike down from the top of the Woodrose Mountain trail without hitting his brakes once. He'd made it almost to the bottom before his spectacular crash—and, of course, never once considered braking to slow his descent. That would have been cheating.

That was years ago. A man didn't become a decorated law enforcement officer without gaining a little wisdom along the way and learning how to pick his battles, right?

"I'm sure we'll have plenty of time to catch up," she answered as calmly as she could manage. "Alex tells me you're renting the old Harper place on Blackberry Lane. That's just down the street from my house. I'm in the red-brick house with the portico."

He smiled again. "Great. Guess I know where to head when I need to borrow a cup of sugar."

How on earth did he manage to make such a simple statement sound vaguely sexy? She decided to ignore it—just as she decided it would probably be better not to mention it had been a long time since she'd loaned anyone a cup of sugar—or enjoyed any other euphemism, for that matter.

"Is it all right if I reopen the store now? I can't afford to be closed all day."

"As far as the police are concerned, sure. Do you need me to send somebody over to help you clean up?"

She shook her head. "I'll check around and see if I can round up a crew."

"Okay. So I'll call you, right?"

She frowned. She was so out of practice at this, she had no idea how to tactfully discourage him. Better to just plow ahead, she decided. "Riley, I don't know if that's such a great idea…"

He gave her a long, amused look. "Funny, I figured you'd want to know what's going on with the case."

"Of course I do!"

"What else did you think I meant?"

She had no way of answering that without sounding like an idiot. *Now* she remembered why he used to drive her and Alex crazy.

"Absolutely nothing. Please do call me. About the case anyway."

"Right. I'll be in touch."

Only after he left and she moved to close the door behind him did she remember that silly horoscope. *Something fun and exciting is heading your way.* That was Riley McKnight, all right. Too bad she wasn't in the market for either of those things—and especially not with her best friend's younger brother.

Two

For the first time in months, Claire was relieved when business was slow. She didn't know how she could provide any sort of decent customer service when she still had hours of work to do clearing up the mess the burglars had left behind.

In desperation, she had finally swept the tens of thousands of spilled beads into one huge bin to be sorted back into compartmentalized trays. If she'd been forced to tackle it by herself, she didn't know what she would have done.

"This is going to take months. You know that, don't you, honey?"

Ruth seemed to read her mind, in that uncanny way her mother had perfected. Claire managed to keep from grinding her teeth, but before she could answer, her best friend chimed in from the other end of the worktable.

"Are you kidding, Mrs. T.?" Alex McKnight's dimple, much like her brother's, flashed with her grin. "You've got the town's best and brightest beaders here. With all of us superwomen working together, we can probably cut the job down to three weeks, tops."

"I say we can do it in two," Evie Blanchard, Claire's assistant manager, spoke in her quietly cheerful way. Monday was supposed to be her day off, but when Evie heard about the burglary, she had insisted on cutting short a late-season cross-country ski outing to help with the cleanup effort.

Evie and Alex were two of the seven women surrounding the String Fever worktable, each with a small kaleidoscopic pile of beads in front of them they were sorting by color and shape into compartmentalized trays that lined the middle of the table. After that, the spilled beads would have to be sorted by size and type—furnace glass, hand-blown glass, semiprecious stones, cloisonné—and organized once more on the shelves.

Claire's mother sat at one end near Maura—Alex's next oldest sister—and Mary Ella, their mother. To Claire's left was Evie and on her right was Katherine Thorne, who had sold her the store nearly two years ago, while Alex sat across the table.

Chester, of course, presided from his place of honor on his favorite blanket, curled up on his side. Sometimes she thought half her customers came into the store just to visit her dog, who was never quite as happy as when he was stretched out in his corner at String Fever, listening to all the chatter.

During those first difficult months after Jeff moved out, String Fever was where she found solace and calm, here amid her friends. Like beads on a wire, they were all connected, linked together by bonds of friendship and family, by shared experiences and a common passion for beading.

"Did you hear about Jeanie Strebel?" Maura, Alex's older sister, was saying.

"No. What happened?" Claire asked.

"She was knocking icicles off her roof with a broom the other night and a big one shot right down and knocked her over. Broke her leg in three places. Jeff did surgery yesterday, from what I hear. Her daughter told me she was going to be in the hospital until Sunday."

"Oh, no!" Mary Ella exclaimed. "And they've already been hit with more than their share of troubles since Ardell had his heart surgery three months ago."

Maura nodded. "I bumped into Brianna at the market this morning before I opened the store and she told me all about it. Have you seen those twins of hers, by the way? They're growing like crazy and have the most darling dark curls and huge eyes. Anyway, guess what happened while her dad was at the hospital with her mom last night?"

They all waited expectantly and Maura let the pause lengthen for dramatic effect.

"Come on, Maur." Alex finally ruined the anticipation. "Just get on with it. What happened?"

"They had a visit from the Angel of Hope."

Excitement seemed to shimmer around the table at the announcement. Even Ruth leaned forward, her eyes wide. "Really? Another one?" she asked.

"It had to be. Somebody left ten crisp hundred-dollar bills in an envelope slipped under their front door to help with medical expenses. You should have seen Brianna's face when she told me about it. That sweet girl. Her eyes were all red and weepy and she just glowed from the inside out."

For the past few months, a mysterious benefactor had been stepping in to help people who most needed it. When Caroline Bybee's ancient Plymouth coughed its final death knell last fall, she woke up one morning to find a later-model used sedan in her driveway, complete with a gift title and a note signed only "Drive Carefully."

A few weeks before that, a young divorced mother who sometimes came into the store told Claire someone had paid her heating bill for the entire winter. She had no idea how or why but the gas company assured her she had full credit on her bill to last into the spring.

During the holiday season, Claire had heard that more than one struggling family—all with young children—had discovered envelopes full of cash on their doorstep with only the words "Merry Christmas from Someone Who Cares."

Those were only the things she knew about. She had to wonder how many acts of generosity had somehow escaped the winding tendrils of the Hope's Crossing grapevine. She didn't know who had first come up with the nickname Angel of Hope, but the whole town had been buzzing about the identity of the benevolent patron.

As tough as she sometimes found living in the same town with Jeff and Holly, stories like this provided another reason to stay. People here cared about each other. How could she doubt it, with her dear friends rushing to her aid in her moment of need?

"You're all my angels of hope," she told them fiercely. "I can't tell you all how much I appreciate your giving up your lives to help me for a few hours."

"Of course we would come in to help you." Mary Ella smiled, her green eyes so much like her son's bright with affection. "You didn't even need to ask, my dear. The moment I heard your store had been robbed and that the little shits had left such a mess behind, I knew I would be spending the afternoon helping you clean it up."

"I still can't believe anybody in town would be so vindictive as to cause such trouble just for the sake of making a mess." Katherine seemed to be taking the burglaries as a personal affront.

"I'm betting it was somebody staying at the ski resort." Evie tucked a strand of blond hair behind her ear. "What are the police saying?"

"Chief McKnight said he would touch base with me later, but I haven't heard anything yet. It's been only a few hours."

"Now there's a familiar story. Another woman waiting in vain for one of Riley's phone calls."

Alex's levity earned her a frown from her mother. "His social life is one thing," Mary Ella said sternly, "but you'd better not let me hear you say anything about your brother's devotion to duty, Alexandra. Riley is an excellent police officer. You know Katherine and the rest of the city council wouldn't have voted to hire him as the police chief if he wasn't."

Katherine looked vaguely alarmed at being dragged into a family discussion. "We feel honored that Riley would even consider coming back to Hope's Crossing. When he agreed to take the job, I was a little worried we would have a hard time keeping him busy."

"Is that a confession, Katherine?" Claire teased. "Are you telling us you broke into a half-dozen stores along Main Street just to keep Riley busy enough that he'll want to stay permanently in Hope's Crossing?"

"Claire Renée!" Ruth sounded positively scandalized. "You know perfectly well Katherine would never hurt our town like that, no matter how good Chief McKnight might be at his job and how much the city council might want to keep him."

Alex rolled her eyes, just out of Ruth's view and Claire bit her cheek, relieved she could find anything funny after this miserable day.

"Of course I know that, Mom," she said. "Joking. Again."

"It's actually a very clever idea." Katherine smiled. "Wish I'd thought of it. Of course, if it had been me, I wouldn't have left such a big mess behind me for you to clean up.

And I *certainly* wouldn't have destroyed poor Genevieve's wedding dress."

That was a phone call Claire had hated making, one she hoped she'd never have to repeat. As any bride would be, Genevieve had been traumatized to learn her wedding dress had been shredded, but another telephone call to the dress designer had ended in prim assurances that another gown could be sent within the next few weeks—for a premium, of course. Claire would have to foot the bill for it until her insurance policy paid up, but she figured it was a small price to pay to keep the peace with the Beaumont family.

"Katherine, you've always got your ear to the ground." The nimble fingers Alex used for slicing and dicing in the restaurant kitchen at the resort didn't stop dancing through the beads as she spoke. "What's the scuttlebutt about who might be behind our dastardly crime spree?"

"I wish I knew. As of an hour ago when I stopped in at the diner, all kinds of rumors were flying, everything from some Ukrainian mafia moving into Hope's Crossing to California gangs setting up a drug operation to some secret government conspiracy. Riley's got his work cut out for him sifting through all the crazy tips."

"He'll figure it out," Mary Ella said, her voice confident. "That boy has been stubborn since he came into the world. He won't stop until he gets to the bottom of the burglaries and puts the offenders behind bars, no matter what he has to do to find them."

"Which is Ma code meaning her only son is sneaky and conniving," Alex said.

"*And* manipulative and underhanded," Maura added.

"Don't forget mule-headed and obstinate," offered Claire, who figured that while she wasn't a sister by birth, she had been the object of his torment enough that she deserved the right to chime in.

All the women laughed, except for Ruth, whose mouth tightened. Despite her friendship with Mary Ella, Ruth held Riley in severe dislike and never found much of anything amusing when it came to him. She couldn't get past the wild troublemaker he'd been in the past, the pain he'd put his mother through. Still, the rest of them were still chuckling when the front door chimes rang out and the man in question walked through the door.

He stood just inside the store, his dark hair slightly ruffled from the cold wind and a brush of afternoon shadow along his jawline, practically oozing testosterone amid all the sparkly beads and chattering women. Claire had a sudden mental image of running her fingers along those whiskers, of tracing that firm jawline and the dimple at the side of his mouth.

Color heated her cheeks. What on earth was wrong with her? The stress of the day. That's what she would blame for her completely irrational response.

Riley surveyed the group of giggling women and Claire noticed she wasn't the only one unable to meet his gaze, although she was quite certain she was the only one whose insides had taken a long, slow roll.

"Okay, now why do I suddenly have the funny feeling my ears should be burning?" he murmured.

"No reason, darling," Mary Ella assured him, although she winked at the rest of them.

"A little narcissistic, are we?" Alex smirked.

He tugged at his sister's dark curls in response before leaning in to kiss his mother's cheek. Claire was close enough to catch his scent, earthy and masculine.

"How nice of you all to help Claire with her mess. This looks like it's going to take months."

"Told you," Ruth muttered.

"I guess you know everyone here," Mary Ella said. "Oh, except for Evie. Evie Blanchard, this is the new police chief of Hope's Crossing and my baby, J. Riley McKnight. Evie works here for Claire."

Riley gave his mother an exasperated frown. "I generally prefer *youngest* to *baby,* thanks all the same, Ma. It's nice to meet you, Evie."

He shook her hand and from his reputation, Claire might have expected him to put out the vibe, maybe offer up the same flirtatious grin he'd employed on *her* earlier. Evie was beautiful, after all, ethereal and blonde and deceptively fragile-looking, especially with those shadows in her big blue eyes. But Riley only smiled at her in a polite but rather impersonal sort of way.

"How's the investigation coming?" Maura asked. "We were just talking about it. Did you come to tell us you've caught the little bastards?"

He raised an eyebrow. "Geez, Maur. Your language! And in front of Mrs. Tatum and Councilwoman Thorne, too. Watch it or Ma will wash out your mouth."

"That's right," Mary Ella said, apparently conveniently forgetting she'd used her own pithy words earlier.

Maura never cared much about what anybody thought of her, one of the reasons Claire admired her so much. "You saw what they did here." She gestured to the mess the women were helping Claire set to rights. "What else would you call them?"

"Point taken."

"I guess I'm just lucky they didn't hit the bookstore."

"So have you caught them?" Alex asked.

"Still working on it. I need to ask Claire a couple of follow-up questions."

"Please. We'd like to know what's going on." In her

quest for information, Ruth had apparently decided to momentarily overlook her dislike of Riley.

"If you all don't mind, I'd like to speak to Claire in private. Certain details of the investigation are somewhat sensitive."

Ruth didn't bother to hide her disappointment as Claire rose and led the way to her office. Riley shut the door, then stretched out in her visitor's chair, rubbing at his forehead. He looked tired, she thought. His day likely had been even harder than hers. She'd only had to deal with one robbery while he'd been faced with a whole crop of them.

"Would you like some coffee?" she asked. "Or I've got tea."

"I'm good, thanks. If I have any more caffeine today, I'm going to be jumpier than a grasshopper on lawn-mowing day."

"You have information for me?" she asked.

"I guess you could call it information. For what it's worth anyway. It's not much, I'm afraid, but I did tell you I would pass along what I could. We found a possible eyewitness who saw a suspicious vehicle pulling away from the pizza place at an odd time in the early hours of the morning. A late-model dark blue or green or black extended-cab pickup truck. The eyewitness didn't get a good look and is uncertain whether it was a Dodge or a Ford."

"Great. That should narrow it down to, oh, maybe half the town."

"I know it's broad, but at least it's something. Not all the security cameras in the other businesses were disabled. We've got security footage at the bike shop that shows three different individuals at the scene, but they're all wearing ski masks and cheap disposable raincoats over their parkas to hide any identifying clothing."

With some degree of shame, she realized she hadn't

given much thought to the rest of the affected stores. "Was the damage serious at the other businesses?"

"It varies. Computers, a little cash. They took a high-end mountain bike from Mike's Bikes." Despite the fatigue still etched into his features, his gaze seemed to sharpen. "Yours was the only store to see actual vandalism."

Lucky her. "I still don't understand why. Maybe they were angry that I didn't have much for them to steal for their trouble."

"Could be. Or maybe it was more personal. I'm sorry, but I have to ask, Claire. Can you think of anyone with a grudge against you, besides Dr. Asshole?"

She stared at him and then started to laugh. She couldn't help herself. "Jeff? You think *Jeff* had something to do with this? That's completely insane! He would never be involved in anything like this. Anyway, he has no reason to have a grudge against me. If anything it's…"

"The other way around?"

Any trace of laughter shriveled. "Jeff and I have tried very hard to get along, for the sake of our children."

"Ah, that rare beast, the amicable divorce." Although he spoke in a light, mocking tone, she saw something in his eyes, some hint of bitterness, and she remembered the raw shock of his parents' breakup. She and Alex had just been starting their senior year, so they would have been about seventeen. Riley would have been about fourteen, she estimated. Although she had seen it all through the prism of her best friend's experience, she knew all six of the McKnight children had been confused and angry, devastated by the destruction of what had always seemed a happy family to everyone in town.

She knew Riley had struggled the most, the lone male left in a household of women after their father abruptly moved away from Hope's Crossing to follow his own scientific ambitions.

"We've worked to make it as amicable as possible," she finally answered stiffly. She really hated talking about her divorce.

"What about the new wife? We believe at least one of the individuals on the security footage might be a female."

She tried to picture Holly skulking around town with a band of cat burglars, breaking into businesses, stealing bikes and computers and trashing String Fever—and Genevieve Beaumont's wedding dress. The image was even more amusing than the idea of Jeff on a wild crime spree.

"You're telling me you suspect that a woman who is five months pregnant might be some ruthless criminal mastermind?"

His dimple quirked. "Hard to say under the plastic raincoat whether she was pregnant. But, okay, probably not."

"A word of advice. You might want to rethink dragging Holly into your little room with the lightbulb for an interrogation."

He gave a full-fledged grin at that, all those shadows of earlier gone. He's a pest, she reminded herself, but it was very tough to remember that when he gunned her engine like it hadn't been revved in a long time.

"It would help the investigation if you could spend some time trying to think if anyone might have reason to be angry with you. Maybe ask your employees if they can come up with anyone who might have a grudge, against either you or them."

She hated thinking someone out there might dislike her or any of her employees. Katherine worked part-time for her sometimes, but she was one of the most admired women in town. Evie couldn't have been in Hope's Crossing long enough to make many enemies—except for maybe

Brodie Thorne, Katherine's son, who for some strange reason seemed to actively dislike the other woman. Brodie was one of the town's most prominent businessmen, though. She could picture Holly and Jeff as some Bonnie and Clyde team before she could imagine Brodie in that role.

That left only Maura's daughter Layla, who worked in the store after school and on Saturdays.

And, of course, Claire herself.

"I'll do that," she said. "I really appreciate you stopping by to keep me up-to-the-minute with the investigation."

"You're welcome." He leaned back farther in the chair. "How about an information trade, then. Are you going to tell me what everyone was saying about me when I walked in?"

She could feel her face heat, for some completely ridiculous reason. "Um, what a good police officer you are," she finally improvised.

He smiled. "Hmm. Now why don't I believe you?"

"Because you happen to have a suspicious mind?"

"Comes in handy when you're a cop. Never mind. I only hope it was juicy."

Before she could respond, she heard the bells jangle loudly out in the store as someone yanked the door open and an instant later, her eight-year-old son raced into her office.

One of the best things about owning a store just a few blocks from both the elementary school and middle school was that her children could come hang out at the store once the afternoon bell rang on those days when their dad didn't pick them up or Claire's mother wasn't available.

Macy loved to bead, creating bracelets and earrings for her friends, and she had a burgeoning sense of style. Claire let her work off the cost of the beads she used by sorting inventory and doing light filing for her.

Owen wasn't much interested in beading, but after he finished his homework under her watchful eye, she allowed him an hour of Nintendo on the console in her office—which the thieves must not have discovered in the cabinet. Because she didn't let him play video games at home, coming to String Fever was usually a genuine treat for him.

She loved having a few extra hours with them when they weren't bickering. This didn't look like one of those times.

"Macy has a boyfriend, Macy has a boyfriend," Owen sang out, his wool beanie covering his dishwater blond hair and his narrow shoulders swamped in the bulky snowboarder parka he insisted on wearing.

"Shut *up!*" Macy followed closely behind with a harsh glare at her brother, somehow managing to look both outraged and a little apprehensive of her mother's reaction at the same time. "You don't know anything."

"I know you were walking after school with Toby Kingston and you were laughing and looking all goofy." Owen crossed his eyes and let his mouth sag open in what Claire assumed was his interpretation of a lovesick twelve-year-old.

"I was not." Macy's color rose and she looked mortified, especially when she saw Riley sitting in the visitor's chair. "Mom, make him stop!"

"Owen, stop teasing," she said automatically.

"I wasn't teasing! I'm telling the complete and total truth. You should have seen her! Macy and Toby sitting in a tree. K-I-S-S…" His voice trailed off when he finally focused on something besides tormenting his sister and realized she had company in her office. "Sorry. Hi."

Riley looked amused at the sibling interchange. Big surprise there because he'd written the playbook on teasing one's older sister. Or in his case, five older sisters. "Hey."

"Owen, Macy, this is Chief McKnight."

Macy dropped her messenger bag next to the desk. "Anna Kramer said a bunch of stores in Hope's Crossing were robbed last night and String Fever was one of them. Is it true?"

Even though she didn't want to unduly alarm her children, Claire couldn't figure out a way to evade the truth. "Yes. They took my computer and a little money out of the till. They also yanked out all the displays and dumped them on the floor. That's what Grandma and the others are doing in the workroom, helping me sort the beads that were spilled."

"Why didn't you call me?" Macy turned the glare she was perfecting these days in her mother's direction. "I had to hear about the store being robbed from Anna, the biggest know-it-all at school."

"I asked your mom not to tell too many people about the robbery yet while we're still trying to figure things out," Riley said.

Macy looked impressed. "Wow, like a real police investigation?"

His dimple flashed. "Just like."

"You're Jace's uncle, huh?" Owen said. Jace was Riley's sister Angie's youngest kid and he and Owen were inseparable.

"Guilty."

"Jace is my best friend. We're in the same class at school."

"So I'm guessing that means you've probably got a part in tonight's Spring Fling."

"Yep. This year the third grade is doing a patriotic show. I get to be Abraham Lincoln."

"You should see his dorky hat."

Owen glared at his sister. "Shut it. You're just jealous. Abraham Lincoln was the Great Emancipator. When your class did the Spring Fling, you had to be a stupid pansy."

Here we go. Claire sighed. The two of them bickered about everything from which row of the minivan they each would claim to whose turn it was to feed Chester.

She fought back her stress headache and opted for diversion, her favorite fight-avoidance technique. Divide and conquer, the time-proven strategy. "Macy, go ask Evie what you can do to help sort the beads."

As soon as her daughter left, she turned to Owen. "When you finish your homework, you can play the Lego Star Wars video game your dad bought you this weekend, before we have to go home and get you in your costume for the pageant."

"Can we go to McDonald's for dinner?"

He always knew how to hit her up when she was tired and stressed, when the challenge of cooking a healthy, satisfying meal for her family seemed completely beyond her capabilities. "We'll see how well you do with your homework first."

In an instant, he reached to whip his homework folder from his backpack at the same time Riley rose to give him space on the desk for the ream of papers he always seemed to bring home.

"I've got to run. Let me know if you think of anything else that might help the investigation. No matter how small or insignificant the information might seem to you, it could provide the break we need."

"I will. Thank you again for all you've done."

"You can wait and thank me after I catch the ba—" He caught himself with a quick, apologetic look to Owen.

"The bad dudes. Good luck tonight, Abe. You were always my favorite president."

Owen grinned as he spread his homework on the desk and reached for a pencil. Claire followed Riley back to the workroom, where he took time to say good-bye to his mother and sisters and the other women still sorting away.

"Wow. This looks like a big mess," he said.

"You let us worry about the beads," his mother said. "You just get back out there and catch whoever did this to our Claire."

"No pressure, right? On my way, Ma." He kissed his mother's salt-and-pepper curls, then headed for the door.

Three

The more things change, the more they stayed the same, and all that.

Riley sat in the auditorium at Hope's Crossing Elementary School, feeling a little like he'd traveled back in time. The place looked just as it had when he was here twenty-five years ago. Same creaky folding chairs, same red-velvet curtains on the stage.

The third-grade class of Hope's Crossing Elementary School had been presenting a Spring Fling Spectacular for more than thirty years. Riley could vividly recall his own stint in their play, which his year had been a salute to the original miners who staked claims in the area. Despite old Mrs. Appleton's stern warnings to the contrary all through their rehearsals, he had been overwhelmed by the crowd and the excitement and had stupidly locked his knees right in the middle of a rousing song about turning silver into gold.

His spectacular dive off the stage as he passed out into the lap of the grumpy fourth-grade teacher holding the cue cards was probably still legendary in the hallowed halls of Hope's Crossing Elementary School.

He smiled at the memory as he sat beside Angie, his

second-oldest sister. Angie's son Jace—Owen Bradford's best friend—was starring as the narrator of tonight's pageant.

He had been away from town for a long time, since he left an angry, troubled punk who couldn't wait to get out. When he was a kid, he had loathed these rituals, these prescribed, hallowed traditions that beat out the quiet rhythm of life in a small town. Now, fifteen years later, he was astonished at the comfort he found in the steadfast continuity of it all.

He might have changed drastically in those intervening years and the town likely had, as well. But certain things remained constant. The hash browns at Center of Hope Café still held the distinction of the best he'd ever tasted, the mountains cupping the town soared just as dramatically imposing as they'd been the day he left, and the elementary school Spring Fling still drew the biggest crowd in town.

Some part of him had dreaded coming home as much as he craved it. His years as a cop in the harsh world of Oakland had shaped him as much as his youth here. A cop couldn't work gang violence task forces, multiple homicides, serial rapes, without some of the ugliness brushing against his own soul. When the former chief of police of Hope's Crossing approached him about replacing him when he retired, Riley had worried those bruises inside him would somehow render him unfit for the quieter, easier pace here.

But that worry seemed far away now as he sat comfortably with his family. The audience applauded energetically when Owen Bradford finished a moving speech about brother fighting brother and Riley slanted his gaze from the stage to the spot across the gymnasium where he'd seen Claire sitting next to her idiot of an ex-husband and the flashy eye candy who'd been in Claire's store earlier. Her daughter sat next to the new wife, not next to Claire, he noted. Awkward.

How could Claire sit there with them and still wear that look of calm indifference in her eyes? Was it a mask or did she really not care that Jeff had moved on, traded her in for a newer, younger model?

None of his business. She could have a half-dozen ex-husbands all arrayed around her like those shiny beads at her store and it shouldn't be any of Riley's concern.

He found it more than a little unsettling that Claire Tatum Bradford still fascinated him like she did when he was just a stupid kid mooning over his older sister's smart, pretty best friend. What would Claire think if she knew he used to fantasize about her?

He shifted his attention back to the stage, where his nephew as narrator was introducing Betsy Ross. What any of this had to do with celebrating spring, he had no idea. He imagined it grew tough after thirty years to come up with something original for the third-grade pageant.

The crowd ate it up, jumping to its collective feet as soon as the last words had been spoken and clapping with broad enthusiasm for the young performers, who beamed as the curtain opened for them to bow once more.

"Thanks for making time to come, Riley." Angie smiled at him as the applause finally died away and people began to gather their coats and belongings. "I know it means the world to Jace that you showed up."

"I've missed a few of these over the years. It's good to be back."

She touched his arm in that Angie way of hers, her eyes sympathetic. His sister had been the little mother to the rest of them. He loved all his sisters and was probably closest to Alex, the next oldest sibling to him, but he would always have a tender place in his heart for Angie. During the dark days after his dad walked out, she had been the one he turned to for comfort when his mom had been too distraught herself to offer any.

"You're staying for refreshments, aren't you? Ang made her famous snickerdoodles," her husband, Jim, said.

Angie and Jim were two of the most sane people he'd ever had the fortune to know. After twenty years of marriage, they still held hands and plainly adored each other.

"And you didn't bring along a few dozen just for your favorite officer of the law?" he teased his sister.

She made a face. "Didn't think about it. Sorry. I'm still not used to having you home for me to spoil again with cookies. I always make a triple batch, though, so I can probably find you a few crumbs lying around. I'll bring them by tomorrow."

"I was kidding, Ang. You don't have to feed me."

"I can if I want. And I want. I'm just glad you're home to give me a chance."

He was still reserving judgment on whether he shared her sentiment. Coming back to Colorado had been a tough decision, one he hadn't yet convinced himself had been right. But being an undercover cop had become intolerable. He had been on the verge of handing in his badge and hanging up his service revolver for good—if not for Chief Coleman's phone call, Riley might be working construction somewhere in Alaska, because that's about all he felt qualified to do besides police work.

Alaska was still an option. He wasn't ruling anything out yet. When he took the job, he'd insisted on a three-month probation to see how he could adapt to the quieter pace in Hope's Crossing. At the end of that time, if he didn't feel the life of a small-town cop was any more comfortable to his psyche than the urban warfare of inner-city Oakland, he might be spending next winter on the tundra.

"Hey, McKnight! Town must be really scraping the bottom of the barrel to drag your sorry ass back."

He turned at the familiar voice and grinned as he recognized an old friend. Monte Richardson had once been the star quarterback of the Hope's Crossing High football team. Now he was balding with a bit of a paunch, a thick brushy dark mustache and the well-fed look of a contented husband and father, at least judging by the sleeping baby in his arms.

"Hey, Monte." Somehow they managed to shake hands around the sleeping baby. "I figured next time I ran into you, it would be when I hauled you in for a drunk and disorderly."

Monte laughed. "Not me, man. I've reformed. Only drinking I do anymore is maybe a beer or two while I'm watching *Monday Night Football* in my man cave. You're welcome anytime."

He shook his head. "How the mighty have fallen. Whatever happened to *party till you drop?*"

"Life, man. Kids, family. It's a hell of a ride. You ought to climb on."

That world wasn't for him. He had figured that out a long time ago. Family was chaos and uncertainty, craziness and pain. In his experience, life handed out enough of that without volunteering for more.

He would have stayed to talk longer but the two of them were interrupted by Mayor Beaumont, who greeted Monte with a polite if dismissive smile and then proceeded to corner Riley for the next ten minutes about the progress of the investigation into what for him condensed to only the most pressing issue, the desecration of his daughter's wedding gown.

"You've got to find the buggers and fast," the mayor finally said, his tone implacable. "Gennie and my wife are out for blood. We all better hope they're not the first ones to find whoever did this or you just might have a murder investigation on your hands."

He took the words to heart. Finally the mayor was distracted by one of the city council members approaching and Riley took blatant advantage of the chance to escape with a wave for the men.

His progress through the crowd was slow and laborious. He supposed that was another one of those curse-and-blessing things about returning to his hometown. Everybody wanted to talk to him, to relive old times, to catch up on the years and distance between them. Add to that the unaccustomed excitement of the day with four—count 'em four—robberies in town, and everyone gathered at the elementary school for the pageant seemed to want to put in his or her two cents.

Wearing the title of chief on his badge in a small town wasn't much different than being an undercover cop whose entire goal had been blending in. The only difference was instead of hanging with drug dealers and pimps, here he was required to be polite, to make conversation, to play the public relations game, something that didn't sit completely comfortably inside his skin.

He did have one uneasy moment when he encountered J. D. Nyman, one of his officers who had also applied for the position of police chief. The man had made no secret that he thought Riley wasn't qualified for the job, which made for some awkward staff meetings.

"Officer Nyman," he said. "Any word from the crime lab on those fingerprints?"

"No," the other man said with blunt rudeness and turned his back to talk to someone else.

Riley almost called him on it, but then decided this wasn't the venue, so he headed out of the gymnasium to the hallway, where he almost literally bumped into Claire Bradford at the coatrack, pulling a charcoal wool coat from a hanger.

She looked tired, he thought. The big blue eyes he used to dream about were smudged with shadows and tiny lines of exhaustion radiated from her mouth. She smiled. "Hello, Chief McKnight."

Her warmth was refreshing, especially after Nyman's rudeness. "Looks like you finally ditched the good doctor."

He gently tugged her coat away to help her into it. Her mouth tightened, at him or at the doctor, he didn't know. "Holly was tired, so they made an early night of it," she answered.

She had always been enamored with Jeff Bradford. He hated the guy for that, alone, especially because from the moment Jeff had noticed her, too, Claire had seemed completely smitten.

Even early on, she had talked about living in one of the town's historic old brick houses, settling down and raising a family here in Hope's Crossing.

Things hadn't quite worked out as she planned and Riley knew a moment's sadness for unrealized dreams. If anyone deserved the life she wanted, Claire Tatum Bradford would have topped his personal list. She'd been through hell as a kid and ought to be first in line for a happy ending.

Was she completely devastated that Bradford had moved on? Riley didn't want to think so. He had been fourteen when his own mother disintegrated for a while after his old man walked out. He could still remember the nights he would wake up to her sobbing in the living room as they all tried to make sense of James McKnight's sudden abandonment of his wife and six children.

Another problem he should have anticipated about moving home. Things he hadn't thought about in years—and didn't want to waste another moment of his life dwelling on—had a way of pushing themselves to the front of his brain. He quickly turned his attention to Claire's son.

"Great show." He shook Owen's hand with solemn gravity. "Your speech was my favorite of the whole pageant."

The boy flashed a grin at him. "Thanks. I'm super glad it's over."

"Me, too." A kid with flaming red hair and freckles who had played a highly unlikely FDR in the pageant grinned at him and Riley couldn't resist smiling back.

"This is Jordie. We're driving him home," Owen announced. "His mom and dad couldn't come see the play 'cause they're both pukin' sick."

His sister rolled her eyes. "Do you have to be so disgusting all the time?"

He shoved his finger in his mouth and made a retching sound until his mother gave him a stern look.

"Carrie and Don have the flu, poor things. I offered to drive Jordan to and from the pageant for them."

That was just like her, always taking care of everybody else. Apparently that hadn't changed. "Well, be careful driving out there. Looks like the snow's finally started. I forgot how lovely spring can be in the Rockies."

"I have four-wheel drive," she said.

"Four-wheel drive won't do diddly-squat if you hit a patch of black ice," he said, but before she could answer, his cell phone buzzed with the urgent ringtone from Dispatch.

"Hang on, Claire. Sorry, I've got to take this."

She shrugged and finished shepherding the boys into their jackets and gloves while he stepped away to answer.

"Yeah, Chief." Tammy, the night dispatcher, spoke rapidly, her words a jumble. "I just got a call from Harry Lange out on Silver Strike Road reporting a possible burglary in progress at one of the vacation homes near his place. He says the owners were just in town from California last weekend and told him they wouldn't be back until June but he's seeing lights inside that shouldn't be there. He thinks it's kids. And get this, Harry also reported they might be driving a dark-colored extended-cab pickup truck, just like our suspect vehicle from the robberies."

"Did he get a plate?"

"No. He said he couldn't see it from his angle in the dark and didn't want to move in too close. What should I do? Jess is in the middle of a domestic disturbance over at the Claimjumper Condos and Marty is taking care of a fender bender out on Highland Road. Do you want me to divert one of them or call the sheriff's department for backup?"

"I can be there faster than anybody else. Have the sheriff send a couple deputies for backup just in case."

"Right, Chief."

He was already heading out the door, his adrenaline pumping at a possible break in the case, when he remembered Claire and the kids.

"Sorry," he said over his shoulder. "I've got an emergency."

He wasn't sure whose eyes were wider, hers or the kids.

"Are you going to catch whoever stole my mom's computer?" Owen asked.

"I intend to," he vowed.

He gave one last apologetic smile to Claire, then raced out the door. Less than a minute later, he pulled out of the elementary school parking lot as fast as he dared and turned toward the canyon road that hugged the mountainside east of Silver Strike Reservoir.

As he had told Claire, the snow that had been threatening all day had begun to fall, plump fluffy flakes that might look like something off a postcard but played hell with road conditions. Welcome to April in the Rockies.

At least there was little traffic in either direction up the canyon. He was still about two miles from Harry Lange's place when his dispatcher's voice crackled through his radio. "Chief, be advised, suspects are believed to have left the premises of the vacation cabin and are now on Silver Strike Road, heading back toward town."

Which meant they would be coming right at him. He might have missed catching them in the act, but he could still possibly nail them with stolen items from the vacation cabin and then link them to the Main Street break-ins.

"Ten-four, Tammy."

He wheeled his department SUV around, grateful for all the years he'd driven the mountain back roads and by-ways around town. This was the only road out of Silver Strike Canyon, which dead-ended at the ski resort. The suspects would have to pass him eventually on their way back to town.

He pulled into a turnoff shielded from view from the road by a large pine, then shut off his headlights and killed the engine, lurking in wait for them in the cold.

Normally he hated waiting for anything. His natural impatience, he figured, a consequence of being the youngest of six and the only boy in a house with only two small bathrooms. Seemed like he'd spent half his youth waiting for somebody to finish blow-drying hair or soaking for hours in a bathtub or writing a novel or whatever the hell they did in there.

This was a different sort of wait, just moments before he expected to apprehend a suspect, and he never minded the anticipation.

The suspects in question didn't give him much time to savor the hunt. Only maybe a minute passed before he heard the rumble of a powerful engine in the cold night, then a dark extended-cab pickup passed him, fast enough that he could nail them for speeding if he couldn't find any other obvious evidence of criminal wrongdoing.

He waited until they took the next curve before he pulled in behind them. He eased closer and despite the snow that seemed to have picked up in the fifteen minutes since he left the school, he had a clear view of the vehicle, a late-model three-quarter-ton Dodge Ram with a lift kit and a roll bar.

He called in the license plate, still following at a sedate pace.

"Affirmative, Chief. That vehicle is registered to…um, Mayor Beaumont."

Oh, crap. Riley considered his options. He'd just left the mayor and Mrs. Beaumont at the Spring Fling, so neither could obviously be behind the wheel. What if their pickup had been stolen?

"Don't the Beaumonts have a teenage son?" he asked on a hunch.

"Yeah. Charlie. Seventeen or so, and a wild one, from what my girls say."

Charlie, you are in some serious trouble. He was close enough now that he could nail the little punk. He hit his flashing lights and accelerated.

For a moment, he thought it would be easy. After a few seconds, the pickup truck started to slow to around twenty-five miles per hour and Riley tried to focus on driving in the snowy conditions instead of the excitement pounding through him.

The truck didn't immediately stop, but Riley assumed Charlie Beaumont was looking for a good place to pull over on this fairly narrow road, with the mountains to their right and the reservoir a dark and sullen void across the oncoming lane to the left.

After perhaps two minutes at the slower pace, suddenly the pickup shot forward, fishtailing on the now icy road.

Shit. The idiot was a runner. And under these conditions, too.

He accelerated to keep pace while he picked up his radio again. "Suspect is fleeing. Unit in pursuit. Requesting backup. How far away is the sheriff's deputy?"

A male voice he didn't recognize answered. "Just approaching Silver Strike Canyon, Chief."

"Set up a roadblock at the mouth of the canyon. Don't let anybody in or out."

As soon as he spoke, he spied headlights heading toward them in the other direction from town and his insides clenched. Too damn late. Somebody was already coming this way. Possibly more than one vehicle.

As much as he wanted to catch the little punk who had run roughshod over his town—no matter how powerful his father might be—Riley had to consider the safety of pursuit when innocent civilians might be in danger. He had to stop the chase before someone was hurt. He would just have to keep his fingers crossed that the sheriff's deputies could set up the roadblock at the mouth of the canyon in time. Even if the kid slipped through, he knew where to find Charlie Beaumont.

Riley eased back and turned off his flashing lights to let the kid know he was curtailing pursuit, but the driver of the pickup, probably juiced up on adrenaline and heaven knows what else, didn't seem to care. The vehicle was still moving dangerously fast, especially on a curvy canyon road in the dark with those big fat snowflakes falling steadily.

After that, everything happened in a blur. At the next

curve, Charlie swung too wide, too fast, and veered into the other lane—directly in the path of the oncoming vehicle.

Riley saw headlights flashing crazily as that driver veered to the shoulder to avoid a head-on collision. He held his breath, hoping the other driver would be able to maintain control. For a second, he thought the other vehicle would make it safely back onto the roadway, but he didn't even have time to offer up a prayer before the vehicle somehow found a gap in the guardrails along the reservoir and a moment later the headlights soared over the side.

"Oh, shit, oh, shit, oh, *shit!*"

Riley hit the brakes and felt the patrol SUV's tires slither to gain traction. He turned into the skid and fought to regain control…and as he did, he vaguely registered the headlights of Charlie Beaumont's pickup were nowhere in sight. How had he escaped so quickly?

He picked up the mic and yelled for the sheriff's deputy to hold the roadblock and for the dispatcher to send emergency vehicles, that he had a vehicle possibly in the water. Without waiting to answer questions, he grabbed his waterproof flashlight and a crowbar from the trunk, then raced to the edge of the slope.

Snow stung his face, but he barely noticed as he scanned below into the dark water. Finally his flashlight picked up the shape of the vehicle about twenty feet from shore. It hadn't rolled, a good sign, but it was leaning nose-down toward the driver's side, submerged in water up to the bottom of the windshield.

Riley made his way down the snow-covered slope as quickly as he dared, sliding a little as he went. He was nearly to the bottom when he heard a voice from above, barely discernible over the wind.

"What can I do?" a man called from the road. "Need me to call for help?"

He didn't recognize the voice and couldn't make out the man's features from this angle. "I've done that already," he shouted back. "Keep an eye out and direct the ambulance."

Until he had a chance to assess the scene, he didn't want another civilian down here for him to worry about.

"Should I go check on the other guys?"

He paused in the act of shoving his flashlight into his waistband and removing his Glock 9 mm and holster. "Other guys?"

"Yeah. The pickup truck. He spun out and crashed into a tree just around the curve."

Riley's gut clenched. He'd been so preoccupied watching in horror as this car sailed into the water that he hadn't seen or heard the other vehicle's collision.

For a second he was torn about what to do, then he yanked off his other boot. As far as he was concerned, the suspects could rot while they waited for help. If Charlie Beaumont hadn't been such an asshole to run, none of this would have happened. Innocent victims got first dibs on rescue, that was his philosophy.

"Yeah, go check on them," he answered the man he now recognized as Harry Lange, although what the wealthiest man in town might be doing spying on intruders at his neighbors' house and responding to accidents in the middle of the night was anyone's guess. "Does your cell work this far up the canyon?"

"It's spotty but I might get lucky."

"Call 9-1-1 and tell the dispatch we've got two accidents to deal with and we're going to need all available units up here."

"Got it."

He was taking too long with this, while the occupants

of the vehicle in the water needed rescue. He just had to trust Lange would be able to reach dispatch to send more help. With a deep, steadying breath, he braced himself and headed into the water.

The shock raced through his nerve endings like ice blocks clamping hard around his feet and calves. He ignored it, pushed past it and waded out.

By the time he had crossed ten yards, the brutally cold water had reached his waist. Snow and wind whipped any exposed flesh and every breath seemed to slice at his lungs like tiny switchblades. He was aware of the bitter cold on some level, but mostly he forced himself to focus on what had to be done.

"Help us. Please, somebody, help us."

The desperate cry chilled him worse than the elements. By the sound of it, that was a kid's voice, a young girl, wet, cold, possibly injured.

Kids. Damn it.

"I'm coming. Hang on."

In the cloudy moonlight, he could finally make out the vehicle was a small SUV, a Toyota, by the look of it. He saw at least a couple of heads and now could hear other young voices crying. The sound of those desperate voices pushed him even faster and he finally just dived in and swam the remaining distance.

With icy hands, he pulled his flashlight from his waistband and aimed it into the vehicle window. He saw a form slumped over the steering wheel where a now-deflated air bag had deployed. He moved the light to the backseat and saw three pale faces staring back.

He tried to pull the doors open but they wouldn't budge because of the water pressing in. "Can you wind down the window?" he yelled.

"No, we tried. They won't work."

Power windows tended not to be real cooperative when the car's battery was submerged in four feet of water. He pulled out the crowbar, grateful for whatever instinct had prompted him to grab it. "Look, I need you to move away from the window and cover your face with your hands. I'm going to break the window, okay?"

"Okay." He heard the muffled response from inside.

"Are you all clear?"

"Yes."

Urgency lent him added strength and he slammed the crowbar into the window. It shattered and he brushed at the glass with his wet sleeve.

"I didn't think anybody saw us. I thought we would be here all night," the girl whimpered. He knew that voice, but he couldn't see her features very well. He aimed the flashlight to get a better look at possible injuries and everything inside him froze.

Macy Bradford.

One of the little figures she cuddled was her brother, Owen, and the other was the freckled, red-headed kid who had been with them at the pageant. Jordie something or other.

He jerked his attention to the motionless form in the front seat. "Claire? Claire, honey? Answer me."

She didn't respond, although he thought he heard a slight moan. He checked quickly for a pulse and found one there, a little thready but strong. He wanted to do a full assessment but his gut was telling him the first priority was to get the terrified kids out of the reservoir and back to shore, where he could now see other rescuers coming down the slope toward the water's edge.

"Are you guys hurt?"

"I'm cold. I cut my face," Jordie said through his scared sobs. "And my shoulder hurts."

"My arm hurts," Owen whimpered. "I think it's broken."

"I'm okay," Macy said, but Riley was pretty sure she was lying. He couldn't wait for stretchers to get here. Not in these conditions. It could be fifteen minutes or longer before the paramedics managed to make it up the canyon and he had no idea what was happening with the other accident.

He was going to have to trust his instincts and go against every stricture he'd ever learned about not moving accident victims who had been injured. Sometimes removing a victim from further injury was the only option and right now hypothermia and shock were both grave concern.

"Macy, I'm going to carry the boys to shore first and then I'll come back for you, okay? There are people who will help you make your way up to the road and get you all warmed up. Got it?"

"Is my mom gonna be okay?" Her voice shook with fear and his chest ached from more than just the effort it was taking to breathe through the bitter cold.

"I promise you, I will do my best to make sure of that. Hang on while I take care of the boys first. You keep talking to your mom while I'm gone, okay? You ready, boys?"

"Uh-huh." Owen sniffled as he slid across the seat. Riley scooped him up over one shoulder and then took the other boy over the other in a double fireman's hold, careful as he could manage of possible injuries.

The trip back through the water was surreal in the moonlight with snow swirling around the inky water. He almost fell once and would have dunked them all but he somehow managed to keep his footing. When he was almost to the shore, several people waded the rest of the way to take the boys from him.

"My wife's a nurse," the man who took Jordie said. "She's waiting on the shore."

"I think they mostly need to be warmed up, although one is complaining of arm pain and the other says his shoulder hurts."

Two of the rescuers carried the boys to shore, but the other one turned to Riley. "Is there anyone else out there?"

He was just a kid, Riley realized. "Two more, one with undetermined injuries."

"I'll help you get them."

He didn't want to endanger anyone else, but the kid was strong, muscled, like a bulldogger. Probably a rancher's kid, who bulked up by hefting hay bales and wrestling steers. "That would be great. If you can carry the girl to shore, I can check on her mom."

Riley hadn't been able to feel his feet for some time now and the snow was falling more heavily, joined now by a vicious wind that churned the water and blasted through his wet clothes. He didn't care. Not when Claire needed help.

"What's your name, kid?" he asked as they made their way back to the SUV.

"Joe Redmond."

There was a coincidence. Redmond was a common name around here, but he was quite sure the kid was somehow related to Lisa, his old girlfriend.

When they reached the SUV, Riley aimed the flashlight into the backseat and the kid made a sound of astonishment. "Mace? Is that you?"

"Yeah. Hey, Joey."

"My mom's gonna *freak* that you guys were the ones hurt."

"How's your mom?" Riley asked Macy.

"I think she might be waking up. I was trying to get her to talk to me and she moaned a few times."

"You did great, honey. Let's get you warmed up, okay,

and I'll take care of Claire from here. Joe, are you sure
you can carry her?"

"You bet. Come on, squirt."

He made sure Macy looked secure in the kid's arms
before he focused all his attention on Claire while they
headed for shore. "Claire? Honey, can you hear me?"

She moaned again, an encouraging sound.

"I need to break another window. I'm going to cover
your face, okay?" He had to hope she could understand
and wouldn't come back to full consciousness in a panic
that she was being suffocated.

He grabbed her scarf and managed to protect her face as
best he could before he hefted the crowbar and half waded,
half dragged himself around to the passenger side across
from her. This window was already cracked and it took
only a hard smack to shatter it completely. He was guessing
by the way the vehicle was tilted toward the driver's side
that the vehicle had landed on that side. Her body would
have absorbed most of the impact and it made sense that
her injuries would potentially be more severe than the children's in the backseat, who probably hadn't braced against
the crash like Claire would have done.

The water inside the car was up to her waist and she
was shaking violently despite her unconscious state. Guilt
crashed over him, colder and more vicious than the waves.
He should never have started the pursuit under these conditions. He should have just waited and set up a roadblock
at the mouth of the canyon to take care of it.

When he pulled the scarf away, she blinked at him and
her huge, dilated pupils and pale features ripped at his
heart.

"Cold," she moaned.

"I know, honey. I know. I'll get you out of here as soon

as I can figure out if it's safe to move you. Where do you hurt?"

She squinted at him, then closed her eyes and he saw blood oozing from her temple.

"What...happened?"

"Accident. You went off the road to avoid a head-on. You probably saved your kids' lives." He batted away the deflated air bag and worked on her seat belt.

A second later, she opened her eyes and started moving frantically. "My kids?"

"Hold still while I get this. They're okay. A little banged up, but they're over on dry land getting warm right now. They're going to be okay."

Her agitation subsided and she sagged against the seat. His radio squawked static and he fumbled with fingers that felt icy and useless to turn it down so he could talk to her.

"Where do you hurt, Claire?" he asked again, more firmly this time.

"Legs. Wrist. Um, head. Everywhere." The last word came out a whimper.

"I don't want to move you until we can get a stretcher out here, unless I absolutely have to. The ambulance should be here soon. We just have to wait it out here a few more moments."

"My kids. I need to take care of my kids."

"They're okay. Someone else is with them."

"Promise. Promise you'll make sure."

"I'll stay right here with you until you're out of the water and then make sure all of you are okay." He brushed a hand over her hair and saw blood oozing from a cut on her forehead. "Just hang on, sweetheart."

"This isn't fun."

Her ragged words somehow managed to shock a laugh out of him in spite of everything. He had never been so frigging cold in his life and he could barely breathe around the icy guilt pressing in on his chest. "No, I can't say that it is. I don't think it's supposed to be."

"First my store, now this."

"I know. You've had a pretty rough day. Got to rank right up there with the worst day ever."

"Stupid horoscope," she muttered, for reasons he didn't understand. He would have asked her, but nothing else mattered except making her safe.

Four

Where the hell were the paramedics?

Riley glared at the shore and the noticeable absence of flashing lights besides his own. He could see the flurry of activity as those on shore helped the children, but the ambulance was nowhere in sight. If this was the way the Hope's Crossing paramedics responded to emergencies, he was going to have to have a serious discussion with the fire chief about the response time of his crews.

"C-cold," Claire whimpered.

"I know, sweetheart. Hang on." He adjusted the blanket around her more snugly. Time was definitely not on his side. The longer she stayed out here in these frigid conditions, the greater the chance of hypothermia.

He'd forgotten how bitterly cold spring storms could turn in the high Rockies. It was the third week of April, for crying out loud, but the temperature had to be in the twenties, with a windchill making it feel much colder.

Claire was already shocky. She seemed to be fading in and out of consciousness and the wound just above her left temple where she must have hit the window was bleeding copious amounts. She needed to get the hell out of the water fast. All his protective instincts were urging him to pluck her out of the car and haul her to safety and it was killing him to just stand here helplessly. But given the extent of her injuries, he couldn't take the risk of injuring her worse. The best thing, the only thing, was to offer whatever comfort he could until the ambulance crew arrived with a gurney to transport her safely.

Her eyes closed again, and he grabbed her scarf for a makeshift compress to the cut on her forehead. "Claire, honey, you've got to stay with me. A few more minutes, that's all."

She moaned a little and he brushed her hair away again. "I know, sweetheart. I'm going to get you out of here. Just hang on."

He thought of how bright and lovely she had looked in her store earlier, even amid her distress at finding her store burglarized. Seeing her like this—scared and injured, like a frightened child—was heartrending.

She seemed to drift off again and he knew it was important that he keep her conscious and alert.

"Claire. Claire!"

Her eyes fluttered open with obvious reluctance.

"Tell me about String Fever."

"My store."

"I know. I saw it today, remember? I never expected you to be running a bead store. I thought you were going to be a teacher, like my mother. Isn't that what you went to college to do?"

She nodded a little. "I taught for a few years. Third grade. When… Macy…was little."

"So how did you go from that to running a bead store?" He didn't really care—okay, he found everything about her unexpectedly fascinating—but he mostly just needed to keep her talking.

The tactic seemed to be working. He saw a little more

clarity in her eyes and maybe even a hint of pride. "Worked for Katherine Thorne before…the divorce. Not for the money, just for fun. After… Jeff left…she asked if…wanted to buy it."

He pictured Katherine Thorne, sixty-six years old and a five-foot, ninety-eight-pound dynamo. Although tiny in stature and deceptively fragile in appearance, she packed a powerful force of will. Had Katherine really wanted to sell the store or had she only offered it to Claire to give a newly divorced, struggling mom something solid to hang on to? Knowing Katherine's generosity, he wouldn't be surprised.

He also hadn't missed Claire's phrasing. *After Jeff left,* she had said. He had assumed her divorce had been a mutual decision. He didn't know why he'd jumped to that conclusion, but Claire's subconscious at least didn't view the end of her marriage that way.

Although he was completely focused on Claire's precarious situation, some tiny corner of his brain couldn't believe any man could be such a moron that he would walk away from someone like Claire for a twentysomething bimbo.

Right now, it was a toss-up whether he was more furious with Jeff Bradford or the stupid little prick who caused the accident.

Her eyes flickered closed again and he cursed to himself. Where the hell were the paramedics?

"How do you like being a businesswoman?"

"Wh…what?"

"Your store. Do you like running it?"

"My store was robbed."

He didn't like how disoriented she sounded. "I know. The good news is, I think it's safe to say we found the bad guys."

He would have preferred a thousand unsolved crimes in his first month on the job to this outcome and he was kicking himself all over again for his handling of the pursuit when the flash of red lights finally heralded the arrival of paramedics on the scene.

Through the hazy filter of snow, Riley watched impatiently while the paramedics conferred on the bank of the reservoir before they finally returned to the ambulance for the gurney.

He spoke nonsense words to Claire while he waited for them. He couldn't have told anyone what he said. Something about how his mom and his sister were both going to kill him for making Claire stay out here in the cold water this long and about the house he was renting down the street from hers and about the trip he wanted to take somewhere hot—maybe down to the bowels of the earth at the bottom of the Grand Canyon—when this was all over.

Finally, just when he could feel her slipping back into unconsciousness and he was pretty sure he could no longer feel his legs, a couple of paramedics in wetsuits waded through the frigid water toward them.

"It's about damn time," he growled. "You stopped for coffee first?"

"Sorry, Chief." The first paramedic to reach him was some kid who looked barely old enough to drink, with blond streaked surfer hair and the raccoonlike goggle tan of a die-hard skier or snowboarder, didn't look thrilled to be reamed by the new police chief.

"Took us a while to make it around the other accident scene," the older one, dark with a bushy dark mustache, explained. "What have we got here?"

Riley put away his irritation to focus on Claire. "Female, age thirty-six, possible head, arm and leg injuries. Definitely in shock. I'm concerned about hypothermia, obviously, and also the head injury. She's been in and out of consciousness for the last ten minutes. Because I couldn't get a proper assessment of her injuries, I didn't want to move her without a stretcher, but if you guys had taken much longer, I would have figured something out on my own."

"We're here now." The older paramedic looked inside and Riley saw his eyes widen.

"Hey, there, Claire."

She opened her eyes slightly and then Riley realized why the guy looked familiar. It was a cousin of hers, Doug Van Duran, a couple years behind him in school.

"Hey, Dougie."

"You're in a real mess, Claire."

"I know." Her eyes were wide with confusion and panic as the paramedics' powerful flashlights shone into the vehicle. "My kids?"

"They're okay," Riley told her again. "Remember, I told you we got them to shore. Just relax and let the guys here take care of you."

He had to admit, despite their late arrival at the party, the paramedics seemed competent. He stood by and watched while they assessed her condition, stabilized her neck and back and then prepared to carefully remove her from the vehicle and transfer her to the gurney.

"We've got this under control, Chief, if you need to head down the mountain to the other scene," Van Duran said after a moment.

"I'll stay until Claire and the kids are in the bus before I check out the situation down there."

In the gleam of the other kid's flashlight, he didn't miss the careful look Doug aimed at him. "You sure about that? I mean, Claire's got some pretty bad injuries but they seem to be fairly straightforward and her kids are just banged up, from what I understand."

"Yeah. So?"

"I'm just saying, that's an ugly scene down there. One DOA and two serious injuries. While we were there, the sheriff was calling in Medivac."

Fatality. Damn it. He closed his eyes. How many kids had been inside that pickup truck? Yeah, they were robbery suspects and had stupidly chosen to run instead of facing the consequences, but nobody deserved to die because of a chain of idiotic choices.

"We can certainly use another man getting her out of the water, but we can make do without you if you need to head down to the other scene."

He should be on the scene of a fatal accident in his jurisdiction, especially one he'd been involved with, however inadvertent, but he couldn't leave Claire. Not yet.

"No, let's get her into the ambulance. I promised her and her kids I'd stay with her."

Over the next few moments, he was forced to retract every negative thought he'd had about the paramedics as he watched their quick, efficient efforts to extract her safely from the vehicle. But it still seemed like a lifetime before she was finally loaded onto the gurney and they began to wade back through the icy water.

The trickiest part—besides making his painstaking way through the water with legs that no longer felt attached to his hips—was safely maneuvering the rack up the slick, snow-covered slope from the water's edge to the roadway. When they finally crested the top, one of the passenger doors opened and a moment later, Macy Bradford rushed to them, her face white and scared in the snow-filtered light of the headlights and her eyes trained only on Claire.

"Mom!" she exclaimed.

Claire's eyelashes fluttered in the icy snowflakes as she tried to remain alert. "Macy. My brave girl."

"Are you okay?"

"I will be. You and Owen and Jordie?"

"I'm fine. We're okay. Some people wanted to take us to the hospital, but I...we wanted to wait for you."

Claire had been through hell and back and she was bloody and broken. But when she still managed to muster a smile for her daughter and reach for the girl's hand, Riley felt like something sharp and hard had just lodged against his heart.

"We've got to get her inside so we can roll," Claire's cousin Doug said, not unkindly, and they pushed the gurney up into the back of the ambulance.

Without warning, the moment the doors were closed behind her mother, Macy suddenly burst into noisy sobs. Even though Riley was exhausted and soaking wet, frozen to the bone, he placed a comforting hand on her shoulder. "She's going to be okay, you hear me? She'll be okay."

The girl drew in a deep, shuddering breath. "I was so scared."

"I know, honey. You've been a champ about this. Now we need to get you and the boys to the hospital. I'm going to see if I can round up another ambulance for you."

"We've got the boys safe and warm here. Do you want us to take them down the canyon to the hospital?"

He looked up at the voice and found the woman he had seen on shore standing beside her big Suburban, along with the boy who had waded out to help him. "I'm Barbara Redmond. I work at the hospital E.R."

Riley considered his options. If the other accident was as serious as the paramedics had indicated, it might be a while before another ambulance crew could make it for the children. Transported in a private vehicle, the kids could already be in a treatment room at the E.R. at the small Hope's Crossing Medical Center before the other crew could make it back up.

"Thank you. That will help."

The people of Hope's Crossing banded together in crisis situations, with everyone pitching in to help. He'd forgotten that in the years since he'd been gone. In some of the neighborhoods he worked in Oakland, accident victims faced a crapshoot, whether would-be rescuers would call for help or loot their pockets.

Riley made sure the children were safely buckled and settled and watched the SUV slowly pull back onto the road. Just as they made the first turn, he saw the brown and white of a Peak County sheriff's vehicle pull to a stop.

He estimated a half hour had passed since the accident, maybe an hour since he'd left the elementary school. For the first time in his life, he understood what people meant when they talked about living a lifetime in a few moments. He felt as if he'd aged at least twenty years since he sat and listened to the Spring Fling pageant with his older sister beside him.

The cold sliced through his wet clothing and Riley fought shivers as he watched a figure climb from the sheriff's department SUV. The sheriff himself, he realized. Evan Grover.

He tensed and instantly felt kickback from his already-aching muscles.

Evan Grover hated him and had since Riley was a punk-ass kid always in trouble and Grover was a wet-behind-the-ears deputy looking to make his mark. From what he understood, the sheriff had thrown his support behind J. D. Nyman and wanted him to be wearing the chief's badge.

The man headed toward him, his brown parka open over

his beer belly. All he needed was a cigar clamped between his teeth to complete the Boss Hogg imagery.

He shook his head. "Hell of a mess."

Riley ground his teeth together to keep his teeth from chattering. No way would he show that particular sign of weakness to the sheriff, even if he had frostbite in every appendage. "You could say that."

"The other scene." The sheriff whistled through his teeth. "Nasty."

He was a professional, Riley reminded himself. He'd been a cop a long time and had dealt with much worse than a two-bit sheriff who used to have it in for him. "I'll have to take your word. Haven't seen it yet. I'm heading down that way myself to assess the scene."

"No rush. Go ahead and change into dry clothes. My guys and the Colorado State Patrol have things in hand."

"Thanks," Riley gritted out. "I appreciate it." Neither department had jurisdiction because this road and the canyon were all part of the Hope's Crossing city limits, but this wasn't the time to be pissy over boundaries, not with a fatality.

The sheriff was acting entirely too conciliatory, which should have tipped Riley off that something was disastrously wrong. But he was still caught completely unaware by Grover's next words.

"I'm real sorry about your niece and all."

Everything inside Riley seemed to freeze. He didn't think it was possible for a person to be even more cold without turning completely to ice, but somehow he managed it. "Sorry, what?"

Grover stared at him for a minute, then he cursed, looking uncomfortable. "You didn't know yet."

"I've been standing in the middle of the reservoir for

the last twenty minutes. I don't know a damn thing. What are you talking about?"

The sheriff looked apologetic, his wide, weathered face a little more red than it had been a moment ago. Despite their history together, there was no malice in his eyes now, only sympathy.

"Thought you knew. The fatality in the other wreck. They're saying she's your niece. Your sister's kid. The one with the bookstore who was married to that rock star. Chris Parker. Sorry to break it to you so hard."

Layla? Not Layla. He pictured her the last time he'd seen her at his mother's house a week ago for dinner: her nose piercing and her battered combat boots and her choppy black hair. She was funny and smart and seemed to think he was among her cooler relatives because he'd lived out of the valley for so long.

He sagged a little, shaking violently now, and had to reach for the open door of his patrol car to support his weight.

He couldn't think, couldn't process anything but shock.

"Are you sure it's her?" he asked, then couldn't believe he sounded like every other victim's family he'd ever had to notify. He was aware of it on some level, but he couldn't help hanging on to whatever fragile, pathetic thread of hope he could find that maybe some terrible, cosmic mistake had occurred.

"Sorry, man. It's her. No question. You didn't hear the chatter on the radio?"

He remembered that moment he had turned it down out in the water. "No, not a word."

"She's been positively ID'd. A couple of the kids in the accident have only minor injuries and they confirmed the fatality was Layla Parker. The responding paramedics, uh, recognized her, too."

Maura. Poor Maura. How would she ever survive? And his mother, losing a granddaughter. His family had already suffered a vast rift. Did they have to endure this unspeakable loss, too?

"You probably need medical attention," the sheriff said after a moment, with surprising concern. Maybe he wasn't a complete asshole after all. "The paramedics said you've been in the water basically since the Bradford car went in."

Riley scrubbed at his face, unable to focus on anything but the crushing pain. "I'm all right. I just need to change my clothes."

"You need something dry to put on? I can probably find something in the back of my unit. Wouldn't come close to fitting, but I don't suppose that matters at this point."

"No, I should have something. Uh, thank you, Sheriff."

The words clogged in his throat, given their track record, but Grover only nodded.

"You should be with your family right now," he said. "Someone needs to tell your sister and your mom. Between my people and the state patrol, we should be able to take care of both scenes."

He was right. Damn it, he was right. Dread lodged in his chest as he gazed after the sheriff, who returned to his vehicle for crime scene tape and the digital surveying equipment necessary to document the accident scene.

Riley had made a few notifications in his career. Not many, but a few back when he was a beat cop. Nothing like this, though. Never in his worst nightmare had he envisioned this scenario, having to tell his sister that her daughter was dead, his mother that she had lost a grandchild.

Numb to the bone, he climbed into the patrol car and turned over the engine. Air blasted him from the heater, prickling over his wet skin, but it did nothing to warm the icy ball in his gut.

He thought of Claire and her children, frightened and cold and hurt, and then of the incalculable, inconceivable pain he was about to inflict on people he loved. Claire had been hurt—Layla was dead, for God's sake—because of him, because for a few heedless moments, he had been focused on taking down a suspect at the exclusion of all else.

The few whispers he'd heard around town since he'd been back seemed to ring in his head. Those who didn't want him in Hope's Crossing were right.

He didn't belong here. He never should have come home.

A terrifying sea creature clutched at her legs, yanking hard, tugging her down, down toward the inky, icy depths of Silver Strike Reservoir.

Her children. She had to get to her children. She fought the creature with all her might, pitting all the strength of a mama bear protecting her cubs. The creature howled, clamping down hard on an arm and a leg and tangling seaweed in her nose, around her face. He could have her, but damn it, she would *not* let him have her children. Claire fought harder, struggling against the constriction around her arm, gasping for air, fighting for her children's lives....

A sudden clatter and a muttered imprecation pierced the nightmare and Claire blinked awake, her heart still pounding in her chest.

She was disoriented for a moment and couldn't figure out why she hurt everywhere. Her mouth felt as if she'd been chewing newsprint and she had the vague sense of something being terribly wrong. For a long moment, she couldn't quite remember what.

"Oh, good. You're awake."

Her mother's face suddenly loomed large in her field of vision and Claire instinctively drew in a sharp breath.

For a moment, she couldn't figure out what was so different and then it hit her. For the first time in Claire's recent memory, her mother wasn't wearing makeup—not even the lipstick she seemed to put on just for a trip to the bathroom. Ruth looked haggard, her eyes red-rimmed and shadowed.

"The kids. Where…are they?" Her throat felt scraped raw and that tangle of seaweed tickled her nostrils again. A nasal canula, she realized dimly. She was in a hospital bed, hooked up to monitors and machines, on oxygen.

"They're fine," her mother said calmly. "Owen has a broken arm and Macy needed a couple stitches in her forehead and has general aches and pains, but other than that, they're just fine. Don't you worry about them right now. They've been staying with Jeff and Holly since the accident."

The single word triggered a sharp burst of memory, that snowy night after the Spring Fling, headlights flashing straight toward them in the darkness, her panicked jerk of the wheel to avoid a head-on…

And then, that terrible moment of sliding out of control, seeing the gap in the guardrail, knowing they were going over.

"Owen has a cast on his arm but that's all. Macy cut her forehead just a little, but Jeff doesn't even think she'll have a scar."

"Jordie?"

"Wrenched a shoulder, that's all. Nothing broken."

Claire sagged against the pillow. How much time had passed since the accident? A few hours? She glanced down and saw her left leg was in traction, a cast running from her toes to just below her knee. Her left arm sported a cast as well, a vivid purple against the white of the hospital sheets.

"You definitely had the worst of it," Ruth said. "Sheriff

Grover figures your car landed on the front driver's side when it hit the water and your body absorbed most of the impact. That's how you came to be so banged up while the kids are okay, for the most part."

Claire closed her eyes, a little prayer of gratitude running through her head. All she remembered thinking in that split second that had seemed to drag on forever was that she'd killed her children.

"They've been begging to come see you," Ruth said, fussing with the wrinkled edge of the blanket. "But I think Jeff has convinced them to wait until tomorrow, at least until you're not so disoriented from your surgeries."

"Surgeries?"

"Technically only one, I guess, but they did two things at once. They had to put pins in your arm and your ankle. You really did a number on yourself."

Usually Ruth would have made that sort of statement in an accusing sort of voice, as if Claire had given herself a bad perm or pierced her eyebrow, but her mother's quiet tone tipped Claire that something was off.

In addition to the hollow look in her mother's eyes, she was acting far more nurturing than normal. She hadn't yet made one complaint about how her knees were bothering her or how inconsiderate the nurses had been or about the bad food they served in the cafeteria. What wasn't Ruth telling her?

Had she broken her back or something? She tried to wiggle her toes and was almost relieved when that tiny movement—plainly visible at the edge of the cast—sent pain scorching up her leg.

"Ow."

"There, honey. Don't try to move. Let me call the nurse. You need pain medication. Trust me on this."

Before Claire could argue, Ruth had pressed a button

on the remote cabled to the bed. Almost instantly, the door opened and a young, fresh-faced nurse with a streaky blond A-line haircut and flowered hospital scrubs pushed open the door.

I used to babysit Brooke Callahan, Claire thought with some dismay. Could the girl really be old enough to legally operate that stethoscope?

"Hi, there." Brooke smiled sweetly and Claire felt about a hundred and sixty years old. "Look at you, sitting up and everything. That's so awesome! I can't believe how much better you look tonight than you did this morning when you came out of surgery."

Right now she felt like she'd just combat-crawled through heavy artillery fire. How bad must she have looked this morning?

"You're a popular person. The phone out at the nurses' station has been ringing off the hook all day with people who want to know if you can have visitors."

She didn't want visitors. She didn't want nurses or doctors or even her mother. She just wanted to lie here, close her eyes and go back to that moment when she'd been standing in line at Maura's place for coffee, when her biggest worry had been whether to use the fire-polished or the cone crystals on Gen Beaumont's wedding dress.

"She's nowhere near ready for visitors," Ruth said firmly, and Claire knew a tiny moment of ridiculous, obstinate contrariness when she wanted to tell little Brooke Callahan to let in whomever she pleased, especially Macy and Owen.

"Could I have a drink of water?"

Brooke was fiddling with the IV pump. She pressed a few buttons, then gave that cheery, toothy smile again. "Why, sure you can."

She scooped up a big clear plastic mug from the rolling hospital tray and held the straw to Claire's mouth.

"I could have gotten you that," Ruth said. "You should have asked."

Claire didn't answer, too busy remembering how delicious cold water could taste on a parched, achy throat.

"You probably feel terrible right now, don't you?" The soft concern in Brooke's voice unexpectedly brought tears to Claire's eyes.

She blinked them away and managed a shrug. She hated this, being helpless and needy. "I've had better days."

"You're due for more pain medicine. I'm going to add it to your IV."

"When can I go home?"

"That's for Dr. Murray to say. I'm guessing at least a few days, given your head injury and the surgeries."

Claire looked at her mother in surprise. "Not Jeff?"

"You know he can't operate on you because of your relationship. But he's been coordinating your care with Jim Murray."

"Dr. Bradford was just checking on another patient down the hall," Brooke offered as she checked Claire's vitals. "I'm sure he'll stop here before he leaves for the night."

Sure enough, the nurse was typing a few notes into the computer on a swing-arm beside the bed when the wide door opened and Jeff came in. His hair had as many blond streaks as Brooke's these days and was cut in a shaggy youthful style that seemed incongruous with his traditional green hospital scrubs and white lab coat.

She was pretty certain he'd had Botox sometime in the past few months, although she was also sure he would rather be tortured with his own scalpel before he would admit it.

"Hello. Claire. Ruth. Brooke."

The nurse gave him her cheery smile, but Claire's mother just lit up, like she always did around Jeff. Her mother adored the man. Claire sometimes thought Ruth considered her and Jeff's divorce the biggest tragedy of her life, even worse than the scandalous end to her own marriage.

Jeff barely looked at her, reaching instead for her chart. As he flipped through it with those familiar blunt fingers she had once loved, Claire sighed, wondering which felt heavier to her right now: the cast on her limbs or the weight of her own failures.

She was very glad she wasn't married to him anymore, for just this reason. She had mostly become invisible to him.

"You didn't operate on me."

He glanced up. "I assisted. Jim Murray was your surgeon. He's a good man. I've just been reading his report."

They were in the same practice, she knew, and she tried to summon a picture of Dr. Murray. A hazy picture formed in her head of a man who was slightly shorter than Jeff with a steel-gray mustache and kind eyes.

The beeper the nurse wore around her neck suddenly went off. She glanced at it, then turned to Jeff. "If you don't need me, Dr. Bradford, I've got another patient to check on."

"Thank you," he said. When she left, he reached for Claire's broken arm, lifted it and wiggled her fingers. For not being her treating physician, he was doing a fairly good impression of it.

"How are the children?" she asked when he turned his attention to her ankle.

"Just fine. I spoke with Holly a few moments ago and she said they had rested most of the afternoon, even Owen. She's making popcorn and when I get home we're going to watch a movie."

Claire felt that absurd urge to cry again. In that moment, she wanted to be cuddled up in her comfortable family room with her children eating popcorn and watching a dumb kids' show more than she remembered wanting anything in her life.

"You don't need to worry about them," Jeff said in that stern, listen-to-me-I'm-a-doctor voice of his. "You should be focusing on yourself."

She didn't know how to do that very well and probably never had.

"That car. The one that drove us off the road. Did the police ever find them?"

Ruth and Jeff exchanged looks and Claire thought she saw her mother give a slight shake of her head. "Don't worry about that now," Ruth said quickly.

"What does that mean?"

They were definitely keeping something from her, but she didn't have the energy to push. Claire really wished she could remember more than those few moments just before the crash and then that terrible moment of flying toward the water.

And Riley McKnight. Good grief. Why would she remember Riley?

Fragments of memory teased at her mind. A quiet voice soothing her, a cold hand smoothing her hair away from her face. Had Riley really been there or was she just mixing things up after seeing him first at her store and then later at the Spring Fling?

"How long will I have to stay here?" she asked Jeff.

"That's for Dr. Murray to decide. If you were my patient, I would probably keep you two or three more days post-op to get you through the worst of the pain and to make sure we don't see any complications from that head trauma."

"I can't stay here four days! The store!"

"You're going to be away from String Fever for more than four days, Claire." Her mother's tone was brisk. "At least three or four weeks. But don't worry, Evaline is taking care of things for you."

"Dr. Murray will go over this all with you, but you're going to have a difficult recovery," Jeff warned. "One ankle is broken, the other is sprained and you've got a broken ulna to boot. Mobility's going to be your biggest issue because you won't be able to use crutches very well at first due to your arm, or at least until the right sprained ankle heals a little. You're going to need help, Claire."

"Don't you worry," her mother said, squeezing her arm. "I'll move into the house with you and take care of everything. We can move you into that guest room you've got downstairs and I'll take your room."

She looked between the two of them and didn't know how to respond. The pain medication Brooke had given in her IV was beginning to take effect. Blessed oblivion lurked just on the edge of her consciousness, enticing her to just close her eyes.

"You rest now, poor thing," Ruth said. "That's the very best thing for you. Am I right, Jeff?"

"Absolutely." Her ex-husband brushed his streaky blond hair from his face, his face twisted into that unnatural botulism-toxin placidity.

Normally she would fight sleep with every ounce of strength she possessed, but right now even battling mystical water creatures in her medication-twisted nightmares was more appealing than contemplating the idea of having her mother living with her for the next few weeks.

She would worry about that later. As long as her children were safe, she could cope with anything.

Five

Hospital sleep was the worst. As she expected, her dreams were tortured and disjointed. Every time she seemed to drift off, the nurses would come in to make her move her arms and legs, to give her more meds, to check her vital signs.

When she awoke to pale morning sunlight streaming through the gap in the blinds that hadn't been fully closed, she was blessedly alone and only in moderate pain.

She gazed at that beam of sunlight and even though she wanted to stay there in the quiet peace of morning, she made herself revisit the accident. Something teased at her, some discordant note she couldn't quite place. Her mother wasn't telling her something and for the life of her, she couldn't figure out what.

With the subtle whir and beep of monitors in the background, she remembered that terrifying soar into the water again, her pain and overwhelming fear for the children, then Riley's quiet voice, offering strength and comfort.

She wasn't imagining. Somehow during the night, full recollection had returned. Riley had been there, out in that cold water with them. He had saved them. She considered it nothing short of a miracle that he'd seen them at all. That stretch of canyon could be sparsely populated at night. If they had gone off the road when no other cars had been in sight, they might have frozen out in that lake before someone else sighted them there below the roadway, trapped and helpless as the car filled with icy water.

She certainly wouldn't have had the strength to extract the children on her own, not with her injuries. If not for Riley, she didn't want to think what might have happened to them.

Riley. The most unexpected rescuer she could imagine. Teasing, tormenting, hell-raising Riley. Somehow he had been there right when she needed him and had risked his own safety to make sure she and the children were okay.

She hoped he hadn't suffered any ill effects from being out in the water so long. She should call Alex. Alex would know. Probably once the doctors allowed visitors today, one of the McKnights—Alex, Angie, Maura or even Mary Ella—would stop by to check on her.

When she heard a quiet rap on her closed door a moment later, she called out "Come in," expecting a nurse to bustle in with more antibiotics or a breakfast tray or something.

Instead, a tall, dark-haired figure appeared in the doorway as if she had conjured him with her thoughts. He wore a dress shirt and tie and a pair of slacks and had obviously dropped in on his way to the police station.

"Riley. Hi!"

In an instant, she was aware of how terrible she must look. Her hair was probably matted and tangled, she was wearing an oh-so-attractive hospital gown and she hadn't seen the inside of her makeup bag in thirty-six hours. She was mortified for just a moment, then gave herself a mental eye roll. She was alive. That was the important thing. She couldn't do anything about the rest of it anyway.

She must be feeling better if she could worry about her vanity, she thought, as Riley moved into the small hospital room, taking up more space than he should given the laws of physics and particle displacement.

"Hi. I hope I didn't wake you."

She worked the button on the bed that raised her head to more of a sitting position. "I've been up for a while. I was just thinking about you, actually."

Surprise flickered in the green of his eyes. "Oh?"

"I was hoping you didn't suffer any hypothermia or anything from the accident. You were in that water with us a long time."

"Nothing some hot coffee and a couple of blankets didn't take care of. I'm fine."

He didn't smile when he spoke and she again had that strange, instinctive sense that something was terribly wrong. Like her mother, he looked haggard and tired. A few more lines fanned from his eyes, a new tightness around his mouth.

"What about you?" he asked. "You're looking good."

She made a face. "And you used to be such a good liar."

Now he did smile, but it didn't reach his eyes as he pulled a chair over closer to her bedside.

"So what does the doc say? What are the damages?"

She thought of her conversation with Jeff and then later in the evening with Dr. Murray, who had indeed been kindly and avuncular. "My arm is broken in two places and my left ankle now has more hardware than the robot Owen built for his science fair project last fall. The right ankle is sprained. The head is okay. Mild concussion and only four stitches. Dr. Murray tells me to expect to feel like I was hit by a truck for at least a month."

His mouth tightened even more. "I'm sorry, Claire. So damn sorry."

The words seemed to vibrate through the room, much

more intense than just casual sympathy for an injured acquaintance. She frowned and studied him more closely.

Through those signs of exhaustion, she saw something else. Something that looked oddly like guilt. "Why do you say it like that?"

He was silent for a moment. "Do you know what caused your accident?"

"Yes. I remember that much. Some joker coming down the canyon took a curve too fast for conditions and veered into my lane. I swerved away to avoid him and went off the road."

"Right. That joker was a suspect trying to get away from me."

She blinked, aware of the machines beeping and the low buzz of activity outside, probably doctors beginning their rounds.

"A suspect? In what?"

He sighed. "Burglary. Multiple burglaries."

In all the craziness of the past few days, it had seemed natural to focus on the accident than on what had come before. "Of my store?"

"Yours and the others hit that night. I had a call about suspicious activity at a house that was supposed to be vacant. The suspect vehicle matched the description of the one seen outside the downtown businesses that were burglarized. I thought I could catch the suspects, maybe with stolen property. When I decided conditions weren't ideal for pursuit, I pulled back but it was too late. They were already spooked. If I hadn't been chasing him, that idiot Charlie Beaumont wouldn't have come around that corner like a bat out of hell and you wouldn't have had to swerve to avoid him and we wouldn't be here having this conversation."

She stared at him. "Charlie Beaumont?"

She pictured Genevieve's younger brother, small for his age and cocky and, like Riley had been, often in trouble.

"He was driving?"

Riley nodded and something bleak and cold swept across his features.

Her brain didn't seem to be working right. She couldn't seem to make the connections click together. "You're saying Charlie robbed my store and all the others in town?"

"He and…a few others."

That bleakness sharpened and she again wondered what she was missing.

"That's the theory we're going with," he went on. "So far the evidence seems to back it up. Charlie's not talking on advice from his attorney."

"Mayor Beaumont," she guessed.

He nodded. "But we have confessions from a couple of the other teens involved and they've led us to some of the stolen items."

"There must be a mistake. I know Charlie has had some trouble, but this is…crazy."

"No mistake," he said.

"But the Beaumonts are rolling in money. Why would Charlie need to take a computer and some spare change from my till? Why would he destroy his sister's wedding dress?"

"Who knows? The thrill of it, maybe? Whatever the reason, Charlie and the others are in serious, serious trouble. I'm sorry you were tangled up in it. One of those wrong place, wrong time kind of things."

She thought of the weird confluence of events that had led her to the canyon at that moment, of Jordie's parents falling ill, of her spontaneous offer to take him home from the Spring Fling, of the late-spring snowstorm that hit so fast and so hard.

"You probably thought Hope's Crossing would be tame compared to what you left in Oakland."

His jaw tightened. "I certainly didn't expect this."

"Okay," she finally said, exasperated with all the layers of subtext that seemed more treacherous than the imaginary tendrils of seaweed in her nightmares. "What aren't you and everyone else telling me?"

His features turned wary. "Why would you think I'm keeping something from you?"

"I have two children, Riley. I've got a built-in lie detector. It's part of the mom job description."

He looked surprised. Good. That was better than that bleak sadness in his eyes. "You're comparing the behavior of your two children trying to get out of trouble to a cop who spent the last five years undercover, lying to keep from being stabbed in his sleep?"

She didn't like thinking about his life before he came home, but that still didn't keep her from picking up on his tactics. "My children also seem to think that if they distract me by changing the subject, I'll forget my train of thought. What aren't you telling me?"

He studied her for a long moment and then released a long, slow breath and looked away. "After he ran you off the road, Charlie Beaumont crashed his pickup a little way down the canyon. Rolled it and hit the trees."

She gasped and the movement hurt her head. "Oh, no. Tell me everyone is okay."

He didn't answer and she shifted on the bed, pulling the blankets higher against the sudden chill.

"They're not okay," she said when his silence stretched on and she didn't need to see the confirmation in his eyes to know she was right.

"A few of them had only minor injuries."

"But?"

For a long moment, she didn't think he would answer her. When he did, his voice was weary and his eyes held a deep sorrow. "Two girls were thrown from the vehicle. One sustained severe head trauma and had to be airlifted to the children's hospital in Denver. And…another one didn't make it."

Claire's hand clenched convulsively on the blanket. How could she lie here feeling sorry for herself, worrying about her store—about her *vanity* for heaven's sake—when a mother somewhere had lost a child?

"Who?" she whispered.

"You don't need to worry about this, Claire. You just need to focus on yourself."

"Who?" she demanded more forcefully.

He sighed. "Taryn Thorne is the girl with the head injuries."

"Oh, poor Katherine!"

Her friend adored her only granddaughter, fifteen and slender and turning into a beauty with her big dark eyes and long dark hair.

Taryn sometimes came into the store. Just the week before, Claire had helped her make a pair of custom earrings for a school dance.

What was Katherine going through? Claire suddenly hated that she couldn't help her friend through this, that she was stuck here in a stupid hospital bed instead of offering solace and aid to Katherine when she needed it.

"And the other girl?" she finally asked, not sure she wanted to hear the answer.

Riley didn't answer for a long time, that bleakness turning his eyes a wintry green.

"You don't need to worry about this right now."

"Stop saying that. Tell me. Please, Riley."

He finally spoke in a voice so low that she almost didn't hear him. "Layla."

When the name finally registered, icy disbelief crackled through her. Layla. Maura's daughter. Riley and Alex's niece. Mary Ella's granddaughter.

Layla, who had worked in her store sometimes in exchange for beads to make the funky Goth jewelry she adored.

"No. Oh, no. Oh, poor Maura."

Her throat was heavy and tears spilled over and she was only vaguely aware of Riley reaching for her uncasted hand.

"I shouldn't have told you. I'm sorry, Claire. You need your strength to recover, not to worry about Maura and the rest of us left to grieve with her."

She wept then, noisy, painful tears that clogged her throat and burned her eyes and hurt her heart. Through it all, Riley held her hand in both of his, looking tortured. She wanted him to hug her as he'd done that day in the store, but she knew he couldn't, not with her casted arm awkward and heavy between them.

He handed her the box of tissues and she must have used half of them before the storm of tears gave way to a deep, primal ache.

"How is your family?" she finally asked.

"Hanging in. We McKnights are tough, but this is…"

"Unimaginable."

"Yeah."

"I'm sorry, Ri. This isn't what you expected."

"No, I'm—"

Whatever he was going to say was cut off when the door swung wide and her mother bustled in carrying one of Claire's beaded bags and her arms loaded with magazines and books.

Ruth stopped in the doorway and did a double take Claire might have found funny if she hadn't been staggering under the weight of her grief for Layla.

"What do you think you're doing here?"

Riley blinked a little at Ruth's outrage, then he shuttered any expression.

"Visiting Claire. I thought she might want to know the status of the investigation into the break-in at her store."

Claire didn't care anymore. She would have gladly endured the violation and outrage of hundreds of burglaries if it meant Layla could still be alive, with her black-painted fingernails and the mascara she would layer on with a trowel.

Ruth squinted at Claire and the scattered tissues on top of the blanket. She advanced on Riley, her features furious. "You told her, didn't you?"

This was what her mother had been keeping from her, Claire realized finally, why she was drawn and upset. She had said nothing to Claire yesterday, had prevented Jeff from telling her, as well.

"Yes," Riley answered. "She asked. I answered."

"You had no right. No right!"

"Why didn't *you* tell me, Mother? Maura is my friend. Alex is my *best* friend. I needed to know. You shouldn't have tried to keep it from me."

Ruth bristled and looked offended, an expression she wore with comfortable familiarity. "I didn't want to upset you. You've been through a terrible ordeal."

"A few broken bones, which will heal," Claire shot back. "I didn't lose a child!"

Ruth aimed another vitriolic look at Riley. If her mother hadn't already disliked him, she would loathe him now for going against her misguided wishes.

"What good does it do for you to know right now? You would find out soon enough. Look at how upset you are."

Ruth would never understand that Claire was angry at *her* for withholding the information, not at Riley. With her classic myopia, her mother could always figure out a way to make herself the injured party in any conflict, so why bother trying to explain?

"I'd better go. I've got to head down to the station."

He seemed so different from the teasing, flirtatious man who had come into her store after the robbery and her heart ached. "I'm so sorry, Riley," she murmured, knowing the words were grossly inadequate, but they were all she had available. "Thank you again for everything that night."

"I'm glad you're doing better. Take care of yourself, Claire."

She nodded and watched him go, then settled in to face an exhausting day of busybody nurses and poking, prodding doctors and, worse, having to cope with her mother.

"Are you sure you're okay back there?" Jeff met her gaze in the rearview mirror.

Claire shifted on the backseat of his Escalade, trying to ignore the pain shooting through her muscles with every rotation of the tires.

She hugged Owen to her and reached across his back to hold Macy's hand. What were a few bumps in the road when she finally had her children close?

"I'm fine. It's only a fifteen-minute drive anyway."

"You really should have taken the front seat." Seated beside Jeff, Holly leaned around the headrest and gave Claire a stern look.

She was absolutely right but Claire refused to give her the satisfaction of agreeing. It had been stupid to insist on taking the backseat, where she didn't have nearly enough legroom for a cast. She had to stop literally bending herself in half to make everyone else happy.

"But then I would have missed the chance to sit by the kids and I've missed them like crazy."

She forced a smile and somehow managed to keep it from wobbling away when Jeff hit one of the town's legendary late-spring potholes and the subsequent lurch sent her meager hospital lunch sloshing around her insides.

It was only the pain pills making her nauseated, she knew. That and the fact that she was actually in motion again after being confined to her hospital room for nearly five days.

"It looks as if most of the snow has finally melted."

Indeed, with the capriciousness of a Rocky Mountain spring, the temperature during her brief trip from the wide hospital front doors to Jeff's backseat had been mild and pleasant. Outside the car window, she saw children playing on muddy lawns already beginning to turn a pale green and as Jeff turned onto Blue Sage Road, she enjoyed the sight of the bright yellow and red tulips beginning to bud in Caroline Bybee's always-spectacular garden.

"It's about time," Macy groused. "It seems like winter went on *forever* this year."

"I know, right," Holly said. "I mean, Sunday is Easter and everything. I was thinking we'd have to hide eggs in the snow this year."

That wasn't an uncommon occurrence in Claire's memory. In the high Rockies, Hope's Crossing had been known to see heavy snowstorms into late May, but usually by the first of April, most of the remaining snow was up at the higher elevation of the ski resort.

"I'm glad it's warmer today, for Maura's sake," she murmured.

Except for those children they passed, the streets appeared quiet, almost deserted. Most of the year-round residents of Hope's Crossing would be at the funeral for Layla Parker. Ruth was there, which was the sole reason Holly and Jeff were the designated drivers taking Claire from the hospital to home.

Her mother couldn't miss the funeral, not when she'd been friends with Mary Ella since they were girls. Claire understood that and had chosen to bite her lip and say nothing when Ruth arranged with Jeff and Holly to take her home from the hospital without consulting her on the matter. She would have preferred to call a taxi. Okay, truth be told, she would rather have tried to wheel herself the four hilly miles from the hospital to home rather than be dependent on her ex-husband.

"Careful on those bumps, honey." Holly rested one of her perfectly manicured hands on Jeff's arm. "Maybe you should slow down a little."

"It's fine. I'm only going twenty-two miles per hour. It's a thirty-five zone."

If he were speeding, he would still probably be safe from a ticket because Riley and most of his police department would probably be at the funeral with the rest of the town.

"How's everything been at home?" she asked Macy quickly.

"Okay. While you've been in the hospital and we've been staying at Dad and Holly's, I've been stopping at the house to take in the newspaper and the mail after school."

"We dropped Chester off at the house before we went to the hospital. He's super-excited to be back home."

She could imagine. Holly wasn't a big dog lover and probably insisted their poor aging basset hound sleep in the cold garage.

"You should have seen him, Mom. He went through

every room, wagging his tail like crazy. You'd think he'd
been gone a month instead of just a few days."

If Claire had possessed a tail, she would probably do
the same thing when they reached her house, she was that
eager to be home. She couldn't wait to be in her own space
again.

Had it really been only five days since the accident?
She felt as if she'd lived a dozen lifetimes in those days.

"I still think it's too early for you to be going home."
Jeff frowned at her in the rearview mirror.

"I'm afraid you're going to have to take that up with
Dr. Murray. He's the one who signed the release papers."

"You can't take care of yourself. Geez, Claire, you can't
even get to the bathroom on your own."

She forced herself to smile patiently, even as she fought
the urge to remind Jeff that while he had the right to his
opinions, she no longer had to listen to them. Truly one
of the better things about not being married to the man
anymore.

"Ruth will be staying at the house the first few nights.
She's insisting."

Unfortunately, she hadn't divorced her mother. It was
a little tougher to ignore Ruth's opinions, much as she
would like to.

While Claire just wanted to go home and crawl into
bed for a few weeks, yank the covers over her head and
forget the rest of the world existed, she had two children
who still needed to eat and do their homework and feed
the dog. Pity parties were for women without obligations.

She had to be realistic about her limitations. Jeff was
correct. Just taking care of herself was going to be enough
of a challenge.

Having her mother there for a few days would be a
big help. For a short time anyway, she could endure her

·mother harping on everything from the smelly dog to Owen's muddy tennis shoes in the hall to the bad haircut of the news anchor on her favorite channel.

Claire had already resolved that she would simply grit her teeth and think how grateful she was that she still had a mother who cared about her and who was willing to step in for a few—and only a few, please God—days.

"What about after she leaves?" Holly asked. "Would you like me to stay with you for a few days? I would be more than happy to."

Claire offered a weak smile while her insides writhed at the idea. The only thing worse than Ruth in her space for a few days would be *Holly,* all big teeth and perfect hair and her desperate need for Claire to be her friend.

"That's a lovely offer, Holly. Really. Thank you. But I'm sure by the first of next week, the kids and I will have figured things out together and I should be a little more self-sufficient. Anyway, you don't need the stress of worrying about somebody else right now. You need to take care of yourself and the little one."

"I *have* had contractions every day since the accident," she confessed, looking so young and worried that Claire was compelled to offer what little comfort she could.

"I'm sure they're simply Braxton-Hicks. Nothing to worry about," she said.

"That's what I've told her." Jeff gave his young wife a fond, indulgent sort of look. "She thinks just because my specialty is orthopedics, I've forgotten my OB-GYN rotation. Not to mention the fact that I've been through this twice before."

If Claire remembered correctly, *she* was the one who'd been through this twice before, but the whole situation was just too strange for her and she wasn't in the mood to point that out.

Jeff turned onto Blackberry Lane just then and a moment later pulled into the driveway, sparing her from having to come up with an answer.

For a moment, Claire just wanted to sit here and gaze at the wonderful familiarity of her house, bricks a weathered red, that charming porch out front, the ironwork fence with the arrowed finials around the perimeter of the yard.

She loved this house and had for years, long before the day she and Jeff made an offer on it three years ago. It was hers alone now, hers and the children's, but she had never been so happy to be there.

Making her way from car to house was a bit of an ordeal. Beyond the difficulties of the transfer from the backseat to the wheelchair she was stuck in for a few weeks at least, her front door had four steps, too many for the portable folding ramp Jeff had wangled from somewhere. Owen finally suggested they use the back door leading to the kitchen because it only had two steps and a slightly larger doorway for the wheelchair, and finally Macy pushed her inside and she was home.

Chester gave a happy bark of greeting—as happy as his barks could sound anyway—but then he freaked out at something, maybe her cast or the sight of the wheelchair, and headed for his safe zone under the kitchen table.

"It's okay, buddy," Owen cajoled. "Come on out. It's just Mom."

"He'll get used to it," Claire said, although she'd been dealing with the whole thing for five days and *she* still wasn't used to it all.

"He's not coming. What a dorky dog." Macy shook her head. "Maybe you should try one of his treats."

As much as she loved Chester, Claire was too achy and exhausted right now to care much about showing up on the dog's popularity list, but because it seemed so important to the kids, she took the treat Macy handed her from the pantry and held it down at the dog's eye level.

Chester hesitated for only a moment before he waddled to her side for the treat, then started sniffing the wheels of the chair and her outstretched toes sticking out of the cast.

"As we talked about at the hospital, you're several weeks from being able to tackle the stairs in this house," Jeff said rather pompously. "We've moved some of your things down to the guest bedroom."

"I know." That part she didn't mind. The guest room was actually one of the nicer rooms of the house, with an en suite bathroom and wide windows overlooking the mountains. She had created such a comfortable little spot there that even after the divorce, Jeff's parents still preferred staying with her whenever they came to visit from their house in Arizona, much to Holly's chagrin.

"We like to be closer to the children," JoAnn had tried to explain to Holly during their last visit, but Claire suspected even after their new grandchild was born, the Bradfords would prefer this place, with its sunny garden and basketball hoop in the driveway to the glass and cedar showplace Jeff and Holly had built up in Snowcrest Estates.

"I brought down all your pillows and your favorite quilt," Macy said. "The Western Star that your Grandma Van Duran made when you were a little girl. Holly helped me put fresh sheets on the bed for you."

"Thank you. Both of you." Claire managed a smile.

"You need to rest now," Holly said sternly. "Jeff and I will stay here with the children until the funeral is over and your mother can get away and come here."

"Can I drive you in?" Owen asked.

She smiled at her eager-to-please eight-year-old. "Of course."

With care and concentration, he maneuvered the chair

through the doors, which were just wide enough for it to fit. She was definitely going to have to come up with another solution than this wheelchair or all the lovely historic woodwork of the door frames she had worked so hard to refinish would be dinged and scraped.

As soon as she reached the bed and started the complicated process of transferring from the chair, she realized with not inconsiderable dismay that she would have to change into a nightgown from the skirt and cotton shirt her mother had brought to the hospital for her trip home.

The enormity of the task, given the cast on her arm, completely overwhelmed her. "Can you send Macy back to help me change?" she asked Owen.

"Don't be silly," Holly exclaimed from the doorway, where she and Jeff had apparently followed them. "I'll help you."

She absolutely did *not* want her ex-husband's young, adorably pregnant wife helping her, but she didn't exactly have a lot of options here. "Thank you," she murmured.

When Jeff made no move to leave, Claire raised her eyebrows. It was an awkward situation all the way around. Although they had been married for ten years and had once been as intimate as two people could be with each other, that was in the past and she wasn't changing clothes in front of him.

Jeff finally clued in and cleared his throat. "Come on, Owen. Let's go see what we can find for lunch. You hungry?"

They left, closing the door behind them, leaving her and Holly alone.

While Claire did her best with the buttons on her shirt, Holly immediately went to the mirror-topped antique dresser and pulled out one of Claire's nightgowns she and Macy must have brought down.

"I have to admit, it's weird for me to see you this way," Holly said.

"What do you mean?"

Holly gestured to the wheelchair and the hospital bed Jeff must have arranged to replace the queen normally in the room. Claire didn't think that was strictly necessary, although she supposed it would help with transfers from the bed to the wheelchair. "I don't know. Needy, I guess. You're the most together person I know. It's just…different to see you otherwise."

"It's not so comfortable for me, either," she said.

"I'm sorry," Holly said quietly. "Really sorry. It must be hard for you."

"Yes," she admitted with reluctance.

"Well, don't worry about it. I'm glad to help. Let's get you more comfortable."

Few moments in Claire's life were as excruciatingly humiliating as being forced to sit, helpless and weak, as her ex-husband's young and beautiful new wife helped her into the loose cotton nightgown.

Holly was actually very considerate and kind about the whole thing, to her relief, but by the time they finished Claire was exhausted and humiliated and could only think about another pain pill. Unfortunately, she wasn't due to take a dose for a few hours yet. She was vigilant about keeping to the correct schedule, afraid of becoming dependent. She didn't know if it was a genetic predisposition, but her mother's dark history was entirely too vivid in her memory.

"There you are, Claire," Holly said when she was finally settled into the bed, the soft quilt tucked to her chin. "Does that feel better?"

"Yes, thank you."

"It's no trouble." She smiled. "If you want the truth, it's kind of nice to have you lean on me for a change instead of always the other way around. You just rest now. Come on, Chester. Let's go."

Claire hadn't realized the dog was there, as well. She opened one eye and spotted his pudgy grumpiness circling around the rug beside the bed, preparing to settle in.

"No, leave him."

Holly frowned. "Are you sure? He can be such a bother."

"I'm sure."

Holly looked skeptical but she shrugged. "Do you need anything else? Water? A book or something?"

"Only my cell phone over on the dresser, please."

She needed to try again to call Maura after the funeral. Every day since the accident, she had tried numerous times, but Maura wouldn't answer the phone. Claire couldn't blame her. She was sure her friend was overwhelmed right now and the last thing she wanted to do was talk on the phone and endure more platitudes. Until Claire could make it in person to see her friend, the phone would have to do and she vowed to keep calling until Maura would talk to her.

"Thank you for taking care of the children so I don't have to worry about them."

"You're welcome. Really." Holly smiled and left the room, closing the door behind her.

Claire scooted as far as she could to the right side of the bed and reached down with her good arm. Chester licked at her fingers for a moment, then nudged at her to be petted.

She scratched his warm fur and thought about how much she hated being on the receiving end of help until she fell asleep.

"What was that man thinking? You can't stay there by yourself. I'm coming over."

Claire shifted her weight on the couch, holding the

phone with one hand while she reached to rub the pain above her left eyebrow and bumped her head with plaster.

After nearly two weeks with the stupid thing, one would think she would remember it was there but she still found she forgot at odd moments.

"That's not necessary, Mom. You don't need to come over. I'm fine. Jeff must think so, right? Otherwise he and Holly wouldn't have taken the kids to Denver for the weekend."

"That doesn't mean anything. He doesn't have a bit of sense when it comes to Holly. If she said she wanted to take the kids to Denver, he would take them even if you were lying unconscious on the floor when they left."

Claire blinked. Wow. That was unusual—for her mother to actually criticize her ex-husband. "Even Dr. Murray was happy with the way I'm healing," she said. "Between the walker and the rolling office chair Alex rigged up for me, I can get anywhere on the main floor on my own and I'm keeping my fully charged cell phone on my person at all times."

"I don't care. I still don't like the idea of you alone in that big house, especially on a night like tonight."

Claire gazed outside at the rain sharply pelting the windows, hurled by the gusting canyon winds. For more than a week, Hope's Crossing had seen lovely weather, which she'd been forced to enjoy from inside while she recuperated. Today had been overcast and cheerless, though, and an hour ago the wind and rain had started in earnest.

She had been looking forward to popping a bag of popcorn in the microwave and enjoying the rainstorm by herself, the first time she had truly been alone since the accident.

She had been home from the hospital for a week and had spent that time constantly surrounded by well-meaning friends. When Ruth wasn't able to be there, she made sure someone else could stay. Evie or Alex or Angie or one of a half-dozen other friends.

Claire was grateful for all they'd done for her. Alex had coordinated so many meals that Claire now had a refrigerator and freezer full of food. Other friends had taken her shopping list to the store for her and brought back an armload of supplies and still another coordinated the car pool for the children so Claire didn't need to worry about getting them to soccer or piano lessons. She knew from her one brief stilted phone call with Maura two days earlier that her friend was receiving much the same.

Claire was deeply grateful for all the help, but she was desperate for a moment to herself just to think.

Ruth didn't seem to agree. "I don't like this. Not a bit. What if you fall down? You could lie there all night and no one would even know. I'll just come and sleep upstairs in your room again and you won't even know I'm there."

"I'm not going to fall. And remember, I've got my phone with me constantly. If I need help, I can call, email or text someone for help in a second."

"Not if you're unconscious."

She held the phone away from her ear and screwed up her eyes, fighting the urge to bang the phone a few times against her head.

After the past six days, she should be an expert on dealing with overprotective people. Her mother, Holly, even the children had joined in the coddling action.

"I'll be fine, Mom," she repeated. *If I trip in the bathroom and break my neck, you'll be the first one I call.* "I'm just going to sit here on the sofa and watch a DVD for an hour and then go straight to sleep, I swear. There's absolutely no need for you to come over. I know how much you hate driving in this weather."

Her mother hesitated a little at that and Claire knew she had pushed exactly the right button.

Ruth didn't like driving at night or in snow or rain—a definite inconvenience when one chose to make a home in the high country of the Rockies. If she had to go somewhere during stormy weather, she inevitably would call Claire for a ride.

"Are you sure?" Claire heard the note of hesitation in her mother's voice and mentally breathed a sigh of relief.

"Positive. I'll be perfectly fine. I've got Chester to keep me company and enough leftovers in the house to last me until July."

Ruth waffled for a few more moments before she finally caved. "All right. Because I guess you don't want my company, I'll stay put."

Claire refused to feel even a twinge of guilt for the slightly hurt note in her mother's voice.

"But call me if you change your mind and decide you want me there."

"I will. Thanks, Mom. Good night."

Her mother hung up and Claire closed her eyes and leaned her head against the couch, just relishing the silence, broken only by Chester's snores on the floor beside the couch.

Dealing with her mother always exhausted her. Sometimes she was deeply jealous of the easy, comfortable relationship Alex and her sisters had with Mary Ella. Claire wanted that, too, but it seemed like every interaction with her mother ended in weary frustration that Ruth could be so needy and demanding.

Ruth hadn't always been like that. Before her father's scandalous death, Claire remembered her mother as a strong, funny, independent woman. Someone very much like Katherine Thorne.

When Claire was eight or nine, her mother had been the PTA president during a tumultuous time when some in Hope's Crossing had been trying to gather support to build a new elementary school. Claire had vivid memories of her mother speaking out with vigor and eloquent prose about the importance of educating young minds in a safe, clean environment.

The memory always made her sad because of the stark contrast between that capable woman and what her mother had become later.

Claire sighed, reaching for the rolling office chair she had found much more convenient than the wheelchair she'd brought home from the hospital. She transferred to it and scooted with her healing sprained ankle into the kitchen, where she opened the refrigerator and scanned the contents for something appealing to warm for her dinner. She finally settled on some of the sinfully divine cream of potato soup Dermot Caine had brought over from the diner a few days earlier—perfect for a cold, stormy night.

She dished some into a bowl, grateful the children hadn't unloaded the dishwasher before they left or she would have had a struggle trying to reach the plates and bowls in the upper cupboard.

As she waited for the soup to warm in the microwave, her thoughts returned to her mother.

She could pinpoint exactly the moment Ruth had changed. April twentieth, twenty-four years ago, 11:42 p.m. She had been twelve years old, her brother eight, the same ages her kids were now. The night had been rainy, like this one. She remembered she had been sleeping when something awakened her. The doorbell, she realized later. Claire had blinked awake and lain there in bed, listening to the branches of the big elm click against the window in the swirling wind and wondering who could be ringing the doorbell so late and if her father would be angry with them because he always rose early for work.

And then she'd heard her mother cry out, a desperate, horrified kind of sound. With a sudden knot of apprehension in her stomach, Claire had opened her door fully and sidled out to the landing, looking down through the bars.

She had recognized the longtime police chief, Dean Coleman, but had been able to hear only bits of his hushed conversation.

Dead. Both shot. Jealous husband. I'm sorry, Ruth.

Everything changed in that moment. Gossip roared faster than a wind-stirred fire. Even though the adults in her life had tried to keep it from her and her brother, their children heard and absorbed snippets about the scandal and a few of them had delighted in whispering about it loud enough so they knew that Claire would overhear.

Her father—the man she had adored, president of the biggest bank in town, a leader of church and community—had been having a torrid affair with a cocktail waitress at the Dirty Dog, the sleazy bar outside of town.

Apparently the woman had a jealous husband, a biker thug by the name of Calvin Waters. When he came home early one night, he caught them in bed together. In a drunken rage, he shot them both with a sawed-off shotgun before turning the gun on himself.

The scandal had exploded in Hope's Crossing. She could still remember those awful days as she had endured stares and whispers and hadn't known what to do with all the anger and shame inside her—or with the grief for her lost innocence.

Claire and her brother had endured those first difficult months by keeping a few friends close and basically sticking their heads down and plowing through.

Ruth, on the other hand, had completely fallen apart.

She had taken to her bed for several months after the scandal, addicted to alcohol and the Valium doctors had prescribed her for sleep.

Left with little choice, Claire had stepped up to take care of the three of them. She had been the one who did laundry, who fixed lunch for her younger brother, who walked him to school and helped with his homework and comforted him when he cried for a mother who had been too absorbed in her loss and humiliation to see her children needed her, too.

Claire knew now, taking charge of her flailing family had been her way of dealing with the chaos.

She sipped at her soup, wishing the rich, creamy taste could wipe away the bitter memories. Ruth had lived in that numb state for about six months, until Mary Ella and Katherine and other friends had forced her to break free of her addiction.

She had fought it with courage and strength and Claire would always admire that in her mother. But even after rehab, Ruth had continued to rely on Claire to make sure her life flowed smoothly.

Claire knew she bore plenty of responsibility for the patterns they had fallen into. Even when she had lived away from Hope's Crossing while Jeff was in medical school, she had handled any crisis of Ruth's long-distance, whether that was dealing with a parking ticket or a doctor bill or calling a plumber to repair a leaky faucet.

She could justify to herself that if she didn't take care of things, her mother's life would fall back into chaos, but she knew that was only an excuse. This was her way of feeling needed, important, to a mother who had basically forgotten her children amid her own pain.

With a sigh, she set down her soup. She wasn't hungry after all. She would just watch the movie, she decided.

She wheeled the chair to the sink and rinsed the bowl, reaching the switch on the disposal only with the help of a large soup ladle.

She headed back to the family room and turned on the movie, eager for any kind of distraction from her thoughts. The movie apparently worked too well. She barely remembered the first scene—when she awoke some time later, the credits were rolling and Chester was standing in the doorway, his hackles raised.

"What's the matter, bud?" she asked.

He gave that low-throated hound howl of his and scrambled for the front door, his hackles raised and his claws clicking on the wood floor.

Claire frowned but curiosity compelled her to transfer to her rolling office chair and follow him. Chester wasn't much of a watchdog but he would sometimes have these weird fits of protectiveness. Probably just the Stimsons' cat or maybe a mule deer coming out of the mountains to forage among the spring greens. For all she knew, her silly dog could be barking at the wind that still howled.

"Come on, boy. It's okay. Settle down."

Still, the basset hound stood beside the door, that low growl sounding somehow ominous in the silent house.

Claire maneuvered down the hallway after him until she reached the window beside the front door, set just low enough that she could peek over the sill from her seated position.

She squinted into the darkness and caught a flash of movement that materialized into a dark shape there on the porch.

Her heart skittered.

Someone was out there.

Six

Claire could hear her pulse pounding in her ears, but she quickly tried to talk herself down.

She was seeing things. A trick of the wind or a shadow or something.

And even if she *wasn't* seeing some weird hallucination, if she really had seen someone standing on her porch, the explanation was probably perfectly benign. This was Hope's Crossing after all. Not that the town was immune to crime—as the recent rash of burglaries would certainly attest—but a home invasion robbery was an entirely different situation.

Settle down, she told herself. She was only freaking out because she was battling a completely normal sense of vulnerability, alone and helpless in her big house on a stormy night. It was only natural to start imagining somebody out there with a chain saw and a hockey mask.

She was seeing things. She was down to one painkiller at night, but maybe even that much of the stuff lingering in her system was messing with her head.

She gazed out into the sleeting rain again, straining her eyes to peer at the dark corners of her lawn. There. Again. This time, she couldn't come up with another rational explanation. That was definitely a person out there dressed in dark clothing, lurking on the edge of the porch.

In a panic, not really thinking about what she was doing, Claire checked to make sure the door was latched and then flicked the porch light rapidly on and off a half-dozen times.

It was probably a stupid thing to do, only serving to let the guy know she had seen him. She would have been better off using that time to barricade herself in the bathroom and calling 9-1-1 or something.

Stupid or not, though, it worked. She had caught his attention anyway. The figure turned quickly toward the front door and she caught the pale blur of a face, but couldn't make out features or any other identifying details—even whether it was a man or woman—before he (she?) turned quickly and rushed down the driveway.

What on earth was that? Her breath came in shallow gasps as Claire reached down to put a comforting hand on Chester's warm fur.

"You're such a good, brave doggie. Yes, you are. Yes, you are. The bad man is gone now. We're okay."

Her voice sounded squeaky, as if she'd been sucking helium and she forced herself to try some of Alex's circle breathing: in through the nose for five counts, fill the diaphragm and hold it for five, then out through the mouth for five counts.

She was only on her second rotation when Chester suddenly gave his howling bark again, his grumpy face concerned, just a second before the doorbell rang. Claire let out a little shriek. Was her intruder back?

After a frantic search for some kind of weapon, she finally picked up a stout umbrella from the holder by the door, then peered through the window again.

This visitor was unquestionably male. Hard chest, broad

shoulders, a slight dark shadow on his face. Relief surged through her, sweet and pure like spring runoff.

Riley!

She fumbled with the dead bolt and the lock and yanked open the door, then shoved herself back in the office chair a few feet to give him room to come inside.

Some of her fear must have been obvious on her face. Riley looked wary. If she hadn't known him since they were both kids, she would have called him dangerous.

"What is it? What's wrong? I saw you flashing your porch lights as I was heading home. Are you hurt?"

Claire wanted to sink into his arms, into that peace and comfort she had found there that day in her store.

"Probably nothing. I feel like an idiot now. Sorry to make you get out of your car in the rain."

She was suddenly aware she was dressed in her night-gown, cotton and shapeless, and no bra. At least it was fairly pretty, a light, sunny yellow that one of her friends from the senior citizen center had embellished with embroidery flowers and brought over a few days earlier.

Claire didn't even want to think what her hair must look like, tangled and flat from falling asleep on the couch earlier. Why could he never see her under better circumstances? She didn't always look like a frowsy invalid, she would almost swear to it.

"What happened?" Riley asked.

"Chester started barking at something, which is unusual for him. I came to investigate and thought I saw someone on the porch. I flickered the lights, I don't know, just as a distraction, I guess. I had no idea you were out there, but I'm so glad you saw them, too. Anyway, it must have worked because he bolted."

"He?"

"I don't know. It might have been a woman. I couldn't

tell. I just saw this dark shape take off down the driveway. Did you see anything?"

He shook his head and she saw a few raindrops that still clung to the dark strands of his hair, gleaming in her foyer light. "Visibility is pretty poor out because of the storm. I didn't see anything except your lights flashing, but I can look around for you. Lock the door behind me and wait right here with Chester."

Did he really think she wanted to be anywhere else? She wasn't a *complete* idiot. "Thank you, Riley. I'll feel really silly when you don't find anything. I'm sorry to bother you."

"You're not bothering me. This is my job, remember?"

He didn't give her a chance to answer before he headed back outside, closing the door firmly behind him. He waited on the other side until she clicked the dead bolt shut, then he began sweeping the lawn with his flashlight. She watched him through the window beside the door as he methodically crisscrossed her yard and then disappeared around the side of the house to check the back door.

What a relief to have Riley there. Not that she necessarily needed a man to protect her, but she couldn't deny she found comfort from knowing she had an armed officer of the law watching her back.

An unaccustomed comfort, she had to admit. Even when she was married, Jeff wasn't the sort to handle this sort of crisis. Once when Jeff was doing his residency, a neighbor in their condo complex had come home drunk in the middle of the night and mistaken their door for his. When his key didn't work, he'd tried to break in through a window.

Jeff had been at the hospital and Claire had been alone with the children. She remembered how terrified she'd been, until she recognized the man and went out to talk him down and help him find his way home.

That seemed a long time ago, but she could still remember calling Jeff at work afterward, needing reassurance or comfort or *something,* even just the sound of his voice.

"Sounds like you handled it just fine," he'd said, dismissing the whole incident.

That was her. She'd been handling every complication since she was twelve years old.

She petted a puzzled but tolerant Chester for another few minutes until Riley rapped on the front door again. Her hands fumbled with the lock and it took her a minute to undo the lock.

"Did you see anything?"

"No murdering psychos. At least as far as I can find."

"You think I was seeing things, then?"

"Nope. You definitely saw someone out there."

"How can you tell?"

He pulled a bundle from behind his back and carried it into the house. "I found this in a corner of your porch, back in the shadows. I probably would have noticed it when I came up to the door if I hadn't been so worried about you."

She stared at the huge basket. "What on earth?"

"Any idea who might have dropped it off for you in the middle of the night?"

"No. That's crazy. Why wouldn't whoever delivered it ring the doorbell?"

"Good question."

He was wearing evidence gloves, she realized. As if this was a crime scene or something.

"You think it's…something weird?"

"I'm sure it's only from one of your many well-wishers. But just to be safe, why don't I take a look since I'm here and all?"

"This is Hope's Crossing, not Oakland, Riley. I highly doubt somebody's left me a pipe bomb in a basket of... of magazines."

His look was wry. "You didn't expect anybody to break into your store and vandalize it, did you?"

She had no answer to that, so she merely pushed her chair out of the way. Riley set the basket on the console table in the entryway and began sorting through the contents.

"Looks like we've got something in a package that says Sugar Rush. What's that?"

"Gourmet sweet shop down on Pine Street, opened about a year ago. They have the best ice cream in town."

"This says blackberry fudge."

"Ooh. Yum. My favorite."

He gave her a sidelong look that made her toes tingle like she'd missed a step. "I'll keep that in mind."

"Though I'm not picky," she confessed. "I like all their fudge. And the ice cream, too. Oh, and their caramel drops. Which is probably why I stay away from Sugar Rush."

He smiled a little and reached into the basket again. "What else do we have here? Looks like lotion."

He opened the lid and sniffed. "Nice. Smells like flowers."

"Christy Powell makes soap and lotion. Maybe the basket is from her."

"I haven't seen a note yet."

He pulled out a thick stack of new magazines, what looked like one issue of just about every offering from the rack at Maura's bookstore, including several beading magazines, she was touched to see.

Usually Claire didn't read many magazines. She preferred a good novel as a general rule, but when she was stressed, sometimes leafing through a magazine that didn't require a major commitment in energy or attention was the perfect thing.

Riley wasn't done yet. He pulled out about a half dozen of the romantic suspense novels she preferred and then a bag of gourmet hard candy, also from Sugar Rush.

"Wow. Somebody knows what I like. I bet it was Alex."

Riley didn't appear convinced. "Why would she bother skulking around your porch and leaving secret baskets instead of what she usually does—barging in and sticking her nose wherever she wants?"

"Good point." She smiled a little. For all his grousing about his sister, she knew Riley and Alex usually had a great relationship. Alex adored her only brother, as did all the McKnight sisters.

"You're right. Alex has a key anyway. If it had been her, she would have dropped off the basket on the kitchen table and then started rearranging my spice cupboard and nagging me about why I haven't replaced the saffron I bought six years ago or something."

He smiled. "Note to self, keep Alex out of my kitchen."

"Wise decision," she answered.

He reached into the basket again. "Check this out. I wonder if it came from Maura's store."

He pulled out a small flowered bookmark with a dangly angel charm.

Claire gazed at it for an instant and then gasped as all the pieces clicked into place. "The angel! Oh, my word!"

"Angel?"

"I must have had a visit from the Angel of Hope. Darn! Now I *really* wish I had been able to see more than just a dark shape out there."

Riley carefully set the bookmark back into the basket, his wary gaze trained on her like he expected her to start speaking in tongues any minute now. "You think you've had an angelic visitation? You haven't been mixing that pain medication with anything, have you? Like bourbon? Or, I don't know, maybe peyote?"

She laughed. "Really? Hasn't anybody in town told you about our angel?"

Riley shook his head and for the first time she realized how tired he looked. His features were drawn and his eyes wore dark smudges underneath.

Between Layla's funeral, the accident and settling into a new job, he must be exhausted and here she was dragging him out on a rainy night for the most ridiculous reason when he probably only wanted to find his bed.

"What angel?" he asked.

"It's not important. Remind me to tell you about it sometime when you're not so worn-out."

"What's wrong with now?"

"Nothing, but you look like you're going to fall over if you don't get some rest. This obviously isn't a bomb or hate mail or anything. I think your work here is done, Chief. Thank you."

"I want to hear about the Angel of Hope. How can I not? If I've got heavenly visitors in my town, I'd like to know."

"I'll tell you, but do you mind if I find a more comfortable spot first?" The chair was convenient but keeping her leg down like this was invariably painful.

He instantly looked contrite. "I'm sorry. I wasn't thinking. Need a push?"

"No, I've got a system."

Using her cane and her right leg, she pushed herself back into the family room, grateful for the wood floors in her old house. In the family room, she went through the laborious process of transferring to the sofa with the aid of the crutches propped beside it, feeling about a hundred years old again.

"Need help?" he asked again.

"I've got it."

"Of course you do." Somewhat to her surprise, Riley took off his coat and draped it over the back of a chair, looking as if he planned to settle in at least for a while.

"What's that supposed to mean?"

He shook his head, an exasperated sort of look in his eyes. "It's freezing in here. You need a fire."

"It's a little tough to start one when I can't quite muck around on the hearth," she admitted. "I can nudge up the furnace, though."

"The furnace won't do you much good if the wind knocks out the power, which it probably will."

Because she knew he was right, she didn't complain when he headed to the lovely old mantel and grabbed kindling out of the basket on the hearth. With efficient movements, he had a little fire blazing merrily in just a few moments. Chester barely waited for Riley to stand up again before he replaced him on the hearth rug, circling his sturdy little body three or four times before settling into his ultimate comfort spot.

"Thank you," she said when the welcome warmth began to seep into the room. "You're right, that's much better."

"Just the thing on a rainy, stormy night."

She had to agree. She had been thinking she needed to replace the drafty old fireplace with a gas insert for convenience's sake, but there was something uniquely comforting about a wood fire.

Riley took the easy chair adjacent to the sofa. He gave a barely audible sigh and leaned back in the chair and she wondered if he'd had time to sit down all day long.

"Perfect. Okay. Now I'm ready. Tell me about the Angel of Hope's Crossing." He smiled slightly, that sexy little dimple in his cheek flashing at her. Her stomach dipped and fluttered and she drew in a steadying breath and told herself to stop being ridiculous.

"Here, have some fudge."

"It's for you," he protested, but when she handed him a piece, he took it and popped it into his mouth. "Mmm. Okay, you're right. Delicious. Now about the angel."

She nibbled the edge of her own piece, letting the sweet, rich taste melt on her tongue. "Well, it all started with Caroline Bybee's car."

"Widow Bybee? Wow. Is she still alive?"

"Hush. She's not that old. And she's got the energy of a woman half her age. Haven't you seen her garden around the corner on Blue Sage?"

"What happened to her car?"

"Well, you know she's on a fixed income. Her husband has been gone a long time and even though she works part-time at the library, I can guess that making ends meet can sometimes be a struggle for the poor dear, especially the way property taxes keep going up."

That was one of the problems with living in a town that had taken off as a tourist destination. People who had lived for years in their family homes often couldn't afford to stay, not when they could make outrageous sums of money by selling their property to be turned into condos or vacation homes.

Many longtime residents had seized their golden ticket and left already, but those who considered Hope's Crossing home and didn't want to uproot their lives were stuck trying to find their place in the new economic reality of high taxes and tourist prices on groceries.

Add to that the fact that most of the jobs in town were relatively low-paying service-oriented positions at the resort or the other hotels that had sprung up—and the restaurants and bars that had followed—and Claire supposed it was no wonder some of the youth in town didn't see a future for themselves here and had turned to crime.

"Caroline had that old sky-blue Plymouth she drove for years, remember?" she said. "It finally died last fall and even though she was much too proud to admit it, I don't think she could afford to replace it. She made do for a few weeks catching rides from friends to church and the library or just walking if she had to do errands in town, but then the cold hit early."

He said nothing for a long moment and when she glanced over, she saw his eyes were closed. He looked loose and relaxed in her recliner, more at ease than she'd seen him since he came back to town. Was he asleep? Was her story that boring or was the La-Z-Boy just too comfortable?

He opened one eye. "Go on. I'm still listening."

Color climbed her cheeks. "Right. Sorry. Um, well, the morning of the first snow, Caroline woke up to find a strange car in the driveway. A Honda Accord only a few years old, complete with snow tires. Of course she called the police right away. Dean Coleman showed up and discovered two sets of keys inside the vehicle, along with a gift title made over to her and a note that said 'Drive Carefully' and that was it."

He opened both eyes and she was astonished all over again at the vibrant green of them, like the foothills in May, lush with new grasses.

Alex had the same color eyes, but they somehow looked more startling amid Riley's masculine features.

She shifted the throw off her a little, too warm now.

"Somebody gave Widow Bybee a car anonymously?"

"Crazy, right?"

"And she has no idea who did it?"

"None at all. You know Caroline. She's not one to take

things at face value. She tracked the purchase to a dealership outside Denver, but that's as far as she could go with her digging. She hit solid bedrock and nobody would tell her anything."

He looked intrigued and she remembered Mary Ella talking about how much Riley had always loved a good mystery.

"Obviously that wasn't the end of it, as your visitor tonight indicates."

"Not by a long shot. The rest of the winter, rumors started trickling around town of others who had been recipients of this unexpected generosity. Money left in mailboxes, baskets of food on porches, bills paid anonymously. Nothing along the lines of Caroline's car, but always coming just at a critical moment when people were most discouraged."

She smiled and gazed at her own basket, touched all over again that someone had gone to so much trouble on her behalf. For the first time, she realized that much of the impact these little gestures had on the recipient came not so much from the tangible gift as from the act of giving itself, the idea that someone had invested time and energy and thought into meeting a need without expectation of even a thank-you.

"Somewhere along the way, somebody coined the mysterious benefactor the Angel of Hope and the name stuck. It's become quite a legend in town, with everyone trying to figure out who it might be. So far no one's been able to catch him or her in the act. I probably came closer tonight than anyone else. It's been really good for the town. I don't think any of us realized just how fractured we'd become as a community until these things started happening."

"Fractured? What do you mean?"

"Hope's Crossing isn't the same place it was when we were kids. It hasn't been for a while."

"Back then, the ski resort was just getting off the ground, only one double lift and a few runs," he said.

"Right. We all thought Harry Lange and the other developers were smoking something funny to ever think they could make a go of another destination ski resort when Colorado was already glutted with them."

"Their gamble paid off."

"Right. Here we are, needing those tourists to survive," she said, a little glumly.

"Any insight into who might be doing the good deeds?"

"There are about as many theories about that zipping around town as I've got seed beads at the store. I was thinking maybe it's your mom."

He snorted. "You're crazy. My mom raised six kids by herself on a schoolteacher's salary and whatever pitiful child support my dad condescended to pay before he died. No way would she be able to afford to buy a car for Widow Bybee, as much as she might love the cranky old girl."

"It was only a theory. I think you're probably right, not necessarily because of the money but because once Mary Ella was out of town visiting Lila when somebody had a cord of firewood sent to Fletcher Jones up in Miner's Hollow."

"Playing devil's advocate here—not that I buy your theory for a minute—but even if my mother was out of town with my sister, she could have arranged the firewood delivery over the phone or before she left."

"True enough, but she's been in the store with me a few times when we heard about something the Angel of Hope had done. She was genuinely shocked and thrilled when we heard someone had paid the entire hotel bill for Mark and Amy Denton when their preemie was in the NICU for three weeks in Denver. I don't think Mary Ella could possibly be that good of an actress. She was crying and everything."

"I don't know. She put on a pretty good show that everything was just fine after my dad left."

She sent him a searching look, surprised he would refer to what had been a traumatic time for his family. He looked as if he regretted saying anything, so she returned to their previous topic.

"After I discarded the theory of your mother being the Angel of Hope, I thought it might be Katherine."

He nodded. "Now *that* I might believe. She and Brodie are loaded. Between the sporting goods store and their condo developments, not to mention that her husband was one of the original investors in the ski resort, Katherine could easily afford to run around town helping people out."

"Except right now, Katherine has far more important things on her mind than bringing me blackberry fudge and a magazine or two. She's in Denver. I've talked to her every day since I've been home and I know she hasn't left Taryn's side at the children's hospital."

She was instantly sorry she'd brought up the accident. Riley's expression grew shuttered and sudden tension seemed to seethe and coil between them.

Chester seemed to sense something was wrong. He lifted his head from the hearth rug and looked back and forth between them. He yawned and clambered to his feet and waddled over to the side of Riley's armchair, as if trying to offer his canine version of moral support.

Riley reached down and scratched the scruff of his neck, his mouth a tight line.

She decided not to tiptoe around the subject. "Have you been to see Maura today?" she asked.

That bleak look in his eyes made her long for the teasing rascal he'd been as a boy. "I try to stop by every day. I swung by on my lunch hour earlier."

"I've only talked to her briefly. Most of the time when I call, I reach her voice mail."

"You're not the only one. She's shutting everyone out. Even when I show up in person, she doesn't want to talk. She pretends everything is just as it was."

"I guess some pain is so deep you have to swim through it on your own."

"True enough."

"How are you?" she asked after a long moment. "How are you *really?*"

"Fine," he said shortly.

When she continued to look at him, he finally sighed. "I've had better months."

She had a feeling he didn't admit that to many people and she was touched that he would share with her. Without thinking other than to offer him comfort, she reached across the space between them and rested a hand on his forearm.

He looked down at her fingers for a long moment and when his gaze rose to meet hers, she wanted to think some of the darkness had lifted from his eyes.

Something flowed between them, something as warm and sweet as the homemade caramel sauce they drizzled over the ice-cream sundaes at Sugar Rush.

"You looked tired when you came in. Have you been sleeping?"

He shrugged but didn't answer directly. "Why are you worrying about me, Claire? You're the one with all the broken bones."

"My injuries will heal," she said softly.

He slid his arm away from her fingers on the pretext of scratching the back of his neck. "Don't worry about me,

Claire. Worry about Maura and the rest of my family and about the Thornes." He quickly changed the subject. "So who's next on your list, if not Ma or Katherine Thorne for the Angel of Hope?"

She decided to let him think he was distracting her, although she wanted to inform him she would worry about him whether he liked it or not. "I don't know. I'm running out of possibilities."

"What if it's a whole group of people? Some kind of loosely structured consortium?"

She laughed. "A what?"

"What if you've got more than one Angel of Hope? An alliance of do-gooders? It could be all of them. Ma and Katherine, maybe even your mother. I could see Angie and her husband joining in."

She considered the idea. "Okay, that's an option. Maybe whoever gave Caroline her car was only the one who started it all, then others joined it."

"I like it. So, really, the Angel of Hope could be anyone. And everyone."

They lapsed into an easy sort of silence while she mulled the likelihood of that. It did fit. She had always considered it a little unlikely that one person could be orchestrating everything.

How would such a group work? Would they act independently or gather for a vote on who to help? While the rain clicked against the windows and the wind howled in the eaves of the old house and the fire simmered in the grate, she imagined the scene. A group of mysterious do-gooders gathered in a room somewhere drinking coffee and discussing the troubles of the people in Hope's Crossing like the court of Zeus on Olympus.

She smiled a little at the image and opened her mouth

to share it with Riley when she noticed his eyes were closed—really closed this time.

His hand had stopped moving on Chester's fur and his chest was rising and falling in a steady, even rhythm.

"Riley?" she whispered. Her only answer was Chester's snuffly breathing.

Definitely sleeping this time. Poor man. He had all but admitted he was struggling to deal with his niece's death. She wished there was some way she could ease his pain. No basket of goodies or envelope full of cash could fix this. Even the Angel of Hope—or angels, as the case may be—wouldn't have any magic cure.

Nor should there be, she thought. Some pain was simply meant to be endured.

Riley looked a different person in the circle of light cast by the lamp at his elbow. When her children slept, they looked peaceful and sweet, but Riley somehow looked much more like the rowdy rascal he'd been as a boy than the contained adult he'd become.

What would it be like to have the freedom to kiss that hard mouth? To dip her fingers in that thick, wavy hair and brush her lips against his ear…

She pressed a hand to her trembling stomach. What on earth was the matter with her? This was *Riley!* She had no business entertaining those sorts of thoughts about him. Besides the age difference…her thoughts trailed off. Okay, three years didn't seem like a big deal when she was thirty-six and he was thirty-three. But she could still remember him so vividly as a nine-year-old pest, driving her and Alex crazy.

She let out a breath. He wasn't that pest anymore. He was a man, tough and muscled, dangerously attractive. And she was a divorced mother whose love life consisted of watching lush, sweeping movies made out of Jane Austen books with a box of tissues and a bowl of popcorn.

The pain pills in her system must be messing with her. Sure, she knew they caused drowsiness and could lead to stomach upset. She found it more than a little disturbing that the prescription label hadn't once mentioned as a possible side effect inappropriate sexual urges—toward *completely* inappropriate individuals.

A smart woman would wake him up and send him home where he could stretch out on his own bed and take all that…maleness…with him.

She opened her mouth to do just that and then closed it again. He had looked so very tired when he came in. If he was comfortable and could rest, it seemed cruel to wake him and send him out into the cold rain.

Hadn't she just been thinking that she wished she knew some way to offer solace? Maybe a few hours' rest were just what he needed.

"Riley?" she whispered again, giving one more try.

He released a long sigh of a breath and seemed to settle deeper into the easy chair. Even though she had a strong feeling she would live to regret this, she didn't have the heart to wake him. Instead, she picked up another soft throw from the back of the sofa and carefully arranged it over him.

She would have done the same thing for Macy and Owen, she told herself as she settled back onto the sofa and tucked her own blanket around her aching leg. She was only being kind to an old friend. The gesture had nothing to do with the crazy, foolish part of her that liked having him there while the storm raged outside and the fire sizzled softly in the grate.

Seven

He had some half-assed dream that he was back in Oakland, deep undercover, his hair shaggy and long and always in the way, the two-day stubble uncomfortable and itchy, wearing clothes that stank of vodka and God only knows what else.

He was hanging with Oscar Ayala, a major player in the *Catorce* gang's drug distribution network. Loud Latino music played over the rockin' stereo in Oscar's crib, its steady, incessant *norteño* rhythm making his head spin.

They were close, so close to dismantling the network. For six months, he'd been playing the part of a midlevel distributor. He had seen horrible things. Done horrible things. A few more weeks and the interagency task force would be ready to move in—if he could only keep his precarious position as confidant to Oscar Ayala. That position was in serious jeopardy because of one reason—Oscar's *chica,* Gabriela, a hot little number from Venezuela who had set her slumberous eyes on Riley.

He'd been discouraging her furtive advances for weeks, but it was getting harder and harder to tactfully keep away from her. Her influence on Ayala was powerful and while Riley couldn't let the man think he was screwing his girl, he also couldn't afford to have a scorned Gabriela whispering trash about him to the dealer he was trying to bring down.

He was in the kitchen pouring drinks, the music pounding, when she cornered him and, apparently tired of playing coy, took the direct route with a determined hand to his crotch.

"Oscar passed out. Now's our chance," she murmured in the dream/memory and wrapped herself around him like a boa constrictor. She kissed him, her mouth hard and practiced.

Short of telling her he was gay—which she could probably tell was a lie by his stupid body's natural response to suddenly finding a lithe, soft female body pressing against all his most sensitive parts after months when he'd been too busy playing a damn role for any kind of social life—he couldn't come up with a single way to get out of the situation.

He was just about to try the gay card anyway when the worst happened. He heard a roar from the doorway and looked up to see Oscar, the prison tats on his face even more menacing than normal.

"He attacked me," the bitch cried out in rapid-fire Spanish. "I just came in for another drink and the next thing I knew, he grabbed me. I was trying to get away, baby."

Riley had stood there for just a moment too long, his brain stalled out, then Oscar lunged into the room, whipping out his Glock.

"Puta," he snarled and before Riley could say anything, he fired into Gabriela's head from six feet away, splattering blood and brain matter all over Riley.

In the dream, the moment moved frame by frame in slow motion, much as it had felt in real life.

"She's a slut," the dream Oscar said, with a hideous

grin on his face. "I'm sick of her shit. One cock after another. I can't take it no more. She's gonna give me crabs
or something."

Riley stood there covered in another person's bodily
tissue. He didn't know what to say, what to do. He was a
cop and he'd just seen a woman murdered in front of him.
Did he arrest the crazy bastard now or let things play out
for another few weeks?

"You messin' with me?" Oscar asked. "You didn't nail
her, right?"

He wiped a hand over his face. "No, man. I didn't touch
her."

The words scraped his throat raw, but he forced them
out anyway. "I didn't touch her. I wanted to but I didn't.
She was yours. Far as I'm concerned, you got the right to
deal with her how you see fit. Ain't my business."

Oscar smiled that hideous smile again. "That's right.
Knew I liked you, man."

In the dream, Riley stepped over the body and grabbed
another drink, the *norteño* music throbbing through his
chest, then watched while rats crawled out from the cup-
boards and started eating the half-gone face.

The slide of something wet against the back of his hand
jerked him awake, heart racing. He yanked his hand out of
reach of the rats, going instinctively for his weapon before
he was even fully awake.

It took him about twenty seconds to realize there were
no rats and he wasn't in that miserable apartment in Oakland, pretending to be the kind of man who could watch
a person's violent death in front of him without any visible reaction.

A dog was licking his hand. Ugly, stout, sorrowful-look-
ing. Claire's dog, he realized. He was at Claire's house,
with its pretty watercolors on the wall and the comfortable

furniture and quiet sense of home surrounding him. He was in her house, in a chair by a dying fire, covered by a nubby-soft blanket. He could just make out a Claire-size shape stretched on the nearby sofa and see the blur of her face in the darkness, her eyes closed as she slept.

He realized he was holding his weapon. Feeling foolish, he slid it back into the harness and drew in a shaky breath, disoriented by the jarring transition from hell to this warm, soft house that smelled of fresh-washed laundry and summer wildflowers and strawberry jam.

It was a smell that was quintessentially Claire. Fresh and sweet. Delicious. Was it some kind of soap she used? Shampoo? Or maybe just her. He had a fragment of memory when he was a kid of walking into his house one day after school and this bright happiness blooming inside him when he realized Claire was there because he caught her scent in the air.

He scrubbed at his face. He hadn't thought about Oscar or Gabriela's murder in months. Why now?

Yeah, it had been the final straw. Two weeks later, as he was coming off the assignment after the task force finally moved in and arrested every freaking one of the *Catorces* because of the evidence he'd collected undercover, Riley had gotten the call from Dean Coleman about his impending retirement, asking him to apply for the job as police chief in Hope's Crossing.

He might not have considered it before, but at that particular point in his life he had been desperate for a little peace. A place where life meant something, where children didn't sleep in filth and learn how to light a crack pipe by the time they were in elementary school.

The discordance between the ugliness of the dream and the soft, pretty colors and textures of her house was still jarring.

Had she covered him with the blanket? She must have done. He had no recollection of finding it for himself. Actually, he had no recollection of falling asleep. They had been talking about the town's Angel of Hope, he remembered, mulling various theories as to the angel's identity. He must have dozed off in the middle of their conversation.

He shifted and automatically began to pet the dog beneath his droopy ears, fairly humiliated that he had relaxed his guard around her. Why had she let him sleep? And gone to the trouble to cover him with a blanket, too, when she could barely move from her injuries?

He studied her sleeping form, baffled by the woman and by his twenty-plus-year attraction to her.

What was it that drew him so strongly to her? Her generosity of spirit? That air of kindness a person couldn't help but notice? He sighed. He wasn't sure. He only knew that he'd had it bad for Claire Tatum Bradford since he was just a stupid kid, fascinated by his older sister's best friend.

Riley had grown up surrounded by women. Even before his father left, James McKnight had been a distant figure in their lives, busy with his career as a science teacher and school administrator, which left Riley possessor of the lone Y chromosome in his house most of the time.

Until he was about ten or eleven, Claire had been just like one of his sisters, always bossing him around and getting after him for one thing or another.

He wasn't sure exactly at what point he figured out she was different, but he could definitely remember the first time he'd noticed her physically.

When he was thirteen, she'd stayed over at the house one summer night, as she often did to escape what he could only guess must have been a depressing home life, knowing what he did of Ruth and how she'd fallen apart after her husband's murder.

He'd gotten up in the middle of the night to use the bathroom. Claire had just been coming out of it and she'd been wearing soft sleep shorts and a tank top without a bra. It had been a cool evening and he clearly remembered being able to see the dark outline of her nipples through the thin, almost translucent cotton.

She had smiled sleepily at him before heading back across the hall to Alex's bedroom and Riley could still remember how he had stood there stupidly far longer than he should have, his mouth dry and his body reacting, well, like a thirteen-year-old boy's does.

That moment had been the highlight of a horny yet relatively sexually deprived adolescence, a memory he had savored far more than he probably should have.

Come to think of it, that moment was still probably one of the hottest of his life.

He stretched a little and glanced at his watch. Two in the morning. He'd been sleeping in Claire Bradford's easy chair for going on three hours, probably the most he'd slept at a time since the accident nearly two weeks ago.

The accident. A chill seeped into his shoulders, wiping away the last trace of any lighter thoughts like that wind blowing down the canyon. A familiar pain pinched under his breastbone.

Layla.

Ah, Layla.

He closed his eyes, picturing Maura as he'd seen her earlier. He checked on her daily, always hoping for a change but his laughing, free-spirited sister was gone. She had aged a decade in the past two weeks, her skin pale and dry, her features gaunt and drawn.

She said she didn't blame him for her daughter's death. Just the day before, she had taken his face in her hands

and told him so. "It wasn't your fault, Ri. Don't you dare
think that. You were doing your job."

Intellectually, he knew she was right, but that didn't
make the guilt any easier to bear.

He had seen ugly things during his time undercover,
things that apparently still haunted his dreams. But in more
than a decade of law enforcement, nothing had affected
him as much as the accident that had killed his sister's
child.

That chill slid deeper into his bones and he glanced
over at the fire and saw it had burned down to embers.
The wind had quieted sometime in the night, but he could
still hear the soft dribble of the rain.

A quick look at Claire assured him that she was still
sleeping soundly and Riley rose and moved quietly toward
the fireplace, her funny-looking dog following close behind. Someone—maybe that idiot Bradford?—had left a
tidy stack of firewood beside the hearth. He stirred the embers for a moment with the poker until they glowed red,
then picked up a nice-size log and tossed it in. It sizzled
for a moment before the embers clawed at it and it caught
fire. He gazed at the flames for a moment, then heard a
slight rustle behind him.

When he turned, he found Claire sitting up, reaching for
the small lamp by her sofa with her good hand. Her hair
was a little mashed on the side where she'd been sleeping
and her cheek was creased from the pillow, but she still
looked soft and sleepy and far more sexy than she'd ever
been at sixteen.

He, not surprisingly, had the same reaction he'd had in
that hallway of his childhood house.

"What time is it?" Her voice sounded husky and low,
which didn't help anything.

"A little past two. You shouldn't have let me fall asleep."

She yawned and massaged her arm just above the cast. "You looked so tired. I figured a few moments might help you feel better."

"A few moments, maybe. That was three hours ago."

She gave a rueful smile. "I guess I fell asleep, too. Sorry about that. Is your neck sore from sleeping in the chair?"

"No, actually. I slept better than I have in…a while."

Her face softened with compassion that he didn't want to see, so he decided to go for the shock factor.

"I have to tell you, this wasn't exactly what I had in mind when I was fourteen and used to fantasize about sleeping with you."

Her jaw dropped and in the dim light from the fire and the area lamp, he watched a tinge of adorable color climb her cheekbones. "You did not."

"Oh, Claire, my dear, I most certainly did. You were the subject of many a heated fantasy. And a fourteen-year-old boy, unfortunately, can have a pretty vivid imagination."

She still didn't look as if she believed him. "Why on earth would you have given me more than a second thought? I was only your older sister's friend. You always ignored us, unless you were figuring out new ways to torment us."

In the age-old dance of idiotic boys, he had mostly teased them as an underhanded way to make Claire pay attention to him. He supposed he was always drawn to her, even before he reached an age where he saw her as a very attractive female.

Despite the emotional toll of the past few weeks, he had to smile a little at the shock in her eyes. She probably had no idea she'd been an object of lust, not just to him but to plenty other adolescent males in Hope's Crossing.

"You're breaking my heart here, Claire. I had a crush on you from the time I was old enough to figure out girls didn't really have cooties. Maybe even earlier than that. I used to have all these really great fantasies where one day you'd come to me with your hair all tousled and sexy—lips pouty, eyes heavily made-up like something out of a Bon Jovi video, you know the drill—and tell me you were into me, too. Now you're basically saying you never once thought of me that way. That's harsh."

Her eyes were huge and he couldn't tell if she was horrified or intrigued. Or maybe both.

She opened her mouth to say something but nothing came out and he finally took pity on her.

"I'm teasing, Claire. Oh, the torrid fantasy part is true, much to my shame and embarrassment, but that was all a long time ago. We were completely different people back then."

He saw her throat work as she swallowed and her hands curled convulsively on the light quilt covering her. Now he'd made her nervous.

"I should get out of here, let you go back to sleep. I never meant to stay so long. Would you like me to take the dog out before I leave?"

She swallowed again, her gaze shifting from him to the dog, then out the window at the rain-soaked darkness before returning to him.

"That would be great. Thank you. There are still far too many things I'd like to do but can't right now, you know?"

He thought of pressing her back on her pillow and burying his hands in her hair and then kissing that delectable mouth. "I think I have a fair idea," he said dryly. "Come on, Chester."

Riley wasn't quite sure how he managed it, but somehow her dog managed to look excited beyond all his inherent basset gloominess. He opened the kitchen door for him and Chester hurried out into the rain.

Riley stood waiting for him, grateful for the cool, wet air to clear out the rest of his cobwebs. He was also grateful he had the next day off so he could try to sleep in a little, though he had a feeling Claire would show up in his remaining dreams.

That beat the hell out of the alternative, though. He would far rather dream about her than those vivid nightmares about his undercover work or about the accident.

As he waited, he did a quick inventory of her lawn in the glow from the porch light.

"Looks like you've lost a few branches from the wind earlier," he said after he'd let the dog back inside, dried him off a little with a towel hanging by the door and then returned to Claire's family room.

"Oh, drat," she muttered.

Who said *drat* these days? he wondered, charmed all over again by her.

That silly word was a firm reminder to him, as if he needed one. Anyone who said *drat* instead of the blue curses he would have uttered was far too sweet for someone like him. He had too many black marks against his soul to deserve a woman like Claire Tatum Bradford.

"I guess that's what happens when I live in a house surrounded by hundred-year-old trees. Do you think they're too big for Macy and Owen to clean up when they get back from Denver with Jeff and Holly Sunday night?"

"I couldn't see all that clearly in the dark, but from what I could tell, I think you're going to need a chain saw for a couple of those limbs."

"Oh. Well, I'm sure I can find someone to help me."

He hesitated for just a moment, obligation fighting against his better judgment. He had to make the offer, even though some part of him knew spending more time with Claire wasn't a good idea. But he was in Hope's Crossing now and that's what people did in a small town. They helped each other when they could. Beyond that, he owed her. If not for him, she could be taking care of her own branches.

"It's been a few years, but I'm sure I can remember how to fire up the Stihl."

Her eyes widened with surprise. "You're far too busy, Riley. You don't have time to be cleaning up my yard. I've got a man I hire to help with the heavy repairs and yard work around here, Andy Harris. If he can't do it, Jeff could probably take care of it after he brings the children home."

He tried to picture the entirely too smooth doctor dirtying his hands with his ex-wife's yard work with his young, lovely wife at his side. The image wouldn't quite come together.

"I'll round up a chain saw and come over later in the morning. Would eleven work?"

"Riley…"

He didn't want to argue anymore, not when it was taking all his concentration to keep his hands off her. "I'll see you in the morning," he said shortly. "Do you need anything else before I leave?"

"No. I… Thank you."

"What are friends for?" he murmured, then let himself out of her warm, pretty house while he still could find the strength to leave.

Eight

She should not be doing this.

As the hungry growl of the chain saw cut through the afternoon, Claire sat in her blasted rolling chair, Chester at her feet, sneaking another peek through the filmy curtains at her bay window, like something out of an Alfred Hitchcock movie. Only instead of spying on her neighbor burying a body in the garden, she couldn't seem to stop watching the very attractive male currently wielding that chain saw on her downed tree limbs.

Something was seriously wrong with her.

Riley had made short work of the storm debris over the last hour. When he finished, he had poked his head in the door to inform her—not to ask, apparently, because he didn't seem to care when she objected—that he was going to trim a few of the lower hanging limbs and any others that had been weakened by the harsh winters and heavy snows in Hope's Crossing.

She had tried to insist she could hire a tree service, but he had only smiled and headed back out to work.

She shouldn't be gawking at him, noticing the way his T-shirt clung to his chest and the muscles that rippled in his back as he stacked and loaded the larger chunks of branches onto her woodpile.

This was Riley. Alex's pest of a brother, the one who used to jump around corners to scare them at every opportunity, who used to cover the spray nozzle handle on the sink so anyone who turned the faucet on would be drenched, whose favorite summer activity had been lurking in wait for them to sunbathe in the backyard so he could sneak out and soak them with the garden hose.

He was *definitely* all grown up, six feet and change of hard muscles.

You were the subject of many a heated fantasy... I had a crush on you from the time I was old enough to figure out girls didn't really have cooties.

She still didn't buy it. He had to have been yanking her chain. Still, his words had chased themselves around and around in her head since that strange conversation in the early hours of the morning.

She sighed and Chester raised his head, his eyes curious. "Sorry. Go back to sleep. Just reminding myself what an idiot I am."

He barked once as if in agreement, then rested his head on his paws again as Claire suddenly became aware the throb of the chain saw had stilled.

She searched the backyard for Riley and found him kneeling near the trunk of her favorite old honey locust. The bright orange chain saw case gaped open on the ground and he was fitting the saw back in.

Was he finished? Yes. A minute later, she watched him close the case and then stand up again and head for the house. Only by sheer luck and Chester fortuitously lunging out of the way, she managed to wheel away from the kitchen window just seconds before he rapped on the back door and then opened it without waiting for her to answer it.

He filled her house, large and masculine, in the space that had become rather girly since Jeff moved out.

"That should take care of your arboreal needs for a while."

"Until the next big windstorm anyway. Thank you. I appreciate all your help."

He shrugged. "No big deal. I had a free morning. Anyway, I'd rather be outside doing yard work than holed up in my office down at the station filling out reports."

"Will you have some lunch? I made a couple of sandwiches." She pointed to the table with more than a little embarrassment. The sandwiches she'd made looked clumsy and crooked on the mismatched china, all she could find in the dishwasher. She couldn't reach up into the cupboard easily, so she'd been forced to make do.

Riley didn't seem to notice anything wrong with her efforts. He gaped at the table and then looked back at her.

"You're in pain and can barely move, Claire," he exclaimed. "The last thing you need to be worrying about is feeding me."

"I'm feeling fine. Great, actually." She didn't add that she had felt more useful making that pitiful excuse for a sandwich than at any time since the accident. "Anyway, it's only a sandwich, Riley. It's not like a five-course meal Alex would fix or anything."

"Thank you, then," he said after a pause. "It looks delicious and I am starving. I should probably wash some of this dirt and sawdust off first, though."

"The bathroom's down the hall, first door on the left."

When he returned a few moments later, his hair was damp around his face and a couple of water droplets still clung to his neck.

He looked completely delicious. She, on the other hand, was not at her best. She had chosen a plain cotton dress with tiny sprigs of blue flowers, something easy to pull over her various medical hardware. She had pulled her hair back in a headband and even put on a little makeup, but her spruce-up efforts seemed rather pathetic.

He slid into a chair at the table and looked around her sunny, comfortable kitchen.

"I have to say, this place has really changed since the last time I saw it, back when that scary-mean Mrs. Schmidt lived here."

"She wasn't scary *or* mean. Just old and lonely."

"Do you always look for the best in people?"

She could feel her face heat. "If you take the time to see past the gruff, you can usually find something good."

"Maybe you should try being a cop for a day or two. That would probably change your perspective." He picked out a pickle spear from the jar she'd managed to wrangle down off the shelf of the refrigerator and took a chomp out of it.

She sipped at her water. "No, thank you. I'll stick with my bead store. I like being foolish and naive."

"I didn't call you either of those things. I actually think it's…sweet."

She didn't want to be sweet. Not when it came to Riley.

"So tell me about the house," he said. "How did you come to be the proud owner of Mrs. Schmidt's crumbling old brick pile?"

"I've dreamed of living here from the time I used to walk past it on my way to school," she confessed.

"Even as creepy as it used to look, with the grime and the cobwebs and the shutters falling off their hinges?"

"I could always see past all the dusty corners to the

gem inside. The bones were good and I knew with a little elbow grease, this place could truly sparkle."

"So you came back to town ready to make your dreams come true."

"Something like that. Mrs. Schmidt died a few months before Jeff finished his residency and was ready to open his practice. When we started looking around for houses, her children were just a week or so from putting it on the market. Our real estate agent put us in touch with them and we bought it just like that."

Jeff hadn't wanted an old house. He had wanted to build their own place from the very beginning, something modern and airy, but she had convinced him this was the perfect place to raise their children.

Her own ignorance still shamed her. She hadn't wanted to see how different—and how distant—she and Jeff were becoming over the years.

"Did you gut the whole thing?" Riley asked.

"Close enough. It took about a year of hard work to make it the home we wanted." And while she had been stripping layer after layer of wallpaper, painting, refinishing old woodwork to create a warm, lovely home for her family, her marriage had been crumbling around her feet without her noticing.

"I can't imagine how much work you must have had to throw at it."

"Yes, but just like I tell my kids when they're complaining about their homework or having to clean up after Chester, we value the things for which we have to work the hardest."

"True enough."

She took a small bite of her sandwich, thinking how much better it would have tasted if she could have made her famous five-spice mayonnaise, but she hadn't been able to reach into the cupboard for the ingredients.

"Do you find the place too much to keep up since the divorce?"

"Ask me that in the fall when I'm trying to harvest the garden—assuming I can even put in a garden this year—and rake the leaves and prep the house for winter."

"So is that a yes?"

"My mother pushed me to sell after…well, after Jeff moved out, but I couldn't bear to lose it after we'd worked so hard on the renovations. I didn't want to lose *everything,* you know?"

She hadn't meant to say that. The words just slipped out before it was too late to call them back.

Riley's gaze narrowed, his features suddenly dark and extremely sexy. "I'm just going to come out and say this. The man was an idiot not to see what he had."

Goose bumps shivered down her arms at the intense look in his eyes. She stared at him for a long moment, tension coiling between them and a glittery awareness floating in the air like dust motes in a sunbeam.

She set her water glass down, wondering if her face could possibly be as red as it felt, and tried hard for a casual smile. "Thank you, Riley. That's a very sweet thing to say."

"Nothing sweet about it, Claire."

His voice was a low rasp in the kitchen. Before she could stir her brain to function, to speak or move away or *something,* he reached out a roughened thumb and caressed her jawline. Heat surged through her, wild and fluttery, and she wanted to lean into his skin like her silly dog nudging her hand for more petting.

"Claire," he said softly, and then his whole hand curved around her chin and he tugged her forward slightly and kissed her.

His mouth was hard, warm and tasted of the outdoors. Beautiful and slightly wild. He didn't rush the kiss, his mouth just barely moving on hers, and everything inside her seemed to sigh a welcome.

She felt as if she had been frozen solid for years, as if she had been waiting like the mountains for the sun to finally come out after long days of darkness. She closed her eyes, relishing the scent and the taste of him, the strength and heat of his fingers, the brilliant, delicious heat bursting through her.

Don't stop, she thought. *Oh, please, don't stop.*

He made a low sound in his throat and deepened the kiss and she leaned into him as his mouth slid across hers, as his hand tugged a little in her hair....

Through the soft haze wrapping around her, Claire was vaguely cognizant of a jarring sound, a door shutting somewhere in the house and then a voice that didn't belong in this lovely moment she was having.

"Hey, you," she heard Alex call out from the entryway. "What's Ri's pickup doing outside full of branches?"

She froze for only a second, her eyes flashing open. Her gaze locked with the intense aspen-leaf green of his—now somewhat dazed—then Claire scrambled back and picked up her sandwich, trying not to notice how her hands trembled.

She was just in time. An instant later, Alex walked into the kitchen. "Hey. Here you are."

"Right. Um. Here we are. Hi."

Chester, who adored Riley's sister, jumped to his feet and headed over for a little love, which she freely dispensed, though her gaze wandered from Claire to Riley.

Claire knew her best friend well enough to feel more than a little trepidation when her gaze narrowed. What could she see? Were her lips swollen? Her hair messy? She wanted to check but couldn't with Alex still studying her with the scrutiny she usually reserved for fresh produce at the farmers' market to serve at the restaurant.

Claire drew in a shaky breath to quickly divert her, but for some reason, Alex apparently decided to say nothing.

"Hey, little bro. This is a surprise. What are you doing here this lovely May day?"

"Claire had a little tree damage from the wind last night. I was just taking the chain saw to the worst of the downed branches."

"Well, wasn't that neighborly of you?"

Riley didn't seem fazed by the slight sarcastic tone in his sister's voice. He smiled blandly, although Claire thought his expression still looked a little shell-shocked. "I do my best."

He had far more experience even than she did deflecting the sometimes-formidable moods of Alexandra McKnight, Claire remembered.

"Would you like a sandwich?" Claire asked quickly.

"Maybe."

When Claire reached down to maneuver the blasted chair toward the refrigerator, Alex stopped her with a hard glare and a foot in front of one of the wheels.

"If you dare try making me a sandwich, I just might break your other leg," her dearest friend in the world snapped.

"Oh, come on. I can make a sandwich. I made one for me and Riley."

"Leave me out of this, please," he said in an amused voice.

"You should be in bed, not in here babying my little brother."

Was that what she was doing? She risked a look at Riley and found him watching her, an unreadable expression on his features.

Claire cleared her throat. "I'm not babying anyone. All I did was make a sandwich."

"Which you don't need to do for me. If I'm hungry, I'll make my own damn sandwich."

"Just for the record, I didn't ask her for anything," Riley said. "The deed was done when I came inside."

"But then, you're never one to turn down a meal. Or anything else, for that matter."

"What's that supposed to mean?" Riley asked, his expression suddenly dangerous.

Claire didn't want to deal with their bickering right now, when she was already feeling unsteady and weak.

"You know where everything is," she said. "Knock yourself out."

"I will."

While Alex moved around the kitchen pulling out ingredients—with much more fluid, efficient movements than Claire ever could, even before her injuries—she sat petting Chester and trying to avoid meeting Riley's eyes.

So they had kissed. What was the big deal? She had every right to kiss anyone she wanted. She could start a queue of eligible men right here in the kitchen, line them out down the sidewalk and into the street if that was her heart's desire.

Not that she knew that many men she might be interested in kissing. Her divorce had been final for two years and she'd gone on exactly one date, an awkward affair with a widowed insurance adjuster from Telluride she met in line at the grocery store.

The whole thing had been a disaster from the moment he showed up at her house with his three children in the backseat.

"I couldn't get a sitter," he'd apologized, so she spent the entire dinner cutting meat into pieces, wiping faces, ignoring snide comments from his bratty prepubescent daughter.

She hadn't been eager to dip her toes into the dating pool again.

Not that she was thinking about dating Riley. It was just a kiss, for heaven's sake. Okay, a pretty stunning, toe-curling one, as far as kisses went. But still only a kiss.

She didn't need to explain herself to Alex, not with Ms. McKnight's own dealings with the opposite sex. Alex specialized in the short-term relationship, dating only ski bums or guests at the resort who came into her restaurant. She pushed away everyone who wanted anything more meaningful.

"So the kids are still gone with Jeff and the ditz?" Alex asked.

"Until tomorrow. Their tickets for the show are tonight."

Jeff and Holly were taking the children to a traveling Broadway production of *The Lion King*. Claire would have loved to take the kids herself, but she'd decided her budget couldn't quite squeeze out tickets at $150 a pop. That translated into a whole lot of bead sales.

"How are you coping on your own?"

She flashed a look at Riley, who had eased back in his chair, his arm over the back of the one next to him. Claire winced, thinking of her foolish worry over the visit from the Angel of Hope and how she had flashed her porch lights to scare him off.

"I'm fine. Just trying to hang on another few weeks when I can get a walking cast and be able to dump the wheels."

"That's great." Alex finished her sandwich creation, which truly looked like something she would serve at the restaurant, complete with a little carrot peel garnish.

She'd always been that way, even when they were girls.

Claire smiled when she thought of all the hours they'd logged in the McKnight kitchen, making brownies or popcorn balls or snickerdoodles.

"Have you checked on Maura today?" Claire asked, aware even as she spoke of Riley's features going taut.

"I just dropped off a basket of muffins for her."

"How is she?"

"Hard to say. She's numb. The way she's acting, you'd think she was drugged or something, but she refuses to take anything the doctor is trying to give her. She says it will only anesthetize her brain and delay the pain."

"Is someone with her?" Riley asked. Claire heard the grim note in his voice and saw the way his jaw tightened.

"Sage. Thank the Lord for her."

Poor Sage. Claire was somewhat ashamed to realize she'd been so busy worrying about Maura that she hadn't given much thought to her friend's older daughter, who had lost her only sister. Smart and funny and uncommonly pretty, Sage wanted to be an architect. She was in her second year at the University of Colorado at Boulder, finishing her general education credits. This was bound to hit her hard.

"She has to go back Monday," Alex said as she finally slid into a chair around the table. "Finals are the week after next."

"That will be tough on Maura, when she's alone in the house." That had been the roughest times at first when the divorce had been finalized, when Jeff would take the kids and she would be alone here in this big house.

Worry furrowed Alex's fey features. "Sage wanted to just bag school and stay home because she's already missed two weeks of classes, but Maura won't hear of it. I have to agree. I mean, she's this close to the end, it seems foolish to throw away an entire semester. I'm just not sure how

Maura will do once Sage returns to school. I think Ma will probably go stay with her for a while, if she'll let her."

Claire had doubts about the likelihood of that. Like all the McKnight women, Maura was fiercely independent and liked her space, even in the midst of trouble.

Riley's features had grown increasingly wooden throughout the conversation. Now he pushed away from the table and took his plate to the sink, in the way of someone who had been trained well in a houseful of women.

"I'm sure the landfill still closes early on Saturday," he said, his voice gruff. "I'd better head out so I can make it there in time to drop your branches for the wood chipper."

He extended a hand out to snag his work gloves and protective eyewear from the counter, a movement that stretched his T-shirt over strong back muscles. Claire swallowed hard and quickly looked away.

"Thank you again for—" picking up the storm debris, kissing me senseless, making me feel wanted "—everything."

He smiled but his green eyes were still troubled. "You're welcome. Thanks for the chow."

On his way out the door, he reached out and tugged a lock of Alex's hair lightly. "See you, brat."

"Bye, dork."

He headed out the door and Claire watched him go, then turned back to Alex, only to find her friend aiming that narrow-eyed, probing look at her again.

"Okay, what's going on?"

Claire willed herself not to flush. "What do you mean?"

"Was Ri bothering you?"

"Bothering me? No, of course not. He was helping me. You saw the truckload of branches. He's been working in my yard for the last two hours."

"Was that *all* he was doing?"

"What are you implying, Alexandra?"

"I don't know. Call me crazy. I'm just catching a weird vibe."

"Okay, you're crazy," she lied. "No weird vibe here."

Alex didn't look convinced and Claire held up the cast on her arm and gestured to her leg with it. "Look at me. I'm not exactly hot babe material here."

"A little plaster wouldn't stop Riley if he set his sights on a woman. You know how he is."

Claire frowned. She'd heard the way his sisters talked about Riley's reputation with women and it bothered her suddenly. More than that, it made her sad.

"Why do you do that?"

"Do what?" Alex asked around a mouthful of sandwich.

"You make him sound like some frat boy with a drawer full of condoms. He's a decorated police officer. Maybe you ought to remember that and give him a little more credit."

Alex blinked. "O-kay." She drew out the word.

"I mean, what's the difference between the two of you? You're thirty-five years old and you haven't dated any man for longer than two weeks in your life. You've got exactly the same commitment issues. In yourself, you consider it exercising discernment. When Riley does the same thing, you all think he's a dog."

"You implying I'm a female dog, Claire-a-bell? Because I can go there, if that's what you want."

Although Alex's tone was mild, Claire could see the temper spark in her eyes. It jarred her back to her senses. Why was she doing this? Alex was her best friend. She loved her better than any sister.

"I'm sorry. I don't think you're a player, honey. You know I don't. But Riley's not, either." She paused. "He's ripped up by the accident and what happened. Layla and Taryn and…everything. Give him a break, okay?"

"Fine," she said after a moment. "And just to show you what a kind, loving sister I am—not to mention what a good friend—I'm not even going to ask why you're suddenly so quick to jump to his defense."

Claire wasn't sure she could answer that question, even if Alex had not decided to be so magnanimous.

"Now that's out of the way, tell me the truth. How are you really feeling?"

Claire hadn't given any thought to her assorted aches since Riley showed up with his chain saw two hours earlier.

"I don't feel like I was dragged down the mountain behind a snowcat anymore."

"That's something anyway."

"Now I'm just impatient to get back to work. I hate that I had to dump everything at the store on Evie."

"She's coping." Alex rose and carried her plate to the sink, just as her brother had done. She went him one better, though, and started automatically unloading the dishwasher.

"I talked to Katherine this morning," Claire said. Without the lifeline of her telephone, she would have gone crazy stuck here at home while she healed, not being able to even reach out to her grieving friends.

"I haven't called in a few days," Alex answered. "How are things?"

"She said they were placing a feeding tube through Taryn's nose."

"That genuinely sucks." To Alex, who loved food and everything about creating it, Claire imagined a feeding tube would seem the worst trial a person could endure.

"Katherine said they're talking about a long-term rehab facility for her now. Doctors said they can give her another week at the hospital while the rest of her injuries continue to heal and if she doesn't come out of the coma by then, they'll move her."

So much sorrow. She couldn't bear it. She had to do something for her friends to ease the pain a little, but she had no idea what. The usual gestures of a warm meal or a lovely card seemed wholly inadequate. She needed to do more.

"Enough of this," Alex said, her voice firm as she closed the now-emptied dishwasher. "Let's do something fun. I don't have to be at the restaurant until five tonight, so I'm hanging out here with you until then."

"You don't have to babysit me."

Alex raised an eyebrow. "Who said I was talking to you? I'm here to visit Chester."

At his name, her basset hound lifted his head off the rug and gave Alex the happiest look he could muster out of his droopy eyes.

"That's right, you gorgeous cuddle monkey. You're such a good boy. Yes, you are." Chester obediently rose and headed over to Alex to nudge against her leg. "Chester and I are going to snuggle up and watch *Charade,* aren't we, you?"

He licked her hand, his tail wagging hard enough to churn butter.

Alex grinned at the dog, then looked up at Claire. "I guess you can join us."

"Thank you," she said dryly.

"A perfect afternoon, right? We can admire Audrey Hepburn and her hats and moon over the lovely Cary Grant."

It *did* sound perfect, she had to admit.

The only thing better would have been sharing a longer kiss with Riley.

Nine

He wasn't avoiding Claire over the next week, he was only busy.

That's what Riley told himself anyway, as the unusually wet and cool May dripped along. He was still trying to settle into his new role as a small-town police chief, a task made more difficult by a few strident voices who didn't want him there, led by J. D. Nyman.

He had plenty to do preparing for the preliminary court proceedings in the robberies—filling out paperwork, interviewing the other teens involved, trying to inventory the stolen items they'd recovered so that they could be returned to their rightful owners. And it wasn't as if that little crime spree was all he had to deal with.

Throw in a half-assed knife fight at the Dirty Dog between a couple of drunk, stupid tourists, some shoplifters at the grocery store who tried to shove a couple of pot roasts down their pants and a pair of domestic assaults and he had plenty on his plate. His obligations didn't leave much time for social calls.

That's what he told himself anyway. He might almost believe it, too, if not for the annoying little voice in his head that whispered the truth.

In his heart, he knew he was avoiding Claire for one reason. That kiss they shared had rocked him off his foundation and he didn't quite know what to do about it.

Claire wasn't the sort of women he was used to. She was soft and pretty and homey, the kind of woman who could spend months fixing a crumbling old house so her family could have a comfortable nest. She was soft quilts and warm cookies after school and flowers brimming over weathered baskets on the porch steps.

All the things he'd been running from like hell since he reached adulthood.

As he headed home from the station on Thursday evening, nearly a week after he had seen those flickering porch lights as he passed her house, Riley mulled all the reasons he needed to ignore the urge to stop by her place to check on her, the same litany of excuses he'd been telling himself every day since their shattering kiss.

As stunning as he found the experience, he knew he couldn't repeat it.

Claire and he were entirely different. His relationships tended toward fun, casual, no-strings-attached sorts of encounters with women looking for the same thing. He knew it probably had to do with his father deserting them all when he was fourteen. As he had watched his mother's stunned devastation in that first year after James McKnight decided he was being smothered by his family and needed to escape, Riley had decided he wasn't going to ever be in that position, where one person could have that kind of power over him. Nor would he ever be the one doing the hurting.

He had almost married once, when he was seventeen years old and his girlfriend found out she was pregnant. The marriage would have been a disaster, he knew that now. The miscarriage she'd suffered at two months, while a tragedy at the time, had probably been one of those blessings-in-disguise things.

Riley wasn't sure he was cut out for that life. Watching his sisters' various marital misadventures had only reinforced that conviction. Casual and fun and flirty, that was him, where no one could end up with a broken heart.

Claire wasn't like that. She needed a man who would stick around. Because that man wasn't Riley—and because he couldn't seem to spend a moment in her company without wanting to become whatever she needed—he decided he was better off staying away.

He was still telling himself that on his way home from the station that evening when he spied a kid trying to ride a bike with his arm in a cast and making no effort to dodge the puddles left by the steady rain of the day.

He smiled as he recognized Owen Bradford under the blue helmet and the Star Wars clone fighter backpack. Nice to see the kid's broken arm wasn't keeping him from the simple pleasures of puddle jumping. Riley had spent many a drippy day when he was a kid seeing just how high he could make the water splash.

He waved, tapping his horn as he passed, and saw Owen's flash of a grin. The kid raised his casted arm to return the wave, but the movement shifted his weight just enough that he was slightly unbalanced when the front tire hit the edge of a puddle that turned out to be more like a pothole. The bike's rear tire went up in the air and Owen, not holding on well, did a spectacular endo over the handlebars.

Crap on a stick. Riley slammed on his brakes and pulled his patrol vehicle to the side of the road—half on the grassy parking strip of grumpy old Mr. Maguire, who wouldn't appreciate it, he knew—and shoved open the door.

When he reached the kid, Owen was sitting beside his bicycle wearing an expression of mingled pain and disgust.

He had mud from chest to knee where he'd fallen and Riley could see a rip in his jeans and a blood smear glimmering through the frayed threads of cotton. Despite the kid's obvious war wounds, Riley could tell he was trying fiercely not to cry, his mouth pressed in a hard line.

He had been that same kind of kid, stubbornly determined to be tough, and seeing this mini-me version of himself was a little disconcerting.

"You okay, bud?"

"Yeah." Owen's voice sounded a little ragged but he cleared his throat. "I think so. Stupid puddle."

"You've got to watch those. You never can tell how deep they are or what's underneath the water."

It struck him that while Claire probably wouldn't appreciate being compared to a mud puddle, the argument could be made that she was much the same. He had a feeling there were hidden depths and pitfalls to her, just waiting to tangle a man up on his handlebars.

Or maybe he just needed to stop thinking about her every blasted minute.

"I do have to say, that was a truly spectacular dive. I'd give it 10 for form and a 9.5 for precision."

Owen giggled, just as he'd hoped. The shock of the fall was probably beginning to wear off and in Riley's experience, this was the trickiest point, when the adrenaline rush faded and the pain set in.

"How's the cast?" he asked. "Did it get banged up?"

Owen lifted his arm and gave it an appraising look in the gathering twilight. "Muddy. My mom's gonna be mad."

"I doubt that. It was an accident and we should be able to wipe it down because it's fiberglass. Can I help you up?"

"Thanks."

Owen grabbed his hand and rose to his feet. Now that

his initial bravado began to fade, he started to look more upset. "I think my bike's messed up."

Riley pulled the bike up so he could look. "Well, the forks are bent. That's going to be a bit tricky to fix but not impossible."

"I really need it. Now that the snow's melted, I ride my bike to school a lot."

"Then we'll have to make sure we fix it right. Come on, let's get you home before that rain starts up again. I can throw your bike in the back of my vehicle."

Owen chewed his lip. "Yeah, only, I'm not supposed to get in a car with anyone else."

For a half second, Riley remembered his days under-cover, grungy and rough. The kids in those desperate neighborhoods didn't have the same suspicions as their parents. They used to flock around him for candy or the little toys he always seemed to have on hand. It hadn't been great for his cover as a ruthless criminal and he'd taken heat from his superiors on the outside, but he hadn't been able to stand their misery. It had become a game between him and the neighborhood kids, trying to come up with creative ways to sneak the goodies on the sly.

"You're absolutely right to be cautious," he said now to Claire's sweet-faced kid, who was always warm and dry and loved. "But let me ask you, what does your mom say to look for if you're ever in trouble?"

Owen gave him a sideways look, a smile lurking. "A cop, I guess."

"Well, I'm the police chief, Owen. The top cop in Hope's Crossing, as a matter of fact. I've known your mom since I was younger than you are. You're safe with me, I swear it. Do you want to call your mom to make sure?"

Owen looked undecided for a moment and then

shrugged. "It should be okay, I guess. Sorry. You probably think I'm a dork."

"I think you're one smart kid to be careful. Come on, let's get you buckled up. You'll have to sit in the backseat. That's where I put all my tough customers."

"Do you have handcuffs and everything?"

Riley opened his jacket to the inside pocket where he stowed his cuffs and pulled them out for Owen, whose eyes grew large. "Cool!"

Riley smiled and helped him in, then ensured he fastened his seat belt before he closed the door and headed to the back to make room for the bike.

When he returned to the front seat and pulled back into traffic, he cast a glance in the rearview mirror and was amused to see Owen's fascination with the patrol vehicle.

"A little late to be coming home from school, isn't it? Don't tell me you were in trouble and had to stay after."

"No way! I've never even had I.S.S. That means in-school suspension."

Riley was familiar with the term. And the regular good old-fashioned suspension and its ugly cousin, expulsion. He had more than a passing acquaintance with every form of school punishment back in his wild youth.

"Did you have soccer practice or something?"

Owen shook his head but didn't elaborate. Riley had enough experience with reluctant witnesses to know when someone was trying to keep secrets.

He firmly believed a kid was entitled to his secrets as long as they weren't dangerous. All the same, he was too much of a cop not to be curious. "So what were you doing so late? Over at a friend's house?"

Owen shook his head.

"Out on a date?" he teased.

"Ew. No!" The kid screwed up his face in horror at the idea.

"Then what?"

"Promise you won't tell my mom?" he asked after a pause.

"That depends," he answered honestly. He had a strict policy not to lie to kids for the sake of convenience. Probably because he felt like the first fourteen years of his life when he thought he had a happy, normal family had been basically a lie.

"Are you doing something illegal or is your secret something that your mom needs to know for your safety or well-being?"

Owen snorted. "No, nothing like that." He paused again. "I've been making a present for my mom."

"Ah, the secret mom present. Got it."

"You know it's Mother's Day on Sunday, right?"

He winced. He'd forgotten that particular day and made a mental note to ask his sisters what Mary Ella might have her eye on. He had to make up for the dozen years of Mother's Days he'd spent in California. "Thanks for the reminder. Guess I better get shopping."

"My mom's birthday is right after Mother's Day, so I should really be giving her two presents."

"Ooh, double whammy. That's rough, man."

Owen giggled again and Riley grinned into the rear-view mirror, feeling better than he had all week.

"I wanted to do something awesome, but I don't have very much money. So Evie at my mom's store is helping me make her something."

"Something out of beads?"

"Yeah. My mom has this cool watch thing that she can switch like, with different bands, you know? So Evie's helping me make her a new one."

He couldn't have said why that touched him so much,

but something about the image of this very rugged little boy with the bum arm making a bead thingy for his mom slid right to his heart. If he was this mushy over it, he could only imagine Claire would bawl like a newborn calf. "She'll love it," he assured the boy.

"I hope so."

"Where does your mom think you are?" he asked as he turned onto Blackberry Lane.

"I told her I was going to my friend Robbie's house after school."

"What if your mom called Robbie's mom to check?"

"Robbie's mom works at the bank until six. His big sister tends him after school, so I told her I'd have Evie make her some earrings if she…" He paused, and in the mirror, Riley saw guilt flash over his features.

"If she gives you an alibi," he answered for Owen.

"Yeah," he answered, his voice sheepish. "You won't tell my mom, will you?"

Something told him Claire was going to have trouble with this one and his elaborately orchestrated schemes. "Are you kidding? I wouldn't ruin the surprise for her or for you."

Owen grinned. "Thanks a lot."

"You be sure and let me know how she likes it, okay?" Riley said when he pulled into the driveway. The windows of her house looked warm and welcoming in the fading, gloomy light.

Although it went against everything he'd been telling himself all week about staying away from her, Riley knew he had no choice now and he opened his car door.

"You don't have to come in," Owen said. "I'm okay."

"You might need somebody there to help you explain the mud on your cast. Anyway, your mom is an old friend and I need to check on her, see how she's doing. And we've got a bike to fix, right? Between you and your mom, you've only got two good arms. I can give you a hand."

"Do you know anything about fixing bikes?" Owen asked, his voice laced with suspicion. "My dad can never fix my bike when something goes wrong. Or Macy's, either. If we have a bike that needs work, we always have to take it to Mike's Bikes, even for a flat tire."

That's because your dad is a jackass pansy, he thought—but of course didn't say.

"When I was first a beat cop, I used to ride a bike."

Owen looked intrigued. "Like a motorcycle?"

"Nope, like a bicycle. Two wheels, pedals, chain. The whole bit."

"Cops don't ride bicycles."

"Maybe not in Hope's Crossing. It doesn't make a lot of sense here. But in a city without a lot of snow, a bike is a great way to get around quickly."

"Especially downhill."

"True enough." Riley smiled. "When you're chasing a bad guy running down the street with some lady's purse, you don't always have time to stop and take your bike into a shop. We often had to fix our own rides on the fly."

"Do you still like to ride a bike?"

He thought of his three-thousand-dollar mountain bike currently taking up space in the spare room at his rented house. One of the main reasons he'd decided to take the job—besides his burnout in Oakland—had been the recreational opportunities that abounded in Hope's Crossing. In the summer a person could find world-class climbing, hiking, biking, fishing. And of course the winter featured challenging downhill skiing and cross-country trails.

So far, he had been too busy to enjoy any of it, a pretty sorry state of affairs.

"I've got a bike at home. Maybe when you get the cast

off you can show me if there are any new trails around here since I was a kid."

"Sure, that would be fun," Owen said as he pushed open his front door. Claire's droopy-eyed dog greeted them with a polite bark and a sniff at their wet shoes.

"Hey, Mom. I'm home. Where are the bandages?"

There was a pause of about five seconds, before he heard Claire's voice growing louder as she approached them. "In the medicine cabinet in the bathroom, right where they've always been. Why do you need a bandage?"

She came from the kitchen on the last "bandage," without the wheelchair, he was happy to see. She walked on crutches that had been rigged up to compensate for her cast, with a little platform to rest her arm. She wore a flowery cotton dress, a pale lavender this time that made him think of a meadow full of wildflowers.

She stopped in the doorway with an almost comical sort of double take. "Riley! Oh! Hello."

He looked at her mouth and suddenly couldn't remember anything but that shock of a kiss. When he dragged his gaze away to her eyes he saw the memory of it there, in the slight widening of her pupils and the sudden flush on her cheekbones.

"Hi," he said stupidly, unable to think of another damn thing to utter. His mind seemed filled with remembering the softness of her skin, the springtime taste of her, her tiny ragged breaths against his mouth.

"What are you doing here?" she asked. "And why does my son need a bandage? Owen, why are you covered in mud? And blood, apparently."

The boy grinned. "I crashed my bike in a stupid puddle and flipped over the handlebars. It was awesome."

She looked at her son as if he was some strange exotic creature. A clone fighter himself or something. Because she'd never been an eight-year-old boy, she probably didn't grasp the particular nuances of the situation and how very cool it could be to endo your ride.

"Awesome," she repeated.

"Yeah, like something on the X-Games. You should have seen it."

"True story," Riley put in. "A genuinely spectacular crash."

She looked from one to the other. "You're both insane."

Riley met the kid's gaze and they shared a grin. When he turned back to Claire, she was shaking her head, but he thought she looked more amused than annoyed.

"And how exactly were you involved in this, Chief McKnight?"

He offered what he hoped was an innocent smile. It had always worked on his sisters, anyway. "Only an eyewitness, I swear."

She raised an eyebrow and he was compelled to come clean. "Okay, I think I might have distracted him from paying as much attention as he probably should have to the road when I honked and waved."

"It wasn't your fault. It was that stupid pothole's fault."

"Something you can be sure I will be bringing up with the city council in the interest of public safety, of course."

"He says he can fix my bike, Mom. We won't have to take it to Mike's Bikes. Cool, huh?"

She smiled. "Frosty."

Riley gestured to her crutches. "Are you supposed to be walking around? Last I heard, I thought the docs wanted you to use the wheels for a while yet."

She looked slightly guilty. "I tried. I really did. But I got so sick of it. I kept banging into doors and I felt trapped, not being able to tackle even a step. At my last appointment, I made Dr. Murray fix me up with crutches. It's still not easy to get around and most of the time in the house I end up using that office chair to roll from room to room, but it's better than trying to maneuver the stupid wheelchair."

Riley could completely relate. When he'd been shot in the leg a few years back—a minor injury from a drug bust that had gone south, which he had decided not to share with his mom and sisters for obvious reasons—he had lasted about three days on sick leave before he'd been hounding his lieutenant to let him back on the job.

"So you're feeling better?"

"Much. I'm going a little stir-crazy, if you want the truth. I need to get back to the bead store."

"Hey, Mom, I'm starving. What smells so good?"

The house *did* smell delicious, the air rich with something Italian, full of tomatoes and garlic, basil and oregano.

"Your sister's making dinner. It should be ready soon, but we need to clean up that mud before you can eat, young man."

"And I still need a bandage."

"Right." She made a move as if to pivot, but Riley stopped her.

"You need to sit down. Point me in the right direction of your first aid supplies and I can take care of it."

"I'm fine. You don't have to…"

He cut her off. "Bathroom, you said, right? I'm on it. Owen, see what you can do with some paper towels to wipe off the mud, okay?"

He headed into the same room where he'd washed up after he had hauled away her branches the other day, a clean, comfortable space with textured walls painted a rich Tuscan gold and umber.

After grabbing a box of bandages off the shelf and some antibiotic ointment, he followed the sound of voices to the kitchen. He found Owen recounting his fall all over again, this time to his sister who was standing at the stove wearing a red-checkered apron and stirring something in a stockpot on the stove.

"Wow. It really smells good in here."

Macy flashed him a pleased smile, looking very much like he remembered Claire at that age.

"Thanks. Hey, Mom, how much fresh rosemary did you tell me again?"

Claire was standing at the island in the kitchen, quartering tomatoes for the tossed salad in a bowl in front of her, he was annoyed to see. "One teaspoon ought to do it. Do you need me to check the flavor?"

"No. I told you I can handle it. You said you would sit down. So sit down."

He decided Macy was an uncommonly sensible girl.

"Just a minute more. I'm almost finished," Claire insisted.

She shifted her weight slightly on the crutches and he saw a spasm of pain cross her features. With a frustrated sigh, he set the first aid supplies on the kitchen table, where Owen sat near the dark, rain-splattered bay windows, then moved behind Claire and in one smooth motion, he scooped her into his arms and carried her toward the table.

Macy and Claire both made the same shocked sort of sound but Owen just giggled.

"Put me down," Claire insisted. "Right this minute."

Now why would he want to do that when she was soft and warm and smelled like strawberries and springtime? He smiled down at her and had the guilty satisfaction of seeing her gaze rest on his mouth briefly before she jerked it away.

"I plan to," he answered calmly. "See? I'm putting you

down right here in this chair. I'm not going to stand here and watch you overdo."

"Fixing broken bicycles, bandaging boo-boos, carting around invalids. You're just overflowing with helpfulness, aren't you?"

He smiled at her tart tone. "Doing my civic duty, that's all."

He finally decided he'd held her long enough—probably longer than was smart—and lowered her into a chair at the kitchen table adjacent to her son, who was watching the whole thing with amusement.

"What would you like me to tackle first? The boo-boo or the salad?"

She glared. "Oh, do I get a choice now?"

"If you can choose wisely."

She rolled her eyes, but he thought he saw a hint of a smile lurking there. Might have been a trick of the light, though. "I can fix up Owen from here. I could actually slice the tomatoes from here, too, but because I have a feeling you're going to insist on doing something, you can finish the salad."

"Wrong. I'm going to insist on doing both. You've only got one good hand. Just relax."

She looked frustrated, but he also saw the lines of pain around her mouth, so he didn't let her annoyance bother him.

"Let me wash my hands and I'll take care of the BMX casualty here first."

He took off his jacket and hung it over a chair, then headed to the sink where Macy was watching the whole scene with interest. "It really does smell delicious," he said as he rolled up his sleeves and lathered his hands. "What are you fixing?"

"Spaghetti. It's not very hard. I just have to boil the

pasta. Grandma brought over the sauce, but we like it a little spicier than she does, so we always add some stuff to her sauce."

Claire didn't look exactly thrilled by her daughter's confession—or maybe she was still annoyed at him.

"Whatever you're doing, it smells perfect."

"Thanks." She smiled, adding pasta to another stockpot full of burbling water on the stove. "That's probably the bread sticks. They're just made with frozen dough, but they're really good and super-easy."

When he decided his hands were sufficiently degermed, he picked up the cutting board and knife along with the remaining tomato as well as the cucumber next to it and carried them to the kitchen table to Claire. He still didn't think she needed to be fixing a salad, but he knew her well enough to know the small gesture would please her—and even though he knew damn well it was wrong and maybe even dangerous, he wanted to make her happy.

"Thanks," she murmured with a soft light in her eyes.

"You're welcome." He deliberately turned away toward Owen. "Okay, sport, let's take a look at the damage."

The boy rolled up his pants leg, revealing a relatively minor scrape.

Riley cocked his head. "Not bad. I think you probably need only about five shots and oh, about ten, maybe twelve stitches."

Owen giggled and Riley thought how peaceful it was to be in this warm, delicious-smelling kitchen while the rain pattered against the window.

"I do not."

"Okay, maybe only seven or eight." He caught Macy's eye and she grinned just like her brother.

"Just wash it off and put a bandage on it," Owen said in an exasperated tone.

"All right, bossy. You must get that from your mom."

"Hey!" Claire protested. "I'm not bossy. I just usually know what's best."

He smiled at that and risked a look at her, then regretted it when he found her watching his mouth again.

"Hey, Mom, did you know Chief McKnight used to be a bike cop?"

She cleared her throat. "I did. Alex is my best friend, remember? And Riley—Chief McKnight—is her brother. She has always kept me up-to-date on what he was doing on the Coast."

Had she wondered about him over the years? The idea of her talking about him while he was gone made his shoulder blades itchy.

"What did she tell you about me?"

"That you were a good cop and that you sometimes did things you couldn't talk about. Oh, and that you were shot and didn't tell anyone in your family about it but your partner called and spilled the beans so they all played along like they didn't know."

"You got shot?" Owen asked, his eyes huge.

He frowned at Claire. "It was just a minor injury. I was back to work in only a few days. They seriously knew? Why didn't anybody say anything to me?" he asked her.

"I guess they figured if you wanted to talk about it, you'd bring it up. Alex was all ready to head out to Oakland, but Angie talked her out of it."

"Sisters can be a real pain in the...neck."

"Yeah, tell me about it," Owen said in a tone of exaggerated misery, which made Macy glare at him.

"Hey, watch it," she said.

"You think one sister is rough. Try having five, kid."

"My worst nightmare!"

Riley laughed and stuck a large square bandage over the scrape, then rubbed the kid's hair. "That should do it," he said. "Now you're ready to go take on a few more potholes. You might want to go change into clean clothes before you eat that delicious-smelling dinner your sister's working so hard to fix."

"Thanks. It didn't even hurt."

"Well, don't forget, you're still going to need those stitches."

Owen grinned, then his eyes lit up. "Hey, you want to stay for dinner, if it's okay with my mom? We always have tons of leftovers when we have spaghetti."

The knife Claire was holding stilled, then flashed with renewed vigor, he noticed with interest.

"Thanks for the invitation but I'd better not. I'm sure you've got homework and your mom and Macy weren't expecting company."

"I did all my homework before I went over to the…" He stumbled. "Before I went to Robbie's house. Mom, is it okay?"

Claire had a hint of color on her cheekbones and she didn't meet his gaze. "Of course. Riley's always welcome here. I'm sure he knows that. We owe him anyway for cleaning up after the windstorm the other day and for helping you home."

He thought of the sandwich she had so carefully made him and of the sweetness of her kiss. She didn't owe him anything.

He should say no. Should leave this warm, cozy kitchen while he still could. "In that case, I'd love to," he found himself saying. "I'm starving and those bread sticks smell like the most delicious thing I've had in years."

This will be good, he told himself. He could regain his

footing with her. They needed to return to the easy friendship they had shared for years. No more flirting and certainly no more kissing.

No matter how hungry she left him.

Ten

She had a crush on Riley McKnight.

Claire would have been astonished if she could find any room around the mortification that swamped everything else.

She was thirty-six years old, had two children and a failed marriage behind her, but she was still acting as if she were Macy's age, trying to get the cutest boy in school to notice she was alive.

This was humiliating on so many levels. Every time he smiled at her, color soaked her cheeks until she imagined she was redder than the spaghetti sauce—which she was also terrified she was going to spill all over while she tried to wrangle the spaghetti one-handed and listen to his stories at the same time.

"My first week out of the police academy, I crashed a brand-new bike into a parked car."

"You did?" Owen asked, eyes shining with a severe case of hero worship, despite Riley's story showing himself in less-than-perfect light.

"Yep. We were chasing this kid who'd fled the scene of an attempted robbery on foot. My partner and I split up to try to cut him off and I had to book up a hill on a side street to get ahead of him. A car came up behind me and I could hear him coming right at me. We didn't know the kid had an accomplice in a getaway car. I don't know if he was trying to hit me on purpose—and I didn't really care. I just swerved out of the way. My bike hit a parked car and I went sailing over it."

"Was your bike okay?" Owen asked, while Claire was still cringing from that mental image.

"Completely trashed. I had to get a new one. The guys called me McFlight after that."

"Were you hurt?" Macy asked.

"Not bad. I felt it for a few days but I didn't break any bones. Not like you guys."

His gaze met Claire's and she flushed and focused on dabbing at her mouth with her napkin, hoping she hadn't trailed sauce there.

She did *not* have a crush. The very idea was ridiculous. She was only reacting as any woman would to the man who had rescued her and her children from a dire situation. Riley had risked his own health and welfare to stand out in that water for long moments to ensure they were safe. Any mother would be grateful to a man willing to wade into danger for her children, right?

Not to mention that he was an exceptionally gorgeous man, sexy even, with those green eyes and the tousle of dark hair. The part of her ego that felt frumpy and dried-up and *old* after the raw indignity of her divorce wanted to bask in his attention like Chester splayed out in the grass on a summer afternoon.

How foolish could she be?

The common-sense part of her was quietly whispering a warning. Riley was a womanizer. He collected women like Evie collected antique beads.

His mother and sisters delighted in telling about his heroic triumphs as a police officer. But Alex, at least, was just as quick to report with a combination of indulgence and frustration about how the man went through women like the store went through jump rings.

Yes, they had kissed. She couldn't find a better example of just how different they were. That kiss had left her shaky and stunned, while Riley had acted as if the whole thing had been just a casual brush of mouth against mouth.

"Did you catch the bad guy?" Macy was asking and Claire forced herself to focus on the conversation instead of a kiss that never should have happened.

Riley grinned. "Matter of fact, we did. He came running up, trying to make it to his getaway car. I was sprawled out on the sidewalk amid the broken pieces of my bike, the breath still knocked out of me. I was thinking he was going to get away, but right by my hand was my front tire, which had come off in the crash. I wasn't even aware of doing it really, but I chucked the bike tire at him like a Frisbee and down he went. Before he could climb back up and escape in the getaway car, my partner came up behind him just as our backup in a squad car came down the street to cut off their escape route."

The kids giggled and Claire smiled, picturing a battered Riley chucking a bike tire at a suspect.

Her kids were crazy about him, she thought. All through dinner, they laughed at his jokes, they plagued him with questions, they vied to tell him their own stories. She might have thought he would find their simple experiences boring, but Riley acted as if a story Owen told about breaking up a playground fracas was the most fascinating anecdote in the world.

Claire didn't know why she should find it surprising that her kids loved him. Riley had always been good at charming people. Why wouldn't he be? He'd grown up with five indulgent older sisters who probably offered plenty of opportunities for him to practice working the charm.

She had watched his technique in various incarnations dozens of times. She could vividly remember one day when Angie had spent an entire summer afternoon making macaroons, simply because he had mentioned with a passing sort of sigh that he'd woken up with a craving.

As the next oldest sister to him and probably the one most susceptible to sibling rivalry, Alex had been the most immune. She had accused him of manipulation—but even she could fall prey if she wasn't careful.

Riley could nearly always sway people to his point of view by wielding that charm that made everyone want to be around him, at least until he turned into the moody, unhappy teenager he'd become after his father left.

The children tried to prolong the dinner as long as possible, but eventually everyone was full and Chester had planted his haunches beside Claire's chair and waited, a clear indication he needed to go out.

"I got him, Mom," Owen said, pushing his chair away from the table.

"Thanks," she answered.

Owen opened the door for the dog, then returned to the table to clear away his plate, which seemed to be the signal for everyone that dinner was finished.

"I guess we better clean this up," Macy said. She stood and began to help Owen. When Claire started to rise, Riley froze her with a death glare.

"If you try to clear a single dish, I'll be forced to handcuff you to the chair. Don't think I won't," he said, his voice stern.

Both Owen and Macy apparently thought that was hilarious. Claire wasn't nearly as amused as she was forced to sit idle and watch Riley and the kids joke around as they scraped dishes, packaged leftovers and loaded the dishwasher.

Riley was drying a pan with one of the pretty embroidered dishcloths when he took a careful look out the window above the sink. Was Chester digging up her flowers again, as he sometimes did when a particular capricious mood struck?

"Looks like you've lost some shingles from your shed, probably from all the wind and rain we've had."

She frowned. "I hadn't noticed." Usually when she was at an angle where she had a vantage point over the window above the kitchen sink, she was focusing on staying upright on the crutches and not on the shingles of her shed roof. "Have many blown off?"

"I can't tell for sure. It's too dark, but I can see a couple missing in the porch light."

"Oh, dear." Just one more thing she had to add to her fix-it list.

"It shouldn't take long to fix. I bet Owen and I could take care of it in an hour. Don't you think, dude?"

"Maybe even a *half* hour," said her son, who never met a competition he didn't try to conquer.

Claire didn't know what to think. What game was Riley playing? She dearly wished she had some idea of the rules so that she didn't feel as if she were floundering completely in foreign seas.

Why did he seem to feel so compelled to help her every time she turned around? Why would he want to give up an hour of his life to fix the roof on her garden shed? Even as the cautious grown-up tried to figure it out, the silly junior high girl inside her squealed and did a happy little dance.

"I'm going to go work on my homework," Macy announced, bored with talk of shingles.

"Let me know if you need help with anything."

"It's algebra."

"Okay."

"You're worse at algebra than I am, Mom."

True enough. "Between the two of us, we usually figure it out."

Macy shrugged and headed from the room, Chester, whom Owen had let in a few minutes earlier, following behind. The reminder of her maternal responsibilities was exactly what she needed right then to give the mature grown-up the advantage and send the giddy girl to her room where she belonged.

"Thank you for the offer to fix the roof," she said to Riley when Macy left. "But you really don't have to do that. I told you I have a handyman. Handy Andy Harris. Do you know him? His family moved here about five or six years ago."

"Don't think I've met him yet."

"He's a nice guy. His wife comes into the store quite a bit."

"So you pay him to fix things, then she comes in and spends the money on beads?"

She managed a smile at his baffled expression. "More or less. That's how it works in a small town."

"Well, while I don't want to take work away from Handy Andy—or beads away from his wife, for that matter—this is a simple job. Seriously. It wouldn't take long at all and I was planning on fixing the bike anyway. Two birds, right? Consider it my way to repay you for the spaghetti."

Claire sighed. She knew that tone. He was going to be stubborn about it. A stubborn Riley McKnight was as immovable as Woodrose Mountain.

She could be stubborn, too, and she really hated being on the receiving end of help. But arguing was only going to prolong the inevitable. She needed her shed roof fixed,

Riley wanted to do it and she had no real logical reason to refuse.

"I can come over right after school. We can fix the bike first and then take care of the roof. That work for you, kid?"

"Cool!" Owen looked as excited as if Riley were offering a trip to Disneyland. Even though Jeff was good to take him snowboarding and skiing, her ex-husband wasn't a handyman sort of guy and Owen enjoyed working with his hands. He'd been begging her for a year to let him build a tree house in one of the mature maples on their lot.

"Can I go play on the computer?" Owen asked.

"Yes," she answered. "Set the timer for half an hour, then we need to do your reading."

"You don't fight fair," she muttered to Riley after he left.

"When have you ever known me to?"

She rolled her eyes. "Why are you so stubborn about this? I can handle my home repairs on my own. What I can't do myself, I can hire out. I've been coping by myself for two years. Longer, really, because I've always been the one to coordinate these kinds of repairs."

Jeff had always been too busy with school and his residency and starting his practice, so the pesky details of day-to-day survival had fallen to her.

"Then it's about time someone else stepped in to take a little of that load off your shoulders."

"Why does that someone have to be you, Riley?" she asked, exasperated.

He didn't answer for a moment. When he did, his tone was solemn. "If not for me, you'd be up and around and handling your own life with your usual terrifying efficiency."

She stared at him as all the pieces clicked into place. "Are you still hung up on that? I told you, you're not responsible for that accident."

His jaw tightened but he said nothing.

"That's what this is about," she said. "All of it. Why you think you have to help me with my shed roof, why you're fixing Owen's bike, why you picked up my branches the other day. You think you owe me something because of the accident. Because you feel responsible."

He gave her a cool look. "Of course not," he drawled, even though she could see her words had struck home. "Haven't you figured it out yet, Claire? I'm a guy. I just want to sleep with you."

The air suddenly thickened with tension, currents seething in the air like the swirls and rivulets of melting snow running fast and high in Sweet Laurel Creek.

She had a wild image of them together, mouths and bodies tangled, heat and fire and glorious passion.

A shiver rippled down her spine, but she wasn't sure if it sprung from her poor, neglected libido reacting with grand enthusiasm to the idea or the rest of her plunging into full-fledged panic.

"Relax, Claire. That was a joke. I'm not going to jump you right here in your kitchen."

"Of course you're not. I never thought you would."

That incongruous dimple flashed. "One never knows."

Her stomach trembled and for once she was grateful she couldn't stand without difficulty because of her stupid cast. She had a feeling if she tried, her knees would barely support her weight.

Much to her relief, she was spared from having to answer by the return of Owen, followed by a waddling Chester.

"Hey, Mom, something's wrong with the internet. I can't get on the game site."

She drew in a breath and tried to shift gears. "I'll have to figure it out after Chief McKnight leaves."

"Which I'm just about to do." Riley grabbed his jacket off the hook by the back door.

"I didn't mean you had to leave now."

"You've got to help with homework and fix computers and I've got about four hours of paperwork to do. Owen, I'll be by after school tomorrow with a load of replacement shingles. You still in?"

Her son looked suddenly sly. "Can I use a hammer?"

"I'm counting on it, ace. Claire, I'll see you tomorrow. Take care of yourself."

Good advice, she thought as she watched him go. If she were sincere about following it, she would tell him firmly not to bother coming back. She didn't need the sort of heartache that was bound to follow Riley McKnight.

Eleven

This time when Riley worked out in her yard, Claire forced herself not to gawk out the window at him. She focused instead on her first beading project since the accident, a fairly simple bracelet she was making out of recycled glass beads from Ghana in lovely aqua tones, with metalwork starfish charms.

She had her supplies set out in the family room—the beads, the spacers, the pliers and cutters—but the limitations of a broken arm presented definite challenges. Claire had sympathy for some of the senior citizens she used to teach at the community center, their hands gnarled and swollen from arthritis.

Usually she found a quiet sort of peace when she worked, the tactile pleasure of the textures and shapes, the unmatched delight of creating something beautiful from only her imagination, her ever-growing bead collection and a little hard work. But this afternoon, even threading the waxed cord onto the needle was an exercise in frustration and she almost quit a half-dozen times.

Every time she was tempted to put the project away, though, she reminded herself that she was exercising, working her arm, hand and wrist muscles as her occupational therapist insisted.

She found even something as basic as a wrapped loop a challenge. She was struggling to hold the pliers and bend the wire when her cell phone rang.

Usually she hated interruptions while she was beading and tried to remember to turn off her ringer. In this case, she jumped at any excuse to take a rest, especially when she saw the identity of her caller on the phone display.

"Hi, Evie. How's the most brilliant bead store manager in the entire Mountain West?"

Her store manager snorted. "Suck-up. You really think that's going to work with me?"

Claire smiled, her frustration subsiding in the sheer joy of talking with one of her dearest friends. "It's worth a try. How are things?"

"Crazy-busy. You wouldn't believe the pre-Mother's Day business we're seeing. We're rocking right now. That class we did for that memory charm bracelet you designed was standing room only. Seriously."

"That's great, Evie. Thank you so much for covering everything for me."

"No worries."

"I'm still planning to be back Monday. I got the all clear from Dr. Murray today. I hope I can make things a little easier for you then."

"Don't push it. There's no need for you to rush back before you're ready."

"I'm so ready. If I don't get out of this house for something besides doctor appointments and therapy, I might do something crazy. Like take up knitting or something."

Evie laughed. "We wouldn't want that. You've got enough hobbies, hon."

"I can't afford any more."

"You know you're going to have to pace yourself. When you first come back to work, you're going to want to jump back into everything you did before, but you'll have to take things slow."

"Are you speaking as my friend or as a physical therapist?"

"I'm retired," Evie said automatically. "But, okay, both."

"I know, I know. I promise, I'll be good."

Evie made another sound of disbelief but didn't argue. "I'm actually calling because we're running low on our heavy-gauge wire. If I place the order before the close of business today, we can get a shipment Monday, but I thought I'd better run it past you."

"Whatever you think best."

"We need it, obviously, but our usual distributor raised their price five percent a few weeks ago. Do you want me to shop around to try to find a better deal?"

She did a quick calculation in her head of the discount they received buying in bulk. Even though math wasn't her strong suit, she'd become rather more adept than she ever expected at figuring percentages in the two years she'd owned the store.

"Let's do half of what we normally order. What we lose for the quantity discount, we might be able to make up by finding a different supplier with a better price point."

"That's exactly what I was thinking, but thought I should check with you."

"You don't need me, Evie. We both know you could run the store in your sleep."

What a blessing that she had someone she trusted so implicitly to leave in charge at String Fever. Evie was smart and creative and capable…and probably far more business-savvy than Claire.

"The other reason I called was to give you the skinny on Gen Beaumont's wedding. Or have you heard already?"

"You forget I'm living in seclusion, completely isolated from the outside world."

"Except for cell phone, home phone, television, the internet… And your mother, of course."

She laughed. "Well, yeah. Except for that. But I haven't heard anything about Gen. What's up? She knows the designer is rushing to send another gown, right? Don't tell me she's decided to send it to someone else for the beadwork."

"There is no one else in town who can handle the job except you."

"And you. And possibly Katherine."

"Okay. The three of us. Gen knows she won't find anyone better."

Despite her best efforts to keep her attention firmly away from the window, Claire caught a flicker of movement and watched Riley heading toward the street, his arms full of shingles, and Owen following him like a little shadow.

She quickly looked back at the beads, picked up one of the recycled glass barrels and rolled it between her fingers. "Then what's the problem?"

"Well, the good news is you've got an extra six months to work your broken arm back into condition before you tackle her project."

"Why?"

"Gen postponed the wedding."

The bead popped out from between her fingers and rolled onto the area rug and she had to lean sideways and dig through the thick pile to retrieve it. "You're kidding! Why?"

"Their family is in crisis. I gather she talked it over

with her fiancé in Denver and they decided to wait until things settle down."

"Because of Charlie."

"Right. The kid is facing serious consequences for the burglaries and the accident. Last I heard, they were talking maybe vehicular homicide."

Claire gasped. "Oh, no. Poor Laura."

The mayor's wife was a customer at the store. She favored large, flashy, expensive art glass beads and usually managed to finagle one of the store employees into basically creating it for her with sly little interactions like, "Can you just get me started?" or "Will you show me that technique again?" or "You know I always struggle with that particular gauge of wire."

Usually Claire's employees loved to help people with their projects, but Laura Beaumont's ploys to have people do the work for her without compensation of any kind had become so transparent, most of them just rolled their eyes—discreetly—every time she walked in the store.

"Poor Gen. It couldn't have been an easy decision. I wonder how her fiancé and his family are taking the news."

Genevieve Beaumont was marrying the son of one of Colorado's most prestigious families, rich and politically powerful, in what had promised to be the leading social event of the year. She sincerely hoped Sawyer Danforth's family didn't try to distance themselves from the Beaumonts in light of Charlie's legal troubles.

"Why do you think Charlie slashed up the wedding dress? I always thought Gen and Charlie got along fairly well, despite the eight-year gap in their ages."

"Who knows." Claire didn't need to see her friend to sense her shrug. "Maybe Charlie was resentful of all the attention Gen was getting. Or maybe he doesn't like the groom. Or maybe he just thought the dress was ugly."

So much anger had been channeled into that wanton destruction. She couldn't imagine it.

"He must be a very troubled young man to have made such terrible decisions."

"Or maybe he's just a rotten kid. It's possible."

She caught a flash of movement outside as Riley passed by the window. She thought of him and the trouble he had caused in his youth, reacting so fiercely to a confusing, painful world. She would have thought he, of all people, should have some compassion for Charlie Beaumont.

"I'd better go so I can place this order before end of business, Pacific time."

"Thank you, Evie. A few more days and I'll be back to take some of the weight off your shoulders."

"So far my shoulders are plenty wide enough for the load. Don't push yourself too hard. I mean it."

"It's not like I'm Alex, who has to stand on her feet all day in a hot restaurant kitchen. I can sit in the store as easily as I can sit here and at least there I'll have someone to talk to besides Chester."

"Well, he *is* the only reason I want you to hurry back, you know. I miss that ugly mug. In fact, I miss him so much I might be fostering another dog myself. The shelter called and they need a temporary home for a labradoodle. It will probably be a tight fit in the apartment over the store, but I figure for a few weeks we'll cope. I told them I would, but I guess I should have checked with you first."

"You know I don't care."

Claire was probably the most indulgent landlord ever, but since Evie was the perfect tenant, employee and friend, Claire figured that earned her more than a little latitude.

Evie had fostered animals before until a permanent placement could be found, but they'd usually been cats or small-breed dogs. She rarely developed a lasting attachment to anything, something that worried Claire. Her friend had deep secrets in her past, a pain she didn't share with anyone.

"I'll see you Monday morning," she said after a moment.

"Need me to come get you?" Evie asked.

Rats. She'd forgotten about transportation. Oh, she hated being dependent on people. "I'll see if Alex can give me a lift. If that isn't convenient, my mom can probably do it."

"Let me know if you change your mind. I know Ruth isn't always easy to take first thing in the morning."

Claire smiled and they quickly ended the call. She sat for a moment, rolling that silky bead between her fingers again and thinking of the events that had affected so many lives in Hope's Crossing. Charlie Beaumont's life would never be the same. He would always have this tragedy around his neck. The ripples from that moment were expanding out in wholly unexpected ways. Gen pushing her wedding back six months. Riley struggling to find his place in town. Probably in a hundred other lives she didn't even know.

She thought of Maura, whose life had been changed forever. Riley's sister was still avoiding her phone calls most of the time, and Claire was determined to make it to her house as soon as possible, if she had to wheel herself the four blocks there.

With a sigh, she turned back to the bracelet, hoping beading would soothe and quiet her spirit.

She was just beginning to find a rhythm of sorts when the back door opened and Riley and Owen came inside.

"Mom? Where are you, Mom?"

"Family room," she called.

Her son burst through the doorway, baseball cap shoved backward and his face flushed with excitement.

"Did you see me work the nail gun, Mom? I did a whole row of shingles by myself."

The very thought of it caused heart palpitations. Her son on a ladder with a nail gun that could impale his hand to the roof. She supposed it was a good thing she hadn't allowed herself to watch.

"You let him use a nail gun?" she asked Riley in what she hoped was a calm voice.

"With help," he assured her. "I kept my hand on it at all times."

"It was awesome," Owen exclaimed. "I think I'm gonna save up my allowance and buy one. Man, I'd have the best tree house in town!"

Riley laughed. "You've got to build to a nail gun, kid. Start out with some regular tools and see how that goes first. You don't snowboard on the black diamond trails until you've had a few runs down the beginner slope."

Her son seemed to accept that bit of philosophy with his usual equanimity—and short attention span. "Hey, Mom, can we have pizza for dinner?"

She smiled. "I was thinking the same thing. It is Friday night after all." She was always grateful when she had the children on the weekend and tried to make Friday nights fun time for the three of them. "I'll call and put in the order as soon as Macy comes back from soccer practice. Want to watch a movie, too? We have all those DVDs your dad and Holly brought over for me to watch while I recover, plus the instant streaming. Wasn't there some superhero show you've been wanting to see?"

"Can I go check out our queue and see?"

"Sure. My laptop's on the kitchen table."

She was deeply grateful for technology—and even more

grateful that her kids could figure it out far better than she could.

The moment her son headed out of the room, Claire instantly wanted to call him back. His presence provided a buffer between her and Riley. Without him, that ridiculous teenage girl inside her couldn't stop thinking about that kiss.

"Owen is a great kid. You've done a great job with him."

"He *is* a great kid, but I'm not sure I had anything to do with it. He came out of the box that way. He was the easiest, most good-natured baby you could ever imagine and a very sweet toddler."

"He has a good mother who loves him. That's got to count for something."

She smiled. "Thanks. And thank you for your help, Riley." She paused. "You probably have figured out that I don't like being in a position to need help."

"I hadn't noticed," he said, his tone dry as he came closer.

"I'm working on it. So thank you."

"You're welcome. We've still got a bike to fix but that shouldn't take long." He stepped closer and her heartbeat kicked up a notch. He was just so *big*. He crowded out any common sense she might have hoped to cling to. "What are you working on over here?"

"A bracelet. I wanted to give something to Brooke Callahan for taking such good care of me when I was in the hospital. While I was there, I noticed she had several flowered scrubs in that color."

He gave her an exasperated look. "Do you ever do anything for yourself?"

"Beading *is* for me. Oh, I might sometimes give away the things I make, but the process of creating them is all about me. I find pleasure in the whole thing, from coming up with the design to choosing the beads to the feel of them under my fingers. These recycled glass beads from Africa are like sea glass that's been worn smooth by the waves."

He leaned forward to touch the beads, his hands looking incongruously large against the delicate blue. "Soft. You're right."

She couldn't breathe with him this close. He smelled musky and male, like cedar and sage, and he crowded her, made her feel girlish and silly. She eased away a fraction of an inch, but he still noticed the movement.

"Why do you do that?"

"What?" she asked, pretending she didn't know what he meant.

"Flinch away from me."

She thought about lying, pretending he was imagining things, but the casual words just wouldn't come. "You make me nervous," she finally admitted.

His eyes widened. "Why? You've known me forever. You have to know I would never hurt you."

Not physically maybe. Claire wiped suddenly damp palms on her skirt. "I'm not going to be one of those women, Riley. Let's be clear."

He shuttered his expression. "Oh, absolutely. I strive for clarity in all things. Which women would you be talking about?"

"I know you're just teasing me, like you've always done. All these little comments about…about sleeping with me and having a crush on me when we were kids and everything. Kissing me. You're just trying to see what kind of reaction you can get out of me. It's no different from all those times you used to jump around the corner and yell boo just for the pleasure of hearing us squeal. I'm not going to fall for it anymore."

Much to her relief, he stepped back a pace but only so

he could glower at her from a better angle. "You're going to have to help me out here. Clarity, remember?"

She hated feeling stupid and out of her depth and she finally just blurted out, "I won't have a fling with you, Riley."

He blinked. "Okay. Good to know."

"It's not that I'm not…um…that I wouldn't…" Oh, she didn't know how to do this. "I'm not sophisticated or worldly or any of those things. I'm a soccer mom. I've been a room mother for six of the last seven years. I'm the president-elect of the PTA, for heaven's sake."

"And that's pertinent to this discussion because?"

"Because I'm not the sort of woman to jump into bed with anyone. Especially not you."

His jaw tightened and she had the ridiculous feeling she'd hurt him somehow. "Why especially not me?"

"A hundred reasons. For one thing, I know you're not serious about any of this, you're playing some kind of game."

"This is fascinating. Do go on." His jaw had hardened and he crossed his arms across his chest, which unfortunately only served to emphasize the definition of his biceps.

"Well, you're my best friend's little brother."

"Younger. I prefer younger. And only by a few years, Claire."

Okay, that was true. If not for the fact that she'd known him all her life, the difference in their ages would be irrelevant. But she *had* known him. She'd seen him grow from a pesky kid to a surly teenager.

He was close, so close that she could see a muscle flex in his jaw. She wanted to kiss that flutter, just throw caution to the wind and…

The pressure in the room shifted as the front door was yanked open.

"Hey, Mom!" Macy called out from the entryway. "Guess what? Julie Whitaker has a sprained ankle, so guess who gets to play goalie tomorrow?"

Her daughter burst into the family room, overflowing with gangly, slim gorgeousness, even in practice shorts and knee-high socks. She grinned when she saw Riley. "Hey, Chief."

"Yay for you! Goalie, huh?"

"Yeah. Jule's super-good, so I never have the chance to goal tend, but she's out for at least two games, so I get to fill in. Maybe if I do an awesome job, the coach will think about alternating us. I don't mind playing forward, but I really love goalie."

"That's wonderful, honey." With effort, Claire shifted gears to her mommy role. "You've worked hard to improve your skills and you definitely deserve it. Hey, I'm going to order pizza tonight and Owen's picking a movie."

"Okay. I'm going to go change and clean up. The field was super-muddy."

In a rare show of affection, she slid her arms around Claire's neck and hugged her, then bounced past Ruth in the doorway on her way out of the room.

"Thanks for the ride home, Grandma," she said.

"You're welcome, my dear," Ruth answered. "Claire, good grief, who left such a mess out by the garbage can? They look like shingles. Is that Andy Harris here working on something? He needs to do a better job of cleaning up after himself."

Riley stepped forward into her line of vision and Ruth's mouth pursed like she'd just chomped into a peach pit.

"I left the mess, Mrs. Tatum. Claire lost a few shingles in the rains of the last few weeks, so I was replacing them. Don't worry, I'm planning to take care of the garbage before I go."

Her mother's sharp-eyed gaze slid from Riley to Claire and then back again. Claire gave an inward cringe at the questions and suspicions she saw gathering there like an August afternoon thunderstorm over the mountains.

She braced herself, wishing she had some way to warn Riley of the cloudburst about to let loose.

"Chief McKnight. This is a surprise." Ruth smiled with absolutely no warmth. "Isn't there a teenager somewhere you can chase down at dangerously high speeds?"

Riley's only reaction was the twitch of a muscle in his jaw. If this was the attitude he faced around town, no wonder he carried unnecessary guilt about the accident.

"Mom," Claire chided quietly.

Ruth offered up a falsely innocent look. "What did I say?"

"You know that was unfair," she began, but Owen's "Hey, Grandma!" stalled the words.

"Hello, dear. What have you been up to?"

"Me and Riley fixed the roof on the shed and guess what? I got to use a nail gun."

Oh, dear. Here we go. Now Ruth would accuse her of allowing Riley to put her son into danger. "Weren't you two going to take a look at your bike?" she asked, a little desperately.

Riley raised an eyebrow at her sudden uncharacteristic eagerness to accept his help, but he only nodded. "We certainly were. That was our next project. Let's go check out what we're dealing with, kid."

"I found just the show on the computer, Mom," Owen informed her. "I put it at the top of the queue."

"Excellent. I'll order the pizza in a minute."

When the two of them headed outside, Owen pacing his stride to Riley's longer-legged gait, Claire turned to her mother.

"Mom, that was unkind. Riley was only doing his job. You know that."

Ruth began fussing around the room, straightening magazines on the coffee table and picking up the granola bar wrapper Owen had left there after school. "I'm sorry, Claire, but I can't forget that because of the way he did his job, you and my only grandchildren were nearly killed. Look at you. You can't even walk and you haven't been able to work for over two weeks. It's not right."

"If you're going to blame anyone, blame the teenagers who decided to go on a crime spree for no discernible reason. Blame Charlie Beaumont. He's the one who chose to run."

Ruth made a dismissive sort of motion. "Charlie is a thoughtless boy who ran because he was afraid."

"Right. Afraid of being caught. They robbed my store and a half-dozen others in town, not to mention that vacation home in the canyon. None of that is Riley's fault."

"I'm not defending what they did. It breaks my heart, that's what it does, and I don't understand it for a minute. I don't see how anyone can. Children from good homes, robbing people, vandalizing things. Something's wrong, I'll grant you that. Personally, I think it's all those video games you parents let them play."

Because she allowed Owen only a couple hours a week of only rated-E-for-everyone games, she wasn't sure how her mother could justify lumping her into that particular category. Anyway, that wasn't the point.

"Whatever the reason, it was the choices Charlie—and, yes, the others—made that caused this tragedy. *Not* anything Riley McKnight did."

"He should never have chased them," her mother insisted. "Not with those snowy conditions. And now a girl is dead and another might as well be, if she has to live the rest of her life like a…like a rutabaga."

"Riley did nothing wrong."

"Believe what you want. I'll do the same."

Would that waxed cord be strong enough to make a noose? she wondered, although it was a toss-up whether she wanted to use it for her mother or for herself. Five minutes of conversation with Ruth and she wanted to bang her head on her worktable a couple dozen times.

"What would you have him do? Just let the kids drive away? Then you and J. D. Nyman and everyone else in town would be saying he's too soft."

Her mother turned her attention to the entertainment center, stacking loose DVDs and picking up the hundred or so remotes it seemed to take to run everything these days.

"I don't know. He could have discreetly followed them long enough to get a license number and then picked Charlie up later at home. But personally, I think he wanted the big, flashy arrest so he could show off in his first few weeks on the job."

"That's not fair. You don't even know him. Not anymore."

"I know all I need to know. That boy is trouble, just like Charlie Beaumont. He always has been. You know what he was like. A wilder boy I never knew. Running around getting girls pregnant."

"One girl, Mom. One girl."

"That we know about. The city council made a huge mistake bringing him back and I for one am glad they're reconsidering."

Claire caught a flicker of movement and glanced toward the hallway and her stomach dropped. They had been so busy in one of their typical arguments that neither of them had heard Riley come back inside. How much of her mother's ridiculous vitriol had he heard?

"I disagree," she said, locking her gaze with his. "I think Riley is exactly what Hope's Crossing needs."

"A womanizer who acts first and thinks later?" Ruth scoffed.

"A decorated, dedicated police officer who cares about this town and the people in it," she answered with quiet firmness and saw something warm and intense spark in his eyes.

"He's trouble," Ruth repeated. "You'll see. I love Mary Ella, you know that. She's a good friend and I love her girls, too. But that boy has broken her heart more times than I can count. He's trouble and he should never have come back."

Riley apparently decided he'd lurked in the hallway long enough. He took a step forward. "I'm sorry you feel that way, Mrs. Tatum."

If Ruth was discomfited at all, she hid it quickly. "I'm sorry you heard that, but I'm not sorry I said it."

"You're entitled to your opinion. Just like J. D. Nyman and anyone else who doesn't think I'm the right fit for police chief of Hope's Crossing. I'm the first one to accept I made mistakes that night. I have to live with them."

"So does my daughter!" Ruth snapped. "So does Taryn and her family. And your family most of all. You don't belong here. Not in Hope's Crossing and not in my daughter's house."

Claire stared at her mother, appalled at her rudeness and her gall. "You have no right, Mother. Riley is always welcome here."

He shrugged. "It's okay. I was just coming in to let you know we fixed the bike. It only took a moment to straighten the forks and it seems to be as good as new. Owen's taking it for a test-drive around the block."

"It's not okay. You don't have to leave. In fact, I was just getting ready to order pizza and we're going to watch a movie. We'd love you to stay."

The invitation was more to spite her mother and all three of them knew it, but she wasn't about to rescind it.

Ruth gave an offended sort of huff. "I'll go, then, and leave you to your pizza since no one wants to hear my opinion."

Claire was tired suddenly, exhausted from all the years of handling her mother's moods and piques. She missed the fun, happy mother she now barely remembered, the one Ruth had been before the humiliation of her husband's murder. She missed cuddles on the sofa under a blanket during a snowstorm and nature walks on Woodrose Mountain and the mom who used to have a funny story for everything. Ruth had gone from smart and capable to needy and helpless, with a side order of bitterness.

"Thank you for picking up Macy," she said, trying to focus on the positive.

"You know I'm always glad to help. I'll come by in the morning to pick her up before the soccer game."

"Thank you for the offer but Holly and Jeff are planning on it. If I hear otherwise from them, I'll let you know."

Ruth nodded stiffly and headed out the door, her shoulders tight. She closed the front door carefully behind her and Claire winced worse than if she'd slammed it. She would have preferred a temper tantrum. Ruth's quiet outrage was far more deadly.

She was going to have to figure out a way to make things right with her mother, but she had no idea how, short of throwing Riley on the pyre of her mother's animosity, which she wasn't willing to do.

"I'm sorry, Riley. My mother can be…"

"I know how your mother can be. Blunt but truthful."

"She has her opinions. Which I don't share, by the way."

"Plenty others do. J.D. has a lot of friends who think he should be the police chief right now. The events of this past month haven't exactly changed anyone's mind."

"I meant what I said. You're doing a good job."

"Thank you." He gave her a careful look. "Look, I appreciate the invitation for pizza. It was a nice gesture of support but not necessary. I've dealt with worse criticism of my job performance. At least here, nobody's shooting at me yet."

"The invitation was sincere, whatever you might think. The kids enjoyed having you over for dinner the other night. They'll love sharing their pizza."

"What about you?" His green eyes turned dark, intense, and her insides jumped again.

"What about me?"

"Weren't you just telling me all the reasons we weren't good for each other? Do you want me here?"

Here, there or anywhere. But this wasn't a Dr. Seuss book and Riley was definitely not green eggs.

"I wouldn't have invited you if I didn't," she answered. "What I said earlier still stands, but just because we have this…thing between us doesn't mean we can't be friends."

"Right. Friends." He studied her for a long moment, then gave a slight smile. "What could be more normal between friends than pizza and a movie?"

Trouble. That's exactly what he was.

Riley sat on the recliner in her warm, open family room with Claire on the sofa adjacent to him and the kids sprawled out on thick cushions on the floor. They were watching some superhero movie, but he couldn't have recited the plot if he were the one about to get run over by a train.

The echo of Ruth Tatum's words seemed to drown out everything else, ringing there with sonorous, unmistakable truth. He was definitely trouble.

The various women in his life could all take out an ad in the Sunday paper saying the same thing. Riley McKnight had been trouble since the day he was born.

He's broken his mother's heart more times than I can count, Ruth had said. He couldn't argue the truth of that. His mother had cried plenty of tears over him, starting long before his biggest sin in the eyes of the Ruth Tatums of Hope's Crossing, when his high school girlfriend had gotten pregnant his senior year.

If Lisa Redmond hadn't lost the baby just a few weeks after she discovered she was pregnant, Riley knew his life would have turned out completely different. He couldn't even comprehend it. He would have married Lisa at seventeen and taken some blue-collar job around town, maybe construction or maintenance at the ski resort. They probably would have been divorced young, if statistics held true. He would have a sixteen-year-old of his own now, something he could barely comprehend.

Lisa *had* lost the baby, miscarried at nine weeks. Her parents had sent her away to live with an aunt in Idaho for her senior year of high school and Riley had been left here to endure the small-town whispers and finger-pointing, one of the many reasons he had been quick to make his escape while he could.

The whole experience had been painful and difficult, but he knew he had been so wild and angry back then that he probably would have screwed up the kid for life.

As he listened to the thuds and thumps from some fight scene on screen, Riley thought of his own anger in his teens, how he had channeled his sense of loss and betrayal into wild drinking, partying, unprotected sex with his girlfriend.

He had been stupid and thoughtless, had hurt his mother probably even worse than his father had. Ruth was absolutely right about that.

He hadn't known what to do with all that anger after his father abandoned the family. As the lone male in a household of women, he'd needed a father in his life, damn it. He'd needed somebody to guide him, show him how to rein in his impulses, how to respect others. Instead, his father had thrown everything away so he could follow his own dreams, could move to South America and study the archaeological ruins of long-dead civilizations instead of having to face the drudgery of his everyday life as a high school teacher and administrator.

Over the years, Riley knew he'd become an expert at casual relationships. So what was he doing here, then, with a couple of kids and a woman like Claire, who was the antithesis of everything he told himself he needed all these years? He belonged in this cozy picture of domestic bliss about as well as a beach cabana on top of the quad lift at the Silver Strike. She told him outright she didn't want a fling and he had never been able to have anything else.

He sensed her watching him. When he turned his attention, she gave him a tentative smile. He gazed at her mouth for a long moment, remembering the particular softness of it, the angle and shape, then he jerked his gaze back to the screen.

She was so lovely, bright and vibrant like sunshine bursting through the clouds on a dank and cheerless day. He always seemed to forget that until he saw her again, when he would experience that "aah" of recognition.

A vague sense of unease settled between his shoulder blades. He shouldn't be here. He didn't belong.

"You don't have to stay," she murmured and he wondered what in his body language had given away his sudden trapped restlessness.

He should have seized on the exit route she'd offered and headed back down the street to his rental house. It seemed cowardly, however, just one more McKnight who walked away to suit his mood.

"We're almost to the end. I can't leave yet," he answered in the same hushed tone.

She didn't look convinced, something else unique about Claire. Most women were only too willing to believe whatever he told them. Not her. She seemed to filter every word, every phrase, through her own internal bullshit censor. He had a feeling he'd probably set off alarm bells more than a few times in his dealings with her.

This was it, he told himself. He would watch this movie and then work on extricating his life from hers. Claire Bradford had a couple of broken limbs, an idiot of an ex-husband and two active children. She didn't need more trouble in her world.

When the closing credits started rolling up the screen, Claire switched on the lamp beside the sofa.

"Great show. Good choice, Owen. Now it's time for bed. Macy's soccer game is early in the morning."

Neither of them answered and Riley realized he hadn't seen movement from the floor for the second half of the movie, except for Chester's occasional twitches as he snuggled up under Owen's arm.

"They beat you to it, apparently. I think they're both out for the count."

Claire shifted her body on the sofa for a better angle. She smiled a little sadly. "They look like kittens nestled together. It's too bad the only time they get along so well is when they're both asleep."

"They will. My sisters and I didn't always get along when I was a kid."

"No, really?"

He ignored her sarcasm. "Now I find most of them fairly tolerable."

"Something to look forward to, I suppose."

"So what now? Do you want to leave them here for the night?"

"On the floor?" She sounded appalled at the very idea and he smiled.

"My nieces and nephews prefer the floor to a bed half the time."

"That may be, but I think they'd probably sleep better and be more comfortable in their own beds. Macy. Owen. Wake up, kids."

Macy stirred a little but not to full consciousness. Claire repeated her name and the girl blinked her eyes for a moment, then rubbed at them blearily.

"I think I fell asleep."

Claire's daughter was as lovely as her mother, with Claire's blue eyes and warm brown hair. In a few years, she was going to be a stunner. Riley only hoped Jeff Bradford was the sort of dad who could put the fear of God in all the little punks who came sniffing around.

"Sorry." Macy yawned. "How did the movie end?"

"The same way it did the last time we watched it," Claire murmured. "And the time before that. And the time before that."

Macy offered up a sleepy smile as she gathered her cotton throw around her shoulders. "Maybe that's why I fell asleep. We need to pick a movie I haven't seen three times."

"It was Owen's turn and this was the one he wanted to see."

"Only he fell asleep in the middle. Wake up, dork."

Owen grunted in his sleep but rolled over again.

"We've got it, Macy. You can go on up to bed."

Her daughter unfolded from the floor with angular grace. "Night. Love you, Mom." She walked to Claire's sofa and wrapped her arms around her mother's neck.

Claire looked pleased as she returned the hug. "Love you, too, sweetheart."

Macy gave him a sleepy smile. "Night, Chief," she said, then headed out of the room.

"Owen, wake up," Claire said in a slightly louder tone.

Chester opened his eyes and gave them both a bored sort of look, but Owen didn't move.

"Come on, kiddo. Time to head up to bed."

The basset hound gave a jaw-cracking yawn and wriggled out from under the boy's arm and waddled over to Claire. He nudged at her arm.

"Does he need to go out?" Riley asked.

"Probably. Do you mind?"

"Not at all."

He walked to the back door, Chester on his heels. For the first time in more than a week, the night was gorgeous, clear and cloudless and glittering with stars that looked close enough to pluck with his fingers.

The dog seemed content to sniff around the fence line, checking for intruders, so after a moment of waiting for him, Riley returned to Claire and her son, who didn't look as if he'd budged.

"No luck?"

She shook her head. "He's renowned for sleeping through anything. Once he fell asleep on the caterpillar train at the county fair. He rode around three times before we could wake him up."

"Want me to carry him to his bed? I'm assuming his room is upstairs."

"It is, but let me try one more time."

"Owen, bath time."

The boy's eyes blinked open blearily. "Do I have to?"

She laughed softly and something warm and dangerous twisted through Riley, tugging at him. "Not tonight. You can take a bath in the morning. Can you make it up to your room?"

"I guess."

He yawned as big as the dog had done and climbed to his feet. "Why did you let me fall asleep in the middle of the movie?" he asked his mother in an accusatory sort of voice.

"I didn't realize you were asleep until the movie was over. But we can watch it again tomorrow if you want."

"Next time, wake me up," he muttered grumpily.

"Easier said than done, kiddo."

Owen still looked disgruntled, but he gave a halfhearted wave to Riley, then trudged up the stairs.

"I hate not tucking him in," Claire said in the same sort of disgruntled tone. "That's been one of the hardest things about this whole thing, but I just can't tackle all those stairs."

"Want me to do it?"

She looked surprised. "Do you mind? Macy usually takes care of it for me, but she's probably already asleep."

"I don't mind. Why would I?"

"I usually just make sure he's under his blankets and the night-light's on, that sort of thing."

"Claire, I might not have any kids, but I'm not completely helpless here. I think I can handle it."

Color climbed her cheeks and in the low lamplight she looked warm and sweet and completely adorable. "I'm sorry. Of course you can."

Grateful for the distraction, he headed out of the family room, stopping long enough at the back door off the kitchen to let the dog back inside before he headed up the stairs.

Owen was already in his bed, his eyes almost closed. Riley saw in the jumble of bedclothes that he wasn't inside his top sheet, only under a quilt with cowboy hat and boot material Riley wondered if Claire had made.

His eyes widened when he saw Riley. "Hi."

"Hey, kid. Your mom felt bad she can't tuck you in, so I said I'd check on you. Looks like you need to get between the sheets there."

Owen looked down. "Oh. Right."

He quickly adjusted the situation, slithering out of one spot and into the other. "Hey, thanks a lot for fixing my bike," he said when he was settled. "I'm super-glad we didn't have to take it to the shop."

"So am I. Have a good night, Owen."

"Thanks." He paused. "Will you leave my door open? My mom might need help in the night and I can't hear her if it's shut all the way."

Riley stared at this kid with the earnest freckled face and his mother's blue eyes, that peculiar tightness in his chest again. How many eight-year-old boys worried about their mother's comfort in the night? He sure as hell hadn't.

He cleared his throat. "You bet."

"Hey, you want to play basketball sometime? I got a new hoop for Christmas, but it's been too snowy or rainy to use much."

"Can you do that with the cast on your arm?"

"Oh, sure. But my mom can't and Macy would rather play soccer."

"What about your dad?"

Owen shrugged. "He doesn't like basketball much."

Just another mark in the Idiot column for Jeff Bradford. "Sure. Maybe. I'll have to check my schedule."

Owen seemed to accept the noncommittal answer with equanimity. "Okay. See you later, Chief."

"Bye, kid."

He closed the door a bit and headed down the stairs, where he found Claire waiting for him in the living room, Chester at her feet.

"Everything okay?" she asked.

He should leave right now, just walk out the door without another word. This family was seeping under his skin, finding unguarded spaces to settle into. "Owen wants me to come play basketball with him sometime."

She gave a rueful smile. "Sorry. I'm afraid he's a little desperate for someone to play with him right now. He probably assumes because you're male and, um, fairly athletic that you must play basketball."

"I can try to swing by sometime. He's a great kid."

She was silent for a moment. "You're really good with him and with Macy. Have you had a lot of experience working with kids as a police officer?"

More than he liked to think about, both as victims and perps. "A bit."

"Well, you seem to know just the right things to say. I thought so the night of the Spring Fling. You'd make a really great father."

He snorted loudly enough that Chester gave him a jowly faced scowl.

"Hooo. Wrong guy."

"Why? Haven't you ever thought about having kids of your own?"

The very idea made his palms itchy, clammy. "You forget. The McKnight men don't have a great track record in the family department."

She stared at him for a long moment, brow furrowed, then she frowned. "You are not your father, Riley."

He shrugged. "Who's to say I wouldn't become like him? I'm sure when he and Mom took vows, my dad never intended to abandon his wife and six kids twenty years later to follow his own dreams."

"It still hurts, doesn't it?"

He opened his mouth to tell her his father had been gone nineteen years, dead for fifteen of those, and any pain had long since healed. The lie scoured his gut.

"Yeah," he finally muttered. "Stupid, isn't it?"

"I don't think it's stupid. Only sad. I miss my dad, too."

He gazed at her, so lovely and pensive there in the low light, and he couldn't help himself. He leaned forward and brushed his mouth over hers once, then again. She made a tiny gasping sound that sizzled through him. Oh, dangerous. Claire Bradford was a beautiful, hazardous bundle of trouble.

When he moved his mouth slightly to try pulling away in some vain attempt to regain a little sanity, she followed him, leaning forward and up as if she couldn't bear to break the kiss. He closed his eyes, hating himself, but then he kissed her. Really kissed her. Tongue and teeth, heat and hunger.

The kiss went on and on. Just when he was about to climb onto the sofa with her, cover her body with his, reach beneath her clothing to the soft curves concealed there, a canine snort rasped through the room like someone had just fired up that chain saw again.

He froze and gazed at her, mouth swollen, eyes half-closed. She looked lush and gorgeous, so sensual that he had to move away from the sofa, out of arm's reach, or he would have grabbed for her again.

"See that?" His voice was low, raw. "I can't even be trusted to keep my hands off you even when we both know I'm not good for you. I take what I want, regardless of the consequences. Not so very different from my old man, am I?"

She stared at him, blinking back to reality. She gave a shuddering sort of breath, pressing fingers that trembled to her mouth, and he forced himself to look away, hating himself.

"Good night. Make sure you lock up behind me."

He headed out her back door into the May night.

Twelve

Oh, it was good to be back.

Claire shifted position in the overstuffed burgundy tapestry chair that now had pride of place beside the antique console table holding the String Fever cash register.

She had no idea where Evie had unearthed the old chair and its matching ottoman. They had been waiting for her when she showed up a few hours earlier, plump and comfortable and exactly the right height.

From here, she could keep her stupid cast elevated yet still be part of the day-to-day action in the store. Evie had even found a little wheeled worktable that fit precisely over the arms of the chair for her laptop and whatever small bead project she might be tackling.

She listened to the chatter of a couple of customers asking Evie a question about a class on the schedule for a few weeks' time and savored the joy of being back. She felt as if she had been freed from a long, dark winter, tossed headlong into verdant new leaves, warm sunshine, daffodils underfoot.

For the first time in three weeks, she didn't have that little niggle at the base of her neck, that disconcerting sensation of a life spinning beyond her control. Here, she was centered, calm. She only wished she'd come in a week earlier.

The customers signed up for the class and left together and Evie returned to the inventory list they'd been going over before the women came in.

"So it looks like we're running low on earring wires and toggle clasps."

"Wow, already?" Claire exclaimed. "I swear, I just ordered those last week. I guess it must have been longer than that."

Evie checked the computer. "Looks like six weeks. We had a run on both of those before Mother's Day. I see you liked your watchband, by the way."

Claire smile, twisting her wrist to better admire the way the recessed lights played on the gems. "You're a sneaky thing, aren't you? What were you doing, encouraging my son to lie to me about his whereabouts?"

Evie smiled. "Not my idea. He came up with the whole thing himself. Even picked out the spacers himself."

"Well, thank you. It was a lovely gift."

She'd cried buckets when she'd opened it—just as she'd cried when she opened the matching earrings and pendant Macy must have sneaked in to make. Her children knew her well. Handmade beadwork was definitely the way to her heart.

"Did you have a nice day yesterday?"

She thought of the brunch her mother had fixed, which had tasted slightly better than the crow Claire had decided to eat to ease the tension between them from their argument Friday night.

"Nice. My mom made her fantastic crepes. What about you?"

Evie smiled, though Claire thought it was slightly bittersweet and she wondered again at the past Evie never discussed. "Great. I picked up the dog I was talking about. He's gorgeous."

"Where is he?" she exclaimed. "Up in your apartment? You have to bring him down. I want to see! He and Chester can bond!"

"He was sleeping in his crate when I left and I didn't want to wake him. I'll go up in an hour or so and bring him down, see how he does in the store. I thought if you don't mind, I'll let him play out in the yard."

"Of course!" One of the things Claire loved best about her store—in pleasant weather, at any rate—was the garden in the back. The fenced space was only twenty feet by twenty feet, but it had a colorful flower garden and a set of lawn furniture she'd found at a yard sale the summer before. On sunny days, the children liked to do their homework out there or play with Chester.

"This is the bolo tie clasp I was thinking about making for the next class at the art center. What do you think?"

Claire admired the cleverly constructed piece. "I think that is a fantastic idea. Maybe we can get some of the husbands involved, the ones who always sit out in their cars and listen to talk radio while their wives bead."

Evie's smile was mischievous. "That's the plan. Get them hooked by making a project for themselves and then they won't mind when their wives come to the classes in the future."

"You're an evil genius in the making."

"Anything I can do to keep the classes going," Evie said. "It's my favorite part of the week."

Claire completely understood. She had started the senior citizen classes shortly after she took over at the request of some of her regular customers who were looking for an excuse to gather socially while they pursued their favorite hobby. She had found the women hilarious—smart, pithy, immensely creative—and had been delighted with the response. From überwealthy older women with vast vacation homes in the area to humble year-rounders like Mrs. Redmond next door, the ongoing class had been enormously successful and Claire had loved the interaction with Hope's Crossing's more seasoned citizens.

After a few months, many of those who came to the Bead Babes meetings started talking about how their arthritis symptoms seemed less severe while they were beading, with increased dexterity and less pain.

With that in mind—and not without a great deal of regret—Claire decided to turn the Bead Babes group over to Evie when she came to town from Southern California a year ago. Her credentials as a physical therapist made it a logical choice.

"What about next month?" Claire asked.

Evie looked suddenly secretive. "Actually, I wanted to talk to you about that."

"You can't quit," Claire said instantly. "I don't care. I won't let you. I know there's no such thing as indentured servitude anymore, but I'll figure out a way to make it legal again."

Evie laughed. "Relax. I'm not going anywhere. Well, not taking a new job anyway. You know I love it here. But I've been kicking around the idea of going out on the summer craft show circuit. So many of our customers who bead have had their lives tangled up in the poor economy. I was thinking I could take their work out on consignment across Colorado. Charge a nominal fee to them, mainly to cover the booth costs. It's sort of a win-win for String Fever because the beaders will buy their supplies from us, plus we can advertise at the craft fairs at the same time."

"Evie, that's brilliant!" Her mind raced with possible beaders who might be in need of a little extra income. Unfortunately, with the high taxes and cost of living in Hope's Crossing, that list was longer than it should have been.

"I love this idea. Which shows were you thinking?"

"Well, because you asked," she smiled. "I made a list." With her usual efficiency, she pulled out a folder next to the cash register and extracted a piece of paper. "This was just a listing of all the fairs within a two-hundred-mile radius."

"Wow! So many. I had no idea."

"Yes, I was thinking I would start with…"

Whatever she intended to say was cut off by the melodic chimes on the door, heralding a new arrival. Chester looked up with interest, then dropped his head again when he spied Ruth.

"Hi, Mom," Claire said.

"Oh, thank the good Lord. You're here."

Her heart gave a sharp kick at the urgent note in her mother's voice and her cast nearly slid off the ottoman as she straightened in the easy chair.

"What is it? What's wrong? Is it the kids? Did the school call you?"

Ruth's brow furrowed. "The school? No. Why on earth would they call me?"

She ordered her breathing to slow, her shoulders to relax, the visions of mortally ill children to clear. "I don't know. You just sounded so frantic when you came in. I assumed something was wrong with the kids."

"Of course I was frantic. I've been worried sick about you! I went to your house and you weren't there and I called your cell phone and you didn't answer. I thought maybe you'd had to go to the hospital or something. I'm so glad I decided to check here first."

"I'm sure if Claire had to go to the hospital, you would be the first one she called," Evie said in her quiet, calm voice.

"Sometimes I wonder," Ruth muttered.

Claire wasn't so certain, either, but she decided this might not be the best time to mention that.

"I must have turned off the ringer on my phone. I'm sorry." She pulled it out of her purse on the floor beside her and saw she had, indeed, missed six—count 'em six— calls from her mother.

"I never dreamed you were back at work. What are you doing here anyway?" Her mother went on. "You're not at all ready to come back to work!"

Claire swallowed her sigh. "Mom, it's been three weeks since the accident. Dr. Murray cleared me last week and even Jeff said there's no reason I can't return to work, as long as I take it easy."

"Which, for you, is easier said than done. You nearly died. I would say that warrants more than a few days away from work."

Three weeks did not a few days make—and while the accident had certainly been scary and she wasn't at all eager to repeat the experience, her mother's assessment was a bit of a stretch.

"I'm feeling much better now. I was more than ready to come back."

"You're going to be sorry. You watch. You're going to overdo and then you'll pay the price. You always think you can handle more than you should."

Since when? In Claire's view, the opposite was probably more accurate. She always feared she would crack apart under the strain of all she had to do, but somehow, despite the odds, she always managed to get through.

"I *have* been easing into the work, Mom. I promise. I'm hardly doing anything, just ask Evie."

"True enough, Ruth," her friend said helpfully. "She's

been sitting on her lazy butt all morning, just giving orders like the bossy britches she is."

Ruth looked between the two of them as if she wasn't quite sure whether to defend her daughter's work ethic or applaud her good sense.

Claire took pity on her mother's indecision. "Why were you looking for me? Did you need something?"

Ruth fussed at a clear plastic display of business cards on the table in a way that seemed completely unlike her. "Oh, you know. Just checking on you."

"Are you sure that's all?" Claire pressed.

Ruth picked up the bolo tie and rubbed a finger across the stone, avoiding Claire's gaze. "Well, the truth is, I need to ask your opinion about something."

She seemed reluctant to elaborate and Evie, brilliant and insightful friend that she was, stepped away from the counter. "I'm going to run up to check on my dog. Ruth, will you excuse me?"

"Bring him down with you," Claire said.

When she was gone, Claire turned to her mother again. "Mom, is something wrong? What's going on?"

"Nothing's wrong. Not exactly. I just wondered how you would feel if I took a temporary job."

Claire gaped at her. "A job."

"A temporary one. Mary Ella talked to me about it this morning. But I should just say no, especially while you and the children need me so much right now for rides and the like."

"I've certainly been grateful for your help, but I can make other arrangements. What sort of job?"

"Helping at the bookstore. You know Sage has gone back to college for her exams and Mary Ella's been running Dog-Eared by herself until Maura has a little more time to sort things out. Angie helps when she can, but she's busy with those kids of hers and of course Alex has the restaurant."

"I think that's a terrific idea!" Claire smiled. "You love to read. You would really excel in that environment."

"I thought about opening a bookstore myself when I was younger."

She stared. This was the first she'd ever heard that. "Really?"

Ruth shrugged. "I got married instead and then you came along. I wouldn't want to do it all the time, but it should be fun for a few weeks and if it helps Maura, then it's worth it. As long as you're sure you and the children can manage without me."

"While I appreciate all you've done for us, we'll make do," she assured her mother, still rather numb. Ruth sometimes helped at String Fever during busy times and she'd worked on and off at the charity consignment store in town, but she mostly lived off the proceeds of Claire's father's insurance policy and the sale of a hundred acres in Silver Strike Canyon that had been in her family for several generations.

"When do you start?"

"Tomorrow. Mary Ella's going to show me the routine there." She paused. "Do you think I'm crazy?"

"No, not at all! Why would I? I think it will be great for you. You'll love it, Mom."

"We'll see. I probably can't run Maura out of business in only a few weeks."

"You'll be fine. Don't worry."

Her mother decided to stay for a while and work on a few new pairs of earrings to go with her new undertaking. Unfortunately, that meant she was just settling in at the worktable with her findings and the seed beads and

Lucite she had decided to use when Evie came down with her temporary houseguest.

Claire immediately fell in love with the tan, gangly, unusual-looking creature, with a Lab-shaped face and body but tight, wiry poodle hair. Chester, too, seemed to find the new arrival acceptable. His tail even wagged when the dog—whom Evie introduced as Jacques—sniffed around him.

Ruth, not so much. When the friendly animal headed to greet her, her mouth pursed. "I hope you're not planning to bring that dog into the store with you on a regular basis. Chester is already one dog too many in a place of business, if you want my opinion."

Because Claire had heard that particular opinion countless times, she only smiled.

"Come on, Jacques," Evie said. "Out."

The dog obeyed the command immediately—as did Chester, who apparently wanted to make sure the new arrival knew which of them was in charge.

Evie had just come in from the garden with the dogs when the chimes rang again.

"Claire! You're back!"

Mary Ella burst through the door, headed straight for her and hugged her close.

"It's so wonderful to see you here in the store, right where you belong. You must have been more than ready to come back."

She smiled, resisting the childish urge to give her mother an "I told you so" look. "I was. Thank you."

"Ruth, did you tell Claire you're coming to help us out at the bookstore for a few weeks?"

"I did."

"I think it's a wonderful idea," Claire said.

"Ruth's help will be a godsend. Otherwise, I'm afraid

we would have to close the bookstore until Sage is done with school." Mary Ella automatically sat down at the worktable and picked up the beads Ruth was working with and admired them under the light. "These will be gorgeous, Ruthie. Make me a pair, will you?"

"If you help," Ruth said tartly. Mary Ella smiled and Claire felt a deep wave of gratitude for the other woman. She didn't know how, but somehow Mary Ella had remained close to Ruth for years, despite her mother's sometimes-toxic mood. Maybe it had something to do with raising five daughters and a wild son, but Mary Ella, better than anyone else Claire knew, could tease and cajole Ruth out of her most bitter moods.

"How are you?" Claire asked the other woman. "I mean, really."

Mary Ella trickled the cup of seed beads through her fingers and into a tray like water droplets. "My heart hurts all the time," she said after a long moment. "I keep thinking this has all been a mistake, you know? Someone somewhere made some terrible karmic error and any moment Layla will burst through my front door with that ridiculous purple hair and her fingers with all those rings flying away on her cell phone."

Her voice hitched a little on the last word and Ruth reached a hand out and squeezed her friend's fingers.

"We all wish that, more than anything."

"The worst thing is, I feel like this dark cloud has descended on the whole town, affecting us all. Everyone just seems so sad. Even the Angel's wings seem to have been clipped, have you noticed? I haven't heard about a single visit since the accident."

Claire thought of that night when Riley responded to her flickering porch lights. "I had a visit."

The three women stared at her. "What!" her mother exclaimed. "Why didn't you say anything?"

That night when Riley had fallen asleep in her family room seemed such a precious memory, one that still seemed not quite real. "I don't know. I guess I wanted to savor it myself. Anyway, it wasn't a big deal. He...the Angel left a basketful of magazines and books and other cheer-up treats on the front porch one night the weekend before last."

"Did you see the Angel?" Evie asked, her eyes bright and intent, which made Claire wonder once more if her friend could be behind the mystery. Evie had arrived in Hope's Crossing not long before the Angel first started appearing and even though she lived a low-key life, Claire had picked up a few clues here and there that Evie might be secretly affluent, someone who could afford the kind of generosity the Angel had displayed.

Besides, Evie certainly knew her reading preferences and her favorite kind of goodies from Sugar Rush.

She searched the other woman's face for some hint that she might know more about the Angel of Hope than she let on but saw nothing more than curiosity.

"Just a shape in the darkness," she finally said. "Not much more than that. Riley checked around the house and the yard for me and couldn't find any clues."

She probably shouldn't have added that little detail, judging by the various reactions. Ruth's mouth pursed as if she'd smelled something particularly foul. Mary Ella gave her a long, speculative look. Evie, drat her, looked as if she were barely hiding a smile.

"Riley?" Mary Ella said.

Claire cleared her throat. "Funny story. I saw a shape out there and thought it might be an intruder. I flicked my porch lights a couple of times to maybe scare him off or something. Riley happened to be passing by just then and stopped to make sure everything was okay."

"Nice of him," Evie murmured.

"Right. Um, well, he checked around the house and the yard for me and couldn't find any clues."

She decided not to mention that he'd fallen asleep or that when he'd awakened he said wholly inappropriate things to her she couldn't stop thinking about. Or the subsequent times he'd dropped by and kissed her until she couldn't remember her name.

Changing the subject right now would probably be a good idea. "You know, whoever it is," she said quickly, "there's something so magical about the whole thing, don't you think? The mystery of an unexpected kindness. I'm glad I didn't see who it was. I'm not really sure I want to know. Don't you think something will be lost if we ever figure it out?"

Mary Ella nodded. "You know, I think you're right."

"You're both crazy. I want to know who it is," Ruth said.

"But this way, we all think the best of each other," Claire said. "We wonder if it could be our neighbor. We look at people in the street and wonder, is it him or her? It could be anyone. Or everyone."

"What are you talking about?" Ruth gave a baffled frown.

Mary Ella smiled. "She just means all the speculation is part of the good the Angel is doing in town. Maybe we all think a little more kindly toward each other and have become a little more aware of each other's needs. The Angel has lifted all of us, whether we've been direct recipients or not."

Claire stared at the other women as random ideas that had been floating through her mind suddenly coalesced in one grand vision. "That is exactly what Hope's Crossing needs!"

"What? A visit from the Angel?" Ruth asked.

"No. We all need to *be* angels of Hope!"

The three women stared at her. Ruth still looked confused, but Evie looked intrigued and Mary Ella's features lit up with excitement.

"That is sheer brilliance, Claire," she exclaimed.

"What are you thinking? A 'random acts of kindness' sort of thing?" Evie asked.

Ideas raced through her head, faster than she could sort them out. "No. No, but I think that could definitely be a component. We need to do something to bring this town together. Everyone in Hope's Crossing has been affected by the accident in some way or another. Don't you feel like something has been shattered?"

"Other than your arm and your leg?" Ruth said caustically, gesturing to her respective casts.

"Besides a few bones. We've all suffered a great loss."

"We should do whatever we can to heal it," Evie said quietly and Claire smiled at her, grateful beyond words for whatever twist of fate had brought her friend here to the mountains of Colorado.

"What about a day of service? Neighbors helping neighbors," Mary Ella suggested. For the first time since she came in, her lovely green eyes looked clear and unclouded by sorrow.

"Yes. Yes!" Claire thought of the possibilities. Fences that needed to be painted, windows to be washed, blankets to be knitted. "We could involve everyone. Children, families, youth groups."

"We should have something special planned for the teenagers. They've lost so much," Evie said.

Claire thought of Taryn, a cheerleader and popular girl

at Hope's Crossing High School, lying in a hospital bed in
Denver, of Charlie Beaumont, facing serious charges in
the accident, of the other teens involved.

And, of course, of Layla.

She leaned forward suddenly, an abrupt movement that
sent a pain rippling up her leg that she ignored. "What if
we end the day with a dinner dance and benefit auction.
The proceeds can go to a charity that benefits the entire
community. Maybe something with particular impact on
the young people."

"A scholarship in Layla's name," Ruth said abruptly.

"Oh." Mary Ella's features softened.

Claire beamed at her mother. "Oh, perfect, Mom. Just
perfect."

"Maura would be touched, don't you think?" Evie asked.

"How soon could we throw it together?" Claire asked.
"Would a month give us enough time?"

"Layla would have turned sixteen on June fourth," Mary
Ella offered.

Claire calculated. Three and a half weeks. Could they
make it happen in that short amount of time? "A little less
than a month, then."

"It's too much work," Ruth said.

"No, we can do this. I can't imagine a better day for it."

She pulled the rolling table with her laptop toward her,
excitement flooding through her. This is what the town
needed, something to hold on to. The bright beam of hope
piercing the dark clouds that had lingered since the tragedy.

Thirteen

Evenings like this seemed surreal to him. A little spooky even.

Riley drove toward his rented house past the close-set Victorian houses of Old Hope, down streets where he saw neighbors out front talking to neighbors, lawns being mowed, kids riding skateboards on homemade ramps in their driveways.

Through the open window of his patrol vehicle, he could smell fresh-cut grass mingled with the sharp sweetness of blooming sagebrush and the delectable aroma of steaks on the grill somewhere close.

It was about as far from the gritty, dark world of an undercover narcotics cop in the inner city of Oakland as anything he could imagine without leaving the planet.

With all the changes the town had seen in the twenty years since he'd been a kid, the particular sweetness of a warm spring evening seemed timeless.

Oh, he wasn't naive enough to think all was Mayberry-perfect in Hope's Crossing. After a month as police chief, he knew the usual elements of human ugliness simmered under the surface. Domestic violence, assault, embezzlement. Even illegal substances. On his desk right now were reports about ongoing investigations featuring all of the above.

He supposed the difference was that in Hope's Crossing, those things were the exception, not the norm.

It was a nice town. The influx of tourists made life a little more interesting and had certainly changed the dynamics, but Hope's Crossing was still a good place to live.

For most people anyway. The jury was still out for him. Maybe he wouldn't even have a job in a month's time when his sixty-day probationary period expired. J. D. Nyman was certainly doing his best to stir up trouble and raise doubt in people's mind as to his competence.

As he turned onto Blackberry Lane, he lifted a hand to wave at Mrs. Redmond on the corner, pruning back a leggy forsythia of bright blooming yellow. She gave him a sour look and deliberately turned her back.

Lisa's grandmother was one of those old-timers who had genuine reason not to want him there, he admitted, reasons not based on prejudice or malice. He had genuinely wronged her family in his wild youth, something he couldn't repair no matter how many hours of service he gave to the town.

Still, others in town somehow had come to blame him for everything that was wrong with the community, regardless of any rational reason. Somehow they seemed to think he was responsible for a group of teens who had suddenly gone off track, although how the hell they thought he had anything to do with Charlie Beaumont and his band of troublemakers other than being uncle to one of them, Riley had no idea.

He sighed as he drove past Claire's house, the brick a warm, weathered rust in the evening light. A basketball suddenly rolled out of her driveway and he hit the brakes just seconds before he would have rolled over it.

"Hey, Chief," Owen called from the edge of the driveway, where he had safely waited instead of chasing into the road after his ball.

"Hey, kid."

He glanced up at the house and saw her there, sitting on a wicker chair on her front porch. She shaded her eyes against the light filtering through the trees and although her smile was guarded, it was still about a hundred degrees warmer than the look he'd just gotten next door.

He lifted a hand in greeting and she waved back with her broken arm.

"Should I wait for you to go past before I get the ball?" Owen asked him.

"No, go ahead."

The boy hurried to the side of the car and scooped it from where it had come to rest against the front tire. "Hey, you want to play?" he asked. "Macy's not home and my mom can't. I'm tired of just shooting by myself."

He should give some excuse—just let the boy grab his ball, wait for him to return to the safety of his driveway, then drive on by. That was the smart thing to do. The safe thing. But he was feeling reckless suddenly and a quick game of hoops wouldn't hurt anything, right? And besides, he *had* more or less promised Owen he would play sometime.

"Sure," he answered and was rewarded with a gleeful shout.

He parked his patrol vehicle and saw Claire's wary surprise when he stepped out.

Chester greeted him with as much enthusiasm as the hound could muster, then plopped back in the cool green grass.

"Watch this!" Owen said, going for the freestanding basketball standard next to the driveway.

"Wow, Kobe Bryant. Your left-handed jump is wicked."

Owen grinned and tossed him the ball. Riley fired it off and was gratified when it swooshed through the net.

"Nice." Owen grabbed the ball and took a ten-foot jumper. It bounced on the rim for a minute with a boing sort of sound, then fell through.

At his suggestion, the two of them played an informal game of PIG—the younger brother of HORSE—for a while and it was close to a perfect moment for Riley. The warm evening, the setting sun turning everything golden, the sweet Rocky Mountain air that smelled of home and peace and summer just around the corner.

Claire had put down whatever she'd been working on, though she said nothing, only watched them.

He was showing off for her, he realized after one particularly hotdog shot, a one-handed, behind-the-back throw that landed in the sweet spot. It was a rather embarrassing realization, a reminder of all those times when he was a kid trying desperately to make her notice him.

What would she say if she knew he still probably had the road rash scars on his back from a spectacular bike crash when he was twelve, trying to pop a wheelie in front of her house and failing spectacularly?

Hunger curled through him, slow and insistent. Stupid. She'd warned him away the last time he was here, told him plainly she wasn't interested in any kind of one-on-one with him. He would do well to keep that in mind.

"Okay, what's a hard one you can't hit?" Owen said, considering his options. While he set up the shot, Riley risked another glance at Claire and found her watching him. Their gazes locked for a moment, then she quickly looked away, a blush staining her cheeks.

A tensile thread of awareness stretched between them, taut and shimmery, and he was so busy trying to figure out what the hell to do with it that he completely missed Owen's shot except for the swish of the net.

"That's G for you. I win!" Owen exclaimed after Riley took a wild shot and completely missed the hoop.

"Good game, kid."

"How about two out of three?" the boy said.

Riley looked at Claire. "How about another day? I should go say hello to your mom."

"Okay. I have to pee anyway."

Riley set the ball down on the standard's base, paused to pet Chester's brown droopy face, then headed up the three porch stairs, the memory of the kiss they had shared the last time he'd seen her playing over and over in his head. He relentlessly tried to shut it down by reminding himself of all the reasons why kissing her was a lousy idea.

Still, he couldn't resist brushing her cheek with a light, friendly sort of kiss when he reached her. If he inhaled the scent of her, fresh and lovely as the spring evening, that was nobody's damn business but his own.

"Thanks for playing with him for a few minutes," she said and he wondered if he was imagining that slightly husky note to her voice. "It's a little tough for me to go in for a layup right now."

"And I would guess the cast on your arm probably plays havoc with your shooting percentage."

She smiled. "I guess I'm a wuss in that respect. A cast doesn't seem to bother Owen, obviously."

"I hear you went back to work today," he said after an awkward pause, perching on the white gingerbread railing that encircled the house.

"Wow. Really? I wasn't aware it made the *Hope Gazette*."

"I sometimes think the *Gazette* is a waste of paper around here. I mean, who really needs it because everyone knows everything anyway? Donna Mazell apparently stopped in on her lunch break. She told me about how you've got a nice comfortable chair set up by the register like the Bead Queen of Hope's Crossing."

"Queen Claire. That's me. I forgot Donna came in. She was looking for polymer beads for a project she's doing with her grandkids."

He didn't know polymer beads from pinto beans, any more than he'd been able to figure out just how exactly Donna had guessed with such accuracy that he might have a particular interest in the comings and goings of a particular bead-store owner of their mutual acquaintance.

"She said she walked out of the store with about seventy-five bucks in beads she hadn't planned to buy and had no idea what she was going to do with."

Claire smiled. "It's the beaders' curse. Knitters, too. They call it SABLE—Stash Acquisition Beyond Life Expectancy. I've got more beads in my personal collection than I'll ever be able to use. You tell Donna she may as well give in. Resistance is futile."

Now there was something he could relate to. He had no power to resist the inexorable pull tugging him to her.

His bodily functions apparently taken care of, Owen burst through the front door and started to head back to his basketball, but Claire's voice stopped him.

"You need to go make sure you've got everything you want to take to your dad's tonight."

"Oh, yeah. I forgot. Okay."

He turned around and raced back inside at that full-throttle speed Owen seemed to use for everything.

"I didn't realize they sometimes went with Jeff and Holly on weeknights."

"Tonight's a special night. Jeff's birthday."

"Ah."

"We're pretty flexible with the custody arrangements. Right after the separation, we tried fifty-fifty joint physical custody for a while, but it was tough on the kids. One week here, one week there. They never felt like they really lived in either of our places. After Holly and Jeff got married, we decided weekends with their dad worked better all the way around except for special occasions because that's when he had the most time to spend with them anyway."

"Macy doing homework?"

"She actually went shopping with Holly for birthday stuff after school. Owen would have gone with them, but he had Cub Scouts this afternoon, until a little while ago."

This was nice, he thought. Sitting here on her porch in the evening while birds flitted through the trees and a light, mountain-scented breeze ruffled his hair. A curious feeling stole through him, so unaccustomed that it took him a moment to identify it.

Contentment.

Even with his unfulfilled attraction for her, the ache in his gut he knew would never be satisfied, he enjoyed her company so much he didn't mind.

"I interrupted you. What were you working on when I pulled up? Something for your shop?"

Her eyes lit up with excitement. "We had this idea down at the store today."

"I'm guessing by that you mean *you* had an idea."

She tucked a loose strand of hair behind her ear so the breeze couldn't play with it anymore. "It really was one of those group-think situations, everyone throwing out ideas."

"Everyone being?"

"Well, Evie Blanchard. You met her that day in my store, I think. Your mother and mine were part of the discussion, too."

"This sounds like trouble, then. As chief of police, I'd better hear what you're up to so I can be prepared."

She rolled her eyes. "We want to organize a day of service where hopefully everyone in town works together to help someone else."

"Sounds ambitious."

"Maybe, but can't you just see the possibilities? When we're done, not only will the town be better tangibly, but I hope people will also feel a little happier. We're thinking the whole thing should culminate in a charity benefit. A real town celebration. What do you think?"

He pictured it, some Pollyanna-ish utopia of neighbors helping neighbors. Despite a quick cynical vision of fistfights erupting over trees overpruned or fences varnished incorrectly, he couldn't resist Claire's excitement. Her whole face glowed with it and she was so lovely there in the evening light that he couldn't seem to look away.

"You're really into this, aren't you?"

"I am. I think it's just what the people of Hope's Crossing need to...to begin to heal."

She smiled a little and reached a hand across the space between them to cover his fingers with hers. He stared at their joined hands and his stomach swooped as if he'd just missed a couple steps and stumbled down a staircase. He didn't want her to move her hand. Not ever.

What was happening here? His throat felt dry, achy, and his chest was tight. He'd never felt this way about a woman before, he realized, this overwhelming urge to tuck her up against his heart.

He couldn't seem to look away, edgy and uneasy. All his instincts that had protected him through gang shootings and shaky drug deals were warning him to get the hell out of here now while he could.

Unaware of his turmoil, Claire smiled softly. "Riley,

we want the proceeds to go into a scholarship fund to help the youth, in Layla's name. Don't you think that would be wonderful?"

"A scholarship."

Layla should be planning her own college path. Instead his niece was dead and now Claire thought she could make everything better by throwing some kind of work party.

"We want to have it on what would have been her birthday."

"That's less than a month away. How can you possibly pull off something this ambitious in that time?"

"It's definitely going to take work, but we're setting up committees to handle everything. We were thinking of having the benefit dinner at the Grand Ballroom at the Silver Strike. Since it's the off-season, I think we can swing it. And Alex of course can help with the food."

Her voice dwindled when she must have begun to sense his less-than-enthused reaction.

"You don't like the idea," she said, looking crestfallen.

"I didn't say that."

"Is it the idea of a benefit? It doesn't have to be something fancy. In fact, it would probably be better if we kept the whole thing low-key, given our time constraints."

He was angry suddenly. Angry at fate for sending him on that mountain road, at himself for ever thinking he could come home and make this work, especially angry at her for being so decent and good and therefore completely out of his reach.

"Look at you, Claire. You can't even walk, but you still think you have to save the whole damn town."

She blinked a little at his sudden attack. "Not true. I'm not trying to save anyone. I just want everyone to come together. To remind the town that we can forget our pain a little when we're reaching outside of it to help someone else."

"You want people to forget Layla is dead?"

"I didn't say that. Not at all."

"You think if you have people mow a few lawns, wash a few windows, you can stick a bandage on the whole thing and everybody will forget the pain and loss. Just kiss the boo-boo and make it all go away."

Hurt bloomed in her eyes. "No. Never. I want everyone to remember Layla. Honor her in a positive way. That's what the scholarship would be."

"You want to pretend Hope's Crossing is this idyllic little valley town, full of peace and goodwill, hearts and flowers. Love thy neighbor and all that crap. Well, sorry to break it to you, but the people here can be just as greedy and selfish as anywhere else in the world."

Her expression grew frosty. "I'm not an idiot, contrary to what you apparently think. I know life in Hope's Crossing isn't perfect. But what's wrong with trying to make it better?"

He had no idea why he was so upset suddenly, but it burned in him, fierce and hot. Frustration over his job, over the charges pending with Charlie Beaumont, over his impossible attraction to Claire, all meshed together in one big ball of anger.

"It's a complete waste of energy. At the end of the day, you might have a few hundred dollars for some college scholarship that would probably be won by some annoying little overachieving punk. But the town will not change just because you want it to, because you think a few acts of service will suddenly make it so."

"We might not change everything, but we can help a few people."

"For what? At the end of the day, no matter how much

work you put into this, nothing will be different. People here will still be as small and petty as they are anywhere else. You'll still be a divorced mother whose husband left you for a ditz with perfect teeth and a boob job."

As soon as the words left his mouth, he wanted to yank them back. He felt as if he'd just drop-kicked a kitten. She paled with a quick, indrawn hitch of breath as if he'd just shattered bone as surely as that accident.

He closed his eyes, hating himself. "I'm sorry. That was…"

Whatever he meant to say was cut off by the approach of a gleaming black Cadillac SUV that slowed in front of her house and turned into the driveway.

"That would be Jeff," Claire said, her voice tight and hollow.

"Claire…"

She cut him off, climbing to her feet with the aid of her crutches to pull open the door. "Owen, your dad is here," she called, and from inside he heard a distant "Okay."

Tension simmered between them, harsh and angry, as Jeff Bradford climbed out of the SUV and headed toward them. He was wearing a tight Ed Hardy T-shirt and a pair of trendy jeans with a wide belt and artfully scuffed boots, something better suited for someone ten years younger.

He looked surprised and not at all pleased to find Riley on the porch of his ex-wife's home.

"Chief." The word was cool and somehow edged with disdain.

"Doc," he replied in the same tone.

The other man leaned in to kiss Claire on the cheek and Riley watched her force a smile, her color still high. "Happy birthday," she said.

"Thanks."

"Your present is inside on the table."

The woman could barely move, but she'd still managed to figure out a way to find a birthday present for her jerk of an ex. That weird ache in his throat returned, all that terrifying tenderness, and he knew he needed to get out of there.

"I'd better run. I'll see you later, Claire."

He didn't want to leave while things were so tense between them, but he couldn't stay here and be polite to Jeff Bradford, not when he wanted to pound the guy right in the gullet of that stupid winged dragon on his T-shirt for ever hurting her.

As he hurried down the porch steps toward his patrol vehicle, he had to wonder which of the two adult males on her property was the bigger ass.

Fourteen

His words shouldn't have such power to wound her. Claire knew it intellectually, but that didn't keep the echo of them from gouging under her skin and even as she watched Riley drive away, she had to fight angry tears.

You'll still be a divorced mother whose husband left you for a ditz with perfect teeth and a boob job.

There it was, stark and unadorned. Riley saw her as some pathetic figure who hadn't been enough for her husband, only as Jeff's castoff.

She tucked away her hurt and focused on what needed to be done at the moment, hoisting herself up on the crutches and hobbling into the house.

"Owen, hurry. Your dad is ready to go."

"I know. I'm coming. Just a sec," he called down the stairs. "I want to take some Lego guys."

Jeff rolled his eyes. "As if he doesn't have a whole box full of Lego junk at my place."

"He's got his favorites, I guess. Can I get you something to drink?"

"I'm good."

"I need to grab a glass of water. Excuse me."

She wasn't surprised when Jeff didn't offer to get it for

her—not that she would have accepted anyway. Right now she was very sick of frustrating men.

She was so busy making her careful way down the hall that she hadn't realized he followed her until she was pouring a glass from the pitcher of filtered water in the refrigerator.

"You're getting along well," he commented.

"I hate it."

"It's a pain, I know. This is the point where all my patients want to cut off their own legs. But you should be able to change casts in a few weeks to one that allows you to walk around more easily."

"I'm not looking forward to a whole summer of hot, itchy casts."

"Relax. You won't have them all summer. I'm guessing you'll probably be ready to lose the cast on your arm in a month or so. The one on your leg might take a few weeks longer, but I'd still say by June you should be done."

That was in line with what Dr. Murray had told her. "Good," she said with heartfelt relief.

He crossed his arms across his chest and changed the subject. "What was McKnight doing here?"

Besides shoving a knife into my heart and making me feel like a fool? She shrugged. "He lives down the street, you know. In that small rental on the other side of the Stimsons. He was passing by and saw Owen playing hoops, so he stopped for a moment to join him."

"I don't like him hanging around here."

For a long moment, all she could do was stare. "Excuse me?"

"Ruth told me he was here the other night, that he's been hanging around. I don't like it. He's not a good influence on Macy and Owen."

"You don't like it." Her temper, which had already been

simmering like Macy's red sauce after what Riley said, started to scorch and smoke.

"You know his reputation with women. You've been friends with Alex your whole life and you've heard the rumors, too. He's a tomcat and always has been. He goes through women like I go through exam gloves and then tosses them away with as little care. He's not good for you, Claire."

She drew in a steadying breath, but it had little effect against the fury sparking through her. That her husband— currently married to a woman ten years his junior and dressing like he was on an MTV reality show, for heaven's sake—would dare lecture her about her choice of friends was beyond belief.

"I do not want to have this conversation with you."

He ignored her quiet warning. "I care about you, Claire. I know how you can be when you pour your heart into something. You always go all the way and don't hold any part of yourself back. I would hate to see that happen with McKnight. Whatever game he's playing, I just don't want you to be crushed when he moves on."

Did *everyone* see her as some pathetic loser who, first of all, couldn't keep a man and, second of all, fell apart when said man left?

She wasn't, darn it. She didn't need either of them in her world to be perfectly content. She had a great life. Good friends, a thriving business, a comfortable home in a town she loved. She wasn't trying to fill any emptiness in her life with either unhealthy relationships or community events.

She sipped at her cold water in hope that it might cool her temper.

"Riley and I are friends, Jeff. That's all." And right now, truth be told, she wasn't sure she wanted to claim even that.

"Are you sure? Because Riley McKnight does not strike

me as the kind of guy who would hang around playing basketball with a kid and pruning your trees and fixing a roof for you unless he wanted to slurp you up with a spoon."

"Apparently you and my mother have had plenty to talk about."

"I'm concerned about you."

She set her glass in the sink with a loud clank. "Funny, don't we have a divorce decree lying around somewhere that clearly indicates you decided you no longer wanted the right to an opinion about my friends?"

"I didn't stop caring about you just because we fell out of love."

You fell out of love, she wanted to yell at him. That was totally a knee-jerk reaction, though, and not even true. They had become roommates those last few years of his medical training and after they first came back to Hope's Crossing.

Anyway, she wouldn't go backward even if she could. She wasn't the same person anymore and probably wouldn't last a week married to him, always catering to his opinion and working with tireless effort to make his life run smoothly, the same pattern she'd perfected growing up with Ruth.

"Be careful. That's all I'm saying," Jeff said. "The kids don't need to see you making a fool of yourself over him."

Oh, she so wanted to point out his Ed Hardy shirt and the Botox injections, but she was trying to be a nice person, right?

"Riley is my friend, that's all. He has been for years. When you think about it, he's been in my life longer than you have. I'm sorry if you don't like it, but I'm not going to hurt somebody I care about by pushing him away just because you suddenly have some ridiculous notion the two of us are secretly carrying on some hot, steamy affair."

Jeff studied her for a moment, then he suddenly smiled in a self-deprecating way. "You're right. I'm being silly, aren't I?"

Conversely, his capitulation only made her feel more like that pathetic loser Riley apparently thought her.

Just once, maybe she would like to be wild, wanton, crazy. The kind of woman who could have a man make a fool of himself over her. She would prefer he didn't do it by suddenly streaking his hair and going for facials, like Jeff had done for Holly. But, hey, at this point she would take what she could get.

The sound of tromping feet down the stairs effectively ended their discussion and a moment later Owen burst into the kitchen.

"Okay, I'm ready."

"Let's go, dude." Jeff slung Owen's bulging backpack over his shoulder.

"I'll see you after school on Wednesday."

"Love you, Mom. Bye."

She hugged him and felt that little clutch at her heart as she always did when they were going to stay with their father.

"Don't forget your present," Owen said to his father as they headed for the front door.

Jeff picked it up from the console table and gave it a little shake. "Heavy."

"I have one I bought myself with allowance and so does Mace," Owen informed him. "That one's from all of us."

"Great," Jeff said as he opened the door for their son. "The Escalade's unlocked. Go ahead and get in the back-seat."

Owen gave Chester one last squeeze, then raced for the Escalade.

"Thanks for the gift, Claire."

"Sorry about the wrap job. I'm not at my best one-handed."

"I'm sure I'll love it."

She had thought so, too, when she'd purchased the framed photograph at a gallery several weeks ago.

He pulled her into a hug and she thought of all the history between them and how strange it was that, as much as she'd once loved him, she had no desire to share anything with him now except their children.

"Just be careful with McKnight, okay? Even a friendship with him might not be the best course right now, politically. I wouldn't be surprised if the city council tosses him out on his can. This accident has people in an uproar. As a small businesswoman trying to make a living in this town, you can't afford to alienate people by aligning yourself with the wrong sort."

She instinctively wanted to defend Riley, but she had no wish to prolong the argument with Jeff, so she gave him a polite smile. "I'll keep that in mind," she said.

After he left, she closed the door behind him, then sank onto the bench in the foyer, her bones aching. She wasn't at all certain she had the energy to even move to a more comfortable spot. Working all day and then dealing with two frustrating males had completely wrung her dry.

Each creak and groan of the big old house seemed to echo as she closed her eyes and considered her options for the rest of the evening.

What she really wanted right now was a long, luxurious soak in the claw-foot tub upstairs in the master bath that she had insisted on keeping when they renovated the house. But because she still wasn't sure about her ability to handle fifteen narrow steps—and because she couldn't very well soak in the tub anyway given the blasted casts—she would have to settle for the pitiful alternative of a shower using the chair the home care nurses had rigged that first day she was home.

Chester apparently decided he was done with his outdoor nap and ready to try the sleeping accommodations inside. He gave his deep, yowly rarh-rarh-rarh bark and she climbed to her feet—well, foot and crutches anyway—and opened the door for him.

He waddled inside, his tail wagging with more energy than the rest of him, appearing delighted to see her. "You're such a good dog. Yes, you are," she cooed, rubbing his acres-long ears. "You love me, don't you, buddy?"

He gave her a doggy grin that looked so incongruous with his sad, droopy eyes and deep jowls. As she rubbed at the spot he loved just behind his collar, Claire could feel her shoulders relax and a bit of the tension of the past half hour seep away. At least one of the males in her life was relatively trouble-free. Food and a warm bed, that's all he needed.

"You want some dinner, don't you?"

In answer, he waddled toward the kitchen, his paws clicking on the wood floor and his tags jingling.

She followed him and refreshed his water and food dish, a bit of a chore with her limited mobility but not impossible.

When the dog's immediate needs were taken care of, she opened the refrigerator and considered her own options. Right now, that last piece of Alex's sinful chocolate cake with the layer of raspberry sauce and the chocolate curls on top looked mighty appealing.

She could have chocolate cake for dinner if she wanted. After the day she'd had, didn't she deserve it?

"You won't tell, will you, buddy?"

Chester barely looked up from his dinner and Claire decided to take that as a yes.

She pulled out the cardboard box with the resort logo and set it on the table. She was sticking a fork into all that chocolaty goodness when she heard a low rapping at the back door.

Chester didn't bark, only wagged his tail eagerly on the kitchen floor, moving around a couple of chocolate cake crumbs she hadn't realized she dropped.

With a sigh, she pulled out the fork and set it on the plate, then hobbled to the door and peeked through the filmy curtain. She supposed she wasn't really surprised to find Riley on the other side, hands in his back pockets.

He'd changed out of the trousers and dress shirt he'd been wearing earlier for work to jeans and a casual cotton red shirt, the sleeves rolled up to midforearm in the still-pleasant evening.

Her stomach did a long, slow roll and she was tempted for a moment not to answer the door. All she wanted was to eat her chocolate cake dinner in peace, have a lousy, awkward shower with half her body wrapped in plastic and then crawl into bed. Was that too freaking much to ask?

Fighting with Riley again didn't fit into that agenda whatsoever.

The only trouble was, he knew she'd seen him. They'd made eye contact, so she couldn't just go back to her cake and ignore him, much as she would like to.

With a sigh, she opened the door.

"I saw the lights on back here and took a chance you were in the kitchen," he said. "I didn't want you to have to make your way through the whole house to the front."

Drat him for being so thoughtful and kind sometimes. And for making Jeff's pretentious attempts to look young and hip seem so ridiculous in contrast to Riley's completely natural deliciousness.

She wished again that she were that sexy, wanton woman

who could fling open the door and jump into his arms without any regard to the consequences. Not that she would do that. Despite their few heated kisses, Riley was only a friend, right?

Still, a girl appreciated choices.

"Come in," she finally said and held the door open farther. After an awkward sort of pause, he walked past her into the kitchen, bringing the scents of the May evening, of sage and pine and loamy dirt.

He looked at the solitary slice of cake on the table. "I'm interrupting your dessert."

"Right. Yes. My dessert. That's exactly what it is." She wasn't about to admit the cake comprised the totality of her nutritional intake for the evening.

"I'm sorry. This won't take long. I just came to apologize."

She said nothing, not sure if she was ready to forgive that easily. He had made her feel small and pathetic and she wasn't sure she could get past that to act as if nothing had happened.

"I'm an ass."

Since his words still stung, she wasn't about to disagree. "I can see where that might be a problem for you, generally speaking."

He smiled a little, although his eyes were still dark with regret.

"I'm sorry, Claire. What I said before, completely uncalled for. I don't see you that way."

"You must or you wouldn't have said it."

"I think I'd like to see you that way," he admitted. "It would be…safer to help me keep some distance."

"Why?"

He didn't answer her and electricity suddenly crackled in the air. She found her gaze on his mouth again and quickly jerked it away, but not before a couple of wild fantasies flashed into her head, the two of them tangled together, his mouth exploring her skin....

Right. No. They were friends. She wasn't going to wade into those dangerous waters.

"It's a pretty evening," he said abruptly. "Feel like getting out? I thought we could take a walk, if you're up to it."

She should say no, return to her backup plan of cake and a shower. But the night was lovely and the idea of a solitary evening had lost most of its appeal. Riley's presence seemed to have blown away her exhaustion like cottonwood puffs on the breeze.

"Sure. Okay. A walk would be nice," she said quickly before she could let common sense change her mind.

"It's cooling down now that the sun is setting. Do you want a jacket?"

"Probably."

"I'll get it for you. Just point me in the right direction."

She had a half-dozen lovely sweaters she couldn't wear over the cast without stretching out their left sleeves irreparably, so her buttery-soft apricot pashmina would have to do.

"I've been using a wrap. I think I left it hanging over the back of one of the chairs in the living room."

He found it quickly and returned to the kitchen. "Now the wheelchair."

"I can walk, if you have the patience to wait for me."

"I don't mind pushing. I was thinking we could walk over to Sweet Laurel Falls. That's probably a bit too far for you to handle on your sticks here."

She hated the wheelchair, but he was right. She could maybe make it to the end of the street and back, but that was probably her limit before she lost feeling in her arms.

"Okay," she finally said with reluctance.

"What about Chester? Where's the leash?"

At the magic word, Chester let out a single deep bark and his morose expression lifted a fraction of a degree. Riley grabbed down Chester's retractable leash and hooked it onto his collar. The dog gave a snuffle of approval and did a little stubby-legged sidestep of excitement.

Next, Riley wheeled in the chair from the family room where she'd left it and carried it down the stairs. Claire followed him on the crutches, but after watching her un-wieldy efforts, he shook his head, scooped her into his arms and let the crutches fall away with a clatter as he started down the steps.

"Riley," she exclaimed, feeling heat soak her cheeks. "Completely not necessary. I can walk."

"Humor me." His arms tightened around her and she tried not to notice that sexy afternoon shadow on his fea-tures or the enticing scent of him, musky and male. She wished again that she could be light and foolish, could kiss him right here on her back porch.

He carried her easily down the stairs and set her in the stupid wheelchair, gripped the dog's leash and they were off.

The moment they hit the sidewalk, Claire wanted to tell him to turn around. She only needed a pair of granny glasses to look just like an old lady being pushed around the yard of her nursing home, especially with the wool pashmina tucked around her shoulders.

She glanced at her watch, the chunky beaded one Owen had made her, and saw it was past 8:00 p.m. Families on Blackberry Lane were settling down for the night, work-ing on homework, relaxing in front of the television. As the sun slid down behind the mountains, the air took on a bit of a nip, as nights did here even into July and August.

"Tell me more about your plans for this benefit," Riley

finally said after they reached the corner and turned toward the mountains.

She tensed, the echo of his harsh words still loud in her ears, then forced herself to relax. She didn't want to fight with him. Not tonight when the evening was so quiet and peaceful.

"Let's talk about something else," she suggested. "What's been the toughest thing to get used to again about coming back to Hope's Crossing?"

"Old friends who ignore my questions. Seriously, I want to hear about the benefit. Is this a one-woman show or are you setting up committees?"

She turned her head to look at him but found no trace of sarcasm in his expression or his voice. He sounded genuinely interested. "I'm organizing the auction portion of the evening and the service project side of things. Alex agreed to arrange the food for the dinner, with her contacts among the local restaurant scene. Evie's handling the decorations and, uh, Holly, Jeff's wife, insists on doing the publicity."

"You seriously just came up with this whole thing today and now you've got a full raft of committees, and on the very day you returned to work. How is that humanly possible?"

"I told you, once we started talking about it at the store, everything sort of snowballed and everyone jumped on board to help. Everybody we talked to has been really excited about it."

"Except me." His voice was low in the cool air and in the hazy light, she couldn't see his features clearly.

"Was it the benefit you objected to or just my involvement in it?"

"Neither." He grew silent as they approached the twenty-foot waterfall and she could hear the muted rumble. "I'm a cynical jerk, Claire. What you're doing sounds nice and noble on the outside. I'm just not sure it will make any kind of difference in the town or the way people are dealing with the accident."

"I can't say whether it will make a difference or not, but what's the harm in trying? I only know whenever I'm serving some need outside my own inherent selfishness, I always feel better."

He pushed the wheelchair to the small weathered bench some civic-minded person in years past had placed here where it had a lovely view of the falls in one direction and the city slightly below them in the other.

Riley sat down on the bench facing town and the flickering pinpricks of light in the gathering dusk. Chester sniffed around the bench, in full hound-dog mode.

"St. Claire. Always so willing to see the good in people."

"Not true," she protested. She thought of her tangled relationship with Holly, how she tried very hard to like the other woman but just couldn't seem to move past her negative feelings to be truly friends.

"Nobody's all good or all bad, Riley. I'm sure you've seen that in your line of work."

"Yeah, point taken. I've seen hardened criminals sob their beady little eyes out at those made-for-TV movies on Lifetime."

She smiled, enjoying the cool night and the rippling sound of Sweet Laurel Falls and Riley's company.

"Is that really true?"

He cocked an eyebrow. "When have you ever known me to stretch the truth?"

She laughed. "Oh, I don't know. How about the time you told Alex and me you heard on the radio every New Kids on the Block had been killed in a plane crash? We cried for an hour until we turned on the news and figured out you made it all up."

"All right, I may have prevaricated on that one. Give me a break here. I only wanted to make you notice me."

"I think you only wanted to torment your sister and I was just collateral damage."

He shook his head. "No, Claire. It was you. It was *always* about you."

His words curled around her like the May breeze. She didn't know how to answer as that slow, sultry tension eddied between them again.

"Why didn't you ever say anything back then?" she finally asked.

"What was I going to say? You were three years older than me."

"I still am. Thank you for the reminder."

"Three years means nothing now. But back then, we were on completely different social planets. Think about it. I was only a freshman when you were a senior. You might as well have been a movie star for all the chance I figured I had with you. Anyway, all you ever saw was Jeff Bradford."

He was absolutely right about that. She had wanted her happily ever after, a peaceful family life with a man who adored her and would never have an affair with some biker bar cocktail waitress.

She had fallen hard for Jeff because he had been smart and ambitious and had seemed to want the same things she did. His family had seemed so *normal* after the scandal that had rocked her young life and his parents had adored her. Sometimes she wondered if she hadn't married Jeff so she could have his parents for in-laws.

He closed his hand around hers and played idly with her fingers. "What if I *had* said something? What would you have done back then if I had told you how crazy I was about you?"

Her stomach swooped as if she'd just dived off the top of the waterfall into the small pool below. "I don't know," she answered honestly. "The old Claire was pretty stupid."

"What about the new Claire?"

She curled her fingers, nails pressing into her flesh. "She would probably wonder why you're wasting your time with a divorced mother whose husband left her for a ditz with perfect teeth and a boob job."

He closed his eyes. "You won't let me forget that, will you?"

"I would still like to know the answer to the question. Why are you here, Riley? Why do you keep coming back, even though both of us know you shouldn't?"

He gazed at her for a long moment and then he tipped a finger under her chin and kissed her.

Fifteen

She caught her breath at the tenderness of his kiss, sweet as the night air around them. She wanted to curl into him, to wrap her soft throw around both of them and stay there in his arms in the dark while crickets chirped in the bushes and a great horned owl hooted somewhere in the distance.

Some part of her warned her loudly to push him away while she still could, but she ignored it, sliding into the kiss like she had wanted to slide into that warm, scented claw-foot tub earlier.

This was not going to end well. Riley McKnight was going to shatter her heart into a thousand shards of glass and in that moment she knew there was not a single thing she could do about it.

He edged backward, his face a blur in the moonlight. "I can't stay away. I keep telling myself all the reasons we both know this is crazy. But something keeps pulling me back."

She said nothing, trembling a little at the fear and desire that warred inside her.

"You're freezing," he said.

She wasn't about to tell him the reasons why. "A little."

"I'd better get you back to your house. This seemed like

a good idea earlier this evening, but I sometimes forget how quickly the temperature can drop in the mountains."

They were both quiet as Riley pushed her down the slight hill toward her house. She didn't have the first idea what might be on his mind, but *she* couldn't stop thinking about that stunning, tender kiss.

Something was happening here, something she wasn't sure she was ready to face. Her feelings for Riley were a conflicted muddle. This was no longer about simply being attracted to a gorgeous man who made her feel vibrant and alive.

He took a different route home, a little more direct, that led them along the creek and past the small Craftsman cottage where Maura lived. A light was on inside, and Claire could see a figure move across the window.

"Oh, stop. Please stop."

He looked down at her, that unreadable look in his eyes again. "It's late, Claire."

"She's awake. I just saw her. I haven't had a chance to see her in person since the accident. Alex and I stopped this morning on my way to work, but Maura didn't answer the door. We've talked on the phone, but it's not the same. Please."

He didn't want to. She could see it clearly in the hard set of his mouth and the stiffness in his movements, but he finally shrugged and turned her wheelchair into his sister's winding front walk.

The house had four steps leading to the porch, and he parked her at the bottom.

"Wait here. She doesn't always answer the door."

Claire folded her hands together and waited while he knocked softly. After a long moment, just when she thought this would be one of those times Maura wanted to avoid company, the door swung open and his sister stood there in her porch light.

She looked thinner, gaunt almost. Her dark curls were flat and lifeless and she wore a faded Hope's Crossing High T-shirt and sweats. Surprise flickered for a moment in green eyes so much like her brother's, but she quickly blinked it away as if she didn't have the energy to spare.

"Riley, hello. What are you doing here so late?"

"Claire and I were out for a walk and saw your light on."

Maura looked down the steps and saw her. Claire had never hated the limitations of her injuries as much as she did right at that moment, when she longed to climb those stairs and embrace her friend. Without her crutches or at least a cane, she didn't dare attempt it. To her relief, Maura made the move toward her, walking down the steps in her bare feet. Claire gripped the armrests of the chair and forced herself to stand, balancing on her good leg and the tip of her cast. She hugged Maura tightly with both arms, even the casted one, ignoring the pain. Sometimes the only comfort a person could give was a quiet embrace. She had been the recipient of that same comfort many times and just stood for a moment now, wishing she could absorb Maura's pain into herself.

"I'm so sorry I haven't been able to stop by before now."

"Don't be. You've had your own stuff."

"That's no excuse. Not really."

After a moment, Maura moved away and Claire sank back to the wheelchair. She watched as the other woman reached down to pet Chester. The dog looked a little baffled at being the recipient of only a perfunctory pat instead of the ebullient love Maura usually gave him.

"Mom told me about this benefit you're cooking up."

Claire searched her features in the glow from the porch

light, but she couldn't read anything in her expression. "It's not much, but at least it's *something*."

"You can't fix this, Claire."

Maura's low words echoed just what she had already heard from Riley. She shifted her gaze to him and found him watching her steadily, though without a trace of an *I-told-you-so* in his eyes.

Claire sighed. "I know, honey. Nothing can fix it. But we all want to remember her, too. This is a small thing, but if it helps bring a little more peace and maybe makes the town a little better, don't you think it's worth it?"

"I won't come. Don't ask me to."

"Do you want us to forget the whole thing? We can put everything on hold, Maur. It's early days in the planning process."

Maura was silent for a long moment, her fingers working a fraying edge of her T-shirt. Riley was watching his sister, his jaw tight. Finally she shook her head. "No, it's a loving gesture. Don't think I don't appreciate it. But right now, I just... I can't."

Claire reached for her hand and squeezed it tightly. The benefit and day of service wouldn't make things right, but maybe they could make things better.

"Looks like your front door's coming off the hinges."

Riley had a too-casual tone she found grating. Only when she looked hard at his features in the moonlight did she see the vast pain in his eyes.

Maura gazed at the door as if she hadn't noticed. "I've had a few visitors lately. I guess it's been overworked."

"I'll stop by tomorrow after my shift to fix it."

Maura opened her mouth to argue, but closed it again and simply nodded.

He embraced his sister, and Maura, usually so competent and together, seemed as fragile as antique hand-blown beads. "Try to get some sleep," he said, kissing the top of her head.

"Thanks, Ri. Claire, thank you for stopping by."

He waited until Maura returned to the house before he turned and pushed Claire back down the sidewalk toward the road. Both of them were silent as they traveled the remaining distance to her house. Even Chester seemed subdued, although when they turned onto Blackberry Lane he picked up a little more energy, apparently eager to be home.

As they passed Mrs. Redmond's house on the corner, Claire spied the elderly woman, dressed in her favorite pink housedress, wrestling her big garbage can out to the street.

The garbage can probably weighed more than Mrs. Redmond's eighty pounds. She shifted, guilty suddenly at her thoughtlessness. She hated to ask him for something again, but she couldn't ignore a neighbor in need.

"Riley, wait. Can you go help Mrs. Redmond with her garbage can? I usually do it, but I haven't given it much thought lately. I forgot tomorrow was garbage pickup day."

He suddenly tensed, she could see it in the set of his jaw. "Of course," he said after a slight pause. He set the brake of her stupid wheelchair and then approached the elderly woman. "Let me help you with that, Mrs. Redmond."

"Who's there?" She squinted into the darkness.

"It's Claire, Mrs. Redmond," she called quickly to allay the woman's suspicions. "Claire Bradford, along with the police chief. Why don't you let him roll your can out to the street for you?"

"The police chief? That McKnight boy?" Scorn dripped from her voice. "I don't think so. I'll get it myself."

"Come on, Mrs. Redmond. Let him help you. I'm sorry I haven't thought to arrange someone else to take care of that for you."

"I don't want his help. He's rotten to the core, that one. You know he knocked up my granddaughter, don't you? Ruined her, that's what he did. She was a good girl until he came along. Then he gets her pregnant and drops her the minute he found out."

Oh, heavens. Claire had completely forgotten Riley's high school girlfriend was Mrs. Redmond's granddaughter. She knew the old scandal, even though she'd been away at college at the time. Alex had been livid with her brother for the whole thing, for hurting his mother and being stupid enough in the first place not to wear a condom.

"Not true," Riley said now to Mrs. Redmond, his voice tense. "I never dropped Lisa. You and everybody else knew I wanted to do the right thing and marry her. Even after she had a miscarriage, I would have married her."

Lisa Redmond had been a cheerleader, popular, pretty. She'd been sixteen, Riley seventeen, when she'd gotten pregnant. Claire knew from Alex the girl had miscarried just a few months into the pregnancy, while their families were still trying to sort through their options.

"I was ready to marry her regardless," Riley said again. "But your son and daughter-in-law sent her away."

Mrs. Redmond made a disparaging sound. "To get away from *you*. You think they wanted her to marry someone like you if she didn't have to? Being married to you would have been a misery for that girl. You would have ruined her life even more than you already had. A clean break, I told my son. Like yanking off a bandage, do it fast and sure. That's the only way. And I was right. You left town the minute you could, didn't you?"

"Right."

Claire couldn't see his features, but she heard the grim tightness in his voice and her heart ached for him. She could tell he hated this. For the first time, she had a glimpse into how difficult things must be for him here in Hope's Crossing, how there were still plenty of people who would never see beyond the hellion he'd been once.

Riley refused to allow the words of an angry, bitter old woman to wound him, especially when he had earned every ounce of her vitriol. It was difficult, though, especially on the heels of their visit with Maura.

"Mrs. Redmond, please let him help you with your garbage can," Claire said in that soft, persuasive voice. "This is silly. That was all nearly twenty years ago. Lisa is happy now. She married a very nice man, a pharmacist from Highlands Ranch. I went to their wedding. They have a son, right?"

"A lucky escape from *him*."

"I'm sorry you feel that way," Riley said, layering the same thin veneer of calm over his underlying tension he used in difficult police situations. "All I want right now is help you take your garbage to the curb. That's what I'm going to do. You can still hate me all you want—after this moment, if you never want to speak to me again, you don't have to. But like it or not, I'm taking your garbage to the curb."

She blustered as he grabbed the can from her. "I don't want your help. I'll have you arrested for trespassing!" she said, her voice querulous.

"You can try, but I *am* the chief of police, so you might have a hard time convincing anyone in my department to take me in for the terrible crime of wanting to help you."

She followed him out to the curb, blustering the whole way. Riley would have liked to just dump the can on the grass and walk away from the old bat, but he knew he couldn't do that with Claire looking on. Okay, he probably would have stopped to help her anyway, even if Claire hadn't been with him. A month in Hope's Crossing must be rubbing off on him.

When he finished, he turned back to the thin old lady, her features now the same shade as her pink housedress.

"For what it's worth, Mrs. Redmond," he said quietly, hoping Claire was too far away on the sidewalk to over-hear, "I've made a lot of mistakes in my life. I'll be the first to admit that. But what happened with Lisa is one I regret the most. I was seventeen and stupid, but that's no excuse for what happened."

"You're damn right it's not. You took advantage of a naive girl's hopes and dreams."

He bit his tongue to keep from responding that he hadn't been Lisa's first boyfriend or sexual partner—or that she had actually done most of the pursuing in their relation-ship.

"I hope you're not doing the same with Claire, taking advantage of her," the old woman's voice was pitched just as low as his own, thank the Lord. "She's a good girl who's had a hard time of it, just like my Lisa. She doesn't need the likes of you ruining her life."

Her words sliced right to his gut, reinforcing everything he'd been thinking since they left Maura's. She was right, damn it. Claire didn't need him. She had a life here she loved. He would only complicate that for her.

He had to stop this. He couldn't trust himself around Claire obviously. Every time he told himself he could keep their relationship on a friendly level, he ended up sharing another of those mind-blowing kisses with her.

He turned his back on Mrs. Redmond and strode back to Claire. After releasing the brake on the wheelchair, he pushed her back the short distance to her house.

"I'm sorry about Mrs. Redmond," she said when they

reached her driveway and that was all it took for his frustration to explode.

"Will you stop apologizing for the whole damn town, Claire? First your mother, now Mrs. Redmond. Give it a rest. We reap what we sow, right? Isn't that what Father Joe was always cramming down our throats? I made some lousy choices when I was a kid. Now I have to deal with those."

"You shouldn't have them thrown back in your face every moment."

"I was crazy to think I could come back and have any hope of functioning competently in my job, with all this latent hostility that's been simmering for years."

He hadn't meant to say that, but the words were out and he couldn't take them back.

"People here have long memories, but don't underestimate the people of Hope's Crossing. They're capable of moving on and behaving with civility, even if they can't forget. Look at your mom and Harry Lange."

He blinked a little at that non sequitur. "What *about* my mom and Harry Lange?"

In the light from her porch, he saw her eyebrows rise in surprise. "They loathe each other. Didn't you know?"

He scoffed. "My mother doesn't hate anyone. I don't even think she holds a grudge against my *father,* for Pete's sake, after everything he did to her."

"Harry must be the exception, then. She can't stand him and I've heard her say as much. I get the feeling he feels the same."

"Why?"

"No idea. Mary Ella won't say. They're always polite when I've seen them together."

He just couldn't wrap his head around the idea of his calm, even-tempered mother having a feud with anyone.

If he had to pick someone, though, it would probably be Harry Lange. The guy was a lightning rod for resentment and anger. People in town either revered him or despised him. When he gathered the original investors together and sold his own large chunk of property in Silver Strike Canyon for what would later become the ski resort, people either seemed to think he saved Hope's Crossing from eventual extinction or ruined the small-town bucolic lifestyle forever.

"You just need to give the town a chance," Claire went on. "Once they see the good job you're doing as police chief, once they have a little more time to get to know you, people will come around."

She looked so sweet and earnest in the moonlight that his chest ached. "It's a nice theory, Claire, but don't you think I ruined any chance of that when I caused an accident that killed my own niece?"

"Riley—"

He cut her off, not eager to tug any harder on this particular thread of conversation.

"Come on. Let's get you inside."

"You don't have to carry me up. If you could just bring the crutches down, I can show you how much better I'm doing on the stairs."

With that, all the myriad emotions he'd been trying to keep capped and controlled burst out, a geyser of frustration. "Shut up. Just shut up, will you? I'm really not in the mood right now to listen to someone else tell me all the frigging reasons they don't want my help."

Eyes wide, she opened her mouth but closed it again when he scooped her out of the wheelchair and stalked up the stairs and through the door, the dog bounding ahead of them.

"Where do you want me to put you?"

"Um, the family room, I guess," she said, her voice low and he felt like a world-class jerk all over again for taking his sudden bad mood out on her.

He set her on the sofa she favored in her warm, cozy family room. "I'll bring in your crutches and the wheelchair and take Chester off the leash. Give me a minute."

With guilt riding him hard, he lifted the wheelchair inside, setting it in the kitchen, then carried in her crutches. The hard metal retained the cold from being left outside and he appreciated the reminder. He had already done enough to hurt her physically, right? He didn't need to make things worse.

He walked into the family room and set the crutches where she could reach them. "Can you handle things by yourself from here?"

"I... Yes. Thank you."

"Good night, then. Thank you for the walk," he said, his voice more curt than he intended. He turned to go, but her words stopped him.

"Why are you mad at *me,* Riley?" She didn't sound angry, only confused and maybe a little forlorn.

He sighed. All evening, he'd done nothing but take his bad mood out on her. He owed her better than that: He owed her the truth, no matter how difficult it was for him. "Again, because I'm an ass."

He sat beside her on the sofa and took her hand in his again, although it took several moments for him to figure out how to word what he had to say.

"I'm not mad at you. I'm mad at myself."

"Why?"

He sighed. "I've still got a crush on you, Claire. Actually, that's not true and hasn't been since I came back to town. I think my feelings are deeper than that, though

I'll admit I'm not positive because I've never been in this situation before."

Her hand trembled slightly in his but she didn't pull away. "The thing is," he went on, "I'm afraid friendship is not going to be enough for me anymore. At the same time, I know as well as you do that anything more than that is impossible."

"Is it?" she finally asked quietly, her eyes a soft, glittery blue. "As crazy as it seems, I'm beginning to, um, have feelings for you, as well. I wouldn't have thought this a few weeks ago. Or even, maybe, a few days ago, but... I think maybe I would like to see where things go here."

For one instant, joy burst through him, wild and fierce, but as quickly as the next breath went cold and dark like a blazing mountainside doused in fire retardant.

He dropped her hand and eased away on the sofa. "I'll tell you where it will go. Where it always goes, when it comes to me and women. You said it yourself. You won't have a fling with me. That's all this would be. We'll have a hot, passionate relationship for a few weeks and then I'll start to feel edgy and restless, smothering in my own claustrophobia, and I'll do or say something colossally stupid and end up hurting you."

"Nice of you to give me the program notes ahead of time so I can follow along."

He glared at her glibness, at that hint of a smile on her features. "It's not funny, Claire. This is far beyond funny. I'm not willing to do that. This is different. *Everything's* different. You're important to me. Besides that, you're my sister's best friend. You're practically part of the family. You deserve better than to be the latest in a long line of women I've ended up hurting."

What the hell was wrong with him? He couldn't believe he was being so noble. After all her words a few nights ago telling him she didn't want a fling with him, Claire Bradford was basically giving him the green light to see how things might develop between them. He ought to just shut the hell up and kiss her, for crying out loud.

Did he have to pick this moment to do the right thing? Yes. When it came right down to it, he didn't have any other choice. The memory of Maura's pain and Mrs. Redmond's anger only reinforced that.

"I'm sorry, Claire. There's too much at stake here, for you and for me."

He brushed his mouth against her cheek one last time, burning the scent of her into his memory, and then let himself out.

Sixteen

For the first time she could remember, Claire was grateful for the rapid-fire pace of her life. Juggling all the whirling plates in her life left little time and energy for anything else.

Between end-of-school-year parent-teacher conferences, follow-up doctor appointments for her and the children, the business of running String Fever and the rapidly approaching service day and benefit, the only time she could spare for regret were those few moments just before she crashed in bed each night. She would lie under the Western Star quilt her grandmother had made when Claire was a girl and try to ignore the aching sense of loss for what might have been.

The rest of the time, she was frenetically busy, like now. With only two weeks before the Giving Hope benefit, Claire was pushing herself to finish the most ambitious necklace she had ever created for the auction, in between customers at the store.

She had two customers currently in the store, and they couldn't have been more different. Janie Hamilton was a plump, pretty, tired-looking woman who had recently moved to town. She sat at the worktable making a colorful pair of earrings out of wire wrap and lampwork beads, while the thin and elegant Sarah Colville, a summer season regular, leafed through a beading magazine for ideas.

"Thank you again for letting me use your tools." Janie smiled tentatively. "Somehow in the move, I've lost a box of supplies and I haven't had time to replenish them. They were really good quality and I hate to buy inferior products just to get by until I've had a chance to look through everything."

Claire smiled. "No problem at all. I'm glad of the company. How are you and your children settling in after your first few weeks?"

"Good so far. Everyone has been very kind to us."

Claire wondered about the other woman's story. She had heard from Ruth that the woman was a widow who had moved with her three children to be closer to her mother and aunt. Moving this close to the end of the school season seemed an odd choice for a mother, but Claire wasn't about to pry.

"If you don't mind my asking, what are you working on?" Janie asked. "It looks as if it's going to be exquisite. I love that big heart pendant. Is it rose quartz?"

Claire closed a jump ring with her pliers. "It is. It was found by a rock hound friend of mine not very far from here."

"It's a great centerpiece to the design."

"Thank you. I hope it will come together soon. I'm afraid I'm not at my best beading form right now. It's a necklace I'm making for the scholarship benefit."

The challenging piece used various precious and semiprecious gems all found natively in the Rockies. She had designed it using a variety of beading techniques and right now, Claire didn't feel proficient at any of them.

"I imagine the cast makes things awkward."

She smiled. "A bit, but I'll soldier through it. I'm hoping the piece does well at the scholarship benefit."

"Oh, you are a wicked girl. Let me take a look." Sarah shifted toward the table and Claire wanted to hide the whole thing suddenly. Sarah was a true artist, in every sense of the word. The renowned painter owned a vacation home in the area with her husband, but unlike most of those who purchased second homes in the area to take advantage of the skiing, they rarely spent time in Hope's Crossing in the winter. She said they preferred winters at their primary residence in Tucson, but both came to the cooler mountains to paint in the summer.

She was one of Claire's favorite customers and she always enjoyed having her in the store, except today when she was struggling so much with the necklace design.

"It's still a work in progress," she said.

"Oh, don't be coy. You know it's going to be spectacular, especially the contrast between that aquamarine and the topaz. Why don't you let me just pay you for it now and forgo all the trouble of having to bid for it at this auction?"

"What's the fun in that?"

"You're going to be difficult, aren't you?"

"I've got to have *something* to auction off. I'm in charge of the whole thing."

"I hadn't heard about an auction," Janie said. "When is it?"

"Two weeks from tomorrow. We're actually having an entire day of activities to encourage people to help their neighbors. It's in honor of a girl who was killed in a car accident last month."

Janie's eyes softened. "What a lovely idea!"

"You bought a house over on Sage Hill Road, right? If you have anything around your new home you could use help with, please let us know. Right now we have more volunteers than projects."

"I can't think of anything. Our house is quite well-maintained, but I'd love to volunteer my children. If nothing else, it will get them out of the house and perhaps help them make some new friends."

"We're hoping it's fun for everyone who participates. We've got raffles and giveaways, free food throughout the day. We're going to set up a bounce house and several other inflatable attractions like that over at Miner's Park and for every half hour of time they volunteer, the children get a ticket."

"Sounds like you've thought of everything." Janie smiled as she finished off her second earring. "I have to say, I've been really impressed with Hope's Crossing. I didn't expect to feel so welcomed from the very first day we arrived."

"It's not perfect," Claire said, thinking of Riley and the opposition that had become vocal and annoying, led by J. D. Nyman. "But it's a nice place."

"It's why we keep coming back year after year," Sarah said. "Every time we think it's just too difficult keeping up two homes, we remember that's one thing we love most about Hope's Crossing, besides Walter's beloved fishing streams. We don't find that same sense of community during the winter when we're home in Tucson."

"The moving van wasn't parked at our house ten minutes before we had four or five neighbors over asking if they could help us unload," Janie said. "It was a bit disconcerting, if you want the truth. I thought it was because they somehow knew my husband had just died." She forced a smile. "But I don't see how that could be possible. I have a feeling they would have showed up regardless of our situation."

Claire tried to imagine losing her husband after a long, debilitating illness, as Ruth had told her was the case. She couldn't wrap her head around it. She vowed to have Janie and her children over to dinner as soon as the craziness of the benefit subsided and she could breathe again.

"You know," she said as she was ringing up the other woman's bead purchases, "your family might be interested in helping with the construction of new playground equipment at that small park near you, the one that has only a couple measly little swings and a slide now. I can get you the information if you'd like."

"I would love it!"

She handed over one of her many lists. "Write down your contact information for me and I'll let that project coordinator know. Here's my card, too. If you don't hear from someone by next week, call me back and I'll put you in touch with them."

"Thank you!" With her new dangly earrings catching the late-morning sunbeams, Janie looked somehow lighter as she left than she had when she came in. This was why Claire loved owning a bead shop. People came here for pretty little luxuries they might not otherwise allow themselves. Creating the pieces themselves added an extra layer of enjoyment and they invariably left happier than when they'd walked through the doors.

One bead at a time, she was trying to make the world a little brighter.

When she left, Sarah set down her magazine again. "I didn't want to say this when you had another customer, but I think what you're doing for this town is marvelous. I've been thinking about it and I would like to donate a painting to your auction. Just last week I finished an oil on canvas of the resident elk herd browsing in that meadow above Dutchman's Pass. It's quite lovely, one of my favorites in quite a while."

"Are you sure?" Claire asked, awed at the offer. Sarah's exquisite paintings hung in galleries across the West.

"Well, I can't guarantee anyone will buy it, but Walter will at least bid on it so I don't humiliate myself."

No one buy it? Sarah's work was sought after by collectors across the country. She'd heard somewhere her paintings were selling well into five figures. Goose bumps popped out on her arms. "Sarah, my word. Thank you. It's too much."

"It's too much only if I say it's too much. I want to do this. My heart has been broken for Maura since I heard about the accident. She has always been kind to us when we go for coffee at her bookstore. This is just a small thing, but if it helps ease her pain a little, I want to do it."

Maura had a way of drawing people to her. Dog-Eared Books & Brew was as much a town institution as the Center of Hope Café. Earlier in the week, Claire and Alex had stopped at Maura's house and she had been dismayed at the changes in her friend. Everyone who knew and loved her was keeping collective fingers crossed this benefit would help her find a little hope herself.

"I'll warn you," Sarah went on, "you won't catch me out raking leaves or building playground equipment or painting up some rickety old shed or whatever. A painting is all you're getting out of me. But at least it's something."

Claire smiled and on impulse hugged Sarah's whippet-thin shoulders. After a surprised moment, Sarah returned the hug briefly, then stepped away.

"I'd better go. I told Walter I would pick up some of that gooey macaroni and cheese he loves from the café for his lunch. If I don't hurry he'll be grousing around like a hungry grizzly, tearing open kitchen cabinets and knocking shelves out of the refrigerator."

"We can't have that."

"I'll take this magazine. I think I'm going to make that charm bracelet for my granddaughter's birthday. Do you have all the supplies I'll need?"

Claire quickly perused the list and nodded. "We should. I've got another copy of this. I'll have all the findings ready for you when you come back and you'll only need to pick out the beads you want to use."

"That is why I put off all my bead projects until we come back to Hope's Crossing for the summer, my dear. That and, of course, Chester."

At his name, her lazy hound thumped his tail on the rug. Claire smiled at both of them and rang up the magazine for Sarah.

When the other woman left, she let her dog out into the back garden. She had just returned inside and headed for the worktable when her cell phone gave a soft little wind-chime ringtone. It took her a moment to remember she had changed her mother's ringtone to something a little more benign than the nuclear meltdown warning. She supposed that was progress.

"Hi, Mom. How are you?"

"Okay. Are you busy?"

Claire thought of all the phone calls she still had to make today for the benefit, the Venetian glass bead order she had been trying to place for a week and her pitifully slow progress on the necklace she was thinking of naming the Heart of Hope.

"Not bad. What's up?"

"Any chance you can close the store for half an hour and come down to the bookshop? I was going to come over there after the lunch rush, but I've got a handful of customers who think I have all day to hang around."

Claire chewed the inside of her cheek, grateful her mother couldn't see her fighting a smile. Somehow Ruth hadn't quite caught on that running a business had more to do with meeting your customers' needs than vice versa.

"Evie should be coming downstairs in a few minutes. She can cover for me."

"Great. I'll see you in a while. I've got to go. No, sir, I'm afraid we don't carry any climbing guide books with Norwegian translations," she heard her say in the background before Ruth cut off the call.

Claire set down her phone, marveling at the changes in her mother in just a few weeks. Ruth could still revert to her needy, demanding self on occasion, but working at the bookstore in Maura's absence seemed to fill a need in her mother to be useful.

If she'd known how much Ruth would thrive in a retail setting, Claire would have encouraged her mother to get a job years ago. Not at String Fever, of course. The changes in her mother weren't *that* extreme.

Maura's bookstore was across the street and up Main Street on the opposite corner, three storefronts from the café. Fifteen minutes later, after Evie came down for her shift, Claire grabbed the cane she used these days instead of the crutches for stability and headed out into the gorgeous late-May afternoon, warm and sunny.

Everything had greened up beautifully except the very tops of the mountains, which retained their snowcaps year-round.

She couldn't believe school would be out in only a week. The children had a summer full of fun activities planned, from baseball teams to tennis lessons to sleepaway camp. Add to that the impending arrival of their new half brother

n a few months and the summer was bound to be as hec-
ic as the past few weeks.

Claire walked past the bike shop and the year-round
Christmas store the tourists loved, with its twinkling lights
nd the train in the window that ran three hundred sixty-
ive days a year. She crossed at the crosswalk and headed
oward the bookstore. If only they could have this sort
f perfect weather on Giving Hope Day, with only a few
lump white clouds to mar the vast blue sky....

Ooomph. She was so busy sky-gazing that she plowed
ight into a solid bulk and caught her breath as a couple
f strong arms grabbed her to keep her from stumbling.

"I'm sorry, Claire. My fault. Are you okay?"

Riley. Her insides tumbled around and she looked up.
ep. He was as gorgeous as ever. She hadn't seen him up
lose since that night at her house. Even though he had
riven past a few times when she had been outside with
ne children on his way to or from his own rental house,
e hadn't stopped.

Somehow she'd forgotten the shock of those green eyes,
ne angle of his jaw. He wore a tan jacket and a light blue
ress shirt with no tie, his badge clipped to the front breast
ocket, and she had an insane urge to just rest against him
or a moment. Or a hundred moments.

His eyes were dark with concern and he looked as if he
anted to whip out his cell phone and call the paramedics
t the slightest provocation.

"I'm fine," she assured him, feeling her cheeks heat.
Vhy could she never have a single encounter with him
nat didn't somehow result in her coming off as an idiot?
I should have been watching where I was going. I was
ist... It's a beautiful day and I haven't been outside all
norning. I'm afraid I got a little distracted."

"I had something else on my mind, too. You're sure you're okay?"

"Fine. Great."

"You look like you're getting along well. No crutches I see."

She held up her foot. "Walking cast. We're on the home stretch, according to the good Dr. Murray. I'm supposed to get the one on my arm off in a couple of weeks and this one a week or two after that."

"How do you feel?"

She remembered that tender kiss between them, the heat and magic, and hated that they had been reduced to this bland, boring chitchat.

"Better than I expected."

"That's great. I like your bling." He gestured to her cane, covered in glued-on fake jewels.

"Holly and Macy surprised me with it last week. It what all the stylish cane users are wearing these days, apparently."

What she had thought so trendy and cute at the time now made her feel old and decrepit compared to Riley, brimming with strength and sheer gorgeousness.

"How about you?" she asked.

"I'm still here." He said it as if it were a joke, but she knew things couldn't have been easy for him the past few weeks. She'd heard J. D. Nyman was collecting a petition to have the city council reconsider their hiring decision, although she hadn't been approached with it yet. She pitied the first person to ask for her signature.

They stood awkwardly for a moment and she hated again that things had come to this.

"I'm meeting someone for lunch," he finally said, "or I'd offer to buy you a sandwich over at the café."

"Thanks anyway, but I'm actually on my way over to the bookstore to meet my mom."

"Another time, then." After another awkward pause, he leaned in and kissed her cheek and headed on his way.

She drew in a breath and hobbled the rest of the way to Dog-Eared, wondering how it was possible that Riley could manage to scrub all the happiness right out of the day, in five minutes' worth of conversation. She sighed and pasted on a smile as she opened the front door of the shop.

She found her mother ringing up a customer Claire didn't know who was buying a tall stack of children's books. "I think you'll find your grandchildren will very much enjoy this author. I know when I read the books to my grandson, he thinks they're a hoot."

Claire waited, browsing through the new releases while her mother finished up.

"Oh, it's been crazy in here all morning," Ruth finally declared after the bells on the door chimed behind the customer. "I'm *exhausted.* I swear I haven't had a minute to breathe today."

"That's what pays the rent, Mom." She smiled. "I love the window display of gardening and wildflower books. So clever to use seed packets and real potted plants. Did you do that?"

Her mother looked pleased. "I did. I thought we needed a little something to remind us summer is almost here."

"It really works together. I should have you come spruce up my window display at the bead store. You've got a real knack."

Pleasure warmed her mother's eyes, made her look years younger. "I'll have to see. I'm pretty busy right now."

The change in her mother astonished her. Ruth straightened the display Claire had just been looking over with a sense of proprietary pride.

"You're really into this, aren't you?"

Ruth shrugged as she aligned the books with the table's edge "I think it's mostly fun because I know it's only temporary. Sage will be back from university for good in a week or so. She can take charge and I'll fill in until Maura thinks she's ready to come back."

Claire hoped that would be soon, but Maura seemed a long way from ready to return to life.

"What did you want to show me?" she asked.

"Oh. Right. It's in the back."

With a careful look around the bookstore at the few browsing customers, she led the way to Maura's stock room, piled high with boxes, a hand truck, wire shelving

From the quilted book tote Claire had given her mothe for Mother's Day a few weeks earlier, Ruth extracted thin box.

"I know what you're going to say before you even ope your mouth. Let me just tell you I've given this a grea deal of thought and I believe this is the right thing to do I want to donate great-great-grandmother's necklace an earrings for the auction."

Claire gasped. "Mother! You can't! You cherish those.

When she was a girl, she was only allowed to eve look at the antique jewelry set on very special occasions

"I wanted to talk to you about it because, really, it's you legacy. If you don't want me to donate it, I won't."

"It's a piece of Hope's Crossing history."

She knew the story well. Her ancestor, Hope Goodwi Van Duran, had been the first schoolmistress when thi area was just a hardscrabble mining camp. She'd falle in love with a rough miner who had ended up owning th claim where the largest, most pure vein of silver in th entire canyon had been found. Their fortune had once ri valed any of the silver barons of the day.

Silas Van Duran had founded the town, naming it after his beloved wife. Poor investments and the depression had wiped out most of the family wealth, but out of silver mined from that original strike, Silas had commissioned a lovely necklace of fine-worked silver filigree, centered by a trio of semiprecious stones also culled from the mountains. Claire had loved the necklace. Sometimes she thought perhaps that was the inspiration for her own early fascination with jewelry and beading.

"I want to do this," her mother said. "If it helps with the benefit, it's a small sacrifice. I think great-great-grandmother Hope would have agreed."

The generosity seemed so unlike her mother, Claire didn't know what to say.

"Do you mind so much?" Ruth asked at her continued silence.

She felt a small pang of loss for the lovely piece, but her mother was right.

"We can place a fairly high reserve on it," she suggested. "If it doesn't look as if it will exceed the reserve, you can always hold it back and possibly donate it to a museum somewhere."

"You would know more about that sort of thing than I do," Ruth said. "The truth is, the actual value of the necklace is not more than a few hundred dollars, at least according to the appraisal I did a few years ago."

"But historically, it's priceless."

"I'm hoping someone else in Hope's Crossing will think so, as well."

"Mother, thank you."

"Just be careful with it. Put it in a safe place until the Giving Hope benefit."

"I will," Claire promised as she gave her mother an impulsive hug. Ruth tolerated it for a moment, hugged her back rather awkwardly, then eased away.

"I'd better get back out," Ruth said.

"Of course."

Claire followed her mother out of the stockroom and watched with that amusement again as her mother gave a careful look at the few customers in the bookstore to make sure no one needed anything before she turned back to her.

"The children are with Jeff and Holly this weekend, aren't they?"

"They're going shopping for cribs, I think." An activity Macy would love but Owen would abhor. Jeff probably would never clue in that an eight-year-old boy had zero interest in outfitting a nursery.

"Need some company? I'm supposed to go listen to some chamber orchestra concert at the resort with Janice Ostermiller, but I can probably back out if you think you might be lonely."

Where was *that* coming from? She'd been alone every other weekend for the past two years and her mother had never jumped to keep her company unless she needed something from Claire.

"Don't change your plans. I'm fine. The truth is, I'll enjoy the quiet. I've got plenty of work to keep me busy for the benefit."

"Owen told me he hasn't seen the police chief around for a while." Ruth's tone was deceptively casual. "I'm glad to hear you listened to my advice."

And there went the warm glow from her mother's generous gesture. It fizzled and popped a forlorn little death.

She sighed, remembering the heat of his hands on her arms out on the street a short time ago, that ridiculous urge she had to just close her eyes and rest there against him for a week or two.

"I told you, Riley and I are just friends. We still are. Nothing has changed in that department."

"Well, I don't expect he'll be around much longer."

The thought of his leaving clutched at her heart. "Why? What have you heard?"

"Nothing. Not really. Oh, you know how people talk."

"Excuse me, I'm looking for your regional photography section." A man she didn't know, probably a tourist, she guessed, interrupted them before Ruth could answer, much to Claire's frustration.

"Oh, yes. Let me show you."

"I've got to go. I'll see you later, Mom. Thank you for the donation. You can still change your mind, you know."

"I won't," Ruth said firmly, then headed off to help her customer.

Claire paused there for a moment in Maura's cozy, warm bookstore, then she pushed the door open and headed back out into the May sunshine.

The delicious smells of yeasty bread and something spicy and delicious emanated from the café and Claire's stomach rumbled. She needed lunch and right now the idea of the café's hot chicken salad on a croissant was close to her idea of heaven.

She pushed open the door and immediately wished she could back right out again. *I'm meeting someone for lunch or I'd offer to buy you a sandwich over at the café.*

Riley hadn't mentioned that someone was a young, beautiful redhead with long fingernails and a particularly grating sort of laugh.

She wanted nothing more than to hurry right back out, but she was hungry and her foot hurt and Dermot Caine, owner and operator of the café, was greeting her.

"Claire, darlin'. Haven't seen you in here in an age!"

"Hi, Mr. Caine. Hey, can I have a chicken salad sandwich to go? I'm kind of in a rush."

"Coming right up, doll. You sit right there and I'll have it for you quick as a wink."

The five minutes it took him to make her sandwich were excruciating. Even though she studiously avoided looking at Riley's booth, she couldn't help overhearing the redhead's grating laugh, with a very flirtatious edge.

Finally Dermot brought out her sandwich wrapped in a white paper bag. She paid quickly and, steeling herself, finally looked toward Riley's booth and forced a casual wave. He gave her an unreadable look but lifted a hand to return the greeting.

When she was certain she was completely out of sight of any patrons in the café, Claire sank onto a bench against the wall, one of several conveniently placed around the downtown for footsore shoppers.

She leaned her head against the sun-warmed brick and closed her eyes. She was definitely going to have to get a grip on herself. Hope's Crossing was a small town and they were bound to run into each other on a regular basis. Riley was going to date other women, there was no question about it. Claire had no claim on him—he'd made that clear—and she certainly couldn't fall apart every time she saw him with someone else.

Seventeen

Riley eased his patrol vehicle into the driveway of his rental house, looking forward with great anticipation to a cold beer and the last few minutes of the NBA playoff game he'd set the DVR to record when he left home going on fourteen hours ago.

It had been a hell of a day, one that must have been designed to make him question what he was doing in Hope's Crossing. He had alienated a group of older ladies when he'd had to tell them their traveling poker game was technically illegal because Colorado didn't allow games of chance for money, especially when their stake had grown to more than a thousand dollars. He'd been off duty an hour ago when he'd seen a speeding vehicle weaving around over on Pinenut and ended up pulling over and subsequently arresting a drunk tourist going fifty-six in a twenty-five-mile zone. The guy had tried to play the "powerful friends" card, claiming his girlfriend worked in the governor's office. As if Riley cared. He hadn't cared about anything except yanking the idiot off the streets—until said idiot puked on his shoes, splattering his slacks, and Riley had been forced to change into the backup jeans and T-shirt he kept in his office.

The bright spot to the whole day, he was chagrined to admit, had been those brief moments at lunchtime when he'd seen Claire.

He'd missed her these past few weeks. It had taken all his determination not to swing by several times after work. To resist temptation as much as possible, he'd ended up taking a circuitous route home most days, coming in from a completely different direction so he wouldn't even pass her house down the street.

As he climbed out, he thought he saw a dark blur near the garbage can next to the house. Probably those blasted raccoons that could sometimes be a problem in this area. He'd already had his can's contents spilled one night about a week earlier.

He grabbed the bag containing his disgusting slacks and decided just to chuck them rather than wash someone else's puke out. Call him fastidious, but he had his limits.

He lifted the lid, making as much noise as he could to scare away any annoying creatures, threw in the bag and closed it again. Suddenly the shape he thought he'd seen materialized into something furry heading straight at him—familiar tail wagging and ears drooping nearly to the ground.

His trespasser howled a little greeting and waddled over to him. Not a raccoon at all, but a very familiar basset hound.

A disbelieving laugh escaped him. All his determined efforts to keep away from her, and fate just kept sending a completely different message.

"You're not supposed to be here, bud."

Chester gave what looked very much like a "Yeah, so?" sort of look and just continued to sniff around his darkened yard.

He was probably picking up the cat living across the

street that tended to make itself at home with arrogant disregard for property lines.

"Come on. We'd better get you home before the kids start to worry."

Chester headed into his backyard and with a sigh Riley set his beer-and-basketball fantasy on the shelf for a minute and looked inside the patrol car for something he could use as a makeshift leash, finally settling on the leather belt he'd taken from his disgusting slacks earlier.

"Here, boy. Come on, Chester."

The dog rounded the house in answer to his name. Riley quickly clipped the belt through his collar, looping it through the buckle, and headed down the street toward Claire's house.

The evening was lovely, the air cool but comfortable and scented with pine, lilacs and the early climbing roses bordering the house next door. This just might be one of the sixty or so frost-free nights the good people of Hope's Crossing could count on each year.

As he neared Claire's house, he heard her call out softly in that peculiarly pitched voice people use when they're trying to command attention but not wake up their neighbors.

"Come on, boy. Where are you? Chester! Here, boy. Come get a treat. Come on, boy."

Riley should have been braced for the dog to lunge when he heard his name, but with no loop to hold on to, the makeshift leash slipped from his fingers. With more speed than Riley would have ever given him credit for possessing, the dog poured on the juice and hurried to the front porch, leaving him in the dust.

"There you are," Claire exclaimed, relief in her voice. "You scared me!"

When the dog waddled up the steps, she reached down and grabbed hold of the trailing end of the belt, frowning.

"What in the world?"

Riley sighed and stepped into the light from her porch. "Mine. Sorry. I improvised after I found him sniffing around my yard."

"I'm sorry he bothered you," she said. "I don't know what's gotten into him. He never runs off. I think one of the children must have left the gate unlatched and I didn't notice it in the dark when I put him out earlier. I can't believe he went all the way down the block."

"I think the Stimsons' cat was on the prowl tonight."

"That would explain it. Not a big cat lover, our Chester."

"I'm afraid I'd have to agree."

She bent down and struggled a moment to unhook the belt, hampered by the awkwardness of her cast.

"Hang on. Let me get that."

He joined her on the porch, trying not to notice the scent of her, strawberries and springtime, or the way her white cotton blouse gaped open probably a button more than she realized, revealing a tiny hint of the lacy bra beneath.

The belt had seemed a good idea at the time, but removing it proved more difficult than he expected. He finally knelt to the level of the dog—and within perfect view of Claire's legs beneath the knee-length flowered skirt she wore, one in a cast and the other bare and smooth. The toes of both feet had been painted a vivid, adorable pink.

He cleared his throat and yanked the belt free, looping it around his hand to keep from sliding his fingers up that delectable length of leg....

"Thank you," Claire said again. "I'm sure he would have wandered back, but I appreciate your going to the trouble to bring him home."

He rose. "No problem. I didn't want to risk him going into the next block and not being able to find his way."

She studied him for a moment there and he thought he saw indecision on her features. "Want to come in for a moment?" she asked, the words tumbling over each other quickly. "Angie brought some cinnamon rolls over earlier this evening."

"My sister Angie?"

"The Demon Seed is what I like to call her, especially when she comes bearing her cinnamon rolls. She brought a whole dozen over, but the kids are gone all weekend. If I don't find somebody to take some of them off my hands, I'm going to eat the whole pan myself."

"That woman knows how to hold a grudge. I couldn't make it to Sunday dinner at her place last week and to pay me back, she makes you cinnamon rolls and conveniently forgets I live only at the end of the block."

"Maybe she thinks you're able to find your own pastries," she murmured.

Something in her tone had him looking closely for any sort of double meaning, but she only smiled blandly.

"Yeah, it's definitely a job hazard when you're a cop. Seems like there are always doughnuts available, whether you want them or not."

"Those, too." She opened the door. "Angie brought me more than enough rolls. Come in and I'll try to find a container for you to take some home."

"I've always got room for Angie's cinnamon rolls. They'll make a great breakfast before my shift tomorrow. Thank you."

She only limped a little as she led the way into the entry and through the hall.

He was struck again by how warm and welcoming she had made her house. It was the sort of place designed for kicking off shoes and settling in. The kitchen smelled delicious, of lemons and spice and roasting meat. His stomach rumbled, but he ignored it as Chester headed straight for the water dish and Claire bustled around her kitchen, pulling out a disposable plastic container. Riley leaned against the doorjamb as she moved half of the round pan into the container.

"Something smells good in here."

She made a face. "Dinner. I know, it's late, but the kids are at Jeff and Holly's, so I've been catching up on work. I marinated chicken all day and forgot to throw it in until I got home an hour ago. So how was your lunch?" she asked, then immediately looked as if she regretted the question, although he couldn't for the life of him figure out why.

"Good. Do you know Sharilyn Lundberg? She's a deputy county attorney."

"I don't think I've met her, no. She seemed lovely."

He hadn't noticed anything about the woman other than her sharp legal mind and her annoying habit of touching his arm entirely too often whenever she made a point, as if that brush of physical contact would somehow give more credence to whatever she was saying.

"We're working together on the charging documents against Charlie Beaumont and the other teens involved in the crime ring."

"Oh. Right. Of course." Claire's features suddenly seemed a little more rosy than they had a moment earlier. "Where do things stand with the charges?"

All the frustration of the meeting with Sharilyn pushed back onto his shoulders. "Not well. Small-town politics are a bitch."

"You're in a difficult situation, Charlie being the mayor's son and all."

"It's tough." All he wanted was to do the job he'd been

hired for, to be a cop. Instead, he had to wade through this frigging minefield. "The mayor, of course, is trying for a deal, trying to plead down the charges, but that's going to be impossible. The county attorney wants to make an example here and try Charlie as an adult because he just turned seventeen. He was drinking. Not much, true, only point-zero-four in his system, well under the legal limit for an adult. But as a minor, he's not supposed to have any alcohol. Layla's dead and Taryn Thorne is still in a coma and may not come out of it."

"Katherine said there have been encouraging signs the last few weeks."

"We can hope and pray for that. Either way, though, Charlie won't be able to squeak out of this, no matter how many strings the mayor tries to tug."

"My heart is sore for the whole family. Mrs. Beaumont comes into my store sometimes. So does Gen, of course. She's very upset by the whole thing. From what I understand, her fiancé has some political aspirations. Gen worries his family will now see her as a liability."

A timer on the stove went off before he could answer. "That's my chicken," she said.

He straightened. "I'll leave you to your dinner, then."

Again, he had the odd sense she was debating something. "Have you eaten?" she finally asked.

"I'm not going to eat your dinner."

"I made plenty. When the kids are with Jeff, I always make a little extra for leftovers so I don't have to cook for myself. I'll warn you, it's not much. Lemon-rosemary chicken and rice."

His stomach rumbled again. Even though he knew it wasn't smart, he was tempted—and the food was only part of it. In the past ten minutes here in her kitchen, the stress and tension of his day seemed to have seeped away.

He felt more calm than he had in weeks. He wanted to say yes, to sit down and enjoy a meal and conversation with her in this quiet, peaceful kitchen. The ferocity of the desire scared the hell out of him.

"I'd better not. I've got about three hours of paperwork to finish tonight that I've been putting off all week."

"Of course." She hid it quickly, but he didn't miss her disappointment. "I understand. You're busy. Let me fix you a plate and you can take it home and eat it while you work."

She reached into a cupboard and his throat just about closed up. She had been working hard all day, too, struggling with the frustration of double casts, and she still wanted to take care of him.

Oh, he was in deep, deep trouble.

"You know, my paperwork's waited this long. Another half hour or so won't hurt."

"Great. Let me just toss a quick salad."

He took the plates from her and set them on the dining nook table in her kitchen and quickly pulled flatware from the drawer. He found it more than a little disconcerting that he was beginning to know where to find things in her kitchen. A few moments later, Riley sat down to what looked like the best meal he'd had in weeks, even counting the always-good food at the diner.

"This is delicious, Claire," he said after the first bite. "Much better than the cold pizza I probably would have had for dinner."

"Thank you. Fresh rosemary makes all the difference. Alex taught me that, FYI."

"Alex gives you cooking lessons, Angie brings you cinnamon rolls. You're more a part of my family than I am."

"Not true! Your mom and your sisters all adore you."

Would they still feel the same if he decided to leave Hope's Crossing? He quickly changed the subject. "Is it tough for you when Owen and Macy are at their father's, being alone here in this big house?"

She took her time answering. "The house certainly seems quiet. I usually try to work late on those nights whenever I can. I'm still not crazy about the silence."

He was so used to silence that he didn't know any different. He'd never lived with a woman and hadn't had a roommate since his freshman year of college.

"I miss them," she went on, "but it's important for them to spend time with their father and the new family he and Holly are starting. I understand that. Every time I'm tempted to just pack up and go as far away as I can, I remember this is best for the kids."

He stared. "I thought you loved Hope's Crossing and wouldn't dream of living anywhere else."

"I dream," she said simply. "Don't get me wrong, I do love it here. For all the occasional glitz and glam during the ski season, this is a small town at heart, full of good people who care about each other. If I ever wonder again, I only have to remember the overwhelming support we've received for the Giving Hope Day."

"So why would you even think about leaving?"

"I could come up with a few reasons. Wondering what else is out there. Feeling trapped. My mother. Do I need to go on?"

He laughed. "But you won't leave, will you?"

"Not while the kids are young anyway."

"Don't you think most people in your situation would rather escape the awkwardness?"

"I'm no saint, Riley. We've established that. My motives are mostly selfish. I love running String Fever, and my friends and support system are here, too. I'm comfortable here."

"You belong here."

"So do you."

"I'd say the jury is so far out on that one that nobody knows where they are anymore."

She studied him for a long moment. "Why did you come home? Really? Don't tell me it was only because the position of police chief opened up. I'm sure when you decided to leave the Bay Area, you could have found a job in a hundred places."

"Maybe." He sighed. "When I found out Chief Coleman had decided to retire, I had just spent months undercover as a pimp and a drug dealer. Before that, I spent nearly a year posing as a white supremacist. I needed to wash the dirt out somehow and the job here just seemed right."

"You needed to be home," she said softly.

"I wouldn't have put it that way. But yeah, I guess."

"You're doing a good job, Riley. J. D. Nyman is an idiot and he always has been. Just give people a little time. When the wounds of the last month aren't so raw, people will see you're exactly right for Hope's Crossing."

Her staunch defense of him, the faith he knew he didn't deserved, warmed him. He gazed at her, so earnest and lovely. He ached to kiss her, to pull her close and just hold on.

He released a slow breath and pushed away his half-eaten dinner. "This was delicious, Claire, but it's late. I'd better go."

She looked a little disconcerted by his abruptness but nodded. "Thank you for staying. It was nice to have company besides Chester."

He glanced at the dog, now splayed out on the floor. "I'll go check to make sure the gate is latched before I leave so he doesn't escape on you again."

"Thank you."

He left through the back door, grateful for an excuse

to put a little badly needed distance between them. The high mountain air cooled his face and he filled his lungs with it. He should never have walked into that house. He should have just brought back her grumpy little dog, left him on the porch and headed back to his own space where he could be safe.

He had lived among despicable thugs for months, but he found Claire Bradford far more frightening than any of them.

He took his time walking around the backyard, steeling his will against making a stupid move. Finally he knew he couldn't put it off any longer and he returned to the kitchen to find she'd cleaned up and was closing the dishwasher door.

"You're right, the gate was ajar. I latched it now, so your escapee should have a harder time making his break."

"Great. Thank you."

"Good night, then. Thanks again for dinner."

"You're welcome," she said as he headed out onto the back porch. "Oh, wait. You forgot the cinnamon rolls."

Keep them, he almost said but he knew she would insist on his taking them.

He stepped inside while she walked back to the kitchen for the container, then she returned and held it out for him.

"There you go. Throw in a coffee from Maura's place in the morning and you've got the breakfast of champions."

He managed to return her smile, although he kept one hand tight on the doorknob and the other gripping the container of cinnamon rolls like it was loaded with C-4 ready to blow.

"This was nice," she said. "See? We don't have to throw away a perfectly good friendship just because…"

Her voice trailed off and she blushed a little.

He closed his eyes. "Because I can't spend sixty seconds near you without wanting to smear Angie's frosted cinnamon rolls from your head to your toes and then lick it off inch by slow, delicious inch?"

She gulped and her eyes darted to the rolls, then to his mouth, then back to the pastries. With a defeated groan, he threw the box on the counter and grabbed for her, shoving the door closed with his foot.

He devoured her mouth, tasting cinnamon and coffee and a lingering hint of rosemary. Her lips parted and he dipped his tongue inside, sliding along the length of hers. She made a sexy little sound and buried her hands in his hair, pulling him closer, and he lost his grip on the last tangled thread of his shredded calm.

The kiss was wild, heated, tongues and lips and teeth, full of all the pent-up frustration and longing of the past two weeks.

Somehow through the urgent ache, he held on to one semirational thought, that he couldn't leave her standing here when her leg was in a cast. If he wanted to continue kissing her—and did he!—he would have to move her to a more comfortable position.

Without breaking the connection of their mouths, he scooped her up into his arms. She gasped a little but didn't pull away—instead, she wrapped her arms around his neck and held on as he carried her through the kitchen and into the family room.

He lowered her to the sofa, but she didn't release her hold around his neck and he had no choice but to follow her down, careful even in the midst of the wild hunger scorching through him to take care with her injuries.

They kissed for a long time, stretched out side by side on her sofa while the old house shifted and settled around them. He lost track of everything but her softness and heat, the welcome of her mouth, of her body.

"I haven't been able to think about anything else but this for two weeks," she murmured against his mouth. "I dreamed about you every night and hated waking up alone and aching."

He closed his eyes while the silky heat of her words slid down his spine like the flick of her finger.

What was he supposed to say to that? She might have dreamed about it for a few weeks, but he'd been thinking about her for *years*.

He kissed her, overwhelmed all over again that Claire Tatum Bradford was here, in his arms, kissing him as if she couldn't get enough.

That sentiment he certainly shared. None of this was enough. He should have known it wouldn't be. He wanted more, he wanted their bodies tangled together, he wanted to lose himself in the sweetness of her skin, every lush curve and angle.

He eased up on one elbow, entranced by the fluttery pulse at the base of her neck. Thinking only to steal a taste, he dipped his head and flicked his tongue there. She gasped and arched her back a little. The cotton of her shirt was soft, warm from her body, as his fingers moved to the first button and worked it free, revealing more of that delectable lace of her bra underneath. Taking a chance, he unbuttoned the next one down, leaving the shirt only fastened by two or three buttons near the bottom.

His body was hard and heavy with need as he brushed his mouth along the slope of her breast above the lace. The scent of her here intoxicated him, strawberries and wildflowers, and he wanted to sink his face into her skin, drunk with her.

She made a tiny sound of arousal and he slid his mouth to the edge of the lace, licking and tasting as he went.

"More," she murmured, her voice low and throaty, and

with one hand she worked the fastenings of her front-clasp bra and pulled the sides away.

The world receded, everything else fading to nothing except for Claire and this moment and the surge of his blood.

He dragged his gaze away from those alluring curves and found her watching him with a shadow of nerves in her eyes. "I'm thirty-six and I've had two children. Just keep that in mind," she whispered, a hint of color dusting her cheekbones.

"You're beautiful," he growled. "Look at me. I'm shaking, you're so beautiful."

He lowered his head and kissed first one peak and then the other, then he took his time there, flicking a tongue over the rosy nipple, tasting and exploring.

She made that sexy little sound again and gripped his head, holding him in place, her body shifting restlessly on the sofa.

When he couldn't think straight another moment, he slid his hands across her abdomen, loving the way the muscles there contracted under his touch. He needed to touch her, to feel wet, silky heat. He slid a hand to the waistband of her skirt, but just before he would have worked the buttons free, she shifted restlessly and he caught a flash of navy blue.

Her cast.

The sight of that hard, bulky casing on her leg hit him like a bucket of snow dumped over his head.

He sat up abruptly, his breathing ragged and his heart racing and his body just about howling with frustration.

"What's wrong?" she asked, her eyes huge and slightly unfocused.

He scrubbed his face. "I... We can't do this."

She blinked a little and he thought he had never seen

anything as beautiful as Claire half reclined on her sofa, tousled and undone, her lips swollen and her gorgeous full breasts white and lovely in the lamplight.

"You have a broken leg and a broken arm. I don't want to hurt you."

"You're a creative guy. I'm sure you can come up with some clever way to work around them." She gave a tiny, sensual smile. "Those aren't the critical regions anyway."

All those delectable curves, that luscious expanse of skin, made him want to whimper.

"I can't, Claire. Right this moment, I've never wanted anything more in my life. You are…everything."

"Then why stop?"

He sighed. "Haven't we been through this a few dozen times? I don't think either of us wants to face the consequences."

Her smile faded and after a moment, she grabbed the edges of her shirt and tugged them together. She eased up a little higher on the sofa. "Why do there have to be consequences?"

"Because that's who you are, Claire. A woman who needs, I don't know, some kind of a commitment before she takes such a step."

"Maybe I don't want to be that woman anymore," she said a little wildly. "I've been alone for two years. Maybe I'd like to be the kind of woman who wears something besides boring white underwear. Who makes love under the stars or…or who lets a man lick whipped cream off her."

"You are. You absolutely should do and be those things. Just not with me," he said quietly, although the thought of her with another man gutted his insides worse than a prison shank.

He forced himself to rise and move away from the sofa, away from all her sweetness and warmth. "Claire, I feel things for you I've never felt for another woman. Never *wanted* to feel. The truth is, I'm more than halfway in love with you. I think I have been since I was too stupid to know the prettiest girl in town would one day grow into a smart, kind, incredibly sexy woman."

She stared at him and he saw a hundred emotions flit across her expressive eyes. Shock and uncertainty and the remnants of that hunger. And, he thought, a sharp flare of joy, quickly hidden. "Riley—"

"I love you, Claire. But despite how incredible I know it could be between us, not this—" he gestured to the sofa "—but all of it, some part of me can still only think about running, just like my old man did. Like I've always done when anyone gets too close. I won't hurt you like that. I can't."

"What do you think you're doing right now?" she asked, her voice low and filled with pain. "Do you think I would be here with you like this if I didn't care about you, too, Riley? I haven't been with another man in my entire life except my ex-husband. My plan was to wait until the kids were a little older and things were more settled before I even thought about…about letting another man into my heart. And then you came home and everything changed."

He had never hated himself as much as he did in that moment, never wanted so desperately to be a different kind of man.

He wanted to tell his conscience to screw off so he could just take what he wanted. But the images of all the women he'd failed in his life seemed to be crowding his brain, starting with Lisa Redmond, pregnant and scared at sixteen. He thought of Oscar Ayala's *chica,* killed in front of him while he did nothing, of his sisters and his mother.

Of Layla.

If he did this, indulged himself in her arms and her

body, Claire would expect things. That was the kind of woman she was. The hell of it was, he wanted to give her those things. He had a crazy vision of living with her here in this house, of helping her raise her children, of cuddling in bed at night while the January snows blew under the eaves and piled up on the driveway.

That picture seemed rosy and wonderful right now, but how long would it take for him to start panicking and edging toward the door?

Better to just do it now before he could do serious damage.

"I can't, Claire. I'm sorry. So sorry."

For about ten seconds after the front door closed behind Riley, Claire sat clutching the edges of her shirt, stunned and achy and still trying to cope with the jarring shift from delicious heat to this icy, terrible cold.

What just happened here? She drew in a shaky breath and tried to button her shirt with fingers that trembled. After a moment she stopped with a frustrated cry and just whipped the whole thing off and picked the soft knit throw off the back of the sofa. She huddled in it, shirtless, limbs trembling.

Hot tears burned her eyelids, but she refused to let them escape. Damn him. Oh, damn Riley McKnight straight to whatever hell that had spawned him for doing this to her. How could he tell her he loved her with one breath and then walk out the door without looking back *again,* leaving her lost and reeling?

It's not you, it's me. He hadn't said it in so many words, but his meaning had been the same. She wasn't buying it. She felt old and desiccated, about as appealing as a frost-killed flower garden.

Covering her face in her hands, she rocked for a minute

there on the sofa, aching and more lonely than she'd been one single moment since her divorce.

The worst part of all of this? She was in love with the idiot. Somehow Riley—with his solid strength and his blasted charm and his innate ability to make her laugh—had slipped into her heart, filling all those cold, empty corners.

What was she supposed to do now?

Those tears pressed harder and she wanted nothing so much as to give in to them, just sprawl here on this sofa and weep and sob and rail against him.

Chester chose that moment to nudge her leg with his nose. His eyes drooped at her with such empathetic sorrow that, conversely, she gave a shaky laugh and buried her face in his warm, furry neck.

For some strange reason, Claire suddenly remembered that silly horoscope she'd read the morning after her store was robbed, minutes before Riley came back into her life.

Fun and excitement heading her way. That's what the thing had claimed.

Stupid freaking horoscope.

Right now she was pretty sure she would prefer to spend the rest of her life staring down excruciating monotony if it meant she could avoid this agonizing sense of loss for something she'd never had in the first place.

Eighteen

This was working. Somehow, despite the crazy hours, the logistical nightmare, the conflicts and confusion, they had managed to pull it off.

By 3:00 p.m. the Saturday of what would have been Layla Parker's birthday, it was apparent the town's first-ever Giving Hope Day was an overwhelming success.

Claire sat at a worktable outside the community center with her leg propped up on a crate and her hands deep in dirt, transplanting flowers donated by the nursery into containers.

They couldn't have asked for better weather. Someone had definitely been smiling on them. It had rained on and off the previous week and she had been praying they could escape another storm. Much to her relief, only a few high, puffy clouds marred the vast blue perfection of the Colorado sky. The June afternoon was lovely, warm and sunny and beautiful, the mountains a brilliant, gorgeous, snow-topped green.

The scent of dirt and petunias and the sharp, sweet tang of pine mingled on the breeze. It smelled fresh and new and, corny as it sounded, rich with hope.

Vehicles had been coming and going all day from the

community center, which had become command central. Even though she'd witnessed the endless stream of people all day, she still couldn't believe the turnout. Everywhere she'd been today, the crowds had overwhelmed her. Seniors wielded paintbrushes alongside teenagers at the high school as they repainted the flaking old bleachers. Little kids carried tools and nails and water bottles for their parents as they worked to build a new playground on land donated by—surprise!—grouchy Harry Lange. Inside the community center, a dozen quilts at a time had been set up for gnarled hands to tie for the children's hospital in Denver and Claire had even seen two sworn enemies, Frances Redmond and Evelyn Coletti, smile tentatively at each other as they snipped yarn.

She smiled at the memory, pulling out another plant start from the flat on the worktable. She rotated her shoulder, aching everywhere, but it was the kind of satisfied exhaustion she loved.

She couldn't regret any of it, not the long hours of preparation, not the paperwork, not the sleepless nights of worry.

The day wasn't over yet—the dinner and auction were still several hours away—but even without that, she thought maybe the goals of she and the others planning this day had been met. The people of Hope's Crossing were talking to each other more, reaching out to neighbors, working together to lift and help those in need.

The Angel of Hope, whoever it might be, must be smiling right about now.

She picked up the trowel, savoring the feel of it in her unencumbered hand. Three days after her cast had been removed, she still felt strange without it. Although she was a long way from regaining full use of her arm, at least the skin had lost a little of that shriveled, puckered look.

She was setting in the last start of this container and packing down the dirt when a voice spoke behind her.

"This is a good thing you've done for Hope's Crossing."

Claire jerked her head around with a little cry of happiness.

"Katherine!" She instinctively reached to hug her friend, forgetting all about her grimy hands.

"Oh, dear," she said when she pulled her hands away and saw the dirt streaks she left on the older woman's pale peach sweater set. "I'm sorry. I wasn't thinking. Now you're all dirty."

"It will wash. Don't worry. It was never one of my favorites."

Claire gave a rueful smile, shaking her head. Katherine never changed. If someone burned down her house, she would probably claim she had been thinking about moving anyway.

"How wonderful to see you!" Claire exclaimed. "I never expected you to make it, with everything you have going on. How's Taryn?"

Katherine's normally graceful features looked haggard, the lines etched a little deeper. Her hair was a few weeks past needing a color and trim and Claire wished she could bustle her away right now to a hair salon for a quick pick-me-up.

"Things aren't going as well as we'd hoped, to be frank," Katherine said. "I guess we had some quixotic idea that once she finally started to come out of the coma a few weeks ago, things would quickly turn around."

Claire and Alex had visited the hospital in Denver the day after that last devastating encounter with Riley two weeks earlier and both of them had been heartened to see Taryn's eyes open, although the girl had still been largely unresponsive. She had wanted to visit again, but pinning down all the necessary details for this daylong event had sapped her time and her energy.

All that seemed unimportant now. She should have made the effort, figured out some way to make it happen. A visit would have been a much better pick-me-up than a hair color, especially if Katherine had been struggling with this discouragement on her own.

"I thought she was improving."

"Every day is still a struggle." Katherine's elegant chin wobbled briefly and she made an obvious effort for control. "I'm afraid we'll soon have to accept she's never going to be our same Taryn."

"Oh, Katherine." She squeezed her friend's fingers, sad all over again at how one single moment could change so many lives. As devastating as the accident had been for Maura and her family—losing a child must bring unimaginable pain—Katherine and her son, Brodie, had endured setback after setback in Taryn's painstakingly slow recovery, measuring each moment in tiny little steps.

"Maybe she won't ever be the same Taryn," Claire said carefully. "But she's tough. I'm still praying you'll all come through this."

"Thank you, my dear." Katherine smiled and finally released her fingers and stepped back. "You and the others have certainly been busy."

"It's been a wonderful day so far."

"We needed this. A reminder that no matter how difficult our own journey, sometimes the only thing that can ease our path is to stop for a while and gather strength by lifting someone else's burden."

Claire nodded. "You and Mary Ella have taught me that lesson well over the years."

"Hand me that extra trowel there and that six-pack of alyssum."

Claire wanted to argue that Katherine wasn't dressed for it, in her cream trousers and pastel twinset. But because she had already ruined the other woman's sweater—and it "wasn't her favorite anyway"—Claire doubted Katherine would listen.

She handed Katherine the trowel and the six-pack. "I've got an extra pair of gloves around here somewhere. Give me a minute to find them."

"No, don't bother. I think I need to stand in the sunshine and get my hands dirty today."

Although Claire's heart ached, she smiled. The two of them worked side by side in companionable silence and she thought she could see a little more sadness and tension leave the other woman's features with every passing moment.

Katherine finally spoke when she was adding the last plant to the container. "I do think it's a wonderful thing you've done, but you shouldn't have worked so hard. You're still healing yourself."

"What were you just saying about losing your pain in lifting someone else? I needed this, too."

She never would have dreamed how much she would need the solace and comfort. If not for the myriad details she had to deal with, she probably would have fallen completely apart after everything that happened with Riley.

"Anyway," she went on, "I only came up with the idea and then everybody else has just taken off with it. It's been truly heartwarming to see the town come together."

"I miss Hope's Crossing," Katherine said. "Everyone is very kind at the hospital in Denver and at the apartment building downtown where we've rented a place so we can be close to the hospital, but it's not the same as being home. This whole thing has taken a toll on Brodie, I can tell you that. My son has never been the most patient man. He's too much like his father was in that respect."

Claire had generally found Katherine's son to be cool and disapproving. How such a warm and generous woman could produce such a son mystified her. She didn't wonder that Brodie was struggling with a daughter who might end up permanently disabled from the accident.

She opened her mouth to answer, but the words died when she saw a familiar silver extended-cab pickup truck pull into the parking lot, its bed filled with lumber.

Whatever she had been about to say flew out of her head as Riley climbed out of the cab. She hadn't seen him since that night and she braced herself against the pain she knew was stupid and useless.

He turned in their direction but seemed to stop short when he saw her. After a pause, he continued toward them without once meeting her gaze.

"Katherine, hello." He pulled the older woman into his arms and kissed her cheek. When he set her away, they shared an awkward moment when under normal circumstances he might have greeted Claire the same way. Instead, he gave her a strained sort of smile and shoved his hands in his back pockets. "Claire."

"Riley," she murmured, and plucked a hapless dracaena out of the flat.

"Uh, I think we're done at the playground. We've got some extra supplies and somebody at the site said to bring them back here."

Oh, she missed him. Everything inside her wanted to jump into his arms, to wrap her arms around his neck and hold on tight.

For two weeks, she had told herself each morning she could get through this. She'd survived a divorce, the dissolution of a ten-year marriage to her childhood sweetheart.

She could certainly get over Riley McKnight when they'd shared only a few kisses.

So why did her throat ache, her eyes sting?

She cleared her throat. "Um, right. We've temporarily created a pile where people can donate unused building materials to anyone who might need something for a project. A clearinghouse kind of thing. It's on the side of the community center, by the Dumpster. Do you need me to round somebody up to help you unload it?"

"I've got it, thanks. See you, ladies."

He climbed back into his pickup and backed up, then headed for the other side of the parking lot to start clearing out the lumber from his truck.

Claire gazed after him as long as she dared before forcing herself to turn back to her planter. After a moment of continued silence, she looked up and winced when she found Katherine watching her closely, an expression of curiosity and compassion in her eyes.

"I'm sorry things aren't going well for our new chief of police. It makes me so angry that certain people are so wrapped up in their own agendas and ambitions that they don't want to give him a chance."

She dearly hoped none of her naked longing was obvious in her expression. "Why do you say that? What have you heard?"

"Oh, this and that. I haven't completely let my responsibilities on the city council lapse, you know. I came back last night for the city council meeting and we went into closed session to discuss a few personnel issues. There are a few voices who think we ought to part ways with Chief McKnight when his probationary period is over at the end of this month."

"J. D. Nyman among them."

"It doesn't help that his brother is also on the city council. Or that Riley is at the top of the mayor's you-know what list right now."

Claire knew Mayor Beaumont was doing his best to get Charlie cleared of all charges, something everyone else in town except William Beaumont knew wasn't going to happen.

"It's not fair! Riley cares about the people of this town and is a good police chief."

"Relax, Claire. I agree with you."

"He has done *nothing* wrong."

She realized she was crushing the poor dracaena and relaxed her fingers. If she were being truthful, sometimes late at night she thought it might be easier if Riley did end up leaving town. At least then she wouldn't have to worry about the chance encounter at the grocery store or the gas station—but she didn't want to see him go like this.

"This is small-town politics and nothing more," Katherine said. "A few people have grudges for things that happened years ago and they've been whispering in the ears of some of the council members whose memories might not be that long."

"Where do things stand?"

"So far the vote is three to two in favor of keeping him. The mayor can only step in when it's a split vote—if we have someone who's absent or chooses to abstain, which is why I left my granddaughter's hospital bed to make sure I didn't miss the meeting."

"Does Riley know?" Claire asked, risking another glance over at his silver pickup.

"I'm sure the rumors have reached him by now."

If he hadn't made it so plain that he didn't want to talk to her, she would have tried to at least offer words of encouragement, to let him know she supported him no matter what.

The whole thing left her terribly sad and feeling helpless.

"Where are you planning to put the planters?" Katherine asked.

"Along Main Street, on those hooks on the lampposts they put up a few years ago, you know, where they put flags for the summer music festival and the art fair. We're going to stagger them on every other lamppost."

"They'll be lovely, Claire. Really beautiful."

A few other men had stepped in to help Riley unload his truck and she watched him carry the last load of lumber and set it on the pile. A moment later, his pickup backed out of the space and he turned around to leave. She watched for a moment, then jerked her attention back to the work.

"Do you plan to stay in town long for the dinner and benefit tonight?" she asked Katherine.

"Yes. Brodie is staying in Denver with Taryn this weekend. I promised him I would represent the family for him. Is everything ready? Mary Ella tells me you've made an exquisite necklace and earring set. And I heard the news that Ruth is actually putting Hope Van Duran's silver necklace up for bid. I was stunned. I'm definitely planning to take my checkbook."

"Here's hoping everyone else in town decides to do the same thing," she said.

"Hasn't this just been the best day ever?"

Riley looked down at his mother in his arms as they danced to the string combo in the corner of the Silver Strike Hotel ballroom, playing a particularly nice arrangement of "I've Got You Under My Skin."

Mary Ella looked lovely, although she still had dark shadows under her eyes and a few more strands of silver in her hair, reflecting the twinkling lights overhead.

She wore a satiny blue dress he thought he remembered

from the big birthday party a few years ago the family threw at Lila's place in Malibu for her and her twin sister, Rose. Lila was divorced and a hotshot businesswoman in California, while Rose had married a successful dermatologist and moved to Utah several years ago, where the population was young and the skin apparently lousy.

"It's a lovely night following a beautiful day," Mary Ella said.

"How could it not be lovely when I get to dance with the prettiest girl in Hope's Crossing?" he said, earning only an eye roll in response.

"It's true," he protested. "You've still got it, you know."

She smiled a little, her fingers tightening in his. "You're very sweet to say so, son."

"I'm serious, Mom." It seemed a night for questions somehow. Anything to distract him from mooning over Claire. Every time he turned around, she seemed to be directly in his line of vision. She was exquisite in a backless black cocktail dress that set off her lush curves.

As he turned his mother on the dance floor, he caught sight of Claire near the dais being set up for the auction, straightening the cloth on the table, for heaven's sake. As if no one else in the room could take care of that detail.

All evening, she had been in perpetual motion. He wondered if she'd had a chance to get off her walking cast for even five measly minutes. He would have liked to grab her and make her sit down somewhere for a breather, but had to remind himself Claire's typical overexertions were none of his damn business.

He jerked his attention away and focused on his dance partner. "Ma, why didn't you ever marry again after Dad left? You had to have had offers."

He rarely brought up that dark time in their lives after James McKnight left. He would rather forget the whol thing, even though, like a bad patch of stinkweed, it permeated every part of their lives.

Mary Ella looked surprised at the question. "Not as many as all that, but yes, I had a few chances."

"Why not take one?"

"I could ask the same of you. You're thirty-three years old, Riley. Don't you think it's time you stopped acting like you're still in a fraternity somewhere?"

He didn't miss her abrupt change of subject. It was a tactic he employed often when interrogating a subject, but he was no more immune to it than the dumbest criminal.

"Unfair," he said automatically. "I've been in Hope's Crossing two months now and I haven't dated anyone."

"Claire doesn't count?"

He missed a step and barely avoided stomping on his mother's foot. "How did you... I'm not dating Claire."

"Too late. You're not as slick as you think you are. I've seen the way you look at her."

"You're imagining things, you crazy old bat," he said with what he hoped was a casual grin. If he made a joke, maybe she wouldn't notice the heat he could feel rising up his neck. "You must need your bifocals checked."

She pinched the back of his neck.

"Ow!"

"That's for being disrespectful to your mother." She pinched him again. "And that's for whatever you did to hurt our Claire."

"Who says I did anything?"

"I say. You're the reason she's got that lost look in her eyes these days, aren't you? Drat you, James Riley. What were you thinking? Claire isn't one of your stupid California bimbos."

"I know that. Believe me, I know," he said in a low voice.

His mother stared at him, eyes narrowed. He tried to

look away, but she must have seen something in his eyes because she stopped moving, just stood stock-still right there on the dance floor.

She gripped his face in her hand and looked into his eyes and he couldn't look away, although he was grimly aware all the misery eating away his insides must be right there for the world to see.

"You're in love with her. Oh, sweet heavens."

"No," he said quickly and pulled his face away. "So are we done dancing? The music is not quite over."

He should have just pulled a double shift, as he'd wanted to. That had been his master plan, but Katherine Thorne had basically ordered him here to make an appearance. Did the half hour he had been here already cover any political obligation he might have?

"What did you do to her?" his mother asked, a voice loud enough they were starting to draw attention.

"Nothing," he insisted. "Absolutely nothing. Can we talk about this another time?"

"No, I want to know what you did. Did I actually raise my son to be that big of an idiot that he wouldn't recognize a woman like Claire for the best thing that ever happened to him? Yes, she might be a bit older than your usual ditzes, but that only gives her a depth and maturity. She's smart, she's beautiful, she's compassionate. What else do you need, for heaven's sake?"

"Ma, please stop. I agree. Claire is wonderful. You don't think I know that? She's perfect…and I'm not."

She stared at him for a long moment, her eyes wide and slightly stricken.

"Riley—"

"Just give it a rest, Ma, okay? Thanks for the dance."

He walked her to the edge of the dance floor, gave her a brief hug and then walked away before she could say any of the arguments he could see brewing in the green eyes he had inherited.

He had to get out of here. The crowd and the music pressed in on him and he was desperate for fresh air. He headed out the double doors into the lobby of the resort and kept going through the massive carved outside doors.

The cool mountain air was fresh and sweet. No matter where he eventually ended up, that particular scent— sage and pine and wilderness—would always mean home.

The jazz music was still audible out here, though muted. Riley took a deep breath, wishing suddenly for a cigarette. He hadn't smoked since his rebellious teens and had no intention of ever starting again, but once in a great while the fierce craving for that nicotine rush hit him like a fist to the gut.

A thin blur of smoke drifted to him. Cigar. An expensive one. Apparently someone else had the same craving.

He turned his head, squinting into the shadows. He saw only a dark shape there and the red glow of the cigar until the other man stepped into the light from the chandelier of entwined elk antlers that hung from the massive log support beam overhead.

"McKnight," Harry Lange greeted, his voice gruff and the cigar clamped between his teeth.

"Mr. Lange," he said just as curtly. He wasn't in the mood to be polite, especially not to the sour bastard who owned half the town, including this resort. He should just keep walking, maybe stroll around the hotel perimeter just to make sure Lange's security was up to par. He started to take a step, but the other man spoke before he could.

"Big turnout."

Riley sighed. He couldn't be rude, much as he would like to. "I'm surprised to see you here."

Harry harrumphed. "Why? Because I think most of the people in this town have shit for brains?"

Riley couldn't help his small smile. Was it because Harry Lange had more money than God that turned him so contrary or had he been that way even before the real estate deals that had cemented his fortune?

"Yeah, something like that. I didn't think you were generally part of the town social scene."

Harry puffed his cigar. "Seems like a good cause, a memorial for that dead girl. I figured I might bid on the Sarah Colville painting. I've got a couple of hers already. I'd like to add a few more to my collection, but for some reason she refuses to sell me any more, at least not directly. I figure this is a good way to pick one up on the cheap. People around here don't know quality when it bites them on the ass and I figure I've got deeper pockets than anyone else in town. It will probably be a steal."

Using a benefit auction to hunt for bargains. Definitely sounded like a Harry Lange tactic. The man had turned being unpleasant into an art form. He remembered suddenly that Claire had told him Harry and Mary Ella were carrying on some sort of feud. He could easily picture Lange holding a grudge over anything, no matter how inconsequential, if he were in the mood. But Riley still couldn't wrap his head around the idea that his mother would ever retaliate in kind.

"The dead girl was one of your sister's kids, wasn't she?"

Riley released a heavy breath, picturing Layla, all Goth and attitude.

"Yeah. Maura's youngest."

"Maura. She's the one who married that musician, right?" There seemed to be more than normal curiosity in the other man's voice, although Riley couldn't figure out why Harry Lange would be so interested in his family.

"Yeah. Layla's father was Chris Parker. The rock star."

Maura hadn't had the greatest of luck, men-wise. She was another McKnight who struggled in the relationship department. She'd gotten pregnant with Sage when she was only seventeen, although she'd never revealed the father's identity. Whoever the son of a bitch was, he'd never stepped forward to support his kid—just another reason Riley had been so determined to marry Lisa Redmond when they found out she was pregnant. He had seen how rough things had been on Maura and on Sage. No way would he have put a kid of his through that.

Maura started dating Chris Parker when Sage was three or four, although none of the family had been too sure about the relationship, Riley remembered. At the time, Parker's rock band was playing weekend gigs at bars and casinos. They'd married, but stayed together just a handful of years, long enough to have Layla, before Parker hit the big time. Maura didn't talk about it, at least not with him, but Riley had a feeling the guy hadn't wanted the burden of a family on his climb to the top.

"I haven't seen your sister around tonight."

"She didn't make it," he said. No way would Maura have been strong enough emotionally for this. She was still lost and grieving and refusing to let anybody try to help.

Harry puffed on his cigar. "I would have thought she'd at least show up to say thank you, what with everybody going to all this trouble in her kid's memory."

He didn't dislike that many people, but for a brief instant, Riley wanted to reach a hand out and shove that cigar right down Harry Lange's throat. "She's…having a rough time," he managed to say calmly. "Right now she needs to grieve in her own way."

Harry puffed again. "Do you remember I was there?" he said after a moment. "At the scene? There wasn't a thing anyone could have done for that girl. She was dead before I even made it to the scene, just a few minutes after the accident. I guess it's some relief she didn't suffer."

Was that Harry's idea of offering his condolences? It was a damn good thing Maura *hadn't* come. Riley didn't think she would necessarily find that a comfort.

"What were you doing out that time of night in the snow when you spied the break-in?" he asked suddenly, a question he'd wondered but never had the chance to ask in all the craziness after.

"Walking my dogs," Lange said, his voice curt again.

That struck him as both incongruous and rather sad. He knew Lange lived alone in a huge house near here. His wife had died years ago and as far as Riley knew, the man had never remarried. He'd had a son several years older than Riley who'd left town just out of high school and rumor was the two of them had come to blows beforehand.

For all his success, the man had no one except some dogs to share it, and had become bitter and reclusive in his old age.

No parallels whatsoever to his own life, Riley assured himself.

"We should probably go back in," he said. "The music has stopped, which means they'll be starting the auction soon. You've got a painting to steal out from everyone else, don't you?"

The old man tipped his cigar, a look of almost amusement in his eyes. "We've got time. They'll save the good stuff for last. Right now they're probably getting ready to auction a quilt or a flower arrangement or some other garbage like that. I hear you're having a bit of trouble with the city council."

Riley scratched his eyebrow. He should have walked away when he had the chance. "So I hear."

He probably ought to be a little more upset by the apparent wavering of confidence in him by the people who had hired him. He had no doubt he could easily prove himself to the town in time, but the truth was, he couldn't bring himself to care much, especially because he was considering leaving anyway. The last two weeks had been hell, living down the street from Claire, driving past her store on patrol, knowing she was so close but impossibly out of reach.

"I think it's a bunch of hooey, if you want my opinion," Lange said. "That J. D. Nyman's a pissy little prick and always has been. Stirring up trouble behind a man's back. What a pansy."

The words surprised a smile out of him. "Man's got a right to his opinion."

"I guess." Lange gave him a long, measuring look before puffing one last time on his cigar stub, then tossing it in the ashtray. "Doesn't mean his opinion holds a drop of water."

He didn't quite know how to respond to that rather flattering, if unspoken, seal of approval.

"For what it's worth, I've got no beef with the job you've done since you came here. I was there that night. I saw you back off the chase and shut down your lights when you realized how slick the road had become. I don't see how anyone can blame you for what happened."

"I… Thank you."

"Unlike J. D. Nyman's, my opinion does matter around here. One of the few benefits of being the richest man in town. People tend to listen when I open my yap. You want me to, I can make it clear to those boneheads on the city council I still think you're the right man for the job. That should shut them up."

Riley scrambled for an answer. "Uh, while I appreciate

the offer, to tell the truth I'm beginning to think this job might not be the best fit for me after all. Maybe it would be better all the way around if I just saved the city council the trouble and paperwork of firing me."

Harry's expression was scathing. "Your mother must be so proud to know she raised her only son to be a quitter, running away like a little girl at the first sign of trouble."

Oh, right. Now he remembered why Harry Lange was so universally disliked. "What's the shame in admitting I may have made a mistake?" he said stiffly. "Maybe I'm just not sure the life of a small-town police chief is right for me."

Over the other man's shoulder, he saw through the wide windows that the auction had started. He didn't recognize the auctioneer who had taken to the dais and was now holding what appeared to be—as Lange has predicted—a quilt with a big multicolored star in the middle.

Claire stood on the edge of the dais, apparently helping to organize the order of the auction items. Through the window, he could see her smile at something one of the other assistants said and something hard lodged in his chest. He couldn't do this. He had spent his boyhood watching and wanting her. Why put himself through that as an adult?

"Maybe it would be better for everybody if I just stepped down and let Hope's Crossing find a police chief who's a better fit."

At Lange's continued silence, Riley finally turned and found the man watching him with uncomfortable perception. His gaze flicked between Riley and the auction inside and then back to Riley.

"Aah."

Riley glowered. "What the hell does that mean, *aah*?"

"Nothing, kid. Nothing."

"No, tell me. You're the one who said your opinion was so damn important around here. I'd like to know."

"Pretty girl, that Claire Tatum."

"Bradford," he corrected.

Harry made a dismissive sort of noise as if her ten-year marriage meant nothing. "Her mother can be a pistol, but Claire's one of the nicest people in town. Genuinely nice, not just-because-you're-loaded nice."

Riley had no answer to that. This was *not* making him feel better, although he doubted that was Harry's intention anyway. Why did the guy think anything about Claire mattered to him? First his mother guessed his feelings for her, now a virtual stranger. Was he wearing a frigging sign?

"Guess it's a good thing you're leaving, now that I think on it. Stupid asshole like you doesn't deserve a nice girl like that."

Why, again, was he standing here listening to a crazy old man? "Never mind. I don't want your opinion after all."

"That's because you know it's the truth. She deserves better than an idiot with one foot already out the door. I'm going to give you a little advice, kid."

"Please, don't hold back."

Harry ignored his sarcasm. "Most people would say I've got everything I could ever want. Fancy house, priceless artwork, enough money to buy and sell most of the town. But I can tell you this. Regret makes a bitter companion. Think hard about what you're giving up. That's all." He straightened. "Now if you're done yakking at me, I've got a painting to buy."

With an abrupt pivot, he turned and headed back into the hotel, leaving Riley standing alone with the echo of his words mingling with the sounds of the auction as the doors opened and then closed behind him.

Riley stared out at the night and the dark shadows of the mountains. *Think hard about what you're giving up.*

Only everything he had never admitted he wanted.

This town. Home, family.

Claire.

Lange was right. He *was* an idiot.

His father had thrown everything away to selfishly go after his own dreams. How the hell was Riley any better than that? He was throwing away his *dreams*—the chance of a wonderful, joy-filled life here with the woman he loved—because he didn't trust himself not to turn into his father.

He was *not* James McKnight. He never had been. Suddenly Riley knew without question that he would cut off his arm before he walked away from his obligations to pursue his own selfish desires, as his father had done.

He was in no danger of becoming like the man. He had spent nearly the last twenty years proving it. That fear was only one more excuse, a convenient rationalization to avoid allowing himself to be vulnerable. He was afraid of failing, of reaching out to grasp everything he had ever wanted for fear that he would screw up everything.

He had told Claire he didn't want to hurt her. The bald truth was, he was more afraid of this tenderness inside him, this overwhelming need to be with her, to watch her smile, to become a better person just because she thought he could.

Why should he fear it? Claire offered peace and comfort. Every time he was with her, life seemed brighter and richer.

He had told her he didn't want to cause her more pain. He would hurt her by walking away, just as James McKnight had done. Why would he do such a stupid, self-destructive thing when everything he wanted was right here?

Nineteen

The place was packed. He couldn't see an empty chair anywhere. Claire must be thrilled at the turnout. At this rate, maybe they could raise enough green for two or three scholarships.

With nowhere to sit, Riley leaned a shoulder against the back wall to watch. He scanned the crowd, only half listening to the bidding going on for some kind of antique necklace. He could see his sister Angie and her husband, holding hands and looking easy and sweet together. His mother sat with Ruth and Katherine near the front and it looked like she'd already bid on something, judging by the package on her lap. Alex was there with some guy he didn't know.

There were a couple of seats, he finally noticed, near Mayor and Mrs. Beaumont. Nervy of them to come, he thought, when they were trying to extricate their son from the consequences of his actions—one of which resulted in the death of the girl the town had come together to honor.

Was it a coincidence that the two of them sat slightly apart from the crowd? Laura Beaumont looked as composed and distant as always in what looked like a designer dress, her makeup perfect, a flashy piece of bling around her neck. The two sat side by side, not even brushing shoulders and when she turned briefly in his direction, he saw dark circles under her eyes her makeup couldn't completely conceal.

He had been so frustrated with the mayor these past few weeks that this unexpected pang of sympathy took him completely by surprise. Yeah, the man was handling the situation completely wrong, but Laura and William must be heartsick, seeing their son's future implode.

Kids put their parents through hell. He certainly had. It was a wonder his own mother was willing to still talk to him after all his crap.

"Come on," the auctioneer was saying. "Remember, this is a part of Hope's Crossing history, made from silver taken out of the original Silver Strike lode."

Riley turned his attention to the auction and saw the bid was for a flimsy filigree necklace on a velvet-covered form.

"You have the chance to take home a piece of history here, folks. Bid is two thousand dollars. Do I hear twenty-one? Twenty-one? No? Going once, going twice, sold to number seventy-five for two thousand dollars. Sir, you may come up and collect your item and provide your information to our lovely assistants."

Holly Bradford jumped up with a little squeal and hugged her husband, then the two of them headed to the side of the dais, where Claire now stood holding the necklace. He was close enough that he could see her expression. Her mouth seemed tight and he thought he saw a glimmer of sadness in her eyes, but he wasn't sure whether it was a trick of the lighting, especially when she smiled graciously enough when Holly gave her a giggling hug.

He couldn't hear their interaction but he could guess,

especially when Holly turned around, leaving Claire to fasten the necklace on her.

That cheerful smile never left her features even amid her ex-husband's younger wife's excitement, and Riley's throat constricted. In that moment, he loved Claire so fiercely that he couldn't breathe around it.

"Our last piece of jewelry of the evening is this exquisite handmade piece created by the organizer of today's incredibly successful event, our very own Claire Bradford. Folks, let's give her another round of applause."

Riley clapped the loudest and Claire slanted a look toward him. Their eyes met for a long moment, hers guarded, his solemn. Something significant passed between them, unspoken but intense.

When she turned away, she was blushing—and he was determined to take her from here as soon as he could.

The auctioneer picked up the necklace, also displayed on a velvet jewelry form. He didn't know anything about beading but even he could see the piece was exquisite, a tangle of color that gleamed brilliantly in the ballroom lights, anchored by a stunning rose-colored heart.

"Claire tells me this is made out of precious and semiprecious gems, each of which can be found in the mountains of Colorado. We've got aquamarine, the state gem of Colorado, as well as topaz and tourmaline. She estimates about a hundred hours of work went into this—and keep in mind, this was all done while the designer and creator had a broken arm."

The crowd applauded again and Claire gave an embarrassed but pleased smile.

"Claire calls this piece the Heart of Hope. Fitting, don't you think? Let's start the bidding at a hundred dollars. Anyone?"

Riley looked at the necklace gleaming there in the light

and then he turned to the woman he loved, whose strength and beauty would always outshine anything else.

He smiled, knowing just what he had to do. He stepped forward and raised his hand. "Twenty-five hundred dollars," he called out.

All eyes turned to him and a few people gasped. He didn't care about anyone else or about how foolish he felt bidding on a necklace. He only cared about Claire. Her expression was stunned, her eyes huge and her mouth slightly open. After a moment she swallowed, the look of shock changing to something else, something bright and glittery.

"Okay." The auctioneer hesitated for only a beat. "Now *that's* what I'm talking about, folks. The new chief of police starts things out right. The bid is twenty-five hundred, do I hear twenty-seven-fifty?"

"Three thousand," a gruff voice called out.

Riley spun around and found his competitor was Harry Lange, the old bastard. The guy gave him an annoying smirk and Riley wished again he'd shoved that stogie down his throat.

"Thirty-five," Riley said immediately.

"Thirty-seven-fifty," Lange countered.

"Four," Riley said. Oh, he was in it now. He knew Harry had no desire for the necklace, he was only goading him on. He didn't know what Harry was playing at and at this point he didn't care. He had finally figured out just what treasure he had been about to throw away and he wasn't letting some grouchy old man yank it out of his hands.

"We've got a bid of four thousand. Do I hear forty-five?"

"Forty-two-fifty," Lange said before the words were out.

"Forty-two-fifty, going once, going twice."

"Five," Riley said quickly.

"Do I hear fifty-two-fifty?"

He waited for the other guy to counter, holding his

breath. While Lange might have endless pockets, Riley unfortunately did not. He did have a healthy nest egg he had built through shrewd investments and he had no problem using some of it for this cause. At heart, this was about a scholarship fund in his niece's name, not about Claire's necklace.

The silence seemed to drag on while everybody waited for the little drama to play out.

"Five thousand, going once…going twice…"

Lange made a little gesture of defeat to Riley, that smirk still on his features.

"Sold, to the new police chief for five thousand dollars. Chief, do you want to come up and collect your item?"

As he made his way to the dais, he heard the swell of whispers, the speculation about why the unattached chief of police would spend five grand on a pretty piece of jewelry.

"That's going to look smashing with your badge," his sister Angie teased as he passed her.

He ignored her and Alex's narrow-eyed look of suspicion. Out of the corner of his gaze, he caught his mother's bright, delighted smile, but he didn't return it, focused only on moving forward to reach out for his prize.

He supposed while he was up there, he might as well pick up the necklace, too.

As Riley seemed to move toward her in slow motion, Claire couldn't manage to grab hold of her wildly whirling thoughts.

Five thousand dollars for her necklace! It was outrageous. She had been hoping for a tenth of that and would have been over the moon if it had sold for a thousand. Five! What was Riley doing?

She couldn't hear anything over the pounding of her

pulse in her ears as Riley continued moving toward her, his green eyes full of an emotion she couldn't name. He looked delicious in an elegant tux that seemed out of character but absolutely right on him.

She had tried not to stare at him all evening—when he'd been dancing with his mother, when he'd stopped to tease Angie, when he had flirted outrageously with a couple of the older ladies who came to the senior citizen beading group. She couldn't help it if he happened to spend entirely too much time in her line of vision. Purely unintentional, she had told herself.

Now she couldn't seem to look away.

"Hi," he murmured when he was only a few feet away. The auction was continuing on without them. They could have been selling the deed to her house for all she knew or cared right then.

She cleared her throat and worked the fastenings connecting the necklace to the form. "You paid entirely too much for this."

"I disagree. It's for a good cause."

Claire was entirely too aware that several people around them—primarily his family and her mother—were just as oblivious to the auction still going on, focusing instead on their little drama.

"Um, I have a box for it so you can take it home."

"I'll just take it now. No box necessary. Thank you."

He held out a hand and she didn't know what else to do. She handed it to him and couldn't help thinking how incongruous it looked, all those pretty, glittery stones in his masculine fingers.

"Turn around," he ordered.

She stared. "Excuse me?"

"Turn around so I can put the necklace on you."

They were drawing even more attention, Claire thought

as she stood frozen. Harry Lange, of all people, was giving them a very amused look, as close to smiling as she'd ever seen him. Strange. Ruth was glaring, no surprise there. Jeff and Holly were both looking baffled, while Katherine and Mary Ella beamed at each other.

"I don't understand," she finally said.

"What's to understand? I bought it for you."

"You...what?"

"It's yours. It rightfully belongs to you. You named it the Heart of Hope, didn't you?" he said, his voice low. "I figure it's only proper, then, that it should belong to the person who *is* actually the Heart of Hope's Crossing."

She stared at him, her heart pounding at the heat in his eyes and the glittery emotion there.

She knew she was blushing—even more so when he moved behind her and removed the necklace she was wearing, a simple strand of pearls that had seemed to fit her dress better than any of her other pieces. More people had turned in their direction, she saw. Even the auctioneer seemed to sense he had lost the attention of his bidders and he was waiting for the moment to pass before continuing.

Riley fastened the necklace she had made around her neck and she felt the weight of it, cool and smooth.

"There," he murmured. "Perfect. Absolutely perfect."

He wasn't talking about the necklace. Her gaze searched his and she saw a fierce tenderness in his eyes.

He leaned in and kissed her cheek, right there in front of everyone in town.

"You're perfect," he murmured in her ear, so no one else could hear. "And now you've got both of my hearts."

Claire's breath left her in a whoosh. She wanted desperately to trust this was real, but how could she? Love wasn't about grand, romantic gestures. It was hard work, it was struggle, it was compromise. It was cleaning up fallen branches after a storm and fixing broken bicycles and taking care of each other.

Much to her relief, the auctioneer made a funny comment and managed to grab attention back to the item currently on the block, the painting Sarah Colville had donated.

"Do you have to finish things up here or can we go somewhere and talk for a minute?" he asked.

Claire looked around at her well-organized committee, who had handled everything so far with competent flair. She could make an excuse, tell him she had too much to do. Some part of her urged her to do just that. He had already hurt her by walking away. What would be different this time?

But then she thought of her misery the past two weeks, the gray pall that seemed to hang over everything, the regret eating at her insides for what they might have had together.

Riley had risked his life in that accident to save her and her children. What kind of coward would she be if she refused to take any sort of risk in return?

"Okay," she finally answered.

Riley's brilliant smile sent hundreds of glittery butterflies fluttering in her stomach.

He took her hand and headed for the door. Claire wobbled along on her cast and the single strappy heel she wore on the other foot, struggling to keep up with him. After a few steps, he must have realized she was having trouble. He stopped, took a careful look at the crowd where a few people still furtively watched them, then he scooped her up, cast and all, her evening dress fluttering over his arm.

She heard a few gasps and titters behind them, but in that moment, Claire didn't care, not with the bubbling laugh pulsing through her.

He was out the door and through the lobby in the time it would have taken her to lodge a protest—not that he would have listened anyway—and then they passed through the wide, carved doors into a cool mountain evening, sparkling with stars.

"That was quite a romantic gesture, Chief McKnight. I'm sure you set more than a few hearts aflutter."

He grinned, looking dark and dangerous and gorgeous, and Claire fell hard for him all over again. "What can I say? I'm a romantic guy."

"Where are we going?"

"You'll see."

He carried her just a few more feet until they reached a bench angled toward the canyon and the distant gleam of Hope's Crossing.

Even though she could hear the distant sounds of the auction, of a few vehicles coming and going from the hotel, they were completely alone here. She shivered a little and Riley instantly removed his tuxedo jacket and slipped it over her.

"Claire," he murmured. Just that, her name, and then he slid his hands to the lapels of his own jacket, drew her closer and kissed her. She caught her breath and returned the kiss, clutching her hands on his shirtfront and probably hopelessly wrinkling it. Oh, heaven. Right here, in his arms. Tears burned her eyes at the sweet ache of it, the slow, easy tenderness of his mouth on hers.

She wanted so desperately to trust him, to trust this, but that little flag of caution waved tentatively for attention and she finally slid away and released her grip on his shirt.

Striving for calm and sanity, she swallowed and drew in a shaky breath. "I'm sorry, Riley. You're going to have to catch me up here. Last time we talked, you were telling me all the reasons you weren't good for me."

"All still very true."

"Yet here we are."

He was silent for a long moment, then he reached for her hand. "I've been informed by more than one person tonight that I'm a first-class idiot."

"Don't believe everything you hear," she whispered.

"In this case, they're right." He squeezed her fingers. "I'm a cop, Claire. I've never turned away from rough situations. I volunteered for every one of my undercover assignments, even though I knew what I would be facing. I've been in the middle of hostage standoffs, I've had perps try to run me over, I told you I got shot once when a drug deal went bad."

"You dived into the icy waters of Silver Strike Reservoir for us."

He dismissed that with a shrug. "I'd be lying if I said I'd never been nervous in any of those moments. I know what fear is. Or at least I thought I did." He paused. "In all those years on the job, nothing prepared me for this."

"This?"

He gazed into her eyes and she held her breath, her chest achy and tight at the emotion there. "Coming home and falling in love."

She stared at him, that tentative joy flailing, trying desperately to fight its way free inside her. "Riley—"

"I love you, Claire. I've been fighting it with everything I've got since I came back to Hope's Crossing, coming up with a hundred reasons why it was crazy to think anything could come of it. All those things made perfect sense. They still do."

She clamped down hard on that joy and braced herself so she could be ready when he pushed her away again. Instead, he drew her fingers to his mouth and kissed the bead-callused tip of her index finger.

"Here's the thing, though. No matter how hard I run, I somehow end up right here. Tonight I realized that none of those reasons amounts to anything compared to the regret I know will eat me alive if I run for good. I love you, Claire. You're everything I've ever dreamed about, all I've ever wanted. I want a life with you, here in Hope's Crossing."

She pressed a hand to her mouth. She'd never run into a hostage standoff or been shot by a criminal, but she knew plenty about fear. Fear was hearing her father had been murdered by a jealous husband. It was watching her mother slip away into a haze of drugs and alcohol. It was standing by helplessly while her children's secure home life crumbled along with her marriage.

It was wondering if she had the guts to seize this gift he offered.

She drew in another shaky breath. "Your mother once told me that fear and courage are like thunder and lightning. They start out at the same time, it's just that the fear always hits first. If we wait long enough, the courage we need will be along soon."

"My mother is a wise woman. She's one of the ones who told me I was an idiot if I walked away from the best thing that ever happened to me."

Just like that, any remaining doubt shot into the air and disappeared like glowing embers from a campfire. This was right. She loved this man, this strong, kind, wonderful man who made her feel beautiful and alive.

Cherished.

Just as he had the night of that terrible accident that had changed everything, when he had saved her children and stayed with her, murmuring quiet words of comfort, she suddenly knew Riley McKnight would do everything in his power to take care of her.

Finally she released the happiness her fear had been

containing and allowed the joy to burst through her, bright and vibrant. She eased forward and kissed him. "I love you, Riley," she murmured against his mouth.

He let out a sound—of relief or happiness, she didn't know—and then he kissed her fiercely, his arms strong and warm around her. "Thank you for buying my necklace," she said after a long moment. "Making it these last few weeks has been a sort of therapy for me, in a lot of different ways. It would have been hard to see it go."

"I've got big plans for that necklace," he murmured.

"Do you?"

"Don't forget, I've got twenty years of Claire fantasies to turn into reality. In the not-very-distant future, I intend to live out a fairly recent one where you're in my bed wearing nothing but that."

His words sent a delicious, heady heat pulsing through her. "I think that could probably be arranged. Have I mentioned I've been beading a long time? I have lots and lots of necklaces."

He made a sexy sound in his throat. "You're killing me here, Claire."

They laughed together, but her smile faded at the tenderness in his eyes when he kissed her again.

"You didn't want to see the other necklace go to Holly, did you?" he asked. "I wish I'd been in time to bid for that one."

She stared at him. "I didn't think anyone noticed. I thought I was being so casual and okay about it."

"No one else could probably tell it bothered you."

Did he know her so well, then? she wondered. It was a rather overwhelming thought.

"It's a family heirloom my mom decided to auction for the benefit," she said. "Not really worth much monetarily but priceless, history-wise, to our family. Jeff knows that

He'll guard it well. Holly might wear it from time to time, but he'll take care of it and keep it safe for Macy. That's all I would have wanted."

He shook his head, his eyes warm. "You're an amazing woman, Claire."

"I'm not. I've wasted entirely too much of my life trying to make sure everything is just right. That everyone gets along. I didn't want to be my mother, so needy all the time, so instead I told myself I didn't need anyone. I could handle everything just fine and wore myself out trying to take care of everyone else. I'm afraid of how much I need you, Riley."

"I won't hurt you," he promised. "I swear it."

"I know," she answered, rather smugly. "Your sisters and your mother are my best friends. The way I see it, if you screw this up, you've got a lot more to worry about than I do."

He gave a mock groan, although she saw the amusement in his eyes. "I'll just have to be sure not to screw it up, won't I?"

She found it impossible to believe she could go from bleak heartache to this blooming happiness in such a short time. "I should probably get back inside. The auction will be ending soon and I need to make sure someone's taking care of the cleanup and taking down the chairs and arranging for the…"

His kiss made her completely lose her train of thought, but she didn't care. He was right. She didn't have to take care of the world by herself anymore. Someone else in Hope's Crossing could step up.

This was exactly where she needed to be, in the arms of the man she loved.

* * * * *

New York Times bestselling author

RaeAnne Thayne

**brings you back to Haven Point—a small town
made for second chances...**

Pick up your copy today!

"Thayne's beautiful, honest storytelling goes straight to the heart."
—*RT Book Reviews*

Be sure to connect with us at:

Harlequin.com/Newsletters
Facebook.com/HarlequinBooks
Twitter.com/HQNBooks

www.HQNBooks.com

PHRAT506

REQUEST YOUR FREE BOOKS!

2 FREE NOVELS
FROM THE ROMANCE COLLECTION
PLUS 2 FREE GIFTS!

YES! Please send me 2 FREE novels from the Romance Collection and my 2 FREE gifts (gifts are worth about $10). After receiving them, if I don't wish to receive any more books, I can return the shipping statement marked "cancel." If I don't cancel, I will receive 4 brand-new novels every month and be billed just $6.49 per book in the U.S. or $6.99 per book in Canada. That's a savings of at least 19% off the cover price. It's quite a bargain! Shipping and handling is just 50¢ per book in the U.S. and 75¢ per book in Canada.* I understand that accepting the 2 free books and gifts places me under no obligation to buy anything. I can always return a shipment and cancel at any time. Even if I never buy another book, the two free books and gifts are mine to keep forever.

194/394 MDN GH4D

Name _____ (PLEASE PRINT) _____

Address _____ Apt. # _____

City _____ State/Prov. _____ Zip/Postal Code _____

Signature (if under 18, a parent or guardian must sign)

Mail to the **Reader Service:**
IN U.S.A.: P.O. Box 1867, Buffalo, NY 14240-1867
IN CANADA: P.O. Box 609, Fort Erie, Ontario L2A 5X3

Want to try two free books from another line?
Call 1-800-873-8635 or visit www.ReaderService.com.

* Terms and prices subject to change without notice. Prices do not include applicable taxes. Sales tax applicable in N.Y. Canadian residents will be charged applicable taxes. Offer not valid in Quebec. This offer is limited to one order per household. Not valid for current subscribers to the Romance Collection or the Romance/Suspense Collection. All orders subject to credit approval. Credit or debit balances in a customer's account(s) may be offset by any other outstanding balance owed by or to the customer. Please allow 4 to 6 weeks for delivery. Offer available while quantities last.

Your Privacy—The Reader Service is committed to protecting your privacy. Our Privacy Policy is available online at www.ReaderService.com or upon request from the Reader Service.

We make a portion of our mailing list available to reputable third parties that offer products we believe may interest you. If you prefer that we not exchange your name with third parties, or if you wish to clarify or modify your communication preferences, please visit us at www.ReaderService.com/consumerschoice or write to us at Reader Service Preference Service, P.O. Box 9062, Buffalo, NY 14240-9062. Include your complete name and address.

ROM15